GOD'S MERCY

KERSTIN EKMAN
GOD'S MERCY

(Guds barmhärtighet)

Translated by Linda Schenck

University of Nebraska Press : Lincoln

Guds barmhärtighet © Kerstin Ekman, 1999
English translation © 2009 by the Board of
Regents of the University of Nebraska. All
rights reserved. Manufactured in the United
States of America.

Guds barmhärtighet first published by Albert
Bonniers Förlag, Stockholm, Sweden. Published
in the English language by arrangement with
Bonnier Group Agency, Stockholm, Sweden.

Translation of this work was supported by a
grant from the Swedish Arts Council.

Publication of this book
was assisted by a grant from
the National Endowment
for the Arts.

NATIONAL
ENDOWMENT
FOR THE ARTS
A great nation
deserves great art.

Library of Congress Cataloging-in-Publication Data

Ekman, Kerstin, 1933–
[Guds barmhärtighet. English]
God's mercy / Kerstin Ekman ; translated by
Linda Schenck.
p. cm. — (European women writers series)
ISBN 978-0-8032-1074-5 (cloth : alk. paper) —
ISBN 978-0-8032-2458-2 (pbk. : alk. paper)
1. Country life—Sweden—Fiction. 2. Sweden—
Rural conditions—Fiction. I. Schenck, Linda.
II. Title.
PT9876.15.K55G8313 2009
839.7′374—dc22
2008051843

Set in Minion by Kim Essman.
Designed by Ashley Muehlbauer.

TRANSLATOR'S PREFACE

This is the fourth novel by Kerstin Ekman that I have had the privilege of translating, and the process has become more exciting with each one. I hope that English language readers will feel they have had a peek at the very special world in which these novels are set and the ways in which that world is both unique and universal at once.

God's Mercy is set mainly in the very special environment of early twentieth-century rural northern Sweden and contains many languages: the local Swedish dialect, standard Swedish, Norwegian, German, the occasional French expression, and, not the least, South Sami, one of the languages of the nomadic Sami peoples of the Nordic region. Very few speakers of standard Swedish understand Sami, making it nearly as exotic for Swedish as for non-Swedish readers. The meanings of most of the Sami words become clear from their context, except for the ones in the poems and songs, or *yoiks*. Hence I have left them as unexplained in the English translation as they are in the original Swedish.

The traditional Sami dwelling is rendered here using the southern Sami word *gåetie*. The Swedish word is *kåta*, more or less a transliteration of *gåetie*. For an excellent series of photos of a *gåetie* under construction, the reader is referred to http://www.umealven.com/content/view/34/45/.

God's Mercy is the first volume of a trilogy. Risten, the character the reader meets on the novel's first page, remains the first-person narrator in all three volumes. The trilogy begins in 1916 and ends around the beginning of the twenty-first century and follows the destinies of the characters in *God's Mercy* and their descendants. Kerstin Ekman has also recently written the screenplay for the film *Varg* (*Wolf*) that opened at Swedish theatres in April 2008 and that continues the present-day story of Klemens, one of Risten's children.

My friend and colleague Rochelle Wright has examined the entire manuscript, applying to it both her Ekman expertise and her infallible language skills. My husband Robert has been a thorough and faithful reader. The Baltic Center for Writers and Translators provided Rochelle Wright and me with a week of intensive concentration in the wonderful environment of Visby in August 2007. Ladette Randolph at the University of Nebraska Press showed tremendous patience in bringing the contract to fruition.

LINDA SCHENCK
Göteborg, Sweden

One winter evening when I was six years old, I was walking alone from out by Storflo marsh toward the village. The chill was deep, and the stars seemed high and bright. I was scared of the forest along the road. The snow weighed down the branches of the spruces, and under them it was very dark. I became increasingly frightened when a shadow appeared on the bridge, looming larger and larger as it advanced. The customs house was the only human habitation along the way, and it was unlit. The border guard was long dead. There was nowhere to hide, and the stream was roaring. No matter what, I had to face whoever was approaching, even if it was the water phantom. By the time he was standing in front of me, I was rigid with fear. He said something I couldn't understand, and yet I thought I'd heard it before. Then he reached out and took me by the chin as if to raise my face toward the starlight. I'd forgotten my own language, but now I realized he was asking my name and whose child I was. So I said I was the shopkeeper's foster daughter, called Kristin.

Risten, he said. Risten, *onne maana. Onne maana!*

When he said that, our language came to life in me again. His way of talking sounded like singing. He asked if I remembered him, but I couldn't say I did. Even though it was cold and dark, I could tell that made him sad. Then he started singing to me: *nanana . . . onne maana . . .*

na na nananaaa
little baby, little Risten
little cheek

Then I remembered that he had sung to me long ago. I wasn't afraid any more. He told me he was my uncle, the one I'd called Laula Anut. He went on singing, and I remembered those exact words, the very same ones.

1

voia voia little baby
There's a wood grouse in the tree
na na nanaaa white-cheeked baby
frost bites hard in all this chill
voia voia little downy
Oh don't let the mountain wind
blow you when the black dog's barking
nana nanaa naaa

When he'd finished singing, he put his hands to my cheeks and felt how cold they were, so he told me to hurry on home to the shopkeeper's. When I got home, I didn't tell them I'd met Laula Anut on the bridge or that he'd sung to me. I didn't want them to think my uncle had been drunk. Hillevi said that when they were drinking, the Lapps went around chanting their *yoiks* and even the other Lapps, the ones she called respectable, found it shameful.

I speak four languages now, and for my story I've chosen the one I learned at the Vocational Seminary in Katrineholm. Laula Anut knew three of those four languages.

Hillevi arrived in Östersund by train on March fifth, 1916. Even in those days the streets were paved, and there was electric arc lighting. There were turrets and towers on the building known as the Central Palace, which housed the bank, post office, and bathhouse. On a huge mural painted right on the plaster in Erik Johansson's house a little farther down the street, strange beasts wandered in a forest. The Staverfelt mansion had wrought-iron balconies, ornamented gables, and vaulted arches. The market hall next door had a stately stepped gable; the Mårtensson home on High Street had several. So it wasn't exactly the last outpost of civilization.

On March seventh though, when she reached Lomsjö, she began to wonder.

There were only two people in the taproom at the inn that afternoon. One was an old Lapp, who was sitting on the floor. The other was Hillevi, who was sitting on a bench attached to the wall with her fur hat sliding off and head tipped forward. She was asleep.

Outside, there was silence. The snow sifted down over sledge tracks and horse droppings. The old Lapp was cutting himself a plug of tobacco from a plait. The innkeeper's wife came in and scolded him for sitting on the floor until the old man explained that the seat of his pants was dirty. Their conversation didn't awaken Hillevi. She only woke up with a start when the innkeeper's wife shook her by the arm, calling Miss!

You'd best not be sitting in here.

She rose and followed obediently. At the door of the dining room she stopped and looked back into the taproom as if she'd never seen it before or had forgotten it in her sleep. There was a lantern on the long, bare wooden table. Next to it was a pair of felt mittens, brownish-yellow at the thumb seam. Sitting on the bench, she'd noticed the smell of stable. The man on the floor was wearing an old blue knitted cap. His boots had upturned toes and were dark with wear, greased hundreds of times.

The dining room was not as warm as the taproom, but a fire gleamed behind mica panes in the iron stove. The table was covered with a heavy white linen cloth. In this room there was a kerosene lamp with a white glass shade that modulated the light. Hanging on the wall over the sideboard were enormous portraits of a man and a woman. The woman was wearing a turban like a negress. But these were country people. His hair was cut short around the ears, and he had a thin fringe of beard under his chin. Pinned to the front of her dress was an enamel brooch. Their expressions were wooden, corpselike.

Hillevi had seen corpses. When the loud Miss! of the innkeeper's wife brought her out of a deep sleep, she had been reminded. As if she were there again. Boots soaked. The edge of her hem hanging in the puddle. Her fear of a different voice, coarse, unrestrained, from the darkness. Miss!

Now she was truly exhausted. Her gaze wandered the walls, with their brown and gold patterned paper. She saw paintings, wall hangings, reindeer antlers, and stuffed birds. There were crystal vases and photographers' portraits on the sideboard with its framed oval mirror. The tray under the salt and pepper set was silver-plated. A stale food smell hung in the air.

She thought: As soon as I'm at my own place, I'll be myself again. I'll stop remembering that harsh voice. This is the last outpost of everything revolting and crude. That old Lapp on the floor. Sitting there cutting tobacco. Singing under his breath in his own language. Yes indeed, he was intoxicated. Outside when I arrived, the skinned body of a reindeer in the lantern light. Blood underneath. He's waiting to be paid, the woman had told her. So he must have flayed that reindeer hanging out there. Well, it had to be a reindeer.

The innkeeper's wife brought her some soup. The tureen steamed as she ladled it out. Big doughy balls floated in the cloudy gray liquid. It tasted odd.

It's moose broth, she told her. 'Twill fortify you, Miss.

Had it been reindeer stock she would have pushed it aside. She remembered the blood dripping from the animal's mouth. There was a yellow patch in the snow too. And black droppings. Well, that's what happens. Involuntary elimination.

I'm an educated woman, I know all about these things. It helps keep you from gagging. Knowledge helps.

Whatever Aunt Eugénie might say. It does help.

Oh, Miss, you wouldn't be weeping now?

Just tired, she mumbled into her handkerchief. She hadn't been given a napkin.

Sure y'are. Poor little thing. So young. And so thin. Dear me, what'll become of you? Well, Miss, you'll be having some pancakes now, with cloudberries. Some milk with it? Nothing the matter with the milk, you know. It's fresh and strained.

She declined politely without saying it made her queasy.

When will the driver be here?

Who can say? In this weather. Never imagined it would get this bad. Drifts on the lake. I s'pose it'll take Halvorsen a day or two. You'll just have to wait it out, poor thing. I'll be giving you my very best room. We've lit the fire. And there are hides to keep you warm too.

She'd brought out a bowl of something a strange shade of yellow and a pitcher of milk.

Do have some berries, at least. And I've brought the ledger.

The pen nib kept splitting as she wrote her name. Hillevi Klarin.

Put down midwife, the innkeeper's wife said after she'd already written Miss. For us to remember you by.

That made her realize her arrival was a major event.

Poor little thing, said the innkeeper's wife to the Lapp a little later. They were on friendly terms now and were talking about her. She could hear their voices through the door to the taproom. The old man rambled on and on. The outside door slammed and booted feet tramped across the floor three times while Hillevi sat waiting for her room to be readied upstairs. Three times faces peered in to look at her.

That night the wind began to whistle in the pipes of the tile stove. Soon it was a high-pitched whine, and the whole house shook. When the morning light came, she watched the snow sweep down like gray curtains. The storm howled. Now and then the gusts would die down. There would be a lull for a couple of hours before it picked up again. All day and all night. The cold seeped in through the cracks and drafty windows.

She spent most of the time in bed, wrapped in two heavy gray woolen blankets. She had folded the brightly striped bedspread and set it aside. She was afraid there might be bugs in the wooly side of the sheepskin, but when the chill from the floor crept up toward the bed, she pulled it over herself anyway. That first day she felt frozen to the bone and achy. The tile stove slowly grew cold. She thought it probably hadn't been used for a long time.

Before Hillevi was properly awake, an old woman came up with the wood basket to rekindle the fire. It was a good stove. Gradually it overcame the rawness and the cold. The stove seemed more human than the old serving woman who never responded, no matter what Hillevi said.

Once the room had become more habitable, Hillevi grew bored. The smells of fried herring and salt pork wafted up. In the end she went down to the dining room and had some pancakes after all. Only pancakes. She asked about Halvorsen and the wagon again.

It's likely to be some time, the innkeeper's wife told her.

And it did take time. She opened the suitcases she'd had them carry up. Her chest was still downstairs. She removed all her things and repacked them even more neatly, paying particular attention to the instruments that were wrapped in clean linen towels in her midwife's bag.

In the middle of the night she woke up and started thinking about the instruments. She had a feeling someone had come to get her in spite of the snowstorm. There was a woman in labor who needed help. But it had been her own screams she had heard. She'd been dreaming.

She groped groggily for the lamp. The wick flared and spat reams of black smoke before she managed to get it turned down. Her shadow loomed on the wall, and the wind was howling outside. Aunt Eugénie came to mind:

My dear, are you sure this is a wise decision?

When it was light outside and the silent old woman had been in, first with the wood basket and then with the coffee and finally with the hot water for washing, her aunt came to mind again, but this time Hillevi was amused. She was such an expert at playing the martyr. Actually she must have been relieved.

On her twenty-fifth birthday her uncle and aunt had given Hillevi a diary. It was a thick book with a burgundy velvet cover. There was a subtle fleur-de-lis pattern in the velvet like a damask tablecloth. The diary locked with a tiny key, but her aunt had insisted she was not to think of it as a youthful diary. She might not even want to write in it every day. It was so she could inscribe the main events of her life.

So far, though, she hadn't written anything in it. She had taken it out when repacking. Now she was sitting in bed with it in her lap. On the bedside table there was an inkhorn, a steel nib, and a piece of ragged blotting paper. The innkeeper's wife had warned her they might have to borrow it back if anybody came to register.

She hesitated. Was her arrival at the Lomsjö inn one of the main events of her life?

What settled it was that the nib was so badly used it might leave blotches, so she didn't write anything. Instead, she took the writing set back down and ended up sitting in the warm kitchen. The hands of the taciturn old woman were sticky with something she was rolling into balls.

We're doing some dumplin's. She suddenly spoke. She was dicing pork and lard. The gray balls of barley flour mixed with grated potatoes and water were dropped into a boiling pot. The kitchen filled with steam.

The second day was overcast and the wind had died down. The dark wall of trees on the far side of the fields was mottled. The boughs of the spruces were heavy with snow and hung almost to the ground. She saw a fox that morning. Otherwise nothing. The dogs were silent, though earlier they'd seemed to bark night and day. They were shaggy gray Pomeranians, their eyes peering out from behind the black-and-white masks of their faces.

Are you sure this is a wise decision?

It wasn't really her aunt any more. The insistent voice inside her sounded more like her own.

Long days and nights. She hated idleness as much as she hated indecision. She had applied for the position and made up her mind to go without consulting anyone. Now here she sat not knowing what to do with her hands. Her embroidery was in the trunk, and she didn't want to unpack it.

One of the innkeeper's sons was outside driving a small black horse who pulled the snowplow. He was plowing in circles, making a ring with a stripe across the middle.

On the third day people began to appear. Some on skis, one or two with sledges. But none of them was Halvorsen. She was in bed by eight in the evening, her mind a haze of worry and boredom that gradually faded into heavy sleep.

A loud shout awakened her. She heard barking and men's voices. At first she thought there must have been an accident or a fight. She couldn't see what was going on since her window looked out over a smooth snowy surface that the innkeeper's wife called the near field. She called the area behind the stable the enclosure.

Hillevi put on her socks and drew her shawl tight as she went out into the hall. The gable window gave her a view of the stable. Looking down, she saw a group of men crowding around the body of an animal lit by lantern light.

It appeared to be a big dog. The men had suspended it by its back legs right where the reindeer carcass had been hanging when she arrived. They were laughing and shouting. She could see the Lapp and a man in a black fur cap who she now knew was the innkeeper. His sons, who had been out plowing snow all day, were there too. And a small agile man seemed to be dancing around the dead animal.

She should have gone into her room and shut the door. But she stayed there watching him slit the body from sternum to genitals. The light fell sharply on the gray fur and on the man's hands. It was probably a carbide lantern, although she couldn't hear it hissing through the nailed-down window. Down below everyone was quiet. A gray bundle of entrails spilled out, and the man put his hands into the cavity and dug out other bits and pieces. Clotted blood stuck to his hands and soaked the cuffs of his sweater. The Lapp brayed into the quiet: a long droning hoooo. That was the moment when she realized the dead animal was a wolf.

The men were shouting and laughing again. All the insides of the wolf were on the ground. The man with the knife knelt down and lifted something up from the stained snow. It was big and glistened in the lantern light, bright blue membranes and dripping blood. He slit it, then extracted a little lump and tossed it to the ground. Another. And another. Five times. Each time, the Lapp howled again.

Then she realized the animal was a she-wolf who had been with young. The man had dropped five unborn cubs to the ground. His knife gleamed in the lantern light.

Stumbling in her thick socks, she went back to her room, locking the door from the inside. She sat on the bed too frightened to lie down under the covers, although she was chilled to the bone. She retched, and her mouth filled up with bitter saliva. She swallowed and swallowed, trying to ease the retching, but suddenly she had to lean down and quickly extract the chamber pot from under the bed as everything came up. Some dripped onto her socks.

How she puked. That was what she called it in her mind. Usually she said throw up. At the hospital they used to say vomit. Her aunt said be sick.

But this was puking. It cascaded out. She couldn't stop retching even after she was sure her stomach was empty. The last part was yellow bile, gall. Tears in her eyes and her face burning, she curled up on the bed and waited for the dry heaves to recede.

Then she made the mistake of using the rest of her water. First she cleaned her socks, wetting her towel and rubbing. But they still smelled of vomit, so she held them over her chamber pot and rinsed them. She applied the last few drops to her swollen face.

There was noise in the house, but she wasn't the least bit interested in what was going on down there. She drew the hide over herself, trying to get warm. Her entire body was still shaking. Her stomach was completely empty, and she eventually grew thirsty. She couldn't believe she had been so foolish as to waste the water on her socks. Not a single drop left in the jug. Although she'd covered it with her towel, the vomit in the chamber pot smelled horrible too. In the end all she could think about was how badly she wanted to drink some water and empty the pot.

She went out into the hall and listened. Boots were tramping down there. An accordion whined, and voices shouted. Peals of laughter rang out. The noise seemed to be coming from the taproom. Just to be on the safe side, she pulled her dress over her nightgown, though she thought she could probably make her way to the front steps and empty the pot in the snow without being seen. But when she got downstairs she could hear someone out there stamping the snow off his boots. She retreated quickly into the dining room so as not to be discovered with the chamber pot.

There was no heat in there now. No lamp was lit, only a soft light coming from outside, the shine of the taproom lamps on the snow. She could discern the table and the tall sideboard. There was something shiny on the tabletop. She felt along the tablecloth but found only a vinegar set. Nothing to drink. She pulled out a chair and sat down by the brown curtains.

Boot heels and toe irons clacked against the taproom floor. Men's voices were singing though she couldn't make out the words. The accordion bleated under fumbling fingers. She was frozen stiff, almost as cold as that first night, an aching chill between her shoulder blades. But the front door kept opening and shutting; men went in and out, possibly to relieve themselves. She would just have to wait.

The image of the unborn wolf cubs came back to her. But it no longer made her retch. She felt cold inside, just as she had that time she stood outside the nursing school, the smell of carbide stinging in her nose.

She figured the innkeeper's wife would eventually materialize and help her, but when the woman finally bustled into the room and grabbed a breadbasket, Hillevi failed to attract her attention. Now the door to the taproom was open. She withdrew into the curtains, would have liked to wind herself up in them and hide if they hadn't been so dusty and hadn't smelled of grease.

She watched two men stamp past, their arms around each other's waists. Two more. A bobbing head. Toothy grins, mouths brown with snuff juice. The accordion wailed. They were basically dancing to the rhythm of their own stamping and the singer's voice. Now a man whirled out onto the floor all alone. He was lighter on his feet than the others. His belt was cinched so tight around his narrow waist that his homespun trousers puffed out like a gathered sack at the back. A curved knife hung from his belt. He tossed his head and his dark curls shook. She considered his hair a little too long to be presentable. When he turned his face toward the dining room door, she recognized those gleaming teeth and could see what kind of knife it was.

Fiddledi da fiddledide . . . fiddledi, fiddledita, fiddletay, fiddledi . . .

Not much of a song. More like a drunken racket. The warmth rolled in with the tobacco smoke, and then the innkeeper's wife came back and pulled the door shut. Hillevi made herself known. She hid the chamber pot in the folds of the curtain, still thinking she'd be able to go out into the snow and empty it. The inescapable gossip when a young woman was sick to her stomach was the last thing she needed.

She asked for some water to drink and a jug to take back up. And whether Halvorsen had come. He damn well had, said the innkeeper's wife. Whatever she meant by that.

I thought I might find out when we'll be leaving, Hillevi said.

She was given a glass of water and sat waiting on her chair for a carafe to take upstairs. But the next time the door opened it wasn't the innkeeper's wife at all. It was the man with the knife and the untrimmed hair. A beam of light fell on Hillevi. He stared. And yet he must have known she was in there. Otherwise he wouldn't have come in. Still, he just stood there gaping, openmouthed, teeth gleaming and brown with saliva. Then he took a step back and closed the door without turning around. Again the room was dark.

She was frightened of course. But she said nothing. She felt herself tensing up as he crossed the floor. She could no longer see his face. He stopped by the table; a match scratched a rough surface, possibly a shoe sole, since he was leaning down. Awkwardly he lifted off the white lamp globe with one hand. It wobbled and sang out as it struck the brass lamp foot. He raised the globe again as he touched the match flame to the wick. It hadn't been adjusted properly so it flared up and puffed out a cloud of black smoke. He cursed under his breath and turned it down. When he tried to set the globe back in place, he almost dropped it, and in the end he just set it on the table. He took a deep breath.

Fancy meetin' you, he said, staggering slightly.

He reeked of drink. His eyes gleamed, and his face was ruddy under his dark whiskers.

We'll be leavin' on the morrow, he said.

She realized this was Halvorsen. She had to travel through the forest all alone with a drunkard.

Do y' have a lap fur, Miss, for the sledge? She shook her head. The only thing she had that vaguely resembled a fur was her faux fur collar.

That made him laugh. With pleasure, it seemed. She couldn't figure him out. How could he dance around so gracefully in those huge boots? Almost pirouetting. And with perfect balance, not the least sign of inebriation.

He left, shutting the door behind him. She sighed with relief. However, he hadn't gone back into the taproom but out toward the front steps. She heard the door bang. Lots of noise. Then that wild laugh again. His chortle of pleasure.

She got up and blew out the lamp. Better to sit here in the dark for a while. That way if anyone else came in they probably wouldn't notice her. The minute she could hear Halvorsen carrying on in the taproom again, she would sneak back up to her room. Never mind the chamber pot. Lord knows she wanted to be well behaved, but this was too much.

He came back in. Thumped into the dark room, stood there unsteadily. A soft reflection of light gleamed off his teeth. He had something in his arms.

Here you are m'am. For your lap fur. Someday, he said. Lovely Miss.

And he gave her a wobbly bow, setting it at her feet. Then he headed toward the door of the taproom, stumbling over the bundle he'd just set down. He pulled himself together enough to make it look like a little leap, and shouting Hey ho! he rushed back into the thick haze of tobacco smoke and the harsh fumes from the taproom, and she heard his voice sounding jubilant.

She ran to the door, stumbling over the bundle as he had. It was quite soft. She didn't dare touch it. Her hand trembled slightly as she groped for the box of matches on the sideboard and lit one. She didn't bother to light the lamp; she could see enough by the light of the match. Even the eye sockets, the gray matted fur and damp streaks of blood on back.

In the morning Halvorsen was no longer drunk. He strapped her baggage onto the sledge, to which a little black horse was harnessed. The innkeeper's wife told Hillevi there was no room for her trunk. Someone named Pålsa would bring it when he came from town.

When will that be? Hillevi asked.

That wasn't easy to say because there would soon be the Saint Gregory market in Östersund, and Pålsa might stay for it.

They started off, tucked in side by side. Halvorsen had lent Hillevi his fur coat. The weather was gray, but behind the haze of snow the March day was dawning. She left her trunk behind with the feeling that her whole mission would come to nothing. She imagined having to give up and go home.

She was scarcely twenty-five when she set off for Röbäck, and secretly betrothed to a man named Edvard Nolin. She never moved back.

The faux fur collar and hat were a farewell present from her aunt when she left Uppsala. Both of them imagined she would need something furry up there. She was wearing the hat, but she'd folded the little collar down into her rucksack when Halvorsen lent her his fur coat for the ride.

Lovely wasn't how she thought of herself. But apparently he did.

Sharp little flurries of snow blew into their faces. They were sitting close to each other, but he no longer paid any attention to her. His hat of bushy fox fur was pulled all the way down to his black eyebrows. He was more interested in his horse than in her. The two of them were going to be sitting there rubbing up against each other for many a mile. The woods were striped with snow; the bristly evergreen forest rose straight up like the frozen coat of an animal.

The snow blew harder and harder, and Halvorsen muttered to "maresy," as he called the horse. She wouldn't have been surprised to hear the horse answer. She felt left out in spite of her legs rubbing against his in the foot sack. But he's wearing homespun trousers and no doubt thick socks and woolen underwear too, she thought. And then there are all my skirts. There's a lot in between.

They were driving straight into the haze of snow, a gray whirlwind. Snow-laden spruces flanked the road; the roadside ditch was marked with felled birches.

She would never come to call him anything but Halvorsen when anyone else was listening. He and his father eventually changed it to Halvarsson, the Swedish spelling. The story was that his father, Morten, had come over the mountains on foot, his sack of goods to peddle in a hand cart. Hillevi couldn't possibly know just how well things had gone for him, the Norwegian who hadn't owned so much as a horse when he arrived, and for his son and his daughters Jonetta and Aagot. She couldn't possibly know anything.

Halvorsen clucked to the horse and pulled at the reins to bring the mare to a halt. He wormed his way out of the sack and walked to the front of the cart, inserting several fingers under one side of the harness. It was too tight; he loosened the girth a notch and tried again. When he was satisfied, he returned and stuffed his legs back down next to Hillevi's. Then he gave the horse a slap, and she recommenced her slow, systematic gait. He gazed intently at her swaying behind. The tip of his tongue protruded. He had no whiskers today, and a dark scab was starting to form on the cheek facing her. He'd shaved in a hurry.

She didn't like the thoughts she was having. Shaving and underwear and whatnot. They were sitting too close together. That brought up the kind of thoughts she would never otherwise have had.

Her Aunt Eugénie came to mind, and she wondered what she would have made of all this, sitting for hours, mile after mile, right up next to a man. I'm not going to converse with him, she thought. Not much anyway. He's the driver, nothing else. Her aunt would never have allowed her to ride this way. So close. Alone with a man who, just the night before, had been more than a little tipsy.

But her aunt had no idea.

Halvorsen was pleased with the mare now and slapped her gently with the reins so she fell into a trot, after which he turned to Hillevi and broke into a cheerful stream of chatter she couldn't follow. He didn't seem to mind, just kept on talking, and after a bit she was able to pick out some words. She was mighty alone on a very long journey, and the same kind of comments she'd already heard plenty of at the inn, that she was young and that she was slight. What was she supposed to say? That she would be twenty-six on her next birthday? It was none of his business.

Miss, you're sittin' deep in a thiiink, he said softly, and at first she thought thiiink was the name of the little sledge. But a thiiink was her thoughts.

Thoughts of Uppsala: the black river whirling just above the falls, the scent of carbide, and her own shrill voice with Berta Fors lying on the stretcher, her face ashen.

What a strange language Halvorsen spoke. It was full of diphthongs he enunciated clearly, saying the words as if they were spelled that way. His chatter was now circling around the subject of Hillevi's journey, her destiny, and her life. It was embarrassing.

He was probably trying to figure out her degree of cultivation. He seemed to sense that she had both a cultivated side and a coarser one. Her cultivation was on the surface, as Aunt Eugénie said, fearing that some of the coarseness would shine through. In her opinion Hillevi was being drawn down toward her origins, and she said as much. But only very softly and when she thought no one but her husband, Hillevi's uncle, was listening.

They had brought her up lovingly. But when Hillevi told them she wanted to use her small inheritance from her father to train in midwifery, her aunt pronounced those somber, mysterious words: she's being drawn down.

Shipmaster Claes Hegger had been a heavy drinker, and drink had made him coarse. He only resembled his brother Carl in appearance. Bowed legs, a heavy torso, and a cranelike neck. No one ever told her what Lissen had looked like, but Hillevi must resemble her; where else would her looks have come from? A dainty thing, her aunt called her.

Photographs showed Hillevi's small, straight nose and the chin she tended to tilt upward. Her eyes were neither wide nor deep set. The look in them was matter of fact. But her hair was not at all the mousy color it looked in studio portraits or big group pictures from parties. Many years later, when she cut her hair and stored the plait away in a Freja chocolate box, it was still strawberry blonde.

There was no photograph of Elisabeth Klarin who was known as Lissen and who had done the cleaning and cooking for Claes Hegger, a bachelor. Housekeeper, her aunt had called her euphemistically. But the proper house-keeper had removed all her things from the chest of drawers, packed her bags, and left in a huff when the maid's condition became evident.

Hillevi's mother died in childbirth. Surprisingly, the old, alcoholic former sea captain had refused to give up his daughter. He acknowledged paternity, though of course the girl bore her mother's family name. A new housekeeper was hired. Hillevi had vague memories of her. But she couldn't recall her father in spite of his fondness for her. She's the light of my firmament he had told his brother and sister-in-law, who considered his words irreverent. He, of course, had no idea where the words came from. His life had taken on meaning, and he intended to quit drinking. He really tried, kept himself semisober and became extremely sentimental according to Carl. The whole matter was more than a little grotesque. With his appearance: gorilla and tapir. Not to mention that he was sixty-nine when Hillevi was born. She was three when he died.

They had to spend the night in Kloven. Me mare she needs some rest, said Halvorsen. A farming family put them up: there was one bed in an unheated room and the kitchen trundle bed to share with the grown-up daughter. Hillevi fell asleep in her chair. Thus the trip ended up taking two days. But for how many days and weeks would she dwell on it in her thoughts? Deep in a thiiink.

Not its beauty. Not the big white lakes, where he carefully guided the horse down the banks so that they'd have a long straight ride on the ice with the bristly forest rising and stretching up to the crests above. When the banks of clouds broke up, she glimpsed the brilliant white mountains. At those moments the sky flashed bright blue.

Not her worries either, the thought that she might have to turn back. But the fact that Halvorsen got her to admit she knew Edvard.

However he had managed to do that.

She'd been strictly forbidden to let on. Edvard had stressed that it would be disastrous for his future if anyone found out they knew each other. He had to be irreproachable to have any chance at all of promotion from temporary to permanent minister of the parish.

An irreproachable clergyman would not send his secret intended on ahead of him. Nor had Edvard done so. On the contrary, his nostrils had flared when she told him that she had applied for the opening as midwife in Röbäck.

Halvorsen had caught her out with questions about whether she had any relations up this way, whether she knew anyone at all. In Röbäck? What about in Lomsjö? Or in Östersund? He kept asking questions. She realized he must think she'd have to be insane to be riding straight out into the unknown. Unfamiliar with the language. And without even the right clothes for traveling by sledge.

That was when she mumbled that she knew Edvard Nolin, the new clergyman who was coming. Instantly, three cocks could have crowed. She tried to gloss it over. It couldn't be retracted. She was acquainted with him, she said. Knew of him.

Halvorsen didn't comment at all. He just looked at her sidelong. For ages.

The second lake they descended to was an even wider expanse. She couldn't see a house anywhere along its shores, nothing but the edge of the forest. Points of land extended sparkling white, shifting in blue, tongues shooting into the whiteness where there was nothing to fix one's eyes on. When they were down on the ice, Halvorsen stopped again to adjust the mare's harness. But that wasn't his real purpose. He removed a rifle that was strapped down on top of the cart and loaded it. With a scowl he wedged it in across their laps.

She thought about that disgusting animal skin. She hoped he wouldn't remember his drunken gift to her. They rode in silence for over an hour. Then he pointed to one of the fingers of land.

That's where they were, he said. Four in the pack. I shot the bitch. She was with young. There were five cubs in 'er.

Luckily there was no way of his knowing that Hillevi had seen the dead wolf cubs. She was busy trying to reassure herself. He's not from the village. What he knows or doesn't know is of no consequence. The innkeeper's wife had said he came from Fagerli. God only knew where that was. Far away, she hoped. Preferably in Norway.

The restfulness of white. She would become familiar with that. When snowflakes sift down and shake through the leafless boughs of the aspens. When the air thickens, when the white goes gray and coalesces into blue twilight. Then you sit deep in a thiiink. Uppsala thoughts.

Miss!

It was a coarse voice. That was clear from the single word. It sounded strained. Hillevi was walking from the hospital to make a home visit in Beaver Row. She heard the voice as she was crossing the Iceland bridge. It was dark and misty, and she couldn't see much when she turned around to look. The falls were roaring, and she hastened her pace until she was nearly running.

Miss! Miss!

Behind her she heard heels clattering on the wooden bridge. The water in the river was swirling below. It frightened her.

When she'd arrived at the door and rushed up the wooden stairs, she could no longer imagine why she had been so afraid. It was only a woman's voice after all. But now that six months had passed, thank God, she realized she'd somehow known what that woman wanted. It was because of the word Miss.

You're needed, Miss, they said. Miss is here with her bag. Now she was a Miss, and that was completely different from being Miss Klarin.

The awful thing was that two days later when she'd gone back to look in on the new mother in Beaver Row and was on her way to the dinner party at her aunt and uncle's to celebrate her twenty-fifth birthday, the woman was standing there in the dark waiting for her. The weather was still misty, and when Hillevi noticed it was drizzling, she stopped on the front steps to cover her hat with her shawl. That was when she heard the voice call out again.

She must have been waiting over by the trash shed. Hillevi crossed the cobbled courtyard quickly and headed out into the road, but the woman caught up with her, laying her hand on Hillevi's arm.

Miss, just listen, please! I've got to talk to you!

She didn't really get a look at her until they were at the bridge. By then Hillevi knew what she wanted. It was so crass. All the circumstances were coarse too. Hillevi just kept shaking her head, her hat swaying under her shawl.

Please leave me alone now. It's just not possible.

The woman seized her arm again, forcing her to stand still.

It's not my fault! I didn't even want to!

And now she saw her face in the light from the street lamp. Pale, a pointed little chin. Just a girl. The hair escaping from under her hat was blonde. It crossed Hillevi's mind that many women would give anything for a head of hair like that. And her eyes were large, her gaze deep blue. Was it the reflection of her soul? There was a scab under her nose. Her mouth looked slack. The words came pouring out. Hillevi wanted to brush the hand off her coat sleeve, but it was gripping tight.

Something Miss Elisif, the course director, had once said came back to Hillevi. It had been during the last year of their studies, by which time they were mature enough to hear about some of the things they might experience.

They'll stop at nothing.

Hillevi took hold of the girl's hand, trying to pry it off her sleeve.

I can't help you. I'm not allowed to. I wouldn't want to either. You'll have to go now. I don't understand why you're asking me.

Miss said it was shameful. When a person was as far gone as she was. That she shouldn't have to go through with it!

Who?

Berta Fors. She was bleeding when they brought her to the hospital, expecting her tenth. And she didn't make it. She's dead now.

They'll stop at nothing. There's no limit to what they may try to get you to believe.

Please go now. You're young and strong. You'll be fine. Come and see me at the maternity ward, and I'll put you in good hands. I'll help you with the layette. I'm sure we can pull together what your little one will need. You mustn't lose heart. There will be a way.

Then Hillevi said something about the rain because it was really pouring by then. The wooden planks of the bridge glistened.

Oh my, I shouldn't have gone out without my umbrella, she said.

Then, and not until then, did the girl release her grip on Hillevi's coat sleeve. Hillevi hurried across the bridge. On West Bank Road she turned her head as discreetly as she could and saw that the girl was still standing there. Her face was white as chalk under her hat.

The worst part was that right in the middle of the dinner party at Uncle Carl and Aunt Eugénie's this memory surfaced: a woman, old before her time, on a stretcher. The skin on her face was damp and gray. That girl had conjured the image back into Hillevi's mind by power of suggestion. *There's no limit.*

Now she remembered Berta Fors. It all came back to her while Uncle Carl was making a speech in her honor. In a way it was fortunate that it happened right then because the tears welled up, and she hardly heard a word he said. In the place of a mother and father. Best of luck. A modest but sincere token. We have done what little we could, out of love. And our sense of responsibility. Our concern, dear girl. But your mind was made up. Her aunt gave her the package containing the diary.

Berta Fors had been on a stretcher. She had been bleeding when she was admitted but was not relieved of her burden. Yes, that was the expression Hillevi had used. She didn't lose the baby, the woman herself might have said. There was no release to be had. Our hands are tied, the ward physician said.

Of course they were. But when he'd left the room Hillevi had burst into tears, and her voice was shrill when she said to the older midwife that she thought Berta Fors should have been helped.

Helped?

The expression on her face ought to have been warning enough to Hillevi. But she burst out that the woman should not have to go through it again. She had hemorrhaged heavily after her last three deliveries.

According to the record, said Hillevi. And this time she's already bleeding early on and look at this. Look at this!

She pointed to the admission record in which she herself had registered Berta Fors:

Fourteen deliveries, 47 years old. Three miscarriages, 9 surviving children. Near fatal hemorrhaging 4 times, so heavy she is reported to have been unconscious for 2 to 3 hours. Terrified of the upcoming delivery because she is convinced it will be her death.

It's inhuman!

Yes, in the end she had said it was shameful. She had. That when a person was so worn down she shouldn't have to go through with it.

Behind the screen or out in the hallway, Berta Fors had been lying there listening. In spite of being so worn down. So she had not been unconscious; she had heard every syllable. Afterward she must have spread the word about Hillevi. Probably everybody was talking about her now down in the Dragarbrunn neighborhood. A Miss who was human. Because that was the first thing the girl down by the bridge had said.

Miss, you're human, you are.

But the face of the older midwife was stern, and she didn't even reply. That afternoon Hillevi was summoned to the head nurse's office.

I've seen midwives succumb, said Sister Elsa. During my many years in the medical profession, I have seen it happen now and then to my great disappointment.

Hillevi didn't dare ask what they had succumbed to. She didn't dare say a word, just stood there worrying that there might be a stain on her apron, some dirt on her starched collar, or a wisp of hair that had loosened from the braided bun at the nape of her neck.

I have seen them succumb to appeals for what they call help. Outright help to get rid of the fetus, which brings shame and humiliation on every midwife in the profession, said sister Elsa. There was no getting away from her gray eyes, not for a whole eternity. Not until she looked down at her calendar open on the desk in front of her and tapped her pen against the desktop once, very distinctly, did Hillevi dare to lower her gaze, curtsey, and exit, backing out of the office.

Not until afterward had she begun to cry again. She also wept every time she remembered it, tears of shame and, in truth, tears of anger. Because six months later Berta Fors died after her fifteenth delivery. She bled to death despite the injections and every conceivable medical intervention.

At the dinner party Hillevi's aunt and uncle saw her tears and assumed she was moved. They proposed a toast, wishing her many significant and happy events to enter into the diary. She knew what kind of events they were referring to, but she couldn't even think about her own future or about Edvard, only about what had happened down by the Iceland falls an hour or two ago. It was the most awful thing she had ever experienced.

Cousin Tobias toasted her. He was already a little tipsy. Her aunt always monitored the stages of his intoxication with quick little sidelong glances. It struck Hillevi that she knew why nowadays he often had one too many. Tobias wasn't the life of the party. Nor was he a particularly promising future physician.

Two days later he came into the sluice room when she was standing there pouring a urine sample into a bottle.

Where do you keep the spirits, Hillevi? he asked

In spite of her sudden insight at the dinner table, it never occurred to her what he was really after. She honestly thought he had something to disinfect.

He accompanied her into the treatment room and stood quiet and subservient as a schoolboy as she poured seventy milliliters out of the bottle labeled conc. alcohol. That was the quantity he had specified. With a laugh that was anything but good-humored, he took the measuring cup out of her hand and diluted it with water from the carafe.

Tobias!

He had already downed it, bottoms up.

We simply can't have this, she said quite sharply.

My dear young cousin, let me tell you what things are really like. I have just paid a visit to Miss Ebba Karlsson in her penultimate resting place. She received me in quite a state of dissolution. I performed an autopsy on Miss Karlsson.

She was carrying a child. That's the way it goes. It shouldn't.

He extended the measuring cup again, but she pretended not to notice and went over and stood by the window. She heard Tobias pour himself some more, but she didn't say a word. He was undoubtedly ashamed of himself. That was why he had tried to pass it off as a joke.

To her lovely golden tresses, he said, raising the cup.

Tobias! That's quite enough now!

He backed out the door, suddenly extremely embarrassed.

There are lots of girls. Their names are Beda and Ebba and Alma. Karlsson and Pettersson and Fors. Quite often they live down in Dragarbrunn. Lots of them have blonde hair. Golden you might even call it. Many have a blonde mane anyone at all might envy.

She knew that she had to find out who the dead girl was, or it would plague her forever. But she had no intention of involving Cousin Tobias.

When I have seen with my own eyes that it isn't her, I'll find her. I'll help her in all kinds of ways. I'll collect money. I'll see to it she doesn't have to be afraid anymore or at a loss about what to do. It can't be absolutely impossible to find her again. She might even come back.

But then she remembered her own words about the umbrella and how she had left the young woman under the lamppost in the rain. That was when she'd given up.

They'd been to the hospital morgue during their training course. They'd seen stiff, pale, graying bodies. It was unpleasant but not unendurable. Nor was it the actual autopsy that upset Tobias so badly. It was the girl. By dissolution he must have meant she'd drowned.

Aunt Eugénie had warned her before she started studying midwifery.

You will, of course, be getting married one day, Hillevi, she had said. An attractive and healthy young girl like you. And a man, my dear, wants a woman who's pure. A pure young woman with an unspoilt mind to mother his children. He doesn't want her mind sullied.

Hillevi and Sara had had a good laugh over that one.

The caretaker opened the door. Since she worked at the hospital, he didn't object to showing her one of the corpses. They'd already laid the body out in a wooden box. There was only one young woman right now, so there could be no mistake.

She was covered with a sheet. As he started to pull it down she cried out:

Just the face. That will do.

There was that golden hair that had lain in a wave under the brim of her hat. Her face was swollen but not beyond recognition. It was torn up along the right ear and cheek. That must have happened after she drowned. Her skin had gone spongy and gray. Bruised in places. The puffy eyelids were shut. Something fungous was growing out from under the ridge of her eyebrows. Her lips were cracked. Her teeth shone between them.

I don't need to see any more, she said, knowing that she would regret having come here.

He shut the lid.

Do you know where she was found?

In the river of course.

Where at? Was it by the Iceland bridge?

That's where they usually get stuck, he said.

She said good-bye and walked quickly out onto Garden Road and inhaled deeply. The stink of carbide stayed in her nostrils all day. Although it must have disappeared in the physical sense, she could still smell it.

Before going to the morgue she'd told herself that it was better to know than to have gnawing doubts. But it wasn't. She couldn't talk to anyone about what she'd experienced. Nor could she write about it in the diary.

No, Hillevi never wrote a word about it in the book with the plush cover. Not in her black oilcloth notebooks either. But in the very first one, which she'd bought to draft of her midwifery log in, there are some notes from her room at the inn in Lomsjö:

near field
enclosure

Shrove Tuesday Dumplings
8–12 potatoes. Cold boiled or raw. Or mixed.
2 coffee cups barley flour or crumbled oatmeal
1 liter white flour
2 teaspoons salt
7 coffee cups milk

Serve with:
lightly salted pork and sauce made from soft whey cheese or
melted butter

In a bowl, mix the sifted flour (or oatmeal) with the grated potatoes. Pour the milk over, one cup at a time, until the dough is a good thickness. On a floured baking board, shape it into a roll, then divide the roll into pieces of equal size. Fill each dumpling with diced, fried pork and whey cheese or just butter and whey cheese. Round it and smooth out the cracks.

Boil the dumplings in lightly salted water until they rise to the surface plus a few minutes more.

Serve with fried pork and whey cheese sauce.
Shrove Tuesday dumplings are only eaten during Lent.

Yesterday, a man called Halvorsen from the parish of Röbäck shot a she-wolf on Lake Kloven.

By the time they reached Kloven, she was very tired. She'd been talking to Halvorsen for a whole day. Or perhaps she'd mostly been silent. At any rate, she wrote two words.

wuz

figger

On the afternoon of the second day of their journey, they were driving across Lake Boteln.

There's the chapel, said Halvorsen, waving his whip vaguely in the direction of the other side of the lake. It had been there longer than the church, was from the seventeen hundreds.

They were that keen to make Christians of the Lappfolk, he said with a grimace.

It was a small red wooden building out on a point of land. It looked odd. There were no other buildings over that way. The village was eventually established by the other lake, which was larger, Lake Rössjön. The ridges were deep blue now, with fewer white-spotted stretches. The March sun baked down, and the snow thawed. Heavy loads of snow swept down off shingled roofs in one fell swoop. The church spire became visible in the distance, but it took her a long time to be able to distinguish the white walls of the church from the snow on the ground.

All the joy she had been hoarding up for so long, saving up for the day she would see Röbäck church for the first time, had evaporated. There was nothing left but a cold sinking sensation of having done something irrevocable. Halvorsen, who was whistling between his teeth and waving his whip, knew: Hillevi Klarin was already acquainted with the minister. Indeed.

Although she hadn't said another word about it.

He pointed out the parish hall and the vicarage. There were other low gray buildings he didn't identify. He indicated the schoolhouse with a wave of his whip. That was where she would be living, in an upstairs room.

One room.

Wisely she kept her counsel.

26

The first few days she was mainly alone with her thoughts. It was unpleasant. Worse than unpleasant: she kept remembering when Edvard found out she had applied for the midwife's post in Röbäck. His fury was clear from the flare of his nostrils. She had felt her stomach sink. But she had not withdrawn her application.

The room upstairs in the schoolhouse turned out to be somewhat more than a room. A room with a wood-burning stove and a sleeping alcove, she would have called it back in Uppsala. The ceiling sagged with moisture, yellow lakes with brown edges.

The stove's new, and they've papered the place up special, said the caretaker's wife, whose name was Märta. She showed Hillevi up the steep wooden flight of stairs that was more like a ladder. When she saw the room, she thought she'd be able to make it homier if only her trunk would arrive.

The man who brought it was called Pålsa and drove a big sledge pulled by a pair of horses. They looked like Halvorsen's mare, short, with long, black shag on their hindquarters. He was difficult to get rid of. She'd had enough after traveling two days with Halvorsen and wanted the man to leave. But he just stood there inside her doorway. Afterward she couldn't remember what he looked like. It was as if she'd been visited by a homespun jacket and a heavy corduroy vest. An independent part of him, a black leather cap, was already on the chair inside the door, so she ended up inviting him in for coffee. She'd done her first baking, and the stove was a good one. As the fire died down, the temperature was even, perfect for drying rusks.

He drank slowly, dunking his rusks and telling her that not a single woman in the villages that made up Röbäck parish owned a hat. Except for the minister's wife.

Mysterious words. He talked with his mouth full of sweet rusks. Now he was saying that only about ten of the children had been vaccinated against smallpox. He was glad Hillevi was trained in health care and the use of instruments.

But, he went on, chewing for ages before the rest of what he had on his mind came out, the previous midwife had made one serious mistake. In addition to which she'd worn a hat.

Much of the time he was incomprehensible even without a mouthful of rusks:

They's been tree afore ye, but they's all been tetchy.

The midwives' tetchiness, it seemed, had mostly been about their lodgings. Hillevi could already have enumerated dampness, the smell of mold behind the new wallpaper, drafts along the floor, and leaky window frames. But she said nothing for the moment.

Afterward she thanked God for that, more or less. The man turned out to be Isak Pålsson, chairman of the local council. She was dependent on him for everything, and she wanted the roof reshingled and the ceiling whitewashed. After he left, she went out into the unheated hallway by her upstairs room and took down the hat that was hanging on a nail above her coat.

Hillevi and Edvard Nolin had met when he was standing in as hospital chaplain. The sight of his neck above the starched white collar and the black edge of his cassock had touched her deeply. He often walked her home in the evenings, and one night he put his hands on her shoulders. After that, a whole week passed before she heard the swish of his galoshes behind her again. That night he took off his gloves and groped inside her coat, seeking her waist. He moaned.

Wanting Hillevi weighed heavily on his conscience. Wanting her in that way, as he put it. To her it was also a major issue, but a worldlier one. She was in love with Edvard Nolin. It was meant to be. But they couldn't afford to marry. Some evenings they crept up the stairs to his room. He made tea on the top of his wood-burning heater.

When he had exposed her camisole with its lacy edge and groped his way to one breast, cold on the top, he groaned as if he were in pain. Nothing happened that night either.

When it finally did, he kept his eyes shut. Afterward he sat at his desk in his underwear, head in hands. There was no lamp lit, but outside the house there were streetlights. The slats between the windowpanes cast the shadow of a cross on the wooden floor and extending across the bed. Hillevi lay there with his fluid in a handkerchief. He himself had ferreted the handkerchief to her at a moment very close to the decisive one. Not until she felt something wet growing cold on the inside of her thigh did she realize what he meant her to use it for.

The handkerchief business made it a little more commonplace: it all came to something more tangible than a groan, something that needed to be wiped up. Hillevi thought about it when she watched him baptize newborn babies in the hospital auditorium. His firm hand wiped the baby's brow with a linen napkin, so he did know how.

Hillevi was going to be a minister's wife. She wondered how long it would be before the bans could be read. Edvard was slow at some things, but perhaps by summer, and certainly no later than next autumn, she'd move into the vicarage, which Halvorsen had pointed out with a crack of his whip. How strange that there were curtains and potted plants in the windows.

She asked Märta Karlsa why the curtains were still hanging there and why someone lit the fire in the empty vicarage every day.

But sure those curtains and flowers in the windows belong to the minister's wife. And the house isn't empty at all.

This peculiar statement made Hillevi's stomach contract.

There she is now, said Märta.

The minister's wife had come outside. She was no ghost. She wore a very old-fashioned black coat with a collar that had three ribbon-edged flounces running halfway down to the elbows. She vanished in the direction of the village. Moved! No, indeed, they hadn't moved yet. The minister was paralyzed from a stroke and couldn't budge.

But isn't a new minister coming? Hillevi asked cautiously.

The assistant minister will be living in the garret, said Märta.

So Hillevi decided to pay them a visit. Edvard wouldn't have objected to the garret room of course. When it came to the commonplace, the worldly, he didn't have much gumption.

Twenty-five years old. The brim of her hat covered the wave of her hair, which to tell the truth, was slightly padded. Her Uppsala thoughts came and went. But most of the time she was busy decorating the plastered wall around the stove with indigo flowers she painted with bluing. Still a girl: hasty decisions, feelings making themselves known in the pit of her stomach, in the palms of her hands, in her armpits.

Edvard, her beloved. His parting words had been a final admonition to keep silent. So how could she have let on to the driver before she even got there? She was jittery the first time she knocked on the vicarage door. She knocked harder. Gathered her courage.

Reverend Norfjell was lying on a sofa in the room where for thirty years he had written his sermons. The white whiskers were the only indication that there was still skin covering his skull, the color of which was primarily yellow.

He's been lying right there since Mickelmass, said his wife.

He was propped up under a quilt. His gaze was fixed on the wall. There was no saying whether he could see the faded pattern of lyres. This room will have new wallpaper, Hillevi nearly said out loud. Suddenly something speckled with gray swished from on top of the quilt to under the tablecloth on the little marriage altar. She couldn't decide whether or not to walk over to the stationary figure and introduce herself. His wife started telling her all about his stroke. She realized now that there had been premonitions.

I'd received a crate of apples, she said. From down south of course. You know, Miss, I suppose, that there are no apple trees here?

Hillevi didn't.

They were winter apples, Åkerö. I always worry they'll freeze if I store them up in the attic, so I cut rings and dry them instead. I'm sitting in the kitchen with the chambermaid. She's peeling and I'm slicing. Yes, I call them chambermaids. Up here all they ever say is maid. Or girl. When he calls me. He wants his coffee. It was a little early, but I brought it in of course. We had coffee together. Right here. He was sitting at the desk. Then he gave me this note.

She waddled over to the desk. Hillevi had never seen such old-fashioned clothes. A black satin dress with a gray-brown sheen at the seams. Gathered in tiny little puckers at the breast. From behind, the skirt cloth was pulled into draping folds. One could sense a bustle. But although she had probably put that device, with its horsehair stuffing, away in a drawer when it went out of fashion, no one had altered the dress. On her head she had some little lacy rounds.

Here it is.

Hillevi read: *Plures spes. Una restat.*

He told me he wanted that on his gravestone.

I don't know what it means, said Hillevi.

Nor do I.

No, there was no one to ask.

Two weeks later there he was, face down on the desk when I came into the room.

Hillevi looked at him. Could he hear? Not that she could tell. He looked stern but peaceful. Märta Karlsa had described the minister's wife as a docile person, but Hillevi thought she might have changed some since Mickelmass. It had been a long winter with a kitchen girl and possibly a cat for company. And the immobile shape on the sofa of course. Her voice was high and shrill, as if she hadn't had anyone to talk to in a long time.

This ceiling needs repapering, thought Hillevi. The whole house will have to have new wallpaper and probably new insulation behind the walls too. She had heard that the sawdust clumped up in the damp. She would have liked to ask if the house was hard to keep warm in the winter but couldn't figure out how to slip it into the conversation. And how could she get a peek at the kitchen? I could come back some other day with something I've baked. Go right to the kitchen with it.

Well, we got here in 1884, said the minister's wife.

She looked in his direction when she spoke. Perhaps she was speaking to him. Hillevi was becoming increasingly convinced that the formerly docile woman had changed.

He was appointed chapel minister that year. We never meant to stay, no. The Bishop thought well of him in spite of his youth. But we never left after all. You see, he took such an interest in the Lapps. And they were poor folks, that they were. You'll have a cup of coffee, won't you, Miss?

She'd kept up her routines even after what happened at Mickelmass. She put out several kinds of cookies and was most insistent that Hillevi have a piece of her almond cake. Apparently it had been sliced and ready in its copper pan for a long time. She said the recipe was from Öland.

I come from Kalmar originally. There's no wheat flour in it. You take equal measures of pea flour and potato flour. And beat ten eggs into the sugar. And almonds of course, a full hundred grams, along with a couple of bitter ones.

Hillevi thought she'd bring over a pound cake, pure and simple. She didn't even have an almond mill. How could she arrange to measure the window frames? She could count the windows from outside. She hoped to set up her loom as soon as possible and was already planning to weave thin, attractive summer curtains of tulle netting. But the loom hadn't arrived yet, and it was still too cold to sit and weave in the school attic anyway. She had a feeling that the days were going by much too fast. The minister's wife rambled on about the years and the decades that had passed. She turned toward the bed. It was cruel if he could hear her, Hillevi thought.

The gray-speckled cat, an old thing with a sagging belly, came out into the open. As if by habit she leapt up to the sofa and lay down on the immobile man. His eyes were fixed as before on the wallpaper. The minister's wife got up and straightened the cloth on the marriage altar after the antics of the cat.

Well, this is where he wed couples who were expecting, you know. Most people who get married around here are.

She's speaking so frankly because I'm a midwife, Hillevi thought. As if she could read her mind, the minister's wife said:

You tell the plain truth after thirty years in a parish like this. I've got nothing against the villagers. It's the Lapps.

Now it was perfectly clear that she was addressing him, the man on the sofa. Her puffy little face was constantly turned toward the yellow head with the thin white stubbly hair. It was as if she were waiting for him to protest. Then she smirked. It was anything but a kind smile.

You know, he developed such an interest in them. They are my life's work, he would say.

There was a singular kind of ridicule in her eyes, above the bags. Hillevi looked away.

Miss, I'm going to tell you something you need to know. Because your mission of mercy will also be carried out among them. You mustn't become too involved.

She turned toward the sofa again.

They are beasts, she said. Simply beasts.

It was cold at night, but the sun baked down during the day.

We'd best do sommat with that fur of yours, said Märta Karlsa. It's startin' to stink.

The only fur Hillevi knew she had was the faux fur collar in its box.

I've put it in the loft, said Märta. Under the rafters so's the rats can't get at it.

She led the way to the barn and up the ramp she called the loftway.

It wasn't properly cured. And now it reeks.

Under one of the roof beams she had lodged the rolled up hide.

Hillevi recognized it. Though the ears had been cut off now.

That belongs to Halvorsen.

He says it's yours, Miss.

Well, it's not. Send it north by the first cart.

He's sure to pass by himself one day, Märta mumbled. Her face had gone stiff. But right now Hillevi didn't care.

She didn't want to ask about it again. But she went up the loftway a couple of times when she was sure no one was looking to see if it was still there. She felt an unaccountable sense of relief the day it was finally gone.

There was a war on. They had to use carbide instead of kerosene in their lamps. I had been born by then, but of course I don't remember it. Hillevi told Myrtle and me about the hissing sound the water and the carbide made when they mixed. The light produced by the gas was an unmerciful glare. She had cut an article out of the newspaper and pasted it into her black book. We read it.

Newborn Babe in a Trench

The following strange story comes to us from an Austrian officer. One October afternoon a Bosnian soldier discovered a newborn boy in a trench, in the area where the Austrians and the Russians were fighting. Where had he come from? No one knew. Was he the fruit of a sinful union, a baby the mother was trying to dispose of in the heat of battle? Or perhaps in desperation because the father had been called up to serve the flag? Was that what had extinguished that most sacred feeling of all, motherly love, causing this mother to leave her child to its fate?

The little fellow could not know what dangers were lurking all around him; he seemed to smile at the soldiers. The officers took up a collection, resulting in a sum equivalent to 170 crowns in our currency, which sufficed to purchase the bare necessities. A nearby parish assumed responsibility for the child's upkeep. All kind and caring people are being appealed to for a contribution so that this destitute child, rescued by his guardian angel, may grow up to become a decent member of society.

I found that newspaper clipping again the other day. It had fallen out of one of the oilcloth notebooks; it was brown around the edges and so brittle I had to handle it with great care to keep it from disintegrating.

I thought she must have had me in mind when she cut it out, how she had found me, and that she was my guardian angel.

I was eager to put the yellowed clipping back in its rightful place and started looking for a spot that size with traces of milk-and-flour paste. It took me a long time, but I finally found the notebook in which it belonged. It was from 1916, before I was even born. She couldn't have been thinking about me at all.

Last Tuesday was when I found the spot where the clipping should be. Today is Sunday. For five days I've been tormented by the realization that I had no idea what Hillevi was thinking about.

The lake is still choppy. The water is black outside the window. Off toward Lubben there's a light. The school is dark. There are lights on at one or two houses out at Tangen; almost everything else is dark.

I feel my loneliness intensely. Seeing Myrtle's pink cardigan on the rocking chair, where I'd put it to remember her by, made my heart ache, so I put it away.

You can never know what another person is thinking. Never.

It's evening, and the heartache is exhausting.

Now it's Monday morning, and the sun is strong. It was an extremely cold night. There's a thin film of ice over the water in the inlet. Just now, when the wind picked up, the ice was crackling. It will soon break up, but it won't be long until the whole lake is frozen solid. Then the air will be less raw, and when the ice is covered with snow, it will be lighter outside.

I heard a melody on the radio, and it lifted my melancholy spirits. That was odd since it brought to mind my Uncle Anund's song that begins *There was once a bride and groom upon their wedding day*. It's about a terrible calamity that took place right here on the lake outside my window.

One late summer day three boats were crossing the lake, heading for the outlet up by the border. When the wedding party got that far, they would have to disembark and walk past the falls to a boat landing known as Oppgårdsnostre. From there they would be rowed across Lake Rössjön to Röbäck church.

There were two big families, all the wedding guests, the woman who had dressed the bride, and the little flower girls and ushers. They were in their black churchgoing clothes, and the bride was bedecked with a tiara and a necklace, gaudy stones, and all kinds of baubles that sparkled in the sun.

But the weather it grew dark, and the wind began to roar.
And soon they could imagine what fate might have in store.
As quick as from the mountaintop an eagle may swoop down,
misfortune soon would strike them and in the sea they'd drown.

This lake turns black before you even realize there's a storm brewing—it's transformed into something vicious and evil.

So many dead in this cold water.

When Tore Halvarsson was pulled up onto the shore, Sven Pålsa, who found him, stepped to the side and was sick. That was how awful he looked, though he hadn't been in the water more than a couple of hours.

One of the three boats with the wedding party capsized in the sudden storm that blew up. There were twelve people in it, and they all drowned. They were:

Isak Pålsson, farmer, 64 years of age.
His son Anders who was only 20.
Isak Pålsson's wife Erna, 52 years of age.
Their daughter Märet Isaksdotter, 25, who was to have been the bride.
Jonas Aronsson, farmer, age 40.
His wife Karin Efraimsdotter, the same age as himself.
Their 15-year-old son Aron.
Their daughter Regina Aronsdotter, only 12 years of age.
Jonas and Karin's younger son drowned too. His name was Daniel.
Karl Persson, a farmer's son, 23 years of age.
Ingeborg Persdotter, a maid, 25 years of age.
Berit Halvdansdater, a farmer's daughter from Skuruvatn, Jolet, lost her life as well.

Not until Mickelmass 1876 had all the bodies been found. Every single one was buried in the churchyard at Röbäck except for Berit Halvdansdater. She was buried by Trövika church.

Laula Anut had not experienced this terrible calamity himself of course. Nor had he been standing on the lakeshore to see any of the corpses surface. He was born in 1903. I heard him sing the song at Christmastime in 1928. I was particularly moved by what the young woman in the wedding dress cried out before she sank, and what she was thinking when the water covered her and everything went dark.

> *Death's cold arms embrace me, soon I will close my eyes,*
> *and from the murky billows I never more will rise.*
> *O Lord do hear me calling, I'm sinking as I pray!*
> *Those were the words she uttered, we hear them to this day.*

> *The murky waters clasp her, hold fast her pallid form,*
> *all hope is lost forever, no respite from the storm.*
> *A rocky ledge she rests on, and not a bridal bed,*
> *far from bridegroom, hearth, and home, in chilly waters dead.*

I found it strange that my uncle could sing about things no one had witnessed. Even then I was aware that no one can know what another person is thinking. I attributed supernatural powers to him. I was eleven at the time.

Now I am old and have long since realized how natural it is to be able to imagine a disaster. His songs bring me great comfort, even the mournful ones.

> *Like little birds that fly away, leaving us behind,*
> *so many meet their deaths although still young of heart and mind,*
> *nothing is more certain than the journey we must make,*
> *nothing is more sure, whatever turns our fates may take.*

My father was a Scottish lord; I don't think anyone would deny that today. But people around here have always been more inclined to remember that my mother's father was a thief known as Meat Michael. They credit Hillevi with having raised me from my circumstances, which were poor, and she deserves that credit. But I was actually lifted away from my childhood home for the first time by an eagle, something that people find more difficult to forgive.

But they certainly profited from it for a long time.

Later times changed, and the village council voted to take down the sign.

In any case I reckon the most remarkable man in my kin, on either side, at least the ones I know of, wasn't that lord but Laula Anut, or Anund Larsson as people called him down here.

People loved to listen to his songs and to sing them too. But they were not always prepared to give him credit for making them up. And they were even less generous about his stories. Though only afterward. While he was telling them, they would stop chewing with their mouths full.

They loved child murders and stories about abducted girls.

Not a single childbirth though it was going on three weeks. She was losing confidence. Hillevi needed to prove to herself that she'd be able to deliver a baby knowing there was no help to be had within eighty kilometers. And not really there either since the doctor in Byvången was a fat old man with a bad heart who would only make the trip under duress. She tried to convince herself that most of the time you got there before it was too late. That children tended to come out head first. But at night, in her dreams, her hands fumbled. Disconsolate, she tried frantically to put together bits of a torn placenta, trembled when she touched sharp, bloody instruments. Ran in deep snow and sank down and down. And suffocated. Never before had she dreamt that she died.

That was when she decided to start going from one village to the next offering vaccinations. Besides, the roads wouldn't be passable much longer. Her first stop was Blackwater, named after a big lake that was under ice and snow at this time of year. She made the trip there more than two weeks after her arrival in Röbäck. She had packed vaccine, disinfectant, and a little vaccination knife into her midwifery bag. She had sent Isak Pålsa a message to please post a notice at the shop.

Although the driver took the short way across the lake, the sledge journey still took over an hour, and she was hoping she'd be offered a cup of coffee on arrival. But she didn't get anything until she'd taken a room at the guesthouse after finishing her vaccinations at the school. That was quickly accomplished since only two mothers, with a total of six children, turned up. When she went down to the shop the next morning, she saw why. Next to the notice that a nurse would be coming to the schoolhouse to give vaccinations, there was another piece of paper on which someone had written in aniline pen *Copied from a newspaper article*, and the following:

> *Those medical researchers who have not become obsessed with profit making but who are, instead, compelled to seek the truth, have recently proven beyond a doubt that vaccinations result in baldness, nearsightedness, a pessimistic worldview, suicide, and a decline in the sciences, art, and literature.*

All she could do at that point was to tear the paper down. And not until later, much later, did she realize that if she had not gone down to the shop that morning before returning to Röbäck, none of it would ever have happened, or at least she would never have known about it.

She didn't, thank goodness, see that long-haired Trond at the store, didn't bump into him anywhere. His sister Aagot was behind the counter. A waif of a girl, incredibly thin. She had dark eyes, and her plait was black and thicker than her forearm. She didn't say a single a word. Just took down the knitting yarn and the other things Hillevi asked for. Well, when it came to the cardamom, she did say we haven't got any. Whether she meant they were out of it or whether people up here didn't spice their coffee cake with cardamom was more than she let on to Hillevi.

Two women were whispering in the shadows over in the corner behind the herring barrel. At first she didn't see them. Brushes and rolls of rope hung down from the ceiling and blocked her view. They sounded worried. Once they seemed to be talking about her, saying Miss. Well, since Miss is here anyway . . . but that was all Hillevi could hear. One of them finally left. She pulled her fur hat down over her forehead and drew a thick crocheted shawl up tight, tying the ends in back. With all the layers of clothing she was so broad she had to tie the shawl by the fringes. The other woman opened the door and called after her.

Bäret! she cried. Bäret! Come back.

But she had her skis on and took off.

Shut the door, said young Aagot. No doubt she'd been instructed not to waste the heat from the stove.

Hillevi was on her way up the hill to the guesthouse in the never-ending snowfall when she caught sight of the other woman again, the one who had called out to Bäret. She was standing waiting by a cowshed at the side of the road and stepped out into the middle where the snow was yellow from horse droppings.

Miss ought to get out to Lubben, she said.

Why's that?

She's been abed for four days now.

People spoke telegraphically to Hillevi, and she had to decode the messages herself. But she couldn't.

Abed?

Well, I s'pose she's on her feet some of the time. But she's not getting anywhere.

With contractions?

The woman gave a barely visible nod. It felt like prying to ask for the name. But why was that? She couldn't really understand it herself. So she said:

Who's she married to?

The answer was a grimace that Hillevi was unable to interpret. Then the woman turned around in her bundled shawl and started walking down the hill as fast as the icy, rutted snow permitted. She looked like a stone that had begun to roll and soon vanished in the haze of snow.

Isak Pålsa's wife, who ran the guesthouse, told her the woman in the shawl was called Doris. She was Bäret's sister. Though now Hillevi realized she should have understood the name as Berit. Bäret kept house for Old Man Lubben and his sons. The oldest son's wife was dead after all.

That *after all*. As if you were always supposed to know.

And the girl?

She's her niece.

After which Verna Pålsa would say no more.

Then who's the father?

Can't say as I've heard, said Verna.

Hillevi said she'd just have to make her way out there and asked whether someone might give her a lift.

It's not all that far, said the woman. The best way to get there's on skis. You ken be borrowing a pair. We've got plenty. But Miss, you haven't been sent for.

Hillevi paid no attention to those words.

As she was leaving, a couple of Lapps arrived on skis pulling a sled with four children in it. They were a whole day late but wanted their children vaccinated though they had no money to pay. They offered her reindeer cheese instead, and when she refused to take it, they tried to get her to accept a soft little reindeer hide. She didn't know what to do, and Isak Pålsa wasn't there. In the end she vaccinated them and decided the town council would have to defray the charge. But she was nervous about having taken the matter into her own hands. Afterward she felt slightly weak-kneed in fact. They were so strange, and their faces so dark; they could just barely make themselves understood. The two smallest children had reindeer hair all over their clothes and on their skin from the hides they were bundled up in. She would have liked to have instructed the parents to put a layer of linen in between, but she didn't dare out of fear of offending them. She accepted neither the cheese nor the hide.

It was late by the time she had packed her things and set off on the skis, so late that dusk was falling. It spread out like ashes on milk. She realized she would have to get back somehow, and probably in the middle of the night. That would be a problem.

Lubben was right out at the far end of a point of land extending into this backwoods lake. Of course the villagers wouldn't have called it that. But when she followed the ski track straight out from the shop with the village at her back, there wasn't a single house in sight. Nothing but the tops of the spruces, running along the edge of the ridge and dissolving into a blur in the thick haze of snow. The snow let up a bit as she was crossing the lake.

On her back she was carrying a big, twined birchbark rucksack Verna Pålsa had begun by offering to lend her and ended up agreeing to sell her. Hillevi figured this wouldn't be the last time that she had to get to a woman in labor on skis. Not everyone lived along a road.

In the blue painted pack she had the contents of her bag wrapped in clean towels. She had never been on a pair of skis before, but she didn't tell them that at the guesthouse. It wasn't all that hard. Now twilight had begun to thicken, and she shuffled along the track, slowly crossing the inlet, loops holding her boots in place. When she was still at least fifty meters from the far shore, a hound set up a frenzied howling. Soon she had stirred up a second one whose bark was hoarser. All she could do was hope they weren't loose and keep on skiing. As she got closer, they suddenly went silent.

At the edge of the lake there was an area where the snow was trampled down, a path leading to a hole in the ice. So they got their water from the lake. Didn't they even have a well? Or had it gone dry? She started wondering whether there would be a pot to boil water in and a hand basin that could be made clean enough to use. Towels. Clean bed linen for the woman. And would they have anything to swaddle the baby in?

This wasn't the first time the prickly chill of poverty had brought her up short. But poverty had never before appeared so dark, cowering, lurking, and treacherous.

Yes, treacherous was the word that came to mind.

Once she was able to discern the house, she could see that it was dark. Not even the flickering gleam of a lantern in the cowshed. There was still a residue of thin daylight over the snow, light the night had not yet managed to suck in, so they hadn't yet lit their lamps.

She thoroughly stamped the snow off her feet on the front steps to give them a moment in there. She had no doubt they had seen her. She must have been a visible shape way out on the lake, a thicker darkness on the surface of the snow. Someone had silenced the dogs.

She banged on the door, but there wasn't so much as a sound in response, no footsteps, no voice asking who was there. She shoved it open herself after forcing down the latch. No one here was foolish enough to build a house with a door that opened outward. They wouldn't want to get snowed in.

A gust of indoor air struck her, thick and dense but not very warm. There was no glow from the stove in the corner. They were probably waiting for it to get really dark, and the house grew chilly while they waited. She couldn't see anyone yet. Shapes loomed, a cupboard bed, a sideboard. She couldn't decide whether it was clothes hanging to dry over the stove or someone leaning over it. Mixed with the indoor smells there was a recent odor of barn, probably off Old Man Lubben who had just come inside.

Now she could see him in the thin, rapidly receding light from the window. Something scraped on the cabin floor. Rather than calling out a greeting, she just stamped her snowy boots a few more times. This was not Uppsala. She untied her shawl and removed her mittens without stepping any further into the room.

She took the next scraping sound as acknowledgement of her arrival. She could see a woman sitting by the stove, in the little warmth it still held. Now she could differentiate the sounds: a man's boots with toe irons were rubbing and shuffling under the table. He cleared his throat. The woman rose and could be heard straightening her skirt as if it mattered how she looked in the dark. The first voice was a child's. It asked a question Hillevi couldn't understand. Then came the woman's voice.

I s'pose we'll have to light t'stove. And t'lamp.

When she heard the woman rummaging through the basket of birchbark and kindling, Hillevi said 'evening. No more. The man cleared his throat again. It sounded phlegmy as if he'd been using snuff. Then she heard the snap of the snuffbox lid. He sat there without moving while the woman lit the fire. He didn't even light the oil lamp. After some time the woman went and lifted it down from its hook over the table. She had matches by the stove, and when the wick of the lamp flared up, Hillevi was so startled she felt scared.

There were so many of them! And they were so silent. Children's faces, faded and gray in the dim light. They were sitting on wooden benches and the edges of beds. Grown men and half-grown ones. The woman at the stove was Bäret. She could tell that in spite of the light. All the faces were turned toward her except that of the old man. Bäret was a large woman. She walked heavily, carrying the lamp, and placed it on the table.

Where is she?

She could hear how sharp her own words sounded. She should have said she was the midwife. But they already knew she was sure. When she got no answer, she walked over to the cupboard bed and opened the doors. But it was empty.

I've heard there's a woman in labor here who needs help.

Bäret didn't answer, just looked at the old man at the kitchen table. He was short and wide; you could tell even though he was sitting. He was leaning forward. His head was set low on his shoulders as if he had no neck. He was wearing a dogskin cap shiny with age. What was left of the fur was patchy. Hillevi couldn't see his eyes.

It was a stalemate she didn't know how to break. Their silence in the face of all possible words. Only now did she recall what Verna Pålsa had said: But Miss, you haven't been sent for.

Her eyes were growing accustomed to the dimness. Things were taking on contours even outside the circle of lamplight. She saw the wood pile by the door and the cooking utensils in the corner that they called the pot nook. They were right on the floor. Could one of those pots be scoured clean enough to boil water?

There was a door on that side of the room. She gathered what little courage she had, walked firmly across and opened it. Standing by the wall right inside the door was a girl. It was cold in there. She could make out mattresses and this thin girl, pallid and gray. Hillevi saw her distended belly, her arms around it.

Here she is then, she said, trying to sound like the wonderful Miss Viola Liljeström. Putting her arm around the girl, she could feel her backbone under the shawl.

You come right with me now. We'll get you back in bed.

Never had she imagined having to force someone. The girl stared into the darkness, huddling by the wall, retreating further and further into the room. Hillevi propelled her, gently at first and then more decisively, one arm around the girl's weak back. She was exhausted, offered very little resistance. And yet Hillevi found herself holding her arm more tightly than she'd intended. Everything turned on itself in here: the very words became an act of violence.

How long have the pains been going on?

She couldn't call the girl m'am, and she was afraid to address her as informally as she would a child. Although she was a child. It was so pathetic, the thin body with the huge belly. She was pale and breathing hard through her open mouth, standing bent slightly forward, her arms across the bump of her stomach. Her felt slippers shuffled as Hillevi dragged her across the floor.

What's her name? she asked. Bäret looked to the old man again, and anger flared up in Hillevi. She repeated the question more sharply and finally got an answer.

Serine.

She guided the girl over to the cupboard bed and instructed her to lie down. But she wouldn't.

Boil some water, Hillevi said to Bäret. Then scour a hand basin and pour the water in it.

She could hear from the noise that the men were leaving. But there were still children in the cabin, though they were completely silent. And Old Man Lubben. She saw a fishnet spread across his lap and a netting needle gleaming in the lamplight. She asked Bäret to put the lamp on a stool next to the cupboard bed, thinking the old man would also go out once the lamp was off the table. But he stayed put. She became aware of his stumpy shape every time she turned around.

She held the girl's body, maneuvering her on to the bed, which had no linens. She saw a striped mattress cover full of brownish-yellow stains under the hide they used for a cover, and she heard the straw rustle as the girl lay down.

There's nothing wrong with standing, Serine, said Hillevi. You can stand up for a while again later. But now it's time for an examination. When did the pains start?

She couldn't get a word out of her. But when Bäret finally brought the hand basin, she told Hillevi, softly and hesitantly, that the girl had been abed for a long time. And sometimes up. She'd had pains for several days. She certainly did look worn out.

Now Hillevi removed her glycerin soap and her fingernail brush from the birchbark rucksack, asking Bäret to put the hand basin on the kitchen table and to carry the lamp back there again. She boiled the brush and a nail file in the water that was now simmering on the stove. There was something soothing in the rhythmic sound from the pot. She felt reassured when she heard it. She put on her apron, rolled up her sleeves, and rubbed soap into her hands and forearms. She wished the old man would leave, but he just sat there without moving, staring at her. Now she could see his face in the sheen from a barn lantern Bäret had put on the table. He wasn't all that old. He was short but seemed strong and muscular. His whiskers were yellowish gray.

She was careful to get soap into every little crease and fold and under her nails. Then she began to brush. First she scrubbed her nails and fingertips, and then she flexed her fingers, letting the brush run over them. She had pinned her watch upside down to the bib of her apron, and when she could see she had been brushing for a good five minutes, she took a towel out of the pack and dried her hands. Then she asked Bäret to change the water in the hand basin, cleaning under her nails while she waited. When there was new water, she started over again. Then the old man spoke again. He spoke quite loudly, and he sounded annoyed. But she didn't understand the words.

When she was done with the second brushing, she rubbed her hands with carbolic acid, and then the old man said something again. When Bäret brought her change of water, Hillevi asked softly what he had said. At first she didn't want to tell her. But Hillevi insisted, saying she wanted to know what people had to say to her.

Did she come all the way out here just to wash her hands, Bäret repeated, staring in embarrassment at the floor.

Hillevi said nothing. She raised the girl's body gently from the waist and removed two underskirts. Bäret, who had been ordered to get fresh things, returned with a red wool sweater and an underskirt that seemed reasonably clean. With a joint effort they pulled the sweater over the thin, floppy arms and the emaciated body with its swollen little blue-veined breasts, and Hillevi began washing the girl's genitals. She wanted something clean to put underneath, but Bäret said there were no sheets.

Have you any newspaper, then?

She shook her head. Hillevi took one of her towels and laid it under the girl, who reacted very strongly when Hillevi spread her thin thighs and touched between her legs. She had to speak soothingly to her for a long time and felt she was holding an injured and frightened bird. The inner labia and vulva opening looked fine. And shame on them had it been otherwise. She could hardly be torn or have poorly healed incisions from previous childbirths. She asked Serine when she had had her last monthly but got no answer.

And your first?

Then Bäret started talking to the girl, and Hillevi could hear that she had switched languages. But she didn't get anything out of her either.

How old is she? Hillevi asked and received a mumbled reply. She asked again quite sharply.

Soon fourteen.

And who is the father?

Instead of answering Bäret looked over at the old man by the table.

Hillevi didn't want to believe it. But, thank God, the girl started to sit up, crying No, no. Then she sank back again, and when Hillevi felt her belly, tight and hard, she thought there was a slight contraction.

The girl's no wasn't exactly a relief since even if the old man hadn't abused her, someone had. She spoke to Bäret in a whisper, so the girl wouldn't hear. Such things were crimes; people had been sent to prison for as much as two years.

So it's a serious matter, do you understand? It mustn't continue.

I don't know anything, said Bäret, looking at the old man once more.

Hillevi put her hand on the girl's abdomen; it was extremely hard. She was terrified whenever Hillevi's hands approached her genitals. Hillevi chattered on while she was doing the internal examination, trying to reduce the tension in the thin body. The cervix was dilated, the sac was whole. The baby had descended. She could feel the front fontanel. But the contractions were extremely weak. Hillevi was at a loss; the only thing she could think to do was to give the girl an enema and wait. At least the pains were regular.

When the enema was done and she had washed the girl and then herself again, she asked for a chair, saying she wanted to keep the lamp at hand. With her back turned to the room, she began to keep a log in her black book.

What's her other name besides Serine?

Bäret replied reluctantly that it was Halvdansdatter.

When did her pains start?

I h'aint been here all the time.

Four days I heard in the village.

Nearly five now.

And when had you planned to send for help?

But Bäret didn't answer. She just looked toward the old man at the table and kept silent. Hillevi managed at least to drag enough out of her so she could write down the essential information.

Serine Halvdansdatter, Skuruvatn, Jolet, Norway. Thirteen-year-old girl. Living for the past year with her relation Erik Eriksson at Lubben to help in the household. Date of first menstrual period unknown. Date of latest period ditto. The informant, an aunt, believes the first fetal movements may have been in late November. Carried to term after normal pregnancy with no bleeding. Labor probably began on March 28. I arrived on April 2 at 8 p.m. At that point the girl was suffering from extreme exhaustion with weak but regular contractions at approximately 10 min. intervals. Temperature 37.4°C. Pulse 88. Abdominal circumference 88 cm. Rachitic pelvis, probably from rickets in early childhood. Fetal heartbeat strong, 35 in 1/4 min. Head down, engaged in the pelvic canal.

She sat on a chair by the bed with a stool next to her. She had told Bäret to set the lamp on it. She could see Serine's face the whole time. In the kitchen and the main room adjacent to it, children and men were settling down for the night. Bäret had made gruel and was trying to coax a bit of it into the girl, but she wasn't eating. She had fixed some for Hillevi as well and stood next to her while she ate. Others were waiting to use the bowl. Hillevi didn't eat any of the thin crispbread because she didn't want to crunch or make crumbs. The least she could do was to keep the area around the bed quiet and clean. She tried to tease a spoonful of gruel through the girl's lips and wished she would open her eyes. But her eyelids just remained shut. All Hillevi could do was wipe her cheeks, brow, and neck, which were covered in dewy perspiration. She was waiting for signs of a change. Bäret brought over the Thielemann's drops and smelling salts, but Hillevi refused them. The contractions were so weak now that they seemed almost to have ceased altogether.

One man and two children clambered up to the top bed in the cupboard. She averted her gaze as the men's legs climbed up but still glimpsed the thick gray woolen underwear. One of the children, a little boy who couldn't have been more than four or five, peered out from the bed and stared at Hillevi's face for a very long time. He wasn't trying to get a look at the girl down there. It was as if he was fully occupied with Hillevi's face and her clothes.

You go to sleep now, she said.

But his head didn't vanish until his father dragged him into the cupboard bed. There was the rattling of straw from mattresses and trundle beds. She heard a child crying softly. The adults who had come in had hardly uttered a word all evening, and the children's voices sounded like the cheeping of birds cut short. Mostly they said nothing. Bäret was still on her feet. Hillevi asked her whose the little ones were.

Ville's.

And his wife?

She done packed it in.

Do you mean she is dead?

Bäret nodded.

Well say so then. It's disrespectful talking like that.

Bäret stared at her.

What did she die of?

A bad chest.

In there the girl was lying on her back. The top bed cast a dark shadow over her. Her face was hollowed out by this shadow, and her skin looked like parchment. She was thin and immobile. Hillevi held her fragile bony wrist. She could feel the pulse, and it seemed to have picked up. She checked it with her watch. Nearly ninety. The girl seemed drowsy and wasn't moaning any longer.

Hillevi took little cat naps. When she woke up, her body ached from sitting upright. She had to use the pail Bäret had thought to leave by her, aware of the problem. She would have preferred to go out, but since people seemed to be asleep now, she crouched in the dark corner at the foot of the cupboard bed. Afterward she tried to move around a little to ease her stiffness. But she kept bumping into straw mattresses and sleeping bodies, and she soon sat back down. The place stayed warm because Bäret got up regularly to feed the fire. She wondered if they usually let it die down on early spring nights like this.

A deep longing came over her for the cozy warmth of a tile stove and the light of many lamps. She thought about hot cocoa and voices talking openly and confidently, asking how the woman in labor was faring, answering when they were spoken to, and speaking freely though softly, keeping the everyday clatter to a minimum. She needed to think about soft lamplight and kind voices.

But as she drifted, off she heard Uncle Carl's voice, his loud cry.

There were children out there in the darkness of the cabin. She wondered if they were asleep. Were they holding hands? She heard sighing behind her, rustling and sniffling. Other than that, the silence at Lubben was compact and oppressive. She had no idea why it hung so heavy. Fear was part of it. Even the stolid Bäret lowered her voice when she spoke. Were they afraid of death, that it would come for the girl? Or was it simply force of habit?

Perhaps they were always afraid to speak here. She had a feeling Old Man Lubben wasn't partial to idle chatter. Bäret was a large woman, and there was no question she was doing what she could for this girl who was her niece. But she avoided opening her mouth when it wasn't necessary, and when she did speak, she would glance over at the table at which the old man sat. He had been out for a few minutes just before midnight but had soon come back in. He was in bed now. Where she wasn't quite sure.

She must have dozed off again and woke up suddenly and with a start. The lamp had gone out. She woke Bäret asleep at the kitchen table with her head in her arms and asked her to find a candle so they could fill the lamp. When there was light, she could see there had been a change in the girl's blank face. Her breathing was more forced, and she was moaning softly with each contraction.

When Hillevi stood up, she saw the boy's face again. He wasn't trying to peer down over the edge to look at the girl in the bed this time either. He was staring at Hillevi.

You're supposed to be sleeping, she said. Everyone's asleep. Even Serine.

But that wasn't true, and he could surely tell, however young he was.

She extended a hand for the girl's wrist. Her pulse was at ninety-five. When she lifted the hide to hear the fetal heartbeat, she saw that her underskirt was soaked and the mattress cover dark. The membranes had finally ruptured, but the girl hadn't said anything. The spot was discolored.

She washed again for another examination. The girl was unresponsive, so Hillevi called right into her ear, slapping her on both cheeks:

Serine! Can you hear me? Serine . . .

She didn't open her eyes. Her lips were parched; Hillevi told Bäret to bring a little water. She took brandy out of her pack and mixed a little. First she gave her some calming drops on a piece of sugar, and the dry lips actually responded. But when Hillevi tried to get a little water into her, she gagged. She was cold and clammy and tossing her head in agitation. Her plaits were coming undone, and the strands of hair on the pillow were drenched with sweat. Hillevi wiped her face with a towel she had asked Bäret to soak in clean water and wring out.

The fetal heartbeat was still regular, and the cervix was two fingers dilated. She was just going to note that down and that she could feel the front fontanel angled to the left, when the girl's body arched in a very strong bearing down pain. But it had no effect. The baby's head didn't move down.

Then followed a steady stream of contractions, and the girl pushed but to no avail. She became increasingly agitated between the pains. She was gasping and in a cold sweat, and after a while she began talking softly. But Hillevi couldn't understand and had to call Bäret, who was standing at the stove heating some milk.

What's she saying?

Bäret bent forward, and the two whispered.

Everything's going black before her eyes.

She said something else too about her hands, and although she didn't understand the words, Hillevi could tell the girl's hands were going numb. Her breathing was shallower now and quicker. With the next contraction Serine stared straight ahead and opened her mouth wide, but not a sound came out of her. A voice came to Hillevi, saying words she recognized. Although it was inside her, it was as clear as if someone in the room had uttered them:

She's leaving us.

She was very frightened now. The girl moaned softly with the next pain, but the baby still didn't budge. Hillevi knew what an old midwife would have done. At the hospital they would have called in the doctor because it was clear that forceps were needed. But she just felt weak-kneed, numb, and completely incapable of making a decision on her own.

The next time the girl pushed, the pain ravaging her, Hillevi's numbness passed. Now she knew she had to act, and she gained strength from her own voice as she shouted to Bäret to bring the water back to a boil so she could sterilize her forceps. While they were waiting, they propped the girl up in the bed. She wasn't sure Serine could understand her, so she told Bäret to explain what she was going to do.

Tell her it's almost over now, she said.

While the water bubbled around the forceps and she wiped the girl's face and held her as she pushed, she prayed to God for it to go well.

The fifth day. See to this poor child. Let it end well. Give me strength. And skill, God. Help me, God. I am sinful, I know. She may be too. Or someone here. In this darkness. But do not make the girl pay the price, let her live. Let it go well, dear Lord.

She prayed without letting any words cross her lips. She mustn't let her fear show. She had to sound and act like Miss Viola Liljeström. But she couldn't.

The tongs of the forceps slipped in easily enough but locking them into position proved impossible. The angle of the baby's head made it difficult to get a grip. She had known it would be difficult but had hoped her prayers would do the trick and something would shift. She couldn't pull until the forceps engaged, and she was beginning to feel desperate, afraid there was nothing to be done but let the girl lie down flat again. Then she remembered: you had to lower the handles. So she tried, but it didn't help. She lowered them as hard as she could, but the forceps still didn't grip tight.

I pray to Thee, Lord, with all my heart, she said silently, and then she took a deep a breath to calm herself and began inserting the tongs cautiously. Bäret was behind her, looming like a huge shadow. Hillevi didn't look up, just kept on working the tongs, focused on trying to grasp the baby's temples and get the forceps correctly angled in the pelvis.

I pray to Thee, God. Do not let this tiny creature come to grief. Do not let this girl succumb. I pray to Thee: do not extract from her price for my want of skill. Do not let her die, God.

She felt a pain shoot through the girl's body, and at last the forceps locked into position. Now they were tight. She pulled gently but firmly, repeating to herself the whole time: I pray to Thee, God, with all my heart.

And the baby came.

I do not know what it was like when I myself was born, only that it happened on the side of the mountain called Giela.

Like all women, I was grown up before I could comprehend the anguish of childbirth. Not until I began to feel the movements like a restless bird inside me did it occur to me to ask what it was really like. Then an old woman told me about having been pregnant and nearly at term when it was time to move with the reindeer. She and her part of the herd had dropped behind the others; the pains had started, and she had given birth all alone out there while the reindeer grazed. She had to swaddle the child in the folds of her long skirt and continued walking with the reindeer until she reached the *gåetieh*, the shelters the men had begun erecting. The weather had been vicious. There wasn't much firewood up there, and she had bled a great deal before she could lie down with the baby.

Then I wondered about my mother, whose name I've been told was Ingir Kari, being alone and cold when she gave birth to me. Perhaps she too had to keep moving because her only option was to continue in the direction of the camp. But when I asked Hillevi, she said that Mickel Larsson's daughter (she never called him Meat Mickel) had given birth at the fall and spring camp up in the birch forest on Mount Giela. However, it was a subject she preferred not to discuss.

Other younger women comforted me when I was up there and anxious, assuring me that the kind of horror story I had heard from old Elle didn't really happen even in the old days. At least it wasn't often that women who had just given birth had to drag themselves on in that way through cold weather and slush. No, there was straw under a woman in labor, and there were hides and skins covering the birch roof to keep out the wind and warm furs in the bed, which was changed every day, that was for sure. And the child was swaddled in linen and in the soft hides of reindeer calves, and water was heated and the baby washed. Yes, three times a day for the first three days they washed the infant, then twice, and after a week once a day. That was how women who were good mothers did it.

But Hillevi had told me they never washed their children, at least not after they were a couple of years old.

Who was I to believe?

My grandfather said the midwife had a tube she held up to a woman's stomach, and through it she sucked the life out of her.

I became fearful as I grew heavy; all I wanted was to get down to Blackwater so that Hillevi could deliver me when my time came. I was distraught for the last few weeks, imagining all kinds of terrible things that might happen. But the other women said such things hardly ever occurred, in fact so seldom that there was almost no point in talking about them.

Years later I told Hillevi what old Elle had said. How she had given birth all alone out in the snow. How she had bled.

They're not really like us, Hillevi told me. They feel things differently.

But I said: Us? Who do you mean by us?

Aunt Eugénie used those words too:

People like that don't feel what we feel.

She had said it in such a soft, serious voice. Whenever Sara or Hillevi was upset about something they had seen, she repeated it. There were times when they'd seen what things were like for poor people. For children and animals too. But Aunt Eugénie sounded so certain, so firmly convinced, although she never explained. It somehow didn't seem necessary.

They're not like us, she would simply say.

Once she said:

They're coarse. You can see it in their faces.

But Hillevi remembered something coarse from home. It was Uncle Carl's scream. Her aunt lay in the bed. The lamp flame shone under the shade with the pink flowers. Although the lamplight was as usual, there was pure terror in her uncle's voice.

She's leaving us! he wailed.

She could hardly believe it was his voice. He was bursting with despair and fright and perhaps anger too, and his voice sounded rough and ragged. When they heard his scream, they didn't know if Aunt Eugénie was dead or alive. Hillevi took Sara's ice-cold hand; their fingers remained tightly intertwined.

They sat on the settee in the hall, shivering although it couldn't really have been all that cold. A spring night with rain on the roof. They'd been asleep and didn't know what was happening. Hillevi had woken up because she needed to use the chamber pot. That was when she heard the footsteps and soft voices. She woke Sara, and they went out into the hall and saw the maid, whose name was Anna, running down the stairs. Hangers banged in the closet as she got a coat. She must have taken Aunt Eugénie's since her own was in the closet by the kitchen entrance. How dared she? There must have been a terrible sense of urgency. The door slammed shut behind her. In the middle of the night.

The bedroom door was open. Aunt Eugénie was moaning, and they saw her arms in the soft light of the lamp on top of the dresser. They were pale and resembled the necks of big birds. Their shadows shifted on the wallpaper. It was quite unreal. Sara wept softly. She was a little younger than Hillevi and turned to her for protection. Hillevi had lived with her aunt and uncle for over a year when Tobias was born, and Sara was born another year or so later. Aunt Eugénie was thirty-one by then. Now she was over forty, and it had happened again. She must have been ashamed this time.

But the girls hadn't given it much thought. Hillevi was fourteen and Sara almost twelve. They were hardly even aware of the secret. They didn't know she was in her seventh month that night she began to moan and flail her arms over her head. Time after time her head banged against the headboard. Sara, trembling, cried harder and harder. Hillevi had to pull her back into their room and tuck her into bed to try to keep her from hearing. She thought she would scurry down to the kitchen and see if the Aga stove was still hot enough to heat up some milk for her, but when she ran past the open bedroom door, she heard her uncle cry out those awful words. Then he came out and called for Anna, the maid.

Where is she? Where the hell is that woman? he shouted, although he must have been the one who had sent her to fetch the doctor. Maybe he'd forgotten because he too ran outside now. She heard the door shut; she didn't think he had even put on his overcoat. She had to go in to her aunt who was lying there alone. She was quieter now, but she clung so tightly to Hillevi's arm that it hurt. Sometimes she pinched. The noises she made had nothing to do with Aunt Eugénie. They were as strange and as wild as Uncle Carl's screams. The sounds didn't mesh with their daylight personas. Aunt Eugénie's pale lilac dress with the gray lace edging was on a chair, a cast-off guise from which all control and grace had fled, just as Uncle Carl's fatherly manner and solemnity had flapped away with his dangling suspenders. The two of them had been transformed as in a bad dream; she into a female creature who pinched and moaned, he to a collarless man whose trousers were falling down, with a wild voice screaming: *she's leaving us!* Without even knowing who he was shouting at. He wasn't even aware of his children, Tobias still asleep in his room and Sara weeping under her covers.

In the end Aunt Eugénie insisted on getting out of bed. She held onto Hillevi and raised herself up, leaning heavily and breathing hard and deeply. Hillevi sensed this was the wrong way to inhale; it sapped her strength, wore her out. She stroked her back, smelling the odor of blood mixed with her aunt's own scent, which had survived the transformation as little gusts of everyday normalcy, of elegance and carnation-scented soap. There was blood in the air nonetheless, and her nightdress was wet. Afterward Hillevi had dark spots on her own nightgown. Then there was a movement, a spasm that seemed to seize them both. Hillevi could feel how involuntary it was and what power it had over her aunt's poor body with its bad back. Time and again it wracked her, and her nails dug into Hillevi's arms.

They were still standing there when the nearly full-term fetus came out, although Hillevi didn't realize what was happening. She was holding her aunt up, she could smell her hair, and she was breathing with her, panting heavily. Then her body relaxed, and Hillevi could lay her down. She saw that her nightdress and the sheet underneath her were ruined. She realized she should change the bloody bedclothes and her aunt's nightdress so Sara wouldn't see them if she came in. But first she had to dry her aunt's sweaty face, and then she whispered she would like some water. But Hillevi was unable to extract her own arms from her aunt's grip. She was clinging like a child. Then in the midst of her helplessness Hillevi heard a perfectly calm woman's voice say:

Well good day, Mrs. Hegger, and how are we now?

And then, without waiting for an answer:

Let's see, my dear child. What a good girl she's been, Mrs. Hegger. Dear, do loosen your hold now . . . that's it, Mrs. Hegger . . . I'm here now, you can let the girl go. Everything's going to be fine. We'll just clean up a bit here . . .

Everything they did after that, the maid and Hillevi, they did as the gentle voice talked on and on, describing its doings and its confidence that they would make everything right. Even when she was lifting up the indescribable thing from the bedside rug and when she (quickly and routinely, Hillevi thought with a retch) wrapped it in a towel, she talked on in her soft voice.

Hillevi didn't pass out, and she didn't run out of the room. Anna, the maid, was ordered to light the kitchen stove and put on a pot of water. Hillevi got the sedative drops from her aunt's drawer, but Miss had drops of her own that she administered on sugar cubes. Uncle Carl never appeared. Miss said he was with the children.

This was Miss Viola Liljeström. She wore her midwife's pin between the points of her starched, white collar, a red and white striped uniform over her woolen dress and a big white apron she was quick to change once she had put fresh sheets and a clean nightdress on Aunt Eugénie. The bloody bedside rug was folded up and left for Anna to deal with. When she had brought the water, she was ordered to light the tile stove.

The doctor came too, after some time, but by then everything was clean and calm, and her aunt was asleep. She hadn't left them as Uncle Carl had feared in his anguish. He was himself again. The smell of cigars wafted up from the study where he sat talking with the doctor. Miss Liljeström said she had given Aunt Eugénie morphine drops and that she would now sleep peacefully. They could air the room out a bit but should make sure it stayed warm. She was on her way to a woman who was having her first baby and needed help getting the labor going, but she would be back before noon; it was very close by. She would be seeing to Mrs. Hegger she said, asking Hillevi specifically to stay by the bedside and telling her it was important to check now and then that the bleeding had really stopped. If they were the least bit doubtful, they could come and fetch her again very quickly; she'd be at number 2 Dip Road, three flights up, at the Manders. She would come right away if they sent for her.

Aunt Eugénie was her old self after just a couple of weeks, although somewhat mournful and gray. And she did say how sorry she was that Hillevi had had to see and hear things a girl should be spared. That was in her ordinary tone of voice, modulated and restrained. They never again spoke about the events of that April night.

The baby born at Lubben was a girl. She appeared to be dead at birth, but once the mucus had been cleared she quickened. Hillevi bathed her, noting fetal swelling of both the left and right parietal bones in her log book. On the portable scale her weight came to twenty-six hectograms, and she was forty-seven centimeters long. The fetal swelling distorted the head circumference measurement.

She was diapered and swaddled in what was clearly nothing but a folded flannel underskirt. Bäret had given Hillevi some things that also included a torn man's shirt. Hillevi took a compress from her pack and tended to the navel. There was still some vernix on the crown of the baby's head under her fuzz of red hair, even after the bath. Her breathing was calm and even.

Serine, exhausted, was sleeping. The afterbirth had only taken twenty minutes to be expelled, and it was small, solid, round, and intact.

It was light inside now, and Hillevi could see that there were old newspapers plastered up as wallpaper. Here and there black patches of mold bloomed. At the bottom of the walls were charcoal sketches of horses with buxom hindquarters and bushy tails.

She went out into the cold morning air, thinking it was the first time in hours she had been able to breathe properly. There were ashes strewn along the icy path to the sheep shed. Walking in that direction, she located the privy. On the other side of the wall were the sheep, bleating and bumping. Someone must be putting out hay for them.

She longed to be at home in her own place.

By the time she came back in, the men had had their barley coffee and left, all except the old one. A young boy came back after a little while though and stood silently in the doorway. Bäret seemed to know his question.

It's over now, she said. But it's deformed.

He went and sat down at the kitchen table, looking in the direction of the cupboard bed where Serine was sleeping with the baby beside her. He had removed his leather cap, holding it in both hands. Hillevi watched him gulping and gulping and wringing his cap, his knuckles bony and white.

The old man got up from his seat at the kitchen table, walked over to the cupboard bed, and looked at the child. When he passed the boy on his way to the door, he said:

A freak. As expected.

The tall lanky lad rushed out, shoving past the old man. When they were both gone, Hillevi said to Bäret:

That's nothing but fetal swelling, marks from the forceps. They'll go away. Explain to Serine when she wakes up.

She looked for her log book but couldn't find it. Bäret just stood there, arms dangling, watching. In the end, when Hillevi asked insistently, she said that Eriksson disapproved of her book. Nothing that happens here is to be written down, he had said.

Did he take it?

Dunno, said Bäret. I ain't been in all the time.

The top layer of ice had melted to slush by the time Hillevi left the place. Her skis splashed. The snow was so wet and slushy it didn't even stick to them. Her skirt was so long it dragged, dripping wet and heavy. She'd have to remember to shorten it.

Less than twenty-four hours had passed since she came to Lubben. No one had thanked her for bringing the child into the world alive. It was clear that no one had wanted her there. Well, except possibly for Bäret, that was hard to say. The old man ought really to have given her one crown and fifty öre for midwifery services. But she hadn't dared ask to be paid.

She wondered how things would go for Serine. Would they send her back to Norway with her child? If they were going to do that, she imagined they would have sent her before it was born. So now? Would they go on abusing her? Hillevi had stopped thinking about that part, letting joy take over, the joy of holding the perfect living baby's body and relief that the girl was finally at peace. She had watched her fall into a deep sleep with a little white gruel moustache from the cup Bäret had put to her lips.

Hillevi stood still, leaning on her poles in the swirling snow, falling more heavily now. She would have to file a report. But about which one of the men? And to whom?

There must be a county bailiff, she thought.

She ended up leaving without her log book. The lack of sleep and the tension had worn her out: she was unable to assert her authority. She planned to do so when she came back to check on Serine. By the time she was halfway across the melting sloppy lake, however, she realized that if she waited until the next day she would never see the book again. The old man would burn it in the kitchen stove. It was still there now though; she was certain. He would want to read it first. She was convinced he thought her notes were the makings of a complaint to the authorities.

She could perfectly well write it all down again from memory when she got back to the guesthouse. She stood there leaning heavily on her ski poles, going back over the delivery hour by hour. She remembered the baby's weight and length. What time it had been when she discovered that the membranes had ruptured. Everything. She could rewrite it with no trouble. But it wasn't the way things should be done.

No.

So she turned around.

Skiing back toward Lubben she had a headwind. The snow, swirling from the west and from the mountains, was a gray shimmer. There was strong April sun behind the thick layer of cloud.

Just as when she had come the first time, the dogs began to bark, this time both at once. The whirling snow was flying straight into her face, lashing sharply at her eyes. She had to turn away from the wind and pull her shawl down over her forehead.

She saw shapes by the hole where they got their water. One was bent over it, another crouching down. Then a gray curtain of snow blocked her view, so she just plowed on with her head bent low. The shawl covering her hat was soaked through and heavy with the wet snow.

The next time she was able to see the hole there was only a thickening out there in the whirling snow, one solitary shape, and it was standing. Like a pillar. She skied on in the wet track; it was like skiing through applesauce.

What a strange fellow. Just standing there like that, so still. With no water bucket. It was definitely a man. He was carrying something. He held it in his arms the way a woman does. He had his arms around it, pressing it to his chest.

She pulled the shawl a little further down to protect her eyes from the sweeping curtain of snow, using her poles to pull herself forward. The next time she was able to see through the thick snow he was still standing there.

As she approached, he moved toward her. He passed her the thing in his arms. It happened so fast she just had to drop her poles and reach out. The moment she had the bundle in her arms he turned and headed for shore.

It was the baby. It had no cap on, was not wrapped in a blanket. The man was now quite far away, his boots taking long strides in the wet snow. Actually it wasn't a man. It was the lanky boy. She had seen his face under the edge of his cap. She tore the shawl off her own head and shoulders and tried to cover the baby's head with it. But it was already wet and icy cold.

Stop! she shouted. Help me! I need the poles.

But he kept walking toward the shore without turning around.

Wait! Wait for me!

He was gone now. She stood there in the thick whirling snow.

Trying to shuffle along without poles, her arms tight around the baby, she soon lost one ski. She felt the cold creeping at the corners of her nostrils; her field of vision became even blurrier. Her heart was pounding fast and hard, and she thought: I mustn't pass out now. Her legs buckled under her, and she sat down in the wet snow, the weight of the pack tipping her backward.

Sitting there cleared her head. She held the baby close again and turned up the edge of the ragged shirt to feel her pulse at the throat. Her skin was cold and tinted blue. There was no pulse. Her eyes were tightly shut. The shirt and the old swaddling underskirt were soaking wet.

It was too late. No warmth would help.

Still it felt wrong to lay the child down in the cold and wet while she recovered her poles and the ski. She groped for the pulse a second and a third time, feeling nothing but cold and stiffness. So she tied her tightly to her chest with the shawl and started making her way toward the village. She didn't dare go back to Lubben now.

When the boy named Elis came back from the lake, he was shivering. His sweater felt thin, and his body was a spindly fence pole. The wind blew right through him. His mittens were soaking, and the wetness on his chest penetrated right through his coat and sweater and all the way down to his bare skin.

He didn't dare go inside. Instead, he took the path to the sheep shed. He crept down with the ewes, but the shuddering wouldn't let up. He realized that he was freezing from something more than the cold weather and that this other thing might rattle the life out of him.

He could see through the cracks between the logs that the light was dusky; he wanted to stay just a little while longer, to absorb a bit more warmth from the sheep. There was a powerful odor from the hay underneath them. They radiated heat, but he still couldn't stop trembling. On the other side he heard the goats getting restless. They always knew when it was time. He would have to get out of there before someone came to settle them. He didn't know who it would be. He couldn't remember who had been doing it in place of Serine these last few days. They had sent him, but not every time. He didn't know how often or for how many days.

But the 'wife will warm the kid up. She's doing it right now.

When she got to Lubben, she had unpacked her instruments from that blue birchbark pack; it contained something awful. He was afraid of her. But she was like two women.

The one woman was good. She was warming the baby up now. She was giving life back to that little body. Her hands were giving the child life. They were soft. Now the baby was alive. It was at the guesthouse. She was heating up milk for it now, crushing sugar. Wrapping the sugar in some cheesecloth and dipping it in the milk and giving it to the baby, who was sucking the sweetness and warmth.

He didn't dare go in. He wanted to say something to Serine. At the same time he didn't know what he would have told her if he had dared to go inside.

64

Then his father came into the sheep shed. He did the goats first and didn't see Elis until he got to the sheep pen.

Come here, he said.

Elis didn't move. So the man strode across on his long legs and grabbed Elis by the neck.

What've ya done with 'er?

A girl. Elis hadn't known that before. He said nothing and bent his head to his chest in anticipation of the blows.

Say sommat! Say sommat, his father shouted.

But he kept silent. He thought: You can hit me. You do that. Because the baby's at the guesthouse now. Having heated milk.

His father's beatings were commonplace. But when Old Man Lubben was angry things got really bad. And angry he was, sitting at the table when they came in. Vilhelm still had Elis by the scruff of the neck and was pushing him toward the stove. As if he realized he needed to get warm. Then he said what he believed.

She's got left in the water.

Elis didn't contradict him. He thought it was best if they believed that. He couldn't have been more wrong. He staggered over to the stove and reached out toward the warmth, thinking about the guesthouse.

At that moment a blow came down on the back of his head. He never heard the old man get up. Nor did he ever find out what it was he grabbed and struck him with.

He lay on top of the trundle bed afterward. He never saw the old man again. Everyone but his father had gone out. His father held out the scoop and gave him water to drink. The back of his head was damp. It was dim and dusky out; at first he thought it was evening. But it was just the snowstorm. It was still midday. He heard the wind tearing at the birches and the fire roaring in the chimney pipe. His father kept an eye on him, and it didn't escape Elis that he was relieved to see him move.

Now they'll have the bailiff out here for sure. Didn't you realize that? Or did you drop her?

Elis turned his head away.

Answer me!

But he didn't say a word because there was nothing he dared to say.

He thought he heard an axe chopping outside. Maybe the old man chopping wood. That was what he usually did when his rage didn't abate even after he'd administered a beating.

Elis raised his head cautiously. The wetness on the pillowslip was a dark color. He felt his hair and the back of his head and was frightened. Now he was sitting up; waves of nausea passed over him.

He staggered to his feet and moved toward the door because he didn't want to spew all over everything inside. But he didn't make it. As he threw up on the floor at his feet, a bolt of lightning shot through his head. He was afraid of another beating. So he told the truth. What he knew deep down was true in spite of having thought in the sheep pen about the guesthouse and the warmth and milk. *That she didn't make it.*

She done died, he said. But she's not in the water. She took 'er.

Then his father rose quickly to his feet asking if it was true. His fist was raised.

The midwife took her.

His father grabbed his boots fast and drew them on, cursing when they rubbed. Then the door creaked loudly after him, and Elis was all alone.

He wouldn't be for much longer. He thought: I can't take any more beatings. I can't. So he got his boots and the knife and a warm work shirt, and he grabbed the chunk of pork that was on the kitchen table.

Before he left, he opened the cupboard bed. Serine was asleep. Since he still didn't know what to say to her, he closed it again.

The swirling snow turned into streaming rain as Hillevi skied toward the village. She pulled herself forward as hard as she could in the melting ski track, but time after time her skis stuck in the wet slush and her boots pulled out of the loops. She was worn out and had to stop and rest, her whole weight hanging on the poles. The forested ridges above the village seemed blurry through the thick quivering mist. She didn't think she had made much progress although she had been pulling with all her might.

She heard a dog barking behind her. She skied as fast as she could, but the barking kept getting closer. After a while she looked back over her shoulder and could see his dark shape. He was running along barking, and very soon he was at her heels; she could feel him tearing at her skirt. She tried to fend him off with her ski pole, but this just enraged him, and he jumped up and ripped at her right coat sleeve.

At first he looked absolutely terrifying with big white eyes, unlike any dog she'd ever seen. Then she realized there were white patches on his coat above the eyes. She flailed at him with her pole and managed to make him dance aside. Then she heard a shout, and the swishing and splashing of skis behind her. The dog seemed to calm down, just running circles around her, barking.

She didn't stop. Lowered her head and plowed on. A man skied right up close to her, angling in front of her so abruptly she barged right into him.

He was the one Bäret called Ville. He simply extended his arms. She had no choice. She was afraid of him.

The dog with the white eye patches followed him when he turned around and skied back toward Lubben.

It was as if the awful events at Lubben had happened to someone else. Seemed more like something she'd only heard about.

And yet one thing and another came back to haunt her.

The sound of skis swishing in white slushy snow. The fear.

The hard little ice-cold body. Handing it over.

It had, of course, happened because she was not the only one to have experienced it. But the other person would not tell the story in the same way. In fact, neither of them would talk about it, not even with each other. She realized that much. They would keep silent, keep silent and keep silent.

Their silence was evil. It was like the black water under the ice.

Blackwater was a dreadful name.

She kept her counsel about it at the guesthouse, and she kept her counsel on the sledge journey home. The farmer who gave her a lift was from Skinnarviken. Thank goodness he wasn't the talkative type. Hillevi had only one thing on her mind: telling Edvard. He would know the right thing to do. How to write a report and where to submit it when you lived as far away as this.

She spent the entire trip thinking about her letter to him. She couldn't figure out how to start it. The whole series of events was already blurry and vague. Bäret's clatter with the pot of water. The children's faces. Old Man Lubben's voice coming out of the darkness in the cabin.

The memories floated like curdling milk: lumpy and swirling in a muddled mass. But it had happened. A mattress cover stiff with blood and a sickly smell. Her breathing as it grew sharper. The moaning. Later, sleep.

The sound of skis in slushy snow. Biting fog and bright light and water over the edge of her boots.

The cold infant body.

I need a minister, she thought. And Edvard is a man of the cloth.

Back home again, she sat with her stationary in front of her, but the moment she dipped pen into ink she knew that what she really wanted was to have him there. A minister sitting listening. Preferably not looking her in the eye.

The only minister within reach lay stiff as a board under covers on his sofa, neither dead nor alive. And she just didn't know how to start her letter. The thought even crossed her mind that writing it down might pose a danger to her. A mad thought of course.

Or perhaps it wasn't.

When she folded the paper up and went to bed, it contained one sentence. Oddly enough, she was able to sleep. She was absolutely exhausted.

Hillevi had heard people talk about something they called the Lapp Sickness. It was a nerve condition that affected not the Lapps but others who moved to Lapland. Having been quick to realize how fast gossip spread in this silent community, she didn't want to ask anybody about it. She did her best to be plucky, but she was being eaten away from inside by something that might very well be that sickness of theirs.

She noticed a lot of things now she'd never paid attention to before. For instance, the day the light came back. Or perhaps one day she just became aware that the light had been growing and growing until the sky was filled to bursting with it. Suddenly there was a life to move into here after all. To arrange for. Measurements for curtains. Getting the walls papered. Writing to Edvard about the dining room furniture. Was it possible to buy a dining set by mail order?

She'd been thinking the vicarage ought to have needlepoint cushions to cover the kneeling stools used during the marriage ceremony. And Edvard's study would have to be set up appropriately for marrying couples who had let events get ahead of them, which seemed to happen quite often up here too.

She fantasized about pink and white petit point roses—some in bloom, some in bud—on a black background. Where would she get the stools and a suitable pattern? There was a specialty shop for ecclesiastical items in Stockholm. But would they have roses?

Then it started to snow again, first a gray flurry from the west that made the pine tree outside her window tremble. Gradually the wind died down and the snow sifted more lightly. But it went on snowing, day after day after day. A year ago this month she had been on an outing to Eklundshof and picked blossoming golden trefoil.

The light was intense now, enclosing the world like a bell jar. The daytime silence and the nighttime silence were equally deep, punctuated occasionally by the barking of a dog. It was hoarse and listless at night, more persistent during the day when the April light filled the air. She was sitting, as she often did, by the window embroidering an unbleached linen tablecloth, a project she'd brought with her from Uppsala. In a dresser drawer she had two rolls of beige lace for edging. The cloth had a cutout pattern at the center; she found working on it very restful. There was a clatter on the steep attic stairs; she knew from the sound of felt slippers that it was Märta Karlsa, although there was really not much need to consider who it might be. Hardly anyone else came.

There's a letter.

She just stood there as if she expected Hillevi to tell her who it was from. Although she should probably have asked Märta in for coffee, her eagerness gained the upper hand. Her fingers and chest were tingling. Her first letter from Edvard. She had to be alone. She slit the envelope with her index finger, regretting later she'd torn it.

She started at the end where the right words ought to be. The kind he had whispered. But they weren't. She examined the opening phrase cursorily. She shut her eyes. Eventually she accepted that the words she so badly wanted to see there wouldn't jump onto the page simply because she had been wild with longing for them. *My dear girl!* Her eyes filled with tears of shame when she thought of the three letters she had written. *My own beloved Edvard! Edvard, my dearest beloved! My Love!*

She couldn't go on reading. She sat staring at the windblown top of the pine tree outside the window, touching neither the letter nor her embroidery. Staring at the birches huddling out there in their coats of black lichen. After a while she took up her embroidery again, listening to a bird the whole time. It was in the birch outside the church. A monotonous one. A black bird wanting to build its nest in her heart. Beaks clicking sharply, this time from up in the woods. And the endless fast-falling snow and the droning inside her.

As the light continued to expand, her future contracted until it was nothing but a dim image of rushing back and forth to the vicarage dressed in a hat and coat. In the end it vanished in snow flurries and left her staring out into the murky light.

She still hadn't written to Edvard. Or to the county bailiff.

She sat there with Edvard's unread letter and its ripped-open envelope on the table in front of her. The snow sifted down and dusk fell. What a silly little-girl attitude not to read it. But that was what she was like these spring days. One moment her heart was throbbing with love and longing; the next she felt old and tired. *As your true friend I appeal to you not to subject your nature to more than it can bear.* She had seen that much while skimming the end for terms of endearment.

The fear had passed. It was dark out now, and she got up and lit the lamp. This time she read the letter through starting at the beginning.

Uppsala, March 29, 1916

My dear girl!

Thank you for your long letter. It meant a great deal to me. However, I must admit to a sense of concern after having read it. The situation into which you have cast yourself is a strain on you. That comes as no surprise to me, and perhaps not to you either after our discussions about what I still consider your rash decision to apply for the position in Röbäck. It is an isolated and far-reaching parish, and its poverty and the expanse appear to have over-whelmed a nature such as your own.

As ever, I am overburdened with tasks and have fallen behind in my preparations for the move, including reading the parish reports and other official documents. For these reasons I hope you will show forbearance about letter writing. Moreover, when I arrive, there is no certainty that we will be able to talk as we would both wish. We must continue to bear in mind the sensitivity of the situation.

As your true friend I appeal to you not to subject your nature to more than it can bear. We cannot, in our human frailty, relieve all the suffering that crosses our paths however much we would like to. We must leave it to God and have faith in His mercy.

Your affectionate Edvard

Edvard was a learned man and ordained. She knew he would go far, of that she was certain. The dean of the diocese and the archbishop himself both had their eyes on him. They had reacted with astonishment to the news of his application for a northerly post.

And yet he would never be able to understand what had happened out at Lubben. He would find her account vile and ugly. But the only way she could tell it was the way it had been. Vile and evil and inexorable.

She pulled her own scarcely begun letter out of the drawer. Walking over to the stove and opening the little hatch, she read what little she had written: *My beloved Edvard! Something dreadful has happened.* She stuffed the paper in, and it flared up in an arc, dark brown. Then it crumbled to flakes of ash.

God's mercy, Edvard. God's mercy.

I'm sitting looking up toward the houses on the hill. In spite of the heat, the old man's outside. The Norwegian, they call him. He stumps across the stubbly grass. The seat of his trousers sags. His hand clutches the top of his walking stick. He wears his cap slightly askew. Bravado? Or some kind of jauntiness.

He still wants to be somebody, although he ended up here.

I just can't figure him out. He crosses the grass with short little steps. He raises his stick, lifts his left foot, sets it down, rests his weight on the right one, points the stick forward and sets it down again. Walking is a major undertaking for him. And yet he crosses the grass in front of his house as if he had a destination other than death. Not an urgent one. But important.

Now he's made his way over to where his dog is lying.

The dog is a pointer, black, with matted fur and a few grayish spots on muzzle and chest. He doesn't seem to care much about the old man heading across the sun-soaked yard. He's not going anywhere, the dog seems to be thinking. Seems to know. But when the old man approaches the grain shed, he perks up his ears, and his knot of a tail tightens. He rises stiffly from his sunny resting spot by the timbered wall. Goes off a little way for a pee, spraying the chives.

Now the old man has passed the shed. The dog watches him with those wise brown eyes in their bulging sockets and sees that he's going inside. So he lies down on his side, settles back into the grass and falls asleep.

The bin from the wood-burning stove is on the front steps. Little birds are jumping around in the ashes, chirping and flapping their wings.

Clouds of ash in the sunshine. Whirling particles.

The old man is moving inside his story.

Or has he moved outside it with his stick and his cap at an old-fashioned rakish angle? Stumped onto the grass a new person? A different one.

I imagine he'd like to think so.

The light of a summer night. A girl's body. He had been able to capture it. Some part of him had been sufficiently receptive to her vulnerability.

He is so old now that the rosy nipples he touched have shriveled up and retracted.

Or decomposed.

He caught the erratic light. Painted the cries of birds, the shimmer of skin. Leaves.

When Hillevi was alone and sitting with her needlework, she often thought about Miss Viola Liljeström. About her clean cotton uniform with its narrow red and white stripes, about her midwifery pin with the hospital's initials SSB at the center of a red cross, and about her apron and her stubby clean-scrubbed hands, fingernails cut short. About her mild voice and her steady stream of calming small talk.

She thought about how things would have gone if Miss Viola Liljeström had been the one who delivered the girl out at Lubben.

For the first time she had a contemptuous thought about the object of her admiration: she would undoubtedly have stayed away from places like Lubben. Like Blackwater. Like this godforsaken corner of the world.

Hillevi had presided over two deliveries since then, one in Whitewater and one in Röbäck itself. The first was a twenty-seven-year-old woman, healthy and strong and having her third child. It was a boy, born after thirteen hours of labor, with no complications. There was clean bedding, and although the copper kettle Hillevi sterilized her things in had been standing on the floor in the pot nook as at Lubben, the floor planks weren't rotting, and the house around the woman in childbirth didn't stink of cowshed and mold. The second was a nineteen-year-old primapara. She looked undernourished but proved to be stronger than Hillevi had anticipated. Her labor began at two in the afternoon, and the child wasn't born until nine the next morning. The afterbirth was expelled twenty-five minutes later. Hillevi held it and, to her relief, found it intact. She placed the baby, a thin little girl, in her mother's arms and sat still for a moment with a sense of gratitude she would ordinarily have addressed to God.

She would certainly have liked to talk to Edvard as a minister about her thoughts on the subject of God and his celebrated mercy. Memories punctuated her everyday thoughts and chatter. Piercing, sudden, passing.

But what could she say to Edvard about this? About Lubben. About a kind of misery for which there was no remedy.

She had inquired cautiously. People said the boy had taken off. So surely he was the father. But what had he been doing down at the lake?

She must write to the county bailiff. Or perhaps to the district police superintendent. One evening she took out her stationary again. She had made up her mind.

She woke up at four the next morning bitterly convinced that Edvard would never marry someone who had been involved in such a scandal.

The girl Serine had soon gone back to her own family in Skuruvatn. Hillevi hoped she knew as little as possible. That she had been asleep. That she would be able to forget.

She had imagined that she too would be able to forget. On the way back to Röbäck the whole series of events had been blurry and unreal as if they had happened to someone else. Or not happened at all.

But she remembered. Every detail.

Now her girlhood was over. No longer did she vacillate between regret and desire, no longer did she act instinctively on her impulses. She discovered that when you have a secret you get to know yourself.

She found herself inventing reasons to go down to Märta Karlsa's kitchen with its steady stream of visitors. She wished she could have set up her loom instead of listening to stories about bears and lies about the Lapps. She would have liked to weave something complicated, something that required concentration. If only her loom would arrive.

But what arrived was Edvard. Just before Easter, along with desire and the sun and the rush of melting snow. He came walking down the road, stepping carefully so his galoshes wouldn't slip in the slush, tipping the big wide-brimmed black hat he had acquired. She didn't know whether to laugh or cry.

Finally she took the initiative and went to his office. He exclaimed: Hillevi!

His long slender hands trembled as he extended them toward her. She reached out to take them, only to realize that his gesture had been parrying. He said, in almost a whisper:

We mustn't meet like this. It's absolutely impossible.

But of course it was perfectly reasonable for the midwife in a parish to have an errand at the minister's, as she told him when she saw how nervous he was. She wanted to take his hands and touch his face; she wanted to know him in all the secular and sacred senses of the word. But he was so worried someone might come. And of course Reverend Norfjell's wife did come in and ask if they'd join her for coffee. What Edvard was now calling his parish office was really her parlor. In the proper study, where the minister kept the church records, nothing had changed. Norfjell lay where he was and could not be moved until all the snow had melted and the roads were passable.

Sweet crescent buns appeared on the table, along with butter cookies and tartelettes. There was the almond cake from Öland again too. Edvard said very little, which made Hillevi chatter on nervously. She was animated, to say the least. She started telling a story she had heard in Märta's kitchen, the one about the old man and the Lapp girl. It came to her when Edvard asked where exactly the border to Norway was, and the minister's wife replied that it was out beyond Blackwater, up in the summer grazing lands at Lunäset.

Oh, there, said Hillevi. Where the Lapp wench was abducted!

How do you mean, Miss? the minister's wife asked.

Well an old fellow lived up there with this Lapp wench. He had stolen her away and never let her out of his sight. The old man had long hair, and every evening he plaited their hair together so he'd be sure to know if she tried to run away.

Edvard never raised his eyes from his folded hands.

Anyway, said Hillevi, the wench managed to smuggle a knife into bed one night, and when the old man was asleep, she cut the hair and scarpered. When he woke up and saw she was gone, he chased after her of course, but he never found 'er. She lay under a spruce and heard 'im run past, panting.

The others just sat there silently. So she brought the story to an abrupt close.

She got home to her family, but she was never quite the same. Her mind had gone funny.

It had been stupid of Hillevi to start on the story, but of course she hadn't realized that until it was too late. How am I talking? she thought. She'd said "wench" and "found 'er" and used all kinds of peculiar language. She hoped they understood it was all part of the story.

The minister's wife, at least, gave the story a smile, though a somewhat reserved and not particularly kind one. Edvard mostly seemed disconcerted. He excused himself right away, saying he had work to do in his office. So Hillevi got up as well.

I have a birth to report, she said.

He reacted with relief and was actually pleasant.

When she had shut the parlor door behind her and was standing there in front of him, so close she could smell him, she knew she ought to tell him about the delivery in Blackwater and how it had ended, tell him everything, just as it had happened.

If he had taken her hands, if he had put his arms around her and pulled her toward him, she would have.

But he just stood there behind the desk. So she left having said no more than that a baby girl had been born, apparently dead, in a croft called Lubben. She had resuscitated the child, but it had died anyway of complications from the forceps delivery.

She didn't tell him how old the mother was. It was not likely he would find out. The girl was Norwegian after all, and her name wasn't in his parish register. He'd probably think the baby had been buried in Norway.

Hillevi crossed the road back to her own room in the schoolhouse, astonished at herself but not upset. On the contrary, she felt calmer than she had for a long time.

There are eight seasons.

Winter-spring is called *gyjre-daelvie* and brings the light. The snow is blinding. Not even on cloudy days is it possible to escape the harsh light that makes old people's eyes run. And even on the days when the snow flurries are thickest, the light still works to penetrate the thick layer of clouds. In this season we devour light.

Gyrje, which is spring, comes murmuring in mid-May and lasts a month or so. This is when the water flows. The rivers swell; the streams go murky with everything they drag along as they rush, overflowing, through the woods. One day the ice is black and cracking. The next morning the wind has torn it up, and the slabs are banging against the stones on the shore and melting away in the cold water and bright sunlight.

Now the wild geese arrive. Ducks and mergansers, goldeneyes and divers circle above the water. They settle in at the inlet by the summer grazing land, at the inlets in Skinnarviken, Vackerstensviken, and all the other bays and coves. The song swans descend and float on the surface of the water out where the current pulls, far from the points of land where the foxes and otters have their dens. Their white bodies glisten. The first morning you might think there are pieces of ice floating out on the dark blue water, but it's the swans.

Now the sandpipers and snipers and woodcocks arrive too. One morning the near field is full of sparrows; the next day all kinds of thrushes are there. Thrushes with mottled breasts, with ringed necks, with bright yellow beaks, with black legs or yellow ones. Then come the chaffinches and the redpolls, the ordinary wagtails and the gray wagtails; the air is filled with calls and twittering. The fieldfares chatter; the bramblings hold out their monotonous drone for hours and days.

On southern exposures penny cress appears. Having formed tight buds in autumn, now it will bloom, the very first of all the flowers, honey-scented. In the morning chill the buds still have a violet sheen. Then the sun hits them, and they blossom in white clusters next to the melting snow, which sinks and subsides with every passing hour.

Now the reindeer are in the calving lands, and the does lick their young in the sunlight. The mountain marshes swell; the water gleams on the bedrock. Dwarf birches and catkinned sallows come into view when the snow melts. The leaves begin to push their way out of their waxy sheaths. One morning the air is blue, and the mountain birches have leafed. The green treetops sway, the sun shining right through them, but the crusty snow lies hard and untouched at their feet. If you listen carefully, you can hear the sighing and murmuring of running water underneath.

Spring-summer is *gyjre-giesie*, and it begins with grass pressing upward in sturdy clumps. Soon you can hear shouts and bells ringing as the ewes and the lambs and the goats and the kids and the cows with their calves are herded and led up the path to the summer grazing lands. The curlews circle over the river, warning about the dogs with loud shrill calls. The cows and the rascally goats as well as the matted gray ewes must be taken to the ford in the stream and ferried across to the pastures. On unsteady legs they take their first tottering steps in the blanket of flowers.

Now there is a mat of bright yellow globeflowers along the bank. Some people call them butterballs, what with all the butter that's churned at the summer pasture lands. The white goat cheese will be stored on the shelves of the root cellar and with any luck will age well. All summer long the whey, with the scent of all the flowers of the fields, will simmer slowly in the cookhouse kettle until it becomes a single essence of delicious sweet brown whey cheese.

Yes, then it's summer, *giesie*! That's when you eat the soft creamy curd cheese. That's when you hear the accordion on Saturday evenings and the boys have shaved so their cheeks are smooth and don't chafe. There are violets and maiden pinks in the blanket of grass and a sea of wild chervil.

Tjaktje-giesie, autumn-summer, has to come of course, with all its ripeness and its clear waters, but who thinks about that? Or about *tjaktje*, autumn, when there is so much to do, or about autumn-winter and winter, *daelvie*, when the light will shrink and the cold will bite. It's a long time away.

Everyone knows we've embarked on the journey that leads to black winter, the eighth season. And nothing is more certain than that is where it ends, and nothing is farther from mind when the curlews caw and the night violets bloom in the grass of the summer pastures.

Cold buttocks, Hillevi remembered when she thought about Edvard's visits. Such a shame. In this whorl of sunshine and grass scents and longing: his cold buttocks. And how he brushed and brushed afterward to sweep off all the chaff.

She had taken matters into her own hands. Edvard was so hopeless about arranging for them to see each other. Afraid of gossip naturally, he was quite right about that. But people could be outwitted. So she took charge.

She had started accompanying Märta across to the summer grazing land. The men had ferried the cows and sheep and goats across as soon as the grass was green, and now every morning and evening at five Märta rowed over to do the milking. Some days she stayed to make cheese. Or to reduce the whey for the whey cheese.

Hillevi told Edvard he must take up fishing. He gaped. They were standing in front of the church with him holding onto his big hat to keep it from blowing away. She had to give him a detailed explanation of her plan.

He would borrow the rowboat that belonged to the vicarage and that Norfjell had used to lay fishnets. Edvard didn't know how to do that of course, but he could hold a fishing rod. If he made his way around the point, he could moor the boat and walk through the woods to the pasture hut known as Kalsbuan.

Kalle Karlsson built it on his grazing land, she went on. Märta's only there morning and evening. We'll have it to ourselves all day.

He asked whether it really was appropriate for Hillevi to be spending time out at that hut.

I can row right across if anyone sends for me, she answered.

But of course he meant it in a different way.

Heavens, said Hillevi. There's no need for a midwife to stand on ceremony.

What a fool I am, she thought afterward. He was thinking of me as the minister's wife. I should keep that in mind myself.

The next day was Sunday, and she went to church. Tenderly she watched him genuflect, gazed at his neck above the white linen collar of his cassock. She sensed that his sermon was difficult for the congregation to grasp, but surely it had a powerful effect as well, the contrast between his clear voice and the convoluted church liturgy.

The next weekday he didn't come. She went across with Märta every morning and stayed on at the cottage when Märta rowed back home after her chores. He didn't come the second day either. The third day she saw the boat out in the middle of the lake. He was just sitting there with a fishing rod in his hands. After some time he rowed back to the landing below the church and got out.

She felt a throbbing between her legs. She thought about all the poor young girls whose pounding blood had led them to bitter misery. I'm no better myself, she thought. It doesn't help that I'll be a minister's wife. I suppose we're all the same when it comes to that. Or at least most of us. Though people don't talk about it. Edvard's the same I know. But now he's scared.

She walked back up the path to the cottage, invisible from the lake behind a veil of rowans and birches.

The fourth day she was once again sitting on the rocks at the shore. This time he rowed in the direction of the point, and she saw the boat vanish. She ran across the pasture to the cottage and changed to a clean apron. Stuck Märta's little fragment of mirror into the window casing and twisted the plait hanging down her back into a knot she fixed with hairpins. She was pale with excitement, so she rubbed her cheeks and pinched them to give them some color.

As he became visible at the edge of the woods, she noticed that he was wearing a soft hat, a sporty outfit, and high boots. Unfortunately though, the sociable goats had gone to meet him. They surrounded him, shoving and rubbing up against the cloth of his suit. She lured them away by rattling some crushed barley in a herring pail. The whole spotted herd with their long goatees and curved horns gamboled toward her. Edvard just stood stock still, not knowing what to do with himself.

It took quite a lot of cajoling to get the goats off the path to the cottage so he would walk down it, but it soon became clear he had no intention of going in anyway. He was afraid someone would take them by surprise. It didn't help to assure him Märta never came back before five. So they had to take a walk in the woods as he put it. But thanks to the goats they did manage to get intimate in spite of his fear of being caught. They were so exasperatingly tenacious she had to pull him into the hay shed at the edge of the pasture.

The mud floor still had a thin layer of hay.

The boat appeared at the point. He didn't wave of course. That would be utter madness; someone from the village might see.

The lake sent its clear waters to meet the shore. It licked and rolled the stones.

Sighs, murmurings, and gurgles. Like blood coursing through the veins. Heat that pounded, receded. The stones had been soaking up sunlight and would retain the warmth until late at night. Throbbing.

I need you, Edvard. I wish you understood, wish you weren't so scared of people, of eyes, of whispers, of gossip.

She walked slowly through the thick blanket of grass in the pasture toward the cottage and the cowshed. She saw the milkwort and water avens and the bright patches of butterballs. She picked forget-me-nots and red campions and stitchwort and inhaled the scent, sour and sweet, and got sticky fingers from the stalks of the catchflies. The ewes cavorted toward her with their lambs.

Here lamby lamby, here lamby lamby, she called. After some time she began to weep softly.

They ate up her bouquet.

I don't mind; you're so fine, she said, I don't mind. I don't mind.

That evening she wanted to think about something else. Yes, she had to. So she told Märta she'd like to try her hand at milking and was given a stool, a pail, and an udder cloth.

She liked the smell in there in the dim summer cowshed. She knew each one of them now. They were short, white, and hornless, easy to tell apart by their patches and patterns of black spots: Star-Rose, Saba, Goldenhill, White Beauty, Sugarcrumb, Busy, and Lily. She sat leaning her brow against Saba's warm spotted side. Heard the rumbling as she chewed her cud. The hay rustled when they rummaged with their muzzles, and a strong scent of summer arose from the fresh hay on the fodder rack. When she pulled their soft bumpy teats, the milk squirted into the bottom of the pail, yellow and thick.

Who knows, maybe you'll marry a farmer one day! Märta teased.

Afterward they strained the milk from the pails into jugs they set on the shelves in the root cellar. She had thought separating the milk from the cream must be a very special skill, but she wanted to try it. She copied Märta, balancing an oblong wooden trough of milk on her left knee, full to the brim and with the yellow cream on top. One hand held lightly at the right-hand corner she let the milk run down into the pail slowly and carefully while the cream stayed in the trough. Hillevi didn't really approve of the way Märta did the last step, running her index finger along the edge, so she used a whisk instead, hoping Märta might take after her in the future.

Märta Karlsa was not, however, ignorant about hygiene. After cooking the whey cheese, she scoured the copper pots with a kind of grass she called horsetail, and she never gave up until even the thickest burned black spots on the bottom were gone. She rubbed the insides of all the pans and jugs shiny and put juniper branches inside for the smell. She called it mountain broom.

Märta didn't expect Hillevi to do the heavy chores; she always swept and mucked out the floor of the shed herself after the milking. Hillevi would take the cows and goats up to the salt lick. The salt was there to ensure they'd come back, but they were all real keen on folks anyway as Märta would say. The first time all the goats, with their sharp horns and slanted red eyes surrounded Hillevi, she had been frightened.

But there was nothing to be scared of. The rams were off in the woods, leaving the nanny goats in peace with their kids. Their shoving was playful, and although this kind of tenderness did have a stench to it, she still found it comforting. Märta had once told her in unfamiliar country speech that goats were both useful and friendly. By now Hillevi understood what she meant. Best of all she liked the ewes, and she knew the vicarage had a cowshed with a hayloft. She ought to be able to keep a few ewes. Like in the old days, when clergymen farmed their own land.

But rather than the matted, long-tailed sheep everyone had hereabouts, she wanted ewes with curly coats, soft as silk, so she could spin lovely, fine yarn. Where did a person get sheep like that?

When the chores were all done, they had coffee in the cottage. Märta gave Hillevi a strange look when she saw the curd cheese and cream on the table. She had set it out for Edvard, who had refused to come inside.

Hillevi now saw that perhaps it was just as well, noticing the herring skins with the heads still on; they looked pretty horrid. He wouldn't necessarily have seen them hanging there of course. But she would probably have started explaining that those wrinkly little sacs hanging over there were calves' stomachs they used for rennet, which would likely have made him decline to taste the soft cheese. What would he have thought of the cottage where everything was so low and so ramshackle and rough?

A bench ran along the wall, so old the worn wood gleamed silver. Carved letters appeared in the trailing evening light coming in through the window; the initials of suitors, said Märta with a laugh. Long ago.

It was late evening when they rowed back. The sun was still warm. Märta rowed without oarlocks, the oars just resting in worn-down hollows. They swept along calmly and surely, and the old worn oar blades silently cut the water, which looked like melted glass. Hillevi thought about Edvard, how awkwardly he rowed. He'll just have to learn, she thought.

But deep down she knew he would never come to the pasture hut again.

Right here on the dinner table Myrtle and I spread out the photos. We let the glare of the sixty-watt bulb shine down on them, and we put on our glasses to be able to see all the details.

We could each remember some things too. In the pictures from when we were a little bigger, we ran around barelegged and had no idea we would age.

The photographer was never in the pictures, but we remembered him. He came from Byvången in a horse-drawn cart with his box camera and his tripod. Sometimes we made an appointment for him to come. He would insert the framed glass film into a slot in the camera, and when he finally pressed his rubber ball after endless preparation, the light would etch us into the film in that slot. The houses were in the pictures too, although not everybody wanted them to be because they were gray and crooked. Some of the pictures showed rotting roof shingles too. The hats Hillevi wore were in the pictures, and they were supposed to be, as well as the Sunday clothes and the shirtfronts and the hop vines around the front door. The dogs stood panting, not always with the good sense to hold their curly tails still at the right moment. The photographer didn't like to print pictures where anything was blurry.

So usually the dogs lay still, staring into the black hole that consumed time and transformed it. There were pictures of the cows, not always because they just happened to be grazing in a meadow near the house. People wanted their cows photographed. Much later, in a different time, when the plump cows were long gone and the fields where they grazed overgrown, a few old people could still point out each cow by name. The pattern of black spots and patches on the white cowhide was forever etched into their minds. Horses' pictures got taken too, but that was less surprising.

Myrtle's father had a good hand with horses. We saw a photograph of him, small and agile, dressed in a white shirt and black broadcloth trousers, holding Sooty by the bridle.

And now here I sit with the picture from the thirteenth of August 1916 in front of me. It's pasted on thick beige cardboard and is unusually well preserved and distinct.

That was Hillevi's name day. The date and year are written on the back in her own hand. I have no idea if she had arranged for the photographer to come or if Eriksson just happened to be passing. But she had definitely done the baking herself, and the picture was taken before anyone had messed up the table on which the tall silver-plated cake stand was the centerpiece.

There's Märta Karlsson in black with an old-fashioned lace collar pinned to her dress with a brooch. She would probably have to change in a little while and row across to do the milking. From the shadows, which are beginning to get long, you can tell it's late afternoon.

Märta's husband is there, not quite so dressed up. He has on his heavy vest and a shirt with no collar. There are three women I don't recognize and a Lapp in a high cap with braided edging. He's got quite a handsome longshirt on, with black trousers and newly-brushed boots. I've wondered whether he might be the man from Fröstsjön who taught the Lapp children up at the settlement. He did reading and Christianity with them and the catechism. In the outback, as Hillevi called it.

We must also mention the person who is missing, who couldn't possibly have been there. After all the young minister couldn't go to the name day coffee party at the midwife's.

But Reverend Norfjell's wife is there, in the seat of honor at the center of the group, wearing an incredible hat. Not the large, heavily decorated ones that were in fashion, but a little one, set all the way forward on her head. It's a small straw basket containing a bouquet of silk flowers. She has on a pale gray dress with edging that looks black.

Hillevi doesn't have a hat on in this picture. She's wearing a white blouse with a high lace collar and a gray-looking skirt stretched tight across her stomach and hips. She's got her watch pinned to a black ribbon on the left side of her blouse and is holding a bunch of flowers. The photograph is so clear that you can see they're sweet William. Probably from the minister's wife.

How nice that the only one person of breeding in the entire parish attended her party. Well, beyond Reverend Norfjell of course. In August 1916 he was still bedridden in his study. Often with the cat curled up on him. He died not long after, in the late summer or early autumn. By then lots of things had changed.

Finally, Trond Halvorsen.

There he stands. Black suit, collarless white shirt, boots, round-brimmed hat. His hair doesn't show; it was probably cut very short. No shadow on his cheeks or chin either; I can see he must have spent a long time with his razor and mirror at the window at home in Blackwater. He's holding a crop in his left hand. His horse and cart must have been nearby, maybe over by the corner of the house. In the other hand he's holding up a huge wolfskin.

So he brought her the wolfskin again, then. The gift she had rebuffed. But now it's been tanned and looks nice. I know she kept it.

There's a river people call the Bend. My uncle said it had other names too, mentioning one I didn't understand. Its water comes from the rounded mountains beyond Mount Giela he called *jingevaerie*. There's a photo taken up there in 1916 in autumn-summer, probably a few weeks after Hillevi's name day. It was taken along the river, up where the water is lively and quick. Further down, where it becomes stately and spreads out in big bright calm pools, it flows into the parcels of forest land belonging to Blackwater. In between, in the narrow band of crown forest on the side of Mount Giela, was the autumn and spring reindeer grazing land my grandfather Mickel Larsson lived on year round after he lost his reindeer herd and became a poor man.

If I say the log cabin behind the men is up at Thor's Hole, everyone knows where the picture was taken.

A cart track ran all the way up, so the photographer didn't have to carry his camera and the heavy tripod the four steep kilometers from Skinnarviken. Thor's Hole was on a piece of property belonging to Paul Annersa.

The men were photographed at Thor's Hole before Myrtle and I were born. We used to stare at Edvard Nolin, the young minister. There were four other men, one of whom must have been Eckendal, the merchant. Even I have no idea who the others were. They were wearing tweeds and high boots, just like Reverend Nolin.

These were the huntin' gents. That was what people called them.

The first ones, Admiral Harlow and his hunting party, had arrived on horseback across the mountains with servants and pack animals. They came all the way from Scotland.

That was in 1899. The admiral, his friend Lord Bendam, and their party came to Skinnarviken and had a hunting lodge built up by the Bend. The spruce trees had enormous dimensions in those days, so it was a handsome lodge. A carpenter from Kloven who had a fretsaw decorated the ridges of the roof with gaping dragons. The admiral described himself as descended from Norwegian Vikings, and he called the house Thor's Hall. To the locals, of course, it quickly became Thor's Hole.

I'm sure a picture was taken of those gentlemen in front of the lodge when it was finished too. It had a dog run, grouse shed and baking cabin, ice room, root cellar, stable and woodshed, bathhouse and privy. But there are no pictures left from Admiral Harlow's day.

They didn't actually come many times. Paul Annersa was greedy as a hog, and every year he raised the hunting fee as high as he dared. In the end he went a little too far, thinking that of course he could charge such a rich man as much as he pleased.

When the admiral's company stopped coming, he must have felt foolish. They didn't even send word from Scotland. Paul Annersa asked Reverend Norfjell about it a number of times since they used to write to him, and he would explain what the letters said.

Not until 1916 did the huntin' gents come again, and when they did, the person who wrote and asked to have things put in order wasn't the real owner. This time the money came from a merchant in Östersund called Eckendal. If Paul Annersa's son was doubtful, the cash in the envelope must have exerted a strong appeal. There was a war on after all, and admirals had more important things to worry about than who was using their hunting lodges.

Ladies came along too in 1916. Times had changed, and women were now keen on walking for sport and mountain hiking. The women are in the photo too, standing apart from the hunters. Their skirts are calf length, and they're wearing soft Scots plaid berets.

The men are lined up with their rifles, and the dogs have been ordered to lie down in front of the hunters' mound of grouse. Yes, it's truly a mound, high as a snowdrift, and you cannot help but wonder if they could eat all that grouse or if some just went to waste after appearing in the picture. It was autumn-summer, as I've said, and not yet cold enough to leave them outside 'til they were frozen as the locals did with birds they trapped in winter. There's a red fox lying there that they'd shot too.

I remember Laula Anut's words when I told him about the photograph and about that huge mound of dead birds.

They helped themselves, he said.

Those words I realized applied not only to the huntin' gents. But afterward, even though I was only a child, I couldn't look at that picture of their hunting prowess in the same way any more. The wolf claw had lodged in my heart.

So I sat at the kitchen table with the photograph and attempted to sing in my uncle's way:

nanaanaaa . . . snöölhken goehperh vååjmesne . . .

In the end I gave up and sang in the wrong language because it was the only one I really knew now. Not until I got out into the woods did I let it out. It was my first attempt, and I'll never forget it:

naana na naaa . . .
wolf claw in my heart
red fox naa . . . na and the grouse
all of them are dead now
dead at the hunter's feet
the grouse and the red fox
naaa na na . . .
hounds are panting
naaa na na na na . . .
the wolf stalks the ridge
searching for her cubs
the eyes of the moon
gleaming in the tarn
in its black water they shine
snöölhke, aske jih dan tjaelmieh
na na naaa . . .
the smoke rises
na naaa . . .
the cold water rushes
the cold wind hu . . . uu
frost on the bog now
lu lu luuu . . .
soon there'll be snow
rätnoe lopme båata
then you'll all be gone
then you'll all be gone
lu lu lu . . .

Now I'm old, and I've got the wolf claw in my heart every night. When the timber trucks thunder by on the road, I lie awake listening. They're helping themselves, I think.

But when I sit with the photographs in front of me, I feel different and less bitter. I study the faces closely without knowing quite what I'm looking for.

They're all dead now. They lived longer than the dogs lying stretched out in the grass. And usually longer than the spotted cows they cared so much about and the horses they had groomed particularly well for the photographer's visit. But in the end they were all gone, and their time was no more. When I look at them, I feel something I cannot put into words.

I want to touch their clothes and hands and faces. But I can't. All I have in front of me is a piece of cardboard. At the bottom is the photographer's name in gold print: *Nicanor Eriksson, Byvången.*

I belong to another time. All those who might have wanted to listen to the stories of that time are under the sod now.

Times and times, incidentally. There is only one time, and you are in it until they lay you in the ground in Röbäck churchyard.

Hillevi was given some whey cheese to take home from the grazing land. She mixed it with cream and heated it up, using it as sauce for the dumplings. It was delicious with salt pork.

An essence right out of the blanket of flowers in the meadow; that was the brown whey cheese. This was summer itself, and she couldn't resist it any more than she could keep herself from wading in the lake or leaning against the cracked wood of the barn wall the sun had baked warm.

In autumn-summer the air cleared, and the stinging gnats and biting black flies that were such a nuisance in the heat disappeared. Early in the mornings there was a hint of white frost over the marsh. Soon it would turn into trembling drops of water on the stalks of the sedge and evaporate as the sun rose.

She and Märta went to the bogs above Lake Boteln to pick cloudberries with two girls from Blackwater named Elsa and Hildur, Isak Pålsa's daughters. Considering the future of course, she shouldn't have been mixing with the locals. The last thing she ought to have when she moved into the vicarage were memories of the fits of girlish giggles she shared with Märta Karlsa. She did refuse to listen when they started telling dirty stories. Or at least she should have. But it was difficult because Märta was funny, and funny in so many ways, unfortunately even some dirty ones.

Hillevi blamed it on their closeness to the strong-scented, gentle animals. She had never before encountered such a strong blend of sweetness and pungency.

They picked the cloudberries in herring pails they emptied into wooden kegs. Hillevi too had bought herself one in the shop in Blackwater, and now she had cloudberries for the winter in Märta's root cellar, a space suffused with the scent of the bog and the taste of desire. She told Edvard about her cloudberry keg when she invented errands to go and see him. But of course she said nothing about the burning impatience she had felt when picking them. Nor did she dare to mention the change either, the one that was sure to come when the leaves were gone from the trees. It was simply this: by the time the first snow fell, he and she would be together, eating her cloudberries with creamy milk at the vicarage kitchen table.

Things being as they were now though, time stood still in the dusty sitting room, Reverend Norfjell's empty eyes, fixed or adrift, staring at the same spot on the wallpaper as the first time she had seen him. She had to give his wife a bowl of cloudberries so Edvard might get to taste them. She was careful not to call the berries by their dialect name when she brought them, still embarrassed about the time she had let a story beguile her into using strange words.

She considered Edvard to be living in Röbäck without living there, which sometimes made her anxious. He was so alone in his black garb, his long coat, and his broad-brimmed hat, and so incomprehensible to the locals. She wished she had had the heart to tell him no one understood the conclusions he reached when he sat brooding in Reverend Norfjell's wife's parlor.

He had stacked his theological tomes on her little feminine writing desk. Everything in there stood still, like the Reverend's eyes glued to the wall. Sometimes when Hillevi watched through her window and saw Edvard walking alone on the road, dressed in black, she felt something stab her inside like a fish thrashing its tail.

She had become so accustomed to seeing him by himself that she was taken completely aback one afternoon when he came out of the vicarage dressed in tweeds, high boots, and a soft hat; climbed into a buggy whose driver she didn't recognize; and headed off in the direction of Blackwater.

It was very strange. Particularly the tweeds. He couldn't possibly have been going out on church affairs dressed like that. She made up an excuse to go in and see Mrs. Norfjell, but she was not forthcoming. Märta had the answer: the minister was on his way to Thor's Hole to hunt grouse with a party from Östersund.

She couldn't imagine that Edvard knew how to shoot. Or how had he become acquainted with people from Östersund. Not a word had he said either.

After a couple of days he came back down, wrote his sermon, and held it. He also buried an old farmer from Lakahögen. But then he returned to the hunting lodge, this time in the company of two young women. They were wearing sporty jackets and shorter skirts, and both had on soft Scots plaid berets. They were chatting up a storm with Edvard.

Hillevi was struck by a powerful sense of foreboding combined with a rage for which she didn't bother to reprimand herself. Of course she didn't begrudge him a little social life; the poor man had spent the whole summer so alone and so worried and so mosquito bitten. But she would never have dreamed there would be women up there, and she didn't think it was proper either, though Märta explained that one of the girls was the daughter of Eckendal, the merchant.

So she decided to see for herself. It was easy to arrange. She got someone to take her to Blackwater and went from there with Elsa Pålsa, whose mother Verna was cooking for the huntin' gents. Hildur stayed at home to run the guesthouse where fortunately there was only one guest, a homeopathist from Sundsvall.

I can clean the birds, Hillevi told Elsa. That was something of an over-statement, which Elsa, worried about what her mother would say when they both turned up, seemed to sense. As it turned out, Verna was pleased to have Hillevi in the kitchen. She was more or less gentry after all and knew how they liked their fowl and hare prepared. And she also seemed to have mastered the difficult business of sauces.

We brought the cream jug, said Hillevi. And lard for the grouse breasts. I'm sure they have some Madeira up here, and we'll toss in some juniper berries.

She said she had no intention of robbing either Verna or Elsa of whatever they were being paid. She claimed she was just along for the fun of it, though she didn't appear to be enjoying herself. The girls from Östersund with their jauntily angled tam o'shanters were running around flaunting their legs.

Eckendal the merchant and his hunters had headed out right after breakfast. Edvard didn't go along on the hunt. He seemed to have been put in charge of walking with the merchant's daughter and her girlfriend. She saw them through the kitchen window as they balanced on the plank bridge over the swirling river, sounding like birds when they screeched in alarm. Not until then did she think about what she would say when he noticed she was up here, and her heart sank.

The huntin' gents had had eggs and fried meat for breakfast before going out, along with porridge and milk and coffee. Verna fixed them a picnic lunch with egg sandwiches, flat bread rolled up with reindeer meat, and cold pancakes. When they came back, there would be dinner too, of whatever was on hand: a buffet of cold meats, followed by a fish course, a meat course, and finally a dessert. Verna explained that the evening would end with a *supé* consisting of a hot meat dish, porridge and milk, and tea.

So we've got our hands full, she said

On the steps to the grouse shed, a Lapp was sitting cleaning birds. He was called Mickel Larsson, and he'd brought them a smoked shoulder of venison to supplement the cold meats. The other men, two fellows from Skinnarviken, were the mountain guides and rifle bearers on the hunt.

There's the minister too, said Elsa.

The loony minister.

That's what Verna called him. Hillevi couldn't utter a syllable, and her heart was pounding. She was glad to be standing with her back to them, bent over the cutting board, busy binding a slice of lard around a grouse.

Well, he could've got off to a better start around here, said Elsa knowingly.

How so? asked Hillevi. Although she'd spoken very softly, Verna heard.

He got it into his head that he'd go to Blackwater, she said. And from there he started asking how to cross the lake to Lunäset. Sets people wondering of course.

'Deed it does, echoed Elsa.

That's Norway, they told him. There's a parish priest on their side to take care of the Lunäsers.

Somebody saw him trying to walk out onto the lake after the ice had started melting at the shore. He must've got soaked. How dumb can you be? He also came up to the guesthouse asking about a Lapp wench. Yes, that was how he had put it. *The Lapp wench who was held in captivity by an older man at Lunäset.* He wanted to *get to the bottom of the matter.* He said. That gave us a good laugh. Not until the poor minister fellow had left of course. But then!

What'd you tell 'im?

That it all happened in the eighteenth century. Or earlier.

And what'd he say?

Not a word. He pulled his big black hat on and left. But I could tell even from behind that he was baffled.

Hillevi kept silent. Well, what could she say? People were supposed to think they didn't know each other, she and Edvard. But the whole muddle had been her fault. She bent over the cutting board, binding the grouse tighter and tighter. But Verna had sharp eyes. She saw that Hillevi's cheeks had gone red.

Was't you?

What?

But there was no sense playing dumb with Verna.

'Im!

You wuz the one what told 'im!

You wuz pulling his leg! Elsa hooted, tears of laughter in her eyes.

Hillevi didn't understand the expression until Verna explained. But no! She'd had no intention of misleading him. Hillevi had tears in her eyes as well but for different reasons. She felt not only shame and embarrassment but also a sense of betrayal.

Imagine the minister thinking so badly of the Lapps, Mickel Larsson complained from the doorway where he stood with a load of grouse.

Oh, said Verna. He'd just heard a story. And what's more it wasn't the old man at Lunäset that was a Lapp. It was the girl.

Everybody's always telling lies about the Lapps, Mickel added, heaving the grouse onto the table.

That fellow, Verna said when he had left. He comes along here nice as can be, but I think he's just waiting for his chance to cast a new spell on us.

Hillevi sometimes felt time yielding under her like the ground in a mire. Verna with her little heart-shaped gray face and her loud piercing voice was a perfectly sensible, modern person. She ran the kitchen and kept the accounts at the guesthouse and got to know all kinds of people. She had a separator and was in favor of building a hydroelectric plant in the river so they would have electric light.

And yet she could say things like that. The Lapps cast spells on people. The grouse shed was haunted. Thor's Hole was plagued by misfortune because it was built on an unlucky spot. A place where the little people had their underground passages.

In the admiral's day they had had an open hearth with a winch for the pot, Verna told her. And a spit over the fire to roast the fowl. The bread oven had been mortared into the chimney of one of the outbuildings. Now merchant Eckendal had got Halvorsen to transport a brand new wood-burning stove made by the Pump Separator Company. There was an icebox too in one of the outbuildings. It was painted to look like gray and white marble. Hillevi said it was a shame such an expensive item stood idle for most of the year.

Oh well, said Verna, the last thing they're short of is cash.

Hillevi noted that when Verna Pålsa talked about people down at the guesthouse, she was more diplomatic. Things got a bit wild up here.

Now there was no time for chatter. The hunters had returned with strings of birds. The minute they came up from the bathhouse by the river they'd want dinner.

Hillevi wanted Madeira for the sauce, and Verna told her to go ask for it herself. But she refused. She didn't want to bump into Edvard. He was still out with the girls collecting plants in the younger one's portable press, but he might walk in at any moment. She had no intention of embarrassing him.

So Verna went and asked the merchant, but there was no Madeira. He said that when he and the chief court clerk were done with the bottle of brandy, she could have what was left of it. Mickel Larsson's eyes lit up when Verna came in with the bottle, but she told him sharply that she needed it for the cooking.

O, you wily woman! said Mickel.

The long-legged dogs had to be fed. Fresh water had to be carried to the bathhouse. While the grouse were roasting in the oven, Verna was preparing to poach the fish. The salmon trout turned out to be too big for the steamer, and she got all hot and bothered.

Wrap 'er in moss and cook 'er on a hot stone slab, Mickel Larsson suggested, but Verna just ordered him out to the woodpile to find her something that didn't flame up as hot as birch. Now there was no time for talking. Hillevi had an urgent need for the privy in the middle of all the chaos and headed outside, nibbling at a leftover pancake from the picnic.

One of the fellows from Skinnarviken saw her and shouted: In one end and out the other, as the farmhand said eating a sausage in the outhouse.

Obviously this attention was not what she needed. With firm steps she headed for the dog run and tossed in the rest of the pancake, which brought on howls and an uproar. The dogs sounded ready to kill each other over that pancake. She cowered in the privy. At least the hubub distracted the men. But they wouldn't forget, she knew, not if she became the minister's wife.

She sat there for some time, listening to the wood in the lichen-covered walls cracking softly and looking at the little bit of blue sky that was visible between the rotting shingles. Eckendal had already given instructions for a new roof to be done before the next hunting season, but that roof would soon fall in too. Snapping and slipping, slowly disintegrating or destroyed in a violent storm, roofs didn't hold up long in the mountains.

Her thoughts were interrupted by a woman's clear voice commenting that the purling water was so beguiling.

It sounds like voices calling!

The other woman said it was melancholy and kind of desolate.

Oh, such nonsense. She could hear the river herself. It was gurgling and swishing and sounded, if anything, more like a drunken farmer. They were putting on airs for Edvard. He must be out there too.

She checked the latch. Didn't want them barging in. She had a feeling they'd be too inhibited though to go into the privy when Edvard was around. They wanted to be beguiling and melancholy.

They left. A few minutes later she heard Edvard talking to one of the men from the hunting party. He was going to the bathhouse.

She continued to sit quietly. Her body felt strange perched atop the oval hole. Like one great big artery, throbbing and full to bursting. She grew heavy and imagined Edvard undressing, standing naked by the wooden tub of steamy water he'd scooped out of the cauldron over the fire.

She wasn't thinking about going in there where he was. No, she wasn't really thinking at all. She had an image of him, of walking toward him through the steam. Just as heavy as she was now, almost sluggish, with all her blood gone to her thighs.

And worse yet.

What idiocy. She saw it now, crystal clear: he would turn to face her, his face rigid. The way it was when she told him about having applied for the position in Röbäck.

When the gentry and the dogs had all been fed, they ate too, at the kitchen table. The men came in, Paul Annersa's grandsons from Skinnarviken and Trond Halvorsen. He had come up just before dinner with the provisions they'd ordered from the store. Mickel Larsson and his son Anund, who was one of the mountain guides, were also there.

Verna had poached a fish just for them; the salted kind they preferred to the tasteless fresh ones. And of course there were all the grouse legs. Little but tasty.

And this *souse*, said Mickel, eating the creamy sauce with a coffee spoon. The way to a man's heart!

Before we know it he'll be *yoiking*, said Trond Halvorsen. You can see it in his eyes.

They all laughed at the old man, who was probably not very old at all. It was just that his face was brown and wrinkled, Hillevi thought. He took it the right way and sang them a note or two for a laugh. He sounded like he was gargling.

You should offer to entertain the merchant! He'd give you twenty-five *öre* just to shut up!

True, he's sure not musical, said Mickel. Yesterday he poured himself a big cog-nack when the girls were singing. They sang in parts. Sounded worse than me.

Hillevi was embarrassed when they made jokes at the expense of Eckendal and his party. She caught herself wondering if the girls in the kitchen at Upper Castle Road had talked like this about Aunt Eugénie and Uncle Carl. She had always assumed they admired her aunt and were intimidated by her uncle or respected him deeply. But perhaps they just had been ingratiating like Mickel Larsson. When they were out of earshot, maybe the servants sat twisting their words nastily, roaring with laughter at things like turned-up cuffs on trouser legs and silver toothbrush cases.

She didn't say anything, and regretted having come to Thor's Hole at all. What had she expected? That she would bump into Edvard, and he would invite her into the parlor and introduce her to his friends? Here she sat in the kitchen instead, hoping they'd never know she'd been there. Things were different now that she was really here.

When they started to talk about Edvard again, she ought to have told them off, but she was afraid it would give her away. Verna was extremely sharp; God only knew she might already have sensed something; she was carrying on so unmercifully. She encouraged the lads from Skinnarviken to tell about how Edvard had been reciting poetry to the young ladies by a waterfall.

Draped across the rocks, lying there like they were posing for a picture.

Lying there?

Burst of laughter. Verna said:

Come on Anund, recite it! You were there, weren't you?

So the young man, Anund, recited:

Two souls at last a'swellin' in my chest, each from the other tries to pull and sway.

Jeez, that's what I call poetry.

Didn't it rhyme though?

Yeah, later, said the boy, who was short for his fourteen years, with stick straight brown hair and amber eyes. He went on:

One rushin' at the world with earthly lust and wringing' out a passionate embrace.

Listen to him! It's unnatural how fast he picks things up. He just has to hear something once and it sticks.

Tell us the name for goat willow!

Salix caprea.

And horsetail!

Eqiisetum hiemale.

How the hell can they say things like that about grass?

It's Latin.

Or Hottentot, maybe.

The spruce clubmoss, Anund.

They calls it lycopodium selago.

Well, I never.

They downed the rest of the cognac. Halvorsen had a little moonshine they poured into their coffee to finish off. Not until they were standing washing the dishes and no one else could hear them did Hillevi dare to tell Verna she didn't believe the young minister would recite that kind of thing to the girls.

Oh, they're not all that innocent, said Verna. The older one's twenty-two.

But that kind of thing—no, I just can't believe it. Anund must have heard it someplace else. It's not fair to Reverend Nolin to talk about him that way.

Well, he wrote it into Miss Eckdendal's poetry album. It's on the table in there, so all's you need to do is look.

It wouldn't have occurred to her to go sneaking in there. Was that what went on? Had Anna and Betty at her aunt's gone around reading what people wrote in the guest book and in Sara's poetry album? Maybe they read opened letters while they were dusting too. What kind of people were they really?

It couldn't be true. But she had to know for certain. And so she went into the parlor after all when the gentry had gone out for an evening stroll by the river. She said she was going to empty the ashtrays, but when she saw their cigar stubs, she thought: Over my dead body. Instead, she went right over to a thick leather-bound book and opened it. But it was the hunting log. She found herself in the previous year when the merchant had hunted at Vemdalen.

380 red grouse
43 black grouse
17 snipe
1 ruff
4 wild ducks
1 golden plover
3 hare

She found Miss Harriet Eckendal's poetry album in the cupboard bench alongside the dining table. It had a green velvet cover. And Edvard's writing was certainly in it. She read:

Two souls, alas, are dwelling in my breast,
each from the other strives to pull away;
one clutching at the world in earthbound lust,
and clinging fast in passionate embrace;
the other rising fiercely from the dust,
our forebears' lofty realms its endless quest.

She shut the album. All she wanted was to get far away from everybody, but there was nowhere else for her to go than back into the kitchen. The Eckendal party might come in at any moment and catch sight of her. Even outside. And Edvard.

Earthbound lust.

It can't be true.

But it was.

They were all still sitting there in the kitchen, and when she came in, they stared at her.

Did you empty the ashtrays? Verna asked, and Hillevi didn't find her tone of voice very pleasant.

No. They'll just have to do it themselves.

That made them laugh; they raised their glasses to her. There was a jug of liquor on the table now, and Hillevi realized they must have persuaded Halvorsen to open it. He was supposed to be delivering it to Skinnarviken but had been so late getting up here he put off going there until on the way down.

I think it was meant for us, I do, said Anders Annersa, holding up his coffee cup.

Then they decided to take a walk down to the bathhouse.

They can fix their cog-nacks themselves. And the ice for their fizzery water.

And cocococo with whipped cream, Elsa imitated.

That's right, Elsa, you're not the merchant's housemaid.

They say he's almost done for.

What? He's going to liquidate?

That's right, Elsa. Your father's got at least . . .

Let's be off then, said Verna sharply.

They were wound up. But Halvorsen was serious; he was looking at Hillevi. When she had gone outside earlier in the evening, he'd been standing there shaving. He'd angled a bit of mirror up over the edge of the door to the woodshed and was lathering his black-whiskered cheeks. She was glad he hadn't noticed her because he was naked to the waist in the cold evening air. He looks like one of those men who travel the roads peddling rat traps she had thought. An Italian. With his belt cinched tight around his narrow waist. The end dangling. Like railroad workers wore theirs.

But he wasn't in fact one of those troublemaking railroaders, and now he looked different. He was wearing a white shirt with thin blue stripes and a suit jacket and trousers of black combed cotton. The end of his belt no longer showed, he must have tucked it into one of the loops. And his hat on the bench was brushed clean. All he was missing was a collar, she thought.

They went on eating and drinking in the bathhouse, sitting on overturned wooden tubs. Mickel rekindled the fire to warm the place back up. Verna had taken along what was left of the curd cheese, and cream and cloudberries too. But Hillevi couldn't get anything down.

The river was so clearly audible in here. It swirled in miniature rapids between the stones right outside the bathhouse wall.

Listen to him, said Mickel. He's saying his own name.

No, sure he's not saying Bend, said Nils Annersa.

No, it's something else he's whispering.

And now when everyone was perfectly silent and the only sound was the swishing and murmuring of the river, Hillevi could almost believe it, and she wondered what name Mickel Larsson heard.

The silence sharpened your senses. You could hear the cold wind in the treetops out there. The swishing was sad and heavy. She smelled the sharp scent of ermine droppings. It was as if time itself was yielding and sinking like the earth in a bog. The hunting lodge, the cut ends of its brown-tarred logs, the little panes of glass in the windows, and the second story, on top of which there was an attic loft, had looked old when she had first arrived. But she thought: I suppose it will soon be gone. The river will run here with a completely different name.

It didn't seem strange to her that Edvard had asked about the girl out at Lunäset without realizing the story was from long ago. To her what had happened out at Lubben seemed in the very distant past. Way back in time immemorial Märta would have said. But when was time immemorial?

The water, it ran and ran—she had no idea how long it had been running. Since the Ice Age at least. It wasn't until now that she realized rivers had short-lived names. At school she had been made to memorize the list of southern Swedish rivers as if it were Gospel: Lagan Nissan Ätran Viskan.

But perhaps the names of mountains and rivers don't last all that long. Time devours itself from behind, covering all that has been in darkness. Perhaps one day people would call the time in which she herself had lived immemorial in spite of the arc lights and enormous ocean liners.

Hillevi, what might you be thinking about? Halvorsen asked.

He could at least have called her Miss Klarin, or just Miss. But she forgave him because of the solemnity in his eyes. And because he was sober. The others were guffawing and gabbing at the top of their lungs now.

I'm thinking about strange things that don't usually occupy my mind, she said.

He accepted that answer. But he went on watching her face.

The others were teasing Mickel Larsson for not daring to go into the grouse shed to get the fowl he was supposed to clean.

Cold hands grab at me, Nils Annersa imitated.

But he made the lad go in.

He's got things on, Mickel muttered.

Steel and a cross of course! You're a crafty one, Mickel.

But he was angry now, and Verna sang to annoy him even more:

Lice and nits,
lice and nits
all kinds of little bugs, y'know . . .

Well that's a different matter altogether, Anders Annersa shouted, and he and Verna burst into song:

Little Pelle ran about
at evening time most oft
father and mother were abed,
come with me to the loft!

No, no, no, there I won't go
not if you pay me a thousand!
It's full of lice and nits there and
all kinds of little bugs, y'know.
It's full of lice
it's full of bugs
all kinds of little things, y'know!

That's awful all right, said Elsa. And why are there cold hands in the grouse shed? Is it true?

Mickel kept silent.

Could be, said Verna. All sorts of things have happened there after all.

All kinds of little things, man! said Anders Annersa, extending his cup for more liquor. He ended up having to pour it himself because the others were busy looking at Verna and waiting for her to tell them the story they were all thinking about. Hillevi was sure they had heard it before. Even Elsa, although she was the one who asked.

They say there was a girl who met her fate there.

Did she do herself in?

Yes, but not there.

Where then?

Mickel Larsson got up and left.

Oh, said Verna, it was way back in the eighteen hundreds. Mickel needn't to get all worked up about it.

But she was a Lapp wench, said Elsa, confirming Hillevi's suspicion that she already knew the story. Still she wanted to evoke it. She wanted to hear the words.

A beauty she was, as I've heard tell, said Nils Annersa. Such pale skin.

Right, when she got bathed anyway.

Did she bathe? In here?

Probably. It was in the Scots' time. They was always bathin'. More often than the merchant's people, even. *Baaaaaf,* they called it. That's what Mamma said, *Baaaaaf . . .*

Did he have a lisp, that admiral?

You bet your life. Call Mickel back in now. No need for him to sulk over this old stuff. He knows as well as anybody that she haunts the place. She comes back to the grouse shed where it happened. You never catch sight of her. You just feel her cold hands. Cold clammy hands.

Oh damnation.

Pour me some now.

Pour Mickel some too.

Mickel!

But once he had shouted, Anders Annersa was quick to shut the door.

Out strollin' again, they are.

Not the wholesaler, he said he'd eaten too much.

He's so fat he shits bent candles.

No, it's the Snipe and the Grouse. There's a bit of space between them anyway. But you should see the Lapwing and the Seagull. That's love if I ever saw it.

Hillevi realized Edvard was the one they called the Lapwing. Though she didn't know what kind of a bird that was, she imagined a spindly long-legged one. Trond Halvorsen slowly pushed a coffee cup with a little liquor in it across the table toward her.

You'll have a drop of sommat strong now, Hillevi, just to warm up, he said.

She swallowed it and shuddered.

Too strong for you? Anders Annersa teased.

If I were out there walking with the gentry, he'd call me the Magpie, she thought. Or maybe just the Crow.

She dozed off in spite of the hubbub in the bathhouse. It was late, but the others didn't seem the least bit interested in going to bed. And she didn't know where she was supposed to sleep. She'd never found herself in a dilemma like that before. She woke up when Nils Annersa was pulling Mickel into the shed. He was reluctant and had his right hand deep in his longshirt.

What've you got there?

Pulling didn't help. He was strong and looked furious.

You'd better watch out, Mickel, when you get home. If your old woman's feeling loving and starts touching you up, your days'll be numbered.

You can bet she'd pull out a sausage!

You've been in the food stores, Mickel!

Don't think your old woman will make do with a *sausage*, do you?

Hillevi thought she'd better shut her eyes and pretend she was still asleep. But she opened them when the young man called Anund said gravely:

There was a man who always kept his hand hid. Though it was long ago.

Right, Sigge the Wolfman, Mickel mumbled. He kept his right hand hidden. Always.

Why was that?

Gimme a bit of the strong stuff, and I might recall it.

Halvorsen poured liquor into his cup. He drank it slowly.

Bottoms up! the Annersa brothers shouted.

Let him be now. Tell us, Mickel. Why did he keep his hand hid?

Well, lots of folks wondered that. Not least the girl he married.

In all other ways, according to Mickel, the young woman had made a good match. He was a handsome man and gave her silver to wear at the wedding. He had lots of reindeer, was a reindeer herder who'd made a name for himself. Oh, yes.

But although she got to know him in the way people do when they sleep in the same bed, she never saw his right hand. When she asked what was wrong with it, if he'd injured it, he told her it was none of her affair. And he sounded angry.

You know how women are; they can never let a thing be. They have to find everything out. And she was the same in spite of her young innocent appearance. So one evening when he'd gone to bed, tired from herding his deer in the mountains all day, she decided to have a look. That night, when he was deeply asleep, she neatly turned back the hides covering him, one by one. His hand was hidden as always, but she rolled up his sweater sleeve gently and carefully. There was still a little glow in the hearth, and it flared up with a soft light now and then. So she could see.

What did she see?

His hand of course. Though it wasn't a hand.

What was it then?

A paw. With claws.

Yes, he was one of them. A werewolf. Now she understood. But nothing had happened yet. He hadn't been gone one single night since their marriage. So, poor girl, she thought he was cured.

But he wasn't?

Ooooh, no.

Things went as they usually do. He started going off at night coming home exhausted and wan.

What about her? Did she move back to her own kind?

Nope. She stuck it out until he died.

And how did he die?

He was shot.

The Lapp who shot him had no idea. He skinned the wolf, and he kept the claws, though he said afterward there was something wrong with the front right forepaw. There was no hide on it. And the woman found her husband lying dead in a grain shed with drops of blood at the corners of his mouth.

Then she caught sight of his hand. It had fur and claws.

What nonsense, said a very pale Elsa. They made up things like that in the old days. When they was ignorant.

I s'pose he had a deformed hand, said Verna. That was why he kept it hidden.

They couldn't abide freaks.

Don't talk like that, said Mickel. Telling lies about the Lapps.

Now he's had too much of the strong stuff!

Hang on, said Verna. I wasn't talkin' specifically about the Lapps. Nobody wanted a freak. Down in Blackwater there was a girl who . . .

Who what?

Well, how should I put it? Verna asked, glancing at Elsa. She had a bit of a thing with her own brother. Though they were really just kids.

Kids aren't actually all that innocent.

Who knows? asked Verna. I s'pose people are different. But these were the kind of people who don't mind much either way. And so things happened. The girl had a baby. Not without a lot of misery because she was a tiny little thing. And it was a freak.

How so?

Nobody knows. No one got to see it.

Did it die?

Yeah.

Their faces were nothing but shadows and holes. Except for Verna's because she was sitting with the dying fire shining on her face. Her eyes were the color of pewter, and her skin was yellow tinged and oily.

Hillevi wanted to leave, but she didn't dare move. She was afraid if she did she would start to scream. Straight out.

Did they get rid of it? Nils Annersa asked.

Yeah.

How?

Well, it was winter, and there was a hole in the ice where they would get water for themselves and the cow. That was it.

The old days, Elsa sighed, with a snort.

Hillevi got up but had to grab the edge of the table and almost set her other hand right on the hot mortared chimney.

Watch yourself there, said Halvorsen, taking hold of her.

I need to get out.

He put his arm around her waist and walked her to the low door. When he had opened it for her, he put a hand to her brow, bending her forward so she wouldn't bang her head.

She released herself from his grasp when they got outside and walked around back to the wall facing the river bank where no one could see her. She still felt trapped. Close by, the water was burbling. It chattered and clucked. Little shouts and a wild whispered laugh, very faint in spite of being close by. The sound was just far enough away that the human ear could catch the chatter but not the sense.

I've got to get away from here, she thought.

Halvorsen came quietly around the corner of the building and asked if she was feeling sick. She shook her head.

That was nasty talk, he said.

Yes.

They don't prattle about anything that could do anyone any harm though. It all happened long ago.

When?

Nobody knows. Maybe a hundred years ago. Or more. Or maybe it's all made up.

Hillevi began to cry. The tears welled up in her chest, and he had to put an arm around her and talk as if to a child. He had taken his suit coat off in the bathhouse and had been in too much of a hurry to put it on when they left. His shirt seemed newly laundered, and the skin on his neck smelled of soap.

Halvorsen, when are you driving home? she asked.

Early, if you wish, Hillevi. But we have to wait for daylight so the mare can see to put one foot in front of the other.

That's a long time from now, said Hillevi, crying some more. I'm not going back in there. But I have no idea where I'm supposed to sleep. I should never have come up here.

Oh, Hillevi, you mustn't take it so hard, he said. It's all just drunken nonsense. It's my fault. I oughtn't have opened the jug.

He walked her to the baking shed, telling her to wait inside. He came back with a gray blanket and a reindeer hide. He lay the hide on the baking table and got her to climb up and wrap the blanket around herself. I'll light the oven, he said. The place will soon warm up.

Once the fire was going he left, returning after a little while with her hat and bag. He folded her shawl into a pillow for her.

You mustn't be frightened if I come in now and then to put some wood on the fire.

But Halvorsen, where will you be otherwise?

Outside, he said curtly.

He was thinking about gossip, she realized. That eternal gossip that fingered at everything.

It was barely light outside but not as cold as she'd imagined. Halvorsen had said they would leave at dawn, but in this damp, cloudy weather she couldn't really see the sunrise. The birches flanking the river were spotted with gold, and birds were moving in their leafy crowns. Although they were silent now with autumn coming on, she could tell there were lots of them in there. Sometimes she wasn't sure if she was hearing the cry of a bird or the sound of the water running between the stones.

He had already harnessed the mare and helped her up. Hillevi had never ridden in such a primitive wagon. Just a cart with a trestle for a seat.

Now, she thought. Now he's going to take up the reins, and we'll ride away from here unseen. It will never have happened.

But they didn't get away that fast. First he had to load an empty lamp oil barrel and a sack of pilsner bottles that made such a racket she nearly burst into tears. She huddled on the trestle. If people in the house woke up, all they would see was a bundle of blankets with a hat on top, nothing more.

He lashed the barrel down. He was attentive and thorough about everything he did. She remembered that from the wintry trip to Röbäck back in March.

Finally he climbed up. He shoved his hat down, angled sharply forward, probably by force of habit since there was no sun to get in his eyes. He clucked one single time, not even lifting the reins over the horse's back, but the mare was receptive, bent her neck and began to pull. She felt the lightness of the load and fell quickly into a smooth gait, adapting to the rutted cart track.

She's the horse you had when we drove from Lomsjö.

Oh yes, it's Dolly all right. She always gets through, no matter how muddy the road.

The wagon rattled in spite of the soft ground; sharp stones protruded as well as tufts of grass resembling heads of fuzzy hair. As long as they followed the watercourse, things were all right. But on a little rise after the first marsh, they had to get out and walk. He went on talking about the horse, saying she was a Norwegian *döle*. She'd been a gift to him for his confirmation. She came from his father's place at Fagerli.

She started thinking about how he must have looked, a thin, black-haired lad on his confirmation day. A horse of his own for a fourteen-year-old! They must be well-off after all. He said, as if reading her mind, and perhaps to give credit where credit was due:

My grandpa on my mother's side, from Lakahögen, paid for it.

He had probably had the same look as now when he was given the horse, struggling to appear indifferent and not to reveal his wild joy. But what was he so joyful about today?

What's so funny, Hillevi? he asked.

She wouldn't have thought he could see her face since he seemed to be looking straight ahead the whole time. But perhaps he could sense how she was about to burst out laughing, just as she sensed it in him? They were walking side by side. Sometimes their arms touched.

I was imagining you, Halvorsen, she said. At your confirmation.

Right, he said. I tore off that black suit the instant dinner was done, pulled on my homespun britches and boots, and went right out to the horse.

They had left the spruce grove on the hilltop and were down on flatter ground driving along a narrow mire. They got up to ride again. For a long time the only sound was the gentle plodding of Dolly's hooves on the soft ground. She was dark brown with a little fuzz on the mound just above her tail. Her sturdy thighs glistened. Hillevi thought he must have groomed her that morning. Her long tail and mane were black with a red sheen. She had a curly fringe over her eyes.

Hillevi had spent the night in the scent of horse; the blanket he had covered her with was imbued with it. Now it was like hot steam on the chill morning air. She thought with distaste of the beer wagoners in Uppsala with their big workhorses and about the man who emptied the night soil containers and his thin gelding. A *döle*, Halvorsen explained, was a cold-blooded horse but with something of a warm-blood in her. She was a tough horse with good endurance. And this particular *döle* was sensible too.

A snipe rose, its curved beak pointing skyward like a probe. Hillevi was startled by its cry. Halvorsen smiled. His cheek was still smooth. Or had he shaved again?

She began to wonder.

When he had harnessed the horse and climbed up onto the trestle with her, he pulled the gray blanket over her shoulders and tucked it in tightly and well. He had been unfailingly reasonable and kind. She thought about how young he was; his eyes gleamed like a boy's. Or those of a young stallion.

The sun broke through briefly, and the haze of water over the tarns and the steam over the marsh grew rosy. But they could see the rain pouring down on the mountains, and soon the air was cobweb gray again, cloudy and damp. The willows were already dripping, like a premonition of rain although it was really just the dew rising.

They were down in the woods after less than an hour and had to walk again because of all the rocks and ruts in the cart track. He asked courteously if she wanted a rest, but she shook her head. She was actually feeling a little scared, though she didn't know of what.

It was more summerlike once they were on the regular path to the grazing pastures. The marshes were less reddened by frost, the birches only just beginning to lose their leaves. There were the big lakes down below them, and the high mountains behind them were swathed in wads of cloud. They heard a long call, a woman's voice sounding like a cuckoo, high and then low. Halvorsen of course knew exactly who was calling her cows, Elin from Nisjbuan.

Hillevi felt better because they were closer to people or at least a person. The wind had picked up. The low clouds were rolling in the strong wind; puffs running rapidly from west to east. Dolly plodded on, the fringe swaying over her eyes. The road was smoother now. Hillevi could sit on the wagon with the blanket wrapped around her. Halvorsen was walking alongside again. The empty bottles were rattling noisily. The sound hadn't bothered her before, or perhaps the track had been smoother. She began to wish fervently for silence. But she didn't say anything: it would have sounded ungrateful.

Suddenly the weather was very wet and gray. The wind held its breath for a moment. They were enveloped in the kind of gray mist they had observed on the mountain tops and couldn't see a thing. The water dissolved into the air, the drizzle turned to drops, and it began to pour.

Hell, said Halvorsen. That hat of yours is in for a ruinin', Hillevi!

She removed it and he put it in the sack with the bottles. It would probably take a beating in there too, but she didn't say anything, just pulled her shawl over her head and tied it under her chin. Halvorsen was slowing Dolly down and leading her off the road. The ground around them was quite flat. She was surprised to see him loosen the horse from the cart.

We can keep dry under those spruces over there. And I can't have the mare standing out in this downpour either.

He led the horse over the springy ground to a sparse grove of evergreens. She thought they would just settle in under one of the bushy trees, but he said they were going to one a little way off, a special tree, waterproof as a hut, under which people spent the night during the haymaking.

It was the biggest spruce Hillevi had ever seen. In front of it was a wooden lean-to and the charred remains of a fire. She would never have imagined a tree could be so tall. She didn't even get a glimpse of the top as he ushered her in quickly, tossing the blanket in too. She could hear him working noisily on the other side of the tree, finding a spot for the mare and tethering her.

The bottom ring of boughs was like a huge bell or a wide fringed skirt trailing the ground. There was nothing growing in here, just a slippery mat of reddish-brown needles. Watertight. Outside, the rain was rushing down, but not a drop fell in here.

Hillevi removed her shawl and wiped her face. Halvorsen bent down and entered, spinning his round-brimmed hat upside down so the water would run off it. His hair was wet as well. When he saw that Hillevi's shawl was too wet to put back on, he said:

What a shame.

Why's that?

You looked so kissable in that shawl, Hillevi.

That was when she realized. He was going to get naughty with her while they were sitting close like this. But for the moment he didn't, just removed a bottle, stuffed into a knitted sock, from inside his jacket.

I've got coffee and sandwiches for us.

They had to share the blanket and drink the tepid coffee from the mouth of the same bottle. There was no choice. Outside, the morning was bare and wet, and the sound of the downpour made her a little dizzy. It released the scent of the marsh. She recognized it from cloudberry picking. A moldering, powerful, and intensely spicy smell.

While they were eating their sausage sandwiches, which she was quite sure had been meant for the merchant's picnic lunch, he asked her straight without even a hint of teasing:

Hillevi, you got a fellow?

If she was ever going be firm with him, it would have to be now. But what could she say? He had no right to ask her questions like that. He must have realized he'd vexed her because he added:

No offense meant, Hillevi.

And he started singing softly in a voice intended to deflect the gravity of his question of a moment earlier:

If you catch a local man
love as virtuously as you can . . .

She thought about how insane the whole business with Edvard was. Earthbound lust. The words stood firm like a knife in a block of hard butter. And virtue. That was an Edvard Nolin word for you.

You're angry, Hillevi, he said. I'll have to coax you back into a better mood.

He put his mouth to her neck.

That was what happened. His moist mouth and the rain. He didn't take his lips away. Didn't kiss her either, just let them rest damp against the skin of her neck, and warm.

What happens happens. It's nothing you plan. A wild kind of joy shot through her, a kind she had only seen in little children before. So she turned her head, not away from him but to help him find her mouth. She ran a hand through his black hair, no longer so short. It curled at the nape of his neck and was damp except at the top of his head where his hat had protected it from the rain.

She was out of her mind. She realized where things were heading when he asked:

Hillevi, do you want to do it now?

She was astonished he asked her in words. Even those few.

She wasn't innocent of course. Perhaps he took that for granted? She thought she had known how it was. The urgency, the heated panting. The kisses to distract from hooks being coaxed out of eyes and suspenders coming down. It wasn't that way at all. He removed his lips from hers, running his index finger over her mouth. His eyes were brown and so close she noticed his curly lashes. She thought about his mother, what joy she must have felt the first time she held this baby boy in her arms. She wondered who that mother was.

You might think in a rainstorm everything would have to happen fast, but he seemed to have all the time in the world. He removed her hairpins, letting her plait down with great care. She didn't really want him to unbraid it because her hair would go all frizzy and unruly in the damp. But the idea that they would ever be among people again felt so distant she let him have his way. He did seem to be thinking ahead because he put her hairpins in the inside pocket of his jacket. Then he undid the button on the collar of her blouse and put his lips and the tip of his tongue to her throat. Once again the same swirling shock ran through her. It was a kind of electricity that shot about without wires, but a more wondrous, softer kind than the electricity in lights.

Clearly a person remains the same person no matter what he does. Halvorsen was himself, thorough and patient, irrespective of whether he was loading things into a wagon or harnessing his mare or undressing Miss Hillevi Klarin. She realized too that his desire had been there much longer than hers and that he had grown accustomed to it and was able to contain it as he removed his jacket and laid it across her shoulders.

He wanted to take her corset off. It was almost impossible but he was persistent and managed to unlace it after turning her onto her stomach on the horse blanket, his mouth at the nape of her neck and his lips in a tangle of her damp hair the whole time. Resolutely, she turned back over, showing him the hooks on the front, concealed by a flap. They laughed as both of them fumbled with hooks and eyes, their fingers getting in each other's way. He pulled his shirt over his head and drew his belt out of his trousers, and with a jolt she remembered him shaving by the door to the woodshed up at Thor's Hole. She recalled what she had thought then and was ashamed.

Though his hair was certainly black.

She helped him remove his heavy cotton trousers and was glad she always wore clean undergarments she had embroidered herself. She began putting two and two together: he hadn't put a single wad of snuff under his lip since they'd left. Had he been planning this the whole time? Then they were skin to skin, and she didn't have another thought of any kind.

She wasn't innocent—that was true—but no man had seen her breasts. Everything that had happened with Edvard had happened in the dark and with her camisole on. Halvorsen took such a fancy to them that he forgot himself for a few moments. He misinterpreted her agitation as he pulled down his underwear and his penis emerged. He whispered to her not to be afraid.

He's as soft as a horse's muzzle, he assured her.

Afterward they lay there trying to make his jacket go around them both. He pulled the blanket up over her shoulders. There was a rustling up in the tree, possibly a squirrel. She thought all kinds of creatures could live in such a big tree. They heard the crunching of Dolly eating from her feed bag.

You're cold, he whispered, wrapping the jacket around her. Then he got up, stooped under the boughs, pulled on his trousers, and buckled his belt. But he didn't button his fly. He shuffled across the big shedlike space around the trunk of the spruce tree, breaking dry branches. Soon there was the smell of smoke, and he had made a little fire just outside in the cinders from other fires made by people who had taken shelter there before. The heat came in little bursts, like breath.

There was a drop of coffee left in the bottle, but it was nearly cold. They'd eaten all the sandwiches. They could hear Dolly's jaws working their way down the bag, and the sound made them smile.

She didn't take everything at once, Hillevi said.

Neither did I, he whispered into her ear, and she felt herself blush.

The storm was still howling outside, and she realized they were going to be there for a long time.

That summer Elis lived with the person they called the Russian Hussy, though he never heard that moniker until much later.

On that March day he had crossed the ice to the summer grazing pasture at Lunäset. No one lived there in the winter. He didn't want to be on the north side of the lake where the villages were. He would instantly be recognized there since his mother came from Jolet. So he crossed over to the south side instead. He had planned to get into one of the cabins at Lunäset, make a bit of a fire, and sleep. He had his piece of pork, but it wouldn't last forever. He might find something edible in one of the sheds or in a root cellar.

All there was, though, was a brittle old fishnet and some traps and snares. And rat droppings.

He soon had to move on, so he walked on the frozen lake, staying close to the shore. Toward evening the next day he reached Skuruvasslia. There was smoke from the chimneys. He couldn't make himself known. They'd send him home quick as a flash, or his father would come and get him. He had the idea that if he stayed out of sight, they would eventually believe he was dead.

The dogs growled, but no one paid any attention, so he sneaked into an animal shed. He slept there, but on his guard, afraid of being taken by surprise when they came to do the morning milking. He was nauseous with fear when a door creaked in the middle of the night and he heard heavy footsteps. But soon he could tell they were in the stable, on the other side of the timbered wall. He knew that people who used their horses for the heavy work in the forest got up in the middle of the night to fodder them. Things soon quieted down again. He only heard the grinding of the horses' jaws and the shuffling of their hooves. He couldn't fall back asleep but stayed there resting in the warmth of the animals for another hour or two. The last thing he did was to quickly milk a little spotted cow; he caught the milk in an anchovy tin.

That made him a thief.

He thought about all the things he had done, but it didn't make him want to cry. He didn't feel like an evil person, or depraved, just hungry.

He wondered whether he would have been able to find enough to eat even if it had been summer. He was the great grandson of the man known as the Squirrel, who had lived off what the forest provided. But at least he had had a rifle and his traps and nets. Elis had nothing but a knife.

So he went on stealing things when he had to. People didn't lock their outbuildings. He would always keep something in his pocket to toss to any loose dogs that came rushing at him. A bit of sausage would always shut them up. He began to hold dogs in contempt.

What he really wanted was to cross the mountains and get down to the valleys on the other side. No one there would be able to figure out who he was. But as long as sledges could cross the mountains into Norway, he was afraid one of the drivers might recognize him. So well into May he lived like a starving tramp. Worse even. Sometimes he thought he was more like a fox. Though he never once considered giving up and turning back.

Being on his own had changed him. His sight and hearing were sharper. When he stole a pair of mittens someone had left in a sheep shed, he felt nothing but unadulterated pleasure at having found them. He never worried about being depraved any more.

By avoiding the roads and walking on the ice of the lakes, he had made his way without being seen by a single soul. He was quite sure that back home they reckoned he was dead. Once when his stomach was reasonably full—he had found a round of cheese—he thought that if this was living, it was not the same life. That thought stuck with him.

When the snow had melted and the roads across the mountain dried, people were on the move again. He often spied on travelers. One day he had the good fortune to see someone who could not possibly be from around there; he was wearing a black wide-brimmed hat and a coat buttoned all the way up to the chin. A preacher. He might have gotten stuck on the wrong side of the mountains after an autumn snowstorm and be on his way back home now.

The sight of Elis frightened him. Although Elis could vaguely imagine how he must look, it didn't occur to him that the preacher would be scared. But when he saw that Elis was nothing but a boy, he quickly recovered.

He gave him a lift in a trap drawn by a small pale brown mare. The price, of course, was an endless stream of questions. Elis managed to say very little and tried, when he did speak, to sound like the folks from Jolet with the heaviest accents.

The preacher went on and on about Jesus. Elis hadn't given him much thought, but this man seemed to know for certain what Jesus's dwelling had been like, what he ate, and what kind of shoes he wore. The man seemed like a child. Again Elis noticed how his long solitude had changed him. He had been more intimidated by people before, always thinking they knew more than he did, at least if they were better dressed. And almost everyone was. He had imagined tramps were frightened. They looked it. He wasn't nearly so scared any more though. He remembered his aunt Bäret telling him how shameless some tramps could be.

He never thanked the preacher or said good-bye because he had planned from the very beginning to sneak away so the preacher couldn't ask a bunch of questions or even worse take him someplace where there were people. No one was supposed to know he came from the other side of the mountains.

Even preachers need to piss. When, gentleman that he was, he went behind a spruce, Elis saw his chance and ran off into the forest. He climbed the hilly terrain until he reached a rocky ledge where he sat listening to the preacher calling. He felt like a lynx. The man didn't give up quickly, and in the end Elis was a bit ashamed. That feeling took him by surprise because he figured if he could hear with the ears of a lynx he could no longer feel shame.

They were at the foot of the mountain in a steep valley edged with spruces. From above the big river had looked like a wide glass-green ribbon, but down here it was more like a series of rapids, shaded by the trees. This narrow slit of a valley never saw the sun.

A little way off where the valley widened was a huddle of gray buildings. He sat high up in the woods on the other side and saw that the houses there got a little sun in the mornings.

He didn't dare go down. It was too close. They'd realize he came from the other side, that he was a Swede and a runaway. Nor did he dare pass by on the road. The valley was a narrow trap with the rushing river on one side and the steep spruce forest on the other. So he climbed up into the woods. The foxlike feeling he had almost lost when sharing the preacher's food parcel returned. He smelled smoke from far away.

He lay still until night arrived.

Before sunrise he felt harsh hands and bony fingers grab him. He'd fallen asleep under a big spruce tree. It was a woman, the one they called the Russian Hussy as he later learned.

She wasn't like other people. That was how she took him by surprise. She was up at night, wandering restlessly, searching. For something to eat, he eventually realized. And she wasn't afraid either.

She dragged him down to a hovel with a sod roof. There were also a few small outbuildings. He could have struggled free, but he figured she might have food.

There were no animals in the shed. The roof had collapsed. She said a bear had pulled off the shingling and taken the cow. He'd heard that one before. She was quite a liar.

She was gaunt, and her straggly hair wasn't plaited or rolled into a bun. When she grabbed him, he had been so frightened he thought she was a witch of the woods. She was actually quite young. It seemed to him that her belly might be soft, but in back she would be sharp as twigs.

Worst of all was what he found in the shack: a tiny baby in a cradle hanging from a rafter. He thought he'd forgotten all about Serine and the child. But he hadn't.

He thought he'd just up and leave. But that wasn't what happened. He got the idea this deceitful—and possibly mad—woman would let the baby starve to death. It was a little girl; she pouted her lips and made clucking sounds. Though he felt dizzy, he extended a finger tentatively, and she tried to suck it.

The woman had milk in her breasts, but Elis had never heard of a woman being able to nurse without having milk to drink herself. She ought to go down to the villagers and beg for a bottle of soured milk at least so the child would grow up human. Try to bring back a goat. But she didn't. She said they had driven her away. That was all she told him. The good thing was that she didn't ask him any questions either.

So he ended up staying for a day, and then for another. In one of the outbuildings he found nets, gray and brittle and with big gaping holes.

He found twine in the shack and carved himself a fishnet needle to mend the biggest holes. She said there were tarns with fish higher up and a boat. But he better watch out for the Lapps, 'cause the boat belonged to them.

Afterward when she boiled up the char, which she called cha, he was pleased that there was fat on it, thinking it would put some milk in her scrawny breasts even if it was the wrong kind. He'd brought bog moss down with him so she could clean the baby's bottom. It was chafed. She seemed utterly devoid of common sense.

Everything in the outbuildings was brittle and broken, but he managed to repair a few traps and snares. The first thing he caught was a she-hare with milk in her udder. He knew the fox would gobble up her young.

The only food the woman had to offer him was sorrel that she boiled into gruel. As the summer passed it got very stringy.

They didn't have any salt either. He told her to get some. But she refused. The fish was bland; without salt everything tastes more or less the same. She wouldn't make it through the winter without at least a goat and a bag of salt. She ought to have some flour too.

It was strange how she sneered when he said that.

He actually managed to acquire a bag of salt. Just as she'd said, when he was fishing up in the little mountain tarns, the Lapps appeared. Their reindeer grazing land was a little lower down, and they had come up to fish too. They gave him coffee to drink, explaining apologetically that it was made of boiled birch bracken fungus. They called it *tjaanja*. There was a war on, and nobody could get hold of the real coffee Swedish people preferred. But Elis, who had never had anything but barley coffee himself, thought it tasted fine. He liked their reindeer cheese too. They asked where he came from, and he described the location of the shack to them. They told him they knew it had been abandoned and that he ought to think twice about sleeping there. There might be invisible creatures inside. Hadn't he heard them tiptoeing and whispering at night?

He told them he didn't believe in little people or witches. But the Lapps had scared him just the same. He thought about ghosts with moldy faces and holes where there had been eyes.

When he told them about the baby and the woman who didn't have as much as a goat and nothing to salt the fish with, they clucked and tutted for a long time in their own tongue. They gave him a bag of salt before moving on.

He hid the bag, only taking out as much as he needed every time they ate. He thought she'd waste it. Summer was drawing to a close, and he was trying to fish and trap as much as he could. He told her she'd have to go down to the folks in the houses by the river and lay in a good store of salt. It would be best if she could get some whey as well to preserve the fish. He gave her the summer pelts from two of the martens; she ought to be able to trade them for something.

In one of the outbuildings he had found wooden casks, and he scoured them with meadowsweet. He would salt her some fish before leaving. The woman seemed to be taking it for granted he would stay on. She said he could sell some more pelts on toward autumn and winter and get flour. Maybe even a pregnant goat if he did enough trapping. She had hooked herself a breadwinner, and was looking forward to the winter with Elis.

It was like a nightmare. Although she was young, she had that kind of moldy dead person's face, and she coughed a lot, more than he did.

He chopped wood for her too. He thought of it quite late. But she would just have to use chunks of dead tree stumps until the firewood dried. He was doing it for the child.

When autumn-summer arrived, he told her he was going up to the tarns to put out the fishnets one last time. She should go down and buy salt to store his catch. After that, he was heading off. He'd have to get a job for the winter, see if there was any logging work to be had.

She laughed at him.

A beanpole of a boy. Who'd hire him?

After that he noticed she started pandering to him. She gave him the best bits of the back of the char. In the evenings she groped at his fly. She'd done that before. She used her hand, saying she could at least give him a little pleasure. He'd always sensed, though, that she enjoyed pawing at him and wanted him to do the same to her. But he left her alone, didn't want it to go any farther. He realized she was afraid of getting knocked up again. He didn't like what she did with her bony fingers, but his lust made it difficult for him to pull away.

He headed up the mountains, wishing desperately for less leaky boots and less ragged trousers. His sweater and coat wouldn't keep him warm either, stiff with dirt as they were.

He needed a real job now. But he was afraid of people and didn't know if they would hire him without seeing papers stating who he was and where he came from. In any case he would have to have clothes for the winter and get his boots cobbled.

The hike upward made him dizzy. He was panting and straining. He was sure his exhaustion was a result of the bad food. As he walked, he found himself hoping he might meet the Lapps again. He thought about their reindeer cheese. It made you feel strong.

Something strange was going on with him. He was on the verge of tears. It had been a long time since he had had such an unconstructive feeling.

The Lapps, of course, had moved down to the forested areas. It was cold up there by the rocky lakeshores. He missed them. The wind tore at the leaves of the dwarf birches; they would soon be bare. He caught a lot of fish but couldn't stay more than one night. This high up there was no wood to build a lean-to, and he didn't have the strength to walk back and forth every day.

Up here it was as if there were nothing else in the world than this kingdom of stones. Cold waters. Bones from dead animals. Tufts of fur with brown dried blood. And above it all a windy sky sending forth armies of ragged clouds.

He didn't like this mountain or the valley either, not one bit. There was nothing but stones to see up here, and there was nothing to see down in the valley but the steep forested hillsides. No blue ridges like back home, no distance to fix one's eyes on and long to be beyond. Nothing but what was there.

When he came back down, there was no smell of smoke. He was instantly alert. The two days and a night up on the stony mountain had brought back his fox instincts.

He stopped in the shade of the spruces and looked closely at the buildings. The axe in the chopping block hadn't been touched. He had left it like that. She usually just tossed it aside. He couldn't see that she had carried any wood inside either.

He decided to get the axe before approaching the shack. He surveyed the place. The patch of nettles next to the decrepit animal shed. The rusty fox trap. Next to the steps a herring pail and a spade with tufts of grass rising around it. Everything was precisely as before. And yet it wasn't.

He eventually realized he could stand there forever without figuring out what was so ominous. He took off the birchbark pack full of fish, putting it down in the high grass and crossing quickly over to the woodshed to grab the axe.

The steps creaked as he put his foot down, though he avoided the spot where he'd gone right through the rotting wood a while back. He shoved the door open and inhaled the air of the shack, cold and still.

The baby was lying in her cradle, silent and pale, eyes shut tight. His stomach turned; he hardly dared touch her, but he forced himself. Her skin was clammy, but he could feel the heartbeat in her chest, like a baby thrush.

He wanted to shout for her mother, but she had never told him her name. The thought crossed his mind again that she was a witch woman. Whoever she was, she had left. He was certain of that when he saw the two scruffy marten pelts he'd left on the bench. She hadn't gone to buy salt. She was just gone.

He snooped around, checking for her few possessions. Her shoes weren't there. She never used them at home. Every scrap of her clothing was gone too.

He touched the little girl again. She was sopping wet, so he took a bit of that bog moss and cleaned her up. But he had nothing to feed her. He knew such a small baby should have milk, but he thought he might boil her up a little fish.

He never did. When he took the girl in his arms, he could tell she was barely alive. Her heart hadn't stopped beating, but her mouth was all dry, and she didn't open her eyes.

She'll die on me, he thought.

Pulling the rags out of the cradle, he wrapped her in them and left. He left precisely as he had arrived: with his knife hanging from his belt and his old knitted cap on his head. That was all.

On his way down the slope he could tell she was getting colder and bluer. He tore at the rags to feel her heart again. The soft beat under his fingers was weaker. He undressed her and pulled up his own sweater, holding her right up against his chest. He pulled the sweater back down, checking that her head was sticking up through the neckline and her mouth and nose were free.

He was way in among the houses by the river before anyone saw him. It was a woman. She cried out and stood gaping as if she'd seen a ghost.

At home he had been to the store and to school and with Mamma at the meeting-house in Skinnarviken. Never inside anyone else's place though. Old Man Lubben, his grandfather, had forbidden it. He said people who went to each other's houses were just busybodies.

The house the woman took him to was warm and had a strong, pleasing smell of food and people. There was a painted cupboard. He was so mesmerized by it he hardly noticed what an uproar he and the baby caused; his eyes were glued to the gray-blue flowering vine on the cupboard door.

More people entered. Worry hung heavy that the child might die before the young woman they had sent for arrived, but she finally did, out of breath. They put the child in her arms, and she pulled out her pale blue-veined breast, pressing the nipple into the baby's mouth. Everyone just sat there staring. Elis too. The skin on her breast was shiny and taut. But the baby couldn't suck. She pressed out a few drops with her fingers, but it just ran down the child's lips without being swallowed.

Then the older woman, the one who had discovered Elis, pulled out a little spoon and the young woman milked into it. He went back to looking at the cupboard, although everyone else's eyes were fixed on the baby's mouth and the spoon. There was red mixed in with the little blue-gray dots in the flowers. You could see the brushstrokes. Around the vine the painter had imitated the grain of wood. It was as if the brush had quivered. It looked like wood but had clearly been painted. He could feel the brushstroke pulling through the thick oil paint, felt it in his own hand, a twinge.

When he came to, the women were buzzing with relief. The baby was making little smacking noises. After a while she was nursing, if weakly. The older woman said to take it real slow. Let him suck a little and then wait. Elis was about to say it was a her. But then he thought the best thing was not to say anything at all. And it didn't take long of course for them to see for themselves.

The men had left. The women fussed over the child; Elis just sat in the chair by the door, looking at the cupboard, figuring out how the painting had been done. There were lots of colors that were sort of in-between shades, like in a bog. They shifted. He wondered how they were made, whether you could buy paint of that many different colors.

He suddenly remembered all the fish in the pack he had left up there. He almost said something, then stopped himself. He noticed they weren't paying much heed to him, and when the men came in for their supper, it became clear they thought he was some kind of idiot. He could tell when the farmer began asking questions. Elis mostly just shook his head, and the farmer filled in the answers himself. The Russian Hussy, he called the woman from the shack. Elis was sure that wasn't a real name. They can't know very much around here, he thought. They've no store and no guesthouse. They don't know anything.

So had she gone off? Elis nodded. They weren't surprised, they said. Down to the coast of course, to the herring boats. It was that time of year. They sounded grim when they said it. As if they were talking about a bitch in heat. They didn't call her bitch, but they used that tone. He was taken aback, remembering how he had imagined her as witch of the woods. She had taken her shoes when she left though, so she had to be human.

They gave him some porridge but made him stay on his chair by the door because he was so filthy. They were decent folks he could tell. The farmer said grace before the meal, and they ate in silence. The woman who had nursed the baby was gone. Home to her own child Elis assumed.

The porridge settled in as lovely warmth, lining his stomach. After a while the feeling spread through his whole body, and he was so sleepy he could hardly keep his eyes open and thought nothing in the whole world could bother him. That was when they told him he was going to have a bath. One of the big boys, Bendik, took him out to the brewing shed where there was a huge tub of hot water. He had to scrub himself with Bendik staring at him the whole time. He took Elis's clothes and started to carry them out. He tried to grab them back, but the bigger boy just whopped him across the neck. It didn't really hurt, but it threw him off balance. Bendik said they'd burn his clothes. He was holding them on a long stick.

Elis stood there naked and freezing, not knowing what to do. Even if he ran back to the shack, there wouldn't be any clothes there. He curled up on the floor near the hearth.

After a while somebody opened the door and thrust in a pile of garments. All he saw were hands, a woman's. There were a pair of worn but clean home-spun trousers, a rope he realized was meant to belt them with, and a really old patched blue cotton work shirt. Laughter bubbled up in him. There was also a knitted sweater, mended and darned many times. Bendik had left him his old boots, but he'd need a pair of socks. In due time, he thought.

He briefly considered running off, until he remembered that porridge. He needed food. He was weak, had a cough, and wore out very easily. So he went back up to the house, although it didn't feel good. The older woman set him on a milking stool in front of the fire, pulled out a little pair of wool shears and told him she was going to give him a haircut. He was afraid she would hurt him, cut his scalp, and so he tried to get away. But the men were sitting on the bench at the table looking on and told Bendik to hold him down. He just had to put up with it.

The matted bits were the first to go, and the long strands. She chopped them off and tossed them right into the fire. She was fast with the shears, which were sharp and cut quite short. That was how they discovered his scar.

I'll be damned, said Bendik.

They gathered round him, wide-eyed. It made an impression. He didn't know what the back of his head looked like, but he imagined from the bump he had felt under his fingers that it was a pretty nasty scar. He remembered there had been a big stiff clot of blood in his cap the first day and night.

So of course they asked where that ugly scar came from. He kept silent. But something about their voices told him they didn't intend to give up. So he thought again, hard this time, like in his fox days, and then said:

Dunno.

He tried to sound Norwegian like Mamma. He and his brothers and sisters had all talked that way before she died. After that there hadn't been much talking at home, and before he started school, he had never exchanged a word with anyone from the village. At the same time he didn't want them to think he came from Jolet. Then they might ask people from there if they knew who he was, maybe at church at Mickelmass. So it was better if they thought he was an idiot. They went on asking about how he got that scar:

Could it have been an animal?

A bear?

Or an ox?

A gun? asked the farmer, pointing to Elis's head.

He shook his head and said as before:

Dunno.

And that was true. He didn't know what the old man had slammed him with. He hadn't exactly planned to lie. The only thing that mattered to him was to sound as if he came from up north and not to reveal his Swedish dialect. Now the farmer was saying that when he was young, he'd been out logging with one of his brothers-in-law. The man ended up in the way of a birch that fell wrong. It came down on his head, and he'd been unable to get up. Afterward his memory was gone. It came back after some time, the farmer comforted Elis. In fact, he said, in a tone of voice as if he were reading from the book of the Lord:

The truth will always come out!

Elis thought that if it were up to him, it wouldn't come out for a long time. But he said nothing. They had found themselves an explanation for his "dunnos" and they liked it. They were up later than usual that evening, curious about him. All but one incredibly old man with a white beard asleep in a corner.

They found it hard to believe he didn't remember anything at all. The farmer's wife told her husband to ask Elis if he had been confirmed. She didn't think she could ask him in a way he'd understand.

Are your confirmed, boy? he shouted as if to an idiot.

Elis began, true to form, by responding that he didn't know. Then he realized he was being foolish. If he wasn't old enough to have been confirmed, he could hardly expect to be given a real job. So he added.

I b'lieve so.

They conferred in soft voices, apparently thinking he couldn't understand unless they shouted at him. They decided to see if he knew his pieces. The farmer asked for the catechism book, but his wife had put it over the door to the barn so God would protect her animals, and she refused to take it down in case something might sneak up on the cows and put blood in their milk again. She extended the Bible to him instead. It was too thick to fit in the crack over the door.

They seemed to be planning to interrogate him about it, but the farmer leafed through with his rough fingers and couldn't figure out what to ask. Elis was wild with impatience. He tried to transmit thoughts to the farmer: ask me about the swine of the Gadarenes or the daughter of the ruler of the synagogue Jairus or who was in the mulberry tree or the names of the sons of Zebedee or what happened to the son of the widow of Nain. But the man didn't seem to be able to come up with a thing. So Elis burst out of his own accord:

Ruben! Simeon!

You could have heard a pin drop.

Levi, Judah, Issachar! he shouted. Zebulun, Joseph, and Benjamin!

They stared.

Dan, Naphtali, Gad 'n Asher!

I'll be damned, Bendik finally said.

They agreed he had been confirmed and that with the aid of the Lord he would regain his memory. They would take him to see the parish minister. He would have to decide what should be done with him and the child.

Elis hadn't been confirmed. He would have been that year at Whitsun if he hadn't run away. Now he felt almost confirmed anyway.

They let him sleep in the loft with Bendik. He was full of questions and dared to abandon his reticence, figuring Bendik wouldn't be as curious as the farmer about where he came from. But Bendik was sleepy. He told him that the woman who had run off to the coast and the herring boats was the widow of the youngest son in the family and then fell into a deep sleep, snoring loudly.

Something about the woman didn't make sense. But not until the next morning, when he and Bendik had been given a bowl of soured milk and a slice of bread and been sent out to the barn to shovel cow muck, did he learn that her child wasn't really the grandchild of anyone in this family. She was born much too long after the husband died of consumption: just a couple of months after the wedding he had become weak and unable to lift a finger.

That made Elis think maybe she wasn't an ordinary human being after all. But he didn't mention it.

While her husband was sick, she had gone to the coast to earn some money when the herring boats came in, Bendik told him. People who had been down there told her in-laws she had been a whorin'. They said she went with Russians, heavily bearded louts who looked like animals. They had come with a fishing boat from the north but stayed on because of the war. They lived fearful lives, said Bendik.

By the time she came back home, her husband was dead, and she was not welcome. They hadn't known about the child.

Elis wondered to himself if that was true.

Bendik and he were given the task of pulling up tree stumps for tar boiling. It was all right when they could find dead ones, but twisting up stubborn stumps that held tenaciously to the soil with their long thick root systems was very hard work. He was ashamed of having so little strength with which to ply axe and crowbar.

In the mornings while they were mucking out and he was still full and more or less rested, he could manage to think. At first his thoughts scared him. But he just kept thinking them and once when he was alone he voiced them. They started going around in his head like the verse of a hymn. He would recite it to himself when he was twisting and turning the crowbar. It made him feel stronger.

The hell with working for no pay!
Being a farmer's slave.
A man could waste his life away.
The hell with this path to the grave!

The food was the best part. Once they got pork. He was disgusted by the memory of the green mess of sorrel the Russian Hussy had boiled, though he still didn't feel he had much in common with people any more. He'd developed a taste for solitude, and he missed it.

He'd begun to think people were fools. So easy to outwit. He knew he was lucky that they'd come up with their own explanation for his bad memory.

But they were still fools.

He hadn't forgotten how hollow he'd felt during the time he was hiding from everyone, but he thought the hollow feeling was mostly starvation. Now he was hungry for solitude.

While they were eating, he would stare at the cupboard with the flowers. The little girl was better now too he could tell. She gurgled and smiled, not knowing her mother was a whore. He wondered when they'd take her to be baptized. No one ever mentioned it.

One Sunday evening when they weren't so tired, Bendik said:

I want to go to sea.

And then, as if realizing immediately he'd said more than he meant to, he tried to backtrack:

Or at least I want to see a bit of the world.

Elis, who seldom opened his mouth to say more than nope and yup, started saying how they should run away together before winter came.

He thought he'd gained enough strength from porridge and soured milk to be taken on as a logger. They ought to make their way down to the Namsos valley. Or up into the woods near there. Although he would have preferred to run off alone, he thought he'd be better off if Bendik was with him. Even if he was too scrawny to be hired on his own, they'd want Bendik who was strong as an ox, so they'd probably take him on too.

My uncle Anund said it was wrong to be ashamed of your children and hide them, even if they looked thin and ill. If you hid children they might disappear.

Would they die?

No, but they wouldn't be alive either.

What happened was that that the Others abducted them, and then they were neither dead nor alive. They'd become invisible children.

All the Others, said Laula Anut, originally came from of a couple of children who had been hidden away.

What children?

The very first people had hidden two of their children because they thought something was wrong with them. They hid them from God.

I thought a lot about those invisible children. I asked Hillevi if she knew that people hid away children they were ashamed of, got rid of them. She gave me a strange look and told me to hush up. So I decided it was probably true.

When Reverend Norfjell died, it took his wife a couple of hours to notice; there was so little difference. At least that was what she said. His body went stiff in that same propped up position he had been in the whole time he was bedridden, and the two women who came to wash and lay out the corpse they couldn't get him down flat. Those two knew all about what happens to the dead. Their judgment was that he'd been cold for at least twelve hours.

Since they had to wait a day for him to loosen up, they went back home.

Disappointed about having to return to their mundane chores in barn and kitchen, they dropped by Märta Karlsa's kitchen on the way and spent a couple of hours drinking barley coffee and talking about what they'd seen. Hillevi, who came in to borrow a drop of cream, listened for a while. Then she went back up to her own room and just sat there. She was too nauseous to drink her coffee.

It was even worse on the day of the funeral. She was sick several times that morning and very upset that the walls were so thin the schoolmistress downstairs might hear her heaving. She really didn't feel up to attending the funeral, but she couldn't do that to the minister's wife who, though condescending, had always been kind to her.

In church all she could think about was the minister lying there more dead than alive for months and then having passed on without anyone noticing. She wondered whether there really was a difference between the two states, being alive and being dead. It was all one big muddle; like the disgusting mess she threw up. Like black decaying ice in the spring, it broke up, gave way.

Edvard officiated, and the minister from Byvången performed the funeral rites. She had been avoiding Edvard. When she saw him go out on church matters, she would go over to the vicarage with her birth reports and ask the minister's wife to leave them on his desk. She felt panicky at the thought that he would be applying to become minister of Röbäck church after Norfjell.

Kneeling at the altar, his neck looked thin above his white linen collar, and the soles of his shoes were worn. Memory opened a door into the past that should no longer have been there: the heat from the iron stove in his room in Uppsala, his long back in its undershirt, and the crucifix-shaped shadow cast by the latticed window. I feel sorry for him, she thought. He never wanted me here. He set his mind to a position as far away as possible because he felt guilty about what we were doing. He wanted to get away. From me. I actually feel sorry for him.

The minister said:

Forasmuch as it hath pleased Almighty God in his good providence to take out of this world the soul of Carl Efraim Norfjell, our departed brother, we therefore commit his body to the ground.

The congregation rose and with it the odor of mothballs and the smell of wet leather and horses. She was having terrible trouble with smells lately and thought: What's happened to me?

He raised the spade and said:

Ashes to ashes.

Gravelly earth rattled onto the coffin lid.

And dust to dust.

That was when it happened. She didn't hear him say at the general Resurrection in the last day, we may be found acceptable in Thy sight. Her head was completely filled with the realization that struck her: *he's dead now.*

Even though no one knows when he died, he's dead now.

It's not in between. It *is.*

And at that very moment she also knew she had to tell someone she was with child. She needed to say it. Then it would be real too. Dead or alive, it would be.

A moment later she thought that if only she dared say it, it would disappear from her. It would be. But not alive.

Who could she tell? Absolutely not Aunt Eugénie. Should she write to Sara? She certainly couldn't tell Edvard. And Halvorsen—that was out of the question. Anyway, he was traveling, buying up goods. He had sent her a postcard from Vilhelmina. A mountain landscape with two Lapp children and a black dog in front of a *gåetie.* Greetings Hillevi from your friend Trond Halvorsen.

Coffee was served in the parish hall after the funeral. She considered her predicament. She had been considering it day and night for two weeks now. If you could still call it considering. The combination of smells in the crowded room—newly washed woolen clothing, the scent of coffee, the oppressive odors from hair and mouths—made her queasy again, and she had to get up and go home. She knew precisely how bad that looked.

Girls who went pale in stuffy rooms. Cheerful, sociable girls who turned quiet and withdrawn. Every woman in the world would recognize those signs. Dark circles under the eyes, swelling breasts.

She had known more about all that than any of them. She had studied things they didn't have a notion about and never would. She remembered Tobias's *Human Sexuality* on the shelf among his medical school texts. She would sneak in and read it in his room when he was out. Now she was fully trained. She had also read about artificial methods and French preventatives, and about abortionists who were tried and convicted in the *Journal of Midwifery*. She was a wellspring of information about sexual relations, and yet here she sat on her bed with unspotted underwear and the same anguish that girl Ebba Karlsson had felt, the one who had come up behind Hillevi on the Iceland Bridge. Ebba had finally caught up with her.

That unfortunate girl had made up her mind to say it. When she said it to me, it became real, Hillevi thought. And I responded that it was raining and I shouldn't have gone out without my umbrella. Then I walked away.

To me it wasn't real. It was simply unpleasant.

Before she said it, it was neither alive nor dead. Then it died. When she said it to me, it became dead.

Whimpering as if she had cut herself, Hillevi curled up on her bed.

The initiative had run right out of her. All she wanted to do was sleep, but she couldn't. Doing handiwork was awful; when she sat still, her thoughts went around in her head worse than ever. She borrowed books from Märta. The younger women in Röbäck exchanged novels, tattered and stained. She read *The Little Seamstress on the Boulevard* and *The Pale Countess* and was ashamed.

She felt as alienated from her own body now as when she got her first monthly. She supposed she had grown up after her aunt's late miscarriage, which the chambermaid had referred to alternately as her losing the baby and her avalanche delivery. Her aunt was afraid Hillevi knew more than she ought to after that night. But Hillevi felt it was the other way around: she no longer knew anything. That time too her body had started living a life of its own; shortly afterward she got her first period. It bled. There was nothing she could do about it. Now it had failed to bleed.

It was as if she were watching herself from outside, powerless. Her consciousness was at the level of the mirror over the sink, glowering at those breasts of hers, now plump whether she liked it or not, and at her pale pink nipples that were slowly growing larger. Sometimes she was sure she must be losing her mind.

After some time, precisely the same thing happened to her as to the heroine of one of those romantic novels, *The Fate of the Crofter's Lass*. She heard a horse and cart stop at the house. She heard a man's voice. But unlike the crofter's lass, she didn't get out of bed because she knew it was no baron who had arrived. She felt incurably apathetic. Not until she heard footsteps tiptoeing up the steep attic staircase did she sit up. But she still had the blanket around her shoulders when there was a knock. She tried to pin up her hair and shouted: Wait! but he stepped in.

The first thing that came to her mind was that Trond Halvorsen looked like a shopkeeper's assistant she had once seen in a dingy little shop on Swine Square in Uppsala a long time ago. The young man had very dark hair, and the bangs down over his eyes under the brim of his provision-dealer's cap were nearly black, his whiskers a bluish shadow on his chin and cheeks.

Halvorsen was holding a box of Freja chocolates, a big one with gold trim. Had he been over to Norway? He had an enigmatic air about him.

She knew he had been out buying up goods, but with a war on surely not even he could bring such luxuries across the border, could he?

His eyes were a little red. Had he been partying? Or was it just lack of sleep?

Are you sick, Hillevi? he asked, and she thought he sounded bashful. She shook her head.

I'm altogether too healthy, she said.

He put the box down and walked quietly over and sat next to her on the rumpled bed. She noticed he was wearing not his boots but soft Lapp reindeer skin shoes.

I didn't think it was you, she mumbled.

Why's that?

He spoke with his mouth to her neck, his lips groping a little to get under her hair.

The footsteps, she said. No boots.

He explained that his feet got really cold sitting for hours on end driving the wagon in boots. But there was no need to be concerned; he did have his boots with him. He was on his way to Östersund with goods. What would she like from there?

Like? she asked. I don't know if there's anything I'd like.

What's wrong? he whispered.

And as it turned out, she never had to make up her mind. He asked her himself: Were there consequences?

She didn't even have to answer. There was just a shifting in her body his lips could sense.

Hillevi, are you unhappy about it? he whispered.

Her answer must have come the same way because he went on:

Oh, don't be, Hillevi. If you like, I'll buy rings.

He'd put his arm around her and was sitting with his cheek pressed to hers. Neither of them moved for a long while.

If not, I'll pay of course. But I'd rather buy rings. Would you like that?

So she nodded and burst into tears.

Then he was like a whirlwind in the room. He lit the fire and put on water for coffee. Then he removed a little leather pouch from his inside pocket and asked softly where she kept her coffee grinder. She realized he had real beans in the pouch, the kind not even a wholesaler could get for love or money those days. She wondered what kind of dealings he was involved in, remembering the horse he'd been given for his confirmation and that the Laka King was his grandfather and that his father only traded in timber nowadays. She realized that man, Morten Halvorsen, was going to be the grandfather of her child.

When Halvorsen had left, she found it difficult to remember what he looked like. The dark man, the shop assistant at Swine Square, kept coming into her head, his face blocking out Halvorsen's. It was like a dream.

She realized now that even in those days she had kept secrets. No one had ever found out that she had gone looking for her real mother's mother.

After the night her aunt miscarried, she had begun to think more about her own mother. Before, her mother's death had just been a sentence people uttered: She died in childbirth, my dear. A string of words that didn't mean much of anything except that she wasn't there. Like an enameled sign, white with blue lettering. No peddlers. For deliveries please use service entrance. But of course there had to be something behind those words. She realized it must have been a terrible night. A winter one that time. She began to see that the events of the early hours of November 19, 1890, when she was born had been awful.

She's leaving us.

Had they shouted those words? Had her father run, unshaven, collarless and with his suspenders dangling?

She knew nothing about it. There had never been any point asking Aunt Eugénie, who didn't think they should talk about Hillevi's mother. You could see she found such questions embarrassing. That they pained her.

But her face. What had she looked like?

It took Hillevi a long time to work up to asking if there was a photograph. By then she was already convinced that if Miss Viola Liljeström had been called and had come that night, things would have ended differently for her mother. Her soothing words and clean hands would have stopped the bleeding. Because it had surely been a hemorrhage. Or else fever.

If it was childbed fever, her mother would never have developed it. Not if Miss Viola Liljeström had been at hand with her clean-scrubbed hands, her cotton uniform, her white apron, and the well-laundered sanitary napkins and linen dressings in her bag.

Since they never again spoke either of that awful night or of Miss Liljeström, Hillevi's aunt had been astonished when at the age of eighteen she said she wanted to train to be a midwife.

At some point after her sixteenth birthday, she had gone to see the woman who had been her father's housekeeper when she was little and asked her about Elisabeth Klarin's parents. She was an elderly spinster and had been extremely reluctant to tell what she knew, but in the end she said she believed they lived at Swine Square and were shopkeepers.

Hillevi thought that sounded solid and nothing to be ashamed of, though of course it wasn't very special. But when she found the shop, it was a dank little place reeking of lamp oil and sour milk. She never said anything to her aunt—or even to Sara—about going there.

There he stood, that swarthy fellow behind the counter. He was too young to be her grandfather of course, and he told her impatiently that there was no other owner; he was the one she should talk to if she had business with the owner. So she thought he was probably an uncle of hers. Perhaps her mother Elisabeth had been that dark too. But she didn't dare ask him. And that was lucky because he was absolutely not her uncle. He said that yes some people called Klarin had once owned the shop. But not before him, further back.

It was as if they had vanished into the grayness of Swine Square. That first time she didn't dare to go into any of the courtyards. The place stank of piss. It frightened her. The emaciated dogs. The staring children.

But she hadn't given up. One day when it was lighter out and she felt bolder, she went there again and asked around. In the end she found an old woman who lived in a little room above a coal and wood shop who could tell her about her maternal grandmother.

That had to have been Hanna Klarin, she said. She and her old man owned the milk shop on the corner. But he's dead now, and she lives with her sister in a place out by Boländerna.

Hillevi asked the man's first name, but the woman had never heard it. Now at least she had one name, she had Hanna, her grandmother. It was as if she couldn't take in any more just then.

She thought a lot about the two names, Hanna and Elisabeth. They were ordinary names, and Elisabeth was a pretty one. They could have belonged to any old housewives. Her aunt had a friend named Hanna. She didn't like that dark shop with the sickening smell coming from the milk jugs in the tub of cold water. But perhaps the shop had deteriorated over the years and become dirty and dank; there was nothing neat about that black-haired fellow.

Not until spring, when she could walk all the way out to Boländerna on more or less dry roads, did she ask her way to the little place Hanna Klarin shared with her sister.

What had she imagined? That her mother's mother would weep and welcome her with open arms? The old woman seemed disapproving. Or perhaps intimidated. Although Hillevi was only sixteen, she was an improbable figure here in her rust-red woolen coat with its matching hat and a lace-trimmed white silk scarf tied in a bow at the front. She had worn her new coat and hat to look nice when she met her grandmother, but she regretted it the moment she stepped inside.

They didn't talk like her. They didn't have a photo of her mother. Neither of the two old women would tell her anything about Lissen. That was what they called her. It was the only thing she found out: that her mother, listed as Elisabeth in the parish records, had always been known as Lissen.

In the end there was silence. They had nothing more to say, so they kept quiet. Hillevi was unaccustomed to such behavior. She had been raised to always speak, and to speak clearly and kindly, even to simple people. It was particularly important to keep up the conversation when things began to feel uncomfortable. At such times her aunt's voice would go even softer. It murmured and found ways out of awkward situations. One had an obligation both to oneself and others to break silence and avoid embarrassment. But the two women in the dark cabin where it didn't smell very clean were apparently not aware of this obligation and refused to say any more.

Lissen. That was all she brought away. And the memory of their silence.

Trond Halvorsen returned just over a week later. He had two shiny gold engagement rings with him and a decorative little silver ring with an amethyst. He had bought her a silk dress. It had pink and violet stripes, a lace collar with a narrow black silk band threaded through it, and a black elastic belt with a gilded buckle in the shape of two birds with touching beaks. He had also bought a deep violet velvet plush hat. It was stretched over a wire frame and would have looked like a huge upside down scoop if the milliner hadn't fluffed up the velvet and draped it in soft little folds. It was trimmed with light purple satin ribbon, with a pin in the shape of a Viking shield in the middle.

He'd bought her a puppy too.

Hillevi didn't know whether to laugh or cry. The dog was a female, and he'd fallen for her because she looked like a little black pointer, although she had no tail and her race was a foreign name he'd forgotten.

Hillevi explained why a midwife couldn't possibly have a dog. First and foremost it was a matter of hygiene. And who would look after the dog when she was far away delivering babies?

Trond said Aagot would now that Hillevi was moving to Blackwater to live above the store. There was a room with a kitchen up there; his whole family had lived there before his father built their house.

This summer I'll build us one, he said. As soon as the ground thaws out, and it's dry enough.

He was planning to build them a house. He'd show her how he'd thought it out. Right by the lake.

The door to old Elle's shelter was so low I had to crawl in on all fours. There was a dry rustling under my knees. She was an old woman and should have had help putting down a layer of fresh birch branches.

This was long ago. It was during the war. But just then, for a few weeks or a couple of months, neither the bombs nor Hitler and Churchill worried me. I didn't even care about King Haakon who, only a couple months earlier, had pronounced the famous three no's and marched off on his long legs, and I had no idea that Namsos, only a few dozen kilometers away, had been destroyed by bombs. I was in a world of my own.

No, I was a world of my own.

She was the first person I told. Now that's strange.

Of course Elle was the object of respect as old people always were in those days. But no one bothered to do what she said any more. Her advice only applied to our own little world anyway. She was full of mumbo jumbo about how everything was supposed to be. It came out from between what was left of her teeth after rolling around on her tongue, which protruded far too often. Very old people's tongues do that. It wasn't healthy looking either. Old Elle was on her last legs, drying up like the branches she sat on.

We were at the top of the stretch of birch wood on Mount Skårefjell. We had started moving in mid-April. I didn't know I was pregnant yet, and like everyone else my mind was full of the occupation. We were amazed that those men in steel helmets and green uniforms had found their way in among the houses at Langvasslia where we were. The reindeer does were going to calve, war or no war; we had to leave for higher ground. But we weren't allowed to use the traditional herding paths. Approaching the border was prohibited.

The men didn't know what to do. They knew it was high time to get the does up to the calving lands, but how would they get them to walk new paths, and how would the does be calm enough to nurture their young when they didn't know where they were?

We mostly moved along at night, on the crust of the snow. This was a new experience for me, but I was told that was how they usually did it; the snow got too soft during the day. Sometimes we had to travel during the day anyway, in confusion, blinded by the sun, and on too little sleep. There was weeping and cursing. The old folks said nothing was as usual that year and warned us that things wouldn't go well if the does heard harsh voices and were treated cruelly. The dogs appeared to be going wild. They were in the grip of the war, Elle and the other old ones said. Dogs soon take their cues from people.

The does did calve in any case, and we stayed at places where not much had been arranged in advance. Other Lapps came, demanding grazing rights for their herds on land we needed, and there were constant discussions that sometimes turned into arguments in spite of the fact that everyone knew the German occupation, the harsh language of the German authorities, was the real trouble.

In the very midst of this tumult I realized what was happening in my body. It came to me slowly and gently as if there were no war and no frenzy around me or as if all those things were very far away.

The worry growing in me was not about poison gas or bombs, although that was what everyone was talking about. We expected this war to be like the last one. But none of that got through to me.

I had seen a white calf tottering around on its weak legs. I followed it day by day as it suckled, and soon I realized it was blind and deaf.

But old Elle said the worst dangers for something growing in a womb came in through the door.

Sarakka Uksakka Juksakka, she mumbled. I didn't know what that meant, but it calmed me down. I would really have liked to talk with Hillevi. But the war had separated us. There were tanks barricading the road below Aagot's; I saw them when it was all over.

Hillevi was a treasure house of knowledge and common sense. But I wondered if she knew how mumbled words could possess your soul if you had just recently realized you were expecting.

Elle said there were three wise women who protected mothers and their children. I laughed softly because I thought it was the thing to do, and I gave her the pouch containing the last of my coffee beans. She ground them and said that one of the women, Sarakka, would help me to overcome the danger and pain of giving birth. She would see to it that the afterbirth came out as it should and that I stopped bleeding. Juksakka would protect my child's fragile head from blows and knocks. Yes, far into the future this wise woman would protect the child from falls.

142

But Uksakka was the one I should cling to now because she guarded the entry to the *gåetie* and kept out evil.

That old woman was actually more aware of war and human violence than I was at the time. I went around in a world dominated by the sound of the coursing of my own blood, imagining babies with two heads, babies with club feet, and babies with no eyes. But I still joked with Elle because I thought it was the thing to do, and I said those wise women of hers must be very old and wrinkled by now; they would be difficult to distinguish from a birch root or an old leather pouch.

But sometimes I still think about what she said about the evil that comes in through the door. I wish there had been a wise woman with power over the world. Mothers and their children ought to have more rights.

When Hillevi knew that Edvard Nolin had gone to a regional meeting and would be away for three days, she went over to see Reverend Norfjell's widow, who was now packing her belongings in chests and moving to Östersund. Hillevi told her that she too was going to move and that it would happen within the next few days.

I'm going to live in Blackwater because it's more central, she said. It won't take me so long to get up to Skinnarviken and Lakahögen. And they have a telephone at the store too. A midwife should always have a phone.

Trond Halvorsen and she had agreed that this was what she would tell people to begin with. They wanted to keep their secret to themselves for a few weeks at least. But Mrs. Norfjell instantly attacked the news like a magpie, dragging and pulling at it and examining every angle.

What did the chairman of the local council have to say about this change, and how did the council members react? Would they pay for housing other than that provided for her above the school?

In the long run no one could expect the midwife to put up with such poor accommodations, Hillevi told her. Drafty and cramped. No real kitchen, just a room with a stove. No thank you, they'd just have to understand. Hadn't her predecessor objected as well?

That one had to leave, said the minister's widow. She was too demanding.

On the third of October Halvorsen loaded her trunk and chests onto a wagon, and Hillevi moved.

She papered the shelves and pinned up crocheted lace edging. She hung curtains. Late in the evenings the stairs groaned. She took him into her opened-out trundle bed, where there was a rustling and a scent of barley straw when they moved toward each other.

The straw stuffed into a clean mattress cover was an interim solution. It was a matter of hygiene, she said. He had the impression that was a word he was going to hear often now and immediately put in an order with the saddle maker in Byvången for a horsehair mattress.

The little black dog they called Sissla had won Hillevi over with her brown-eyed gaze. She had a box to sleep in by the door. She was housebroken but needed frequent walking; her bladder wasn't fully mature. Early in the mornings, before anyone else was up, Hillevi went down the stairs with her and let her pee behind the store. Sometimes when the weather was dry, she walked her all the way down to the boathouse.

Do your business now, she would say.

People who heard her say that during the day laughed behind Hillevi's back. They weren't accustomed to euphemisms.

Halvorsen was good about leaving Hillevi around three in the morning. He would pass by the stable and fodder Dolly and Sooty, the big gelding. They assumed no one noticed his comings and goings, but they weren't overly concerned. All would be revealed, Halvorsen had said with a twinkle in his brown eyes.

One morning when she went downstairs in the dark to let Sissla out, she stumbled over something on the bottom step. She never saw what it was, and Sissla didn't notice because Hillevi carried her both up and down the stairs.

On her way out later that morning she saw that what she had stumbled over was a little, neatly wrapped brown paper package with a string around it, crossed in the middle. She felt it. Whatever was inside was both soft and hard at once, and the sensation that rose in her as she fingered it, trying to figure out what it was through the paper, was anxiety. Yes, she was definitely distressed.

It had to be meant for her. No one else lived behind this door. The stairway went right up to her garret room. The little vestibule was full of the smells of the store and the storehouse on the other side of the wall.

That sensation under her fingertips made her refrain from tearing the paper off where she was standing. She took it with her and went back upstairs.

She undid it on the counter by her dishwashing basin. She cut the string. There was a sense of urgency and no time to stand there fussing with the knot. She turned back the paper, which seemed to have been used many times before. Inside lay a chopped-off dog's paw.

Her first reaction was sheer bewilderment. She pulled the paper hastily around the contents again, to conceal it. She had a momentary impulse to open the hatch on the stove and toss it in. But she knew it would smell. Instead she hid the package under the top logs in her wood box. For a long while she stood there completely mystified, just staring at the wood box lid. Her next impulse was to rush down to Trond and tell him what she had found. That urge subsided as well.

She thought about the package having been put where she would stumble over it. But Trond's boots hadn't bumped it when he went down a couple of hours before her. It was in the middle of the bottom step. If it had been there then, he would have found it.

Whoever put the package there must have done so a little later. Was it someone who knew she would be alone then? Was she and no one else meant to find it?

That was how those thoughts began.

The store was originally right next to the house I live in. It was a small building, but it had a second story, although the ceiling was low up there. They say Morten Halvorsen built it when he decided to settle here. He came from Fagerli, on the Norwegian side. People called it t'shop.

He became the son-in-law of the Laka King, and he made his fortune in timber. But from the beginning he was nothing but a peddler with his wares on a cart who would stop at each farm and unpack his notions: papers of pins, brooches, mirrors, dress fabrics, suspenders, snuffboxes, razors, and garters. A lot of junk really. But he made a living.

When he decided to go as far as Blackwater for the first time, it was probably because he had heard there were people there with cash in their pockets. The days of the big lumber companies had begun. The sawmills by the coast needed timber. The gentlemen from the companies purchased forest to be felled, and the men in the village were employed to do the logging and transporting. They were paid in cash but had nowhere to spend it since there was no general store in Blackwater. It wasn't difficult to figure out that they needed things like heavy duty harnesses, horse fodder, and Chicago pork for the lumberjacks.

So this junk dealer from Fagerli who stocked up at Namsos, where goods arrived on heavily laden cargo ships, must have had some idea about staying in Blackwater and setting up shop. He had two barrels of pork lashed to his cart and a sack of Brazilian coffee. Coffee was something both lumberjacks and village women wanted.

Because it was autumn, he had to find somewhere to stay for the winter in any case. The days were still clear and bright but were getting shorter and shorter. The mountain lakes had gone black in the first autumn storms with white froth like rows of vicious bared teeth.

He trudged along, pulling his cart in the deep wheel ruts. There was forest, forest, and more forest. He was keeping an eye out for the milestone, which wasn't really a border stone in those days since we were part of a union with Norway. The forest was like a wall. He couldn't see the glimmering of the lake between the spruce trees, though he knew it must be there. He came to a place where two paths very clearly diverged. He heard the sound of running water and realized he must be near a river since the rushing was quite loud. It probably marked the border.

He stood there for a long time with his pushcart, uncertain about which path to take. A Lapp came along, a little man in a longshirt made of hides, with a faded blue cap on his head.

The peddler greeted him politely:

Peace be upon you, stranger!

The Lapp's pipe rasped, but he didn't say anything. The peddler asked the way to Blackwater. The Lapp looked at his load, so the peddler felt compelled to explain he intended to offer his goods for sale there. To make the Lapp more conversant, he mentioned that there were surely one or two little things on his cart.

For your kids, he said.

The Lapp looked to be thinking very hard. He removed his pipe from his mouth, pointing its short stem at the overgrown track leading down to the right. He continued to stand at the convergence of the roads as the peddler headed that way, pushing his cart. It wasn't easy going. There was a high ridge of grass between the ruts; the cart wobbled on its iron-rimmed wheels. The left-hand road was better; it seemed people usually passed this village by. He turned around to say something about it to the Lapp, but he had vanished. Nowhere to be seen, he must have turned off into the woods or the marsh. He was most definitely not there.

The peddler plodded on with his pushcart, avoiding the stones and staying on course as best he could with his heavy load. The sound of rushing water grew louder and louder. Sometimes he heard a clucking and buzzing like voices, but it was only the water running through the stones. He wished he had someone to talk to. The air was cold and raw that afternoon, and the shadows of the spruce trees were long.

Suddenly there was more light and more space between the spruces. Birch, rowan, and sallow appeared, and soon he was looking down at the river. There was a bridge abutment. But no bridge. On the other side was another stone abutment. But the bridge itself, which hadn't been a very large one, must have been swept off one spring. The river water rushed past.

He was upset, to put it mildly. Then he felt a chill. It was as if the spruce shadows grew blacker and the air nippy. His nose was cold.

He'd have to turn back now, he realized. The people who lived between Blackwater and Gremså had built themselves a new stone bridge, to which the other path had led. Nowadays this one was a dead end. But he didn't want to turn his cart around and start pushing it back up.

Truth be told, he didn't dare.

Damn Lapp, he muttered, teeth clenched.

He was still upset, and he also knew how exposed he was standing by the bridge abutment. The water sighed and chattered against the stones as it had sighed and chattered since time immemorial, whether or not any human creature was listening.

Damnation, he said. Hell and damnation.

He thought he heard a branch snap, but he wasn't quite sure. That accursed water drowned out all other sounds. He grabbed the cart by its shafts and pushed it between the trees. It was no easy task, with rocks and high tufts blocking the way, but he managed. When he had maneuvered it into a clump of sallow and birch saplings, the wheels were concealed, but the load remained perfectly visible from the path. No one would notice it from a distance though.

He went around behind it and unlashed the ropes quickly to retrieve his rifle; it was a comfort to hold. After some rummaging between sacks and barrels, he got his liquor jug as well. He didn't load the rifle until he had taken a couple of deep swigs. It warmed his chest. The heavy throbbing of his heart let up a bit.

When he had sat for a while behind the cart with one hand around the butt of his rifle and the other on the jug, a black grouse hen flapped by. He hadn't heard her rise up. She came from the same direction he had just come from himself with his cart; he was certain something had frightened her.

Now he was warned, though he didn't hear anything. Quickly he broke off a sallow sapling and sharpened it with the knife from his belt. He drove it into the ground, stood it upright and set his cap on it, protruding above the load on the cart. Then he took his rifle and cautiously crept away between the tree trunks, staying very low.

He sat behind a large clump of osiers, in a spot where he could see the path. The Lapp appeared at the bend after some time, not walking along the track but slinking by the edge. Sometimes he was invisible behind the undergrowth. Clearly he knew how to walk stealthily. Not that he would have been audible anyway; all you could hear was that eternal water. The peddler disliked that sound for the rest of his life. He called it the worrying of the water.

The Lapp had been out of sight for some time, probably standing listening. Then he appeared by the bridge abutment, rifle loaded. He was visibly put out when the cart wasn't there and twirled around to withdraw hastily into the low bush. He was padding surreptitiously in the other direction. The peddler was able to catch regular glimpses of him. He saw when the Lapp had spotted the cart, saw him take aim.

There was silence. For at least a minute or more the peddler thought, but it probably wasn't that long. Time had slowed down. The river water, on the other hand, was rushing as fast as ever.

The Lapp shot. He must have hit the cap perfectly because he leapt out onto the path like a cat, heading for the cart as the peddler put the butt of his rifle to his shoulder. There was no reason to hesitate. He had him in perfect range and pulled the trigger without a second thought.

Afterward his heart was pounding again. He could hardly breathe, had to lean against a birch and shut his eyes. His face prickled, swollen and hot.

Then he heard a voice:

Guktie vöölti? Guktie vöölti?

That means did it hit? Did it hit? A little old woman came rushing down the path, waving her pipe eagerly until she caught sight of the bundle on the path. That was what the remains of the Lapp looked like. Then she became like a cat too, not going much closer, but a little. When she saw the blood in the grass, she turned and fled into the woods.

He never saw her again.

The peddler concealed his cart a little better and then dragged the dead body of the Lapp into the bushes. He sat down to think things through. On the one hand, it was clear enough, although there had been no witnesses.

There was the Lapp's rifle, which had been fired, and there was the hole in his own cap.

He had acted in self-defense. No one could dispute that.

On the other hand, it wasn't a very auspicious beginning to arrive in Blackwater with a corpse on his cart or to direct people to the place where that poor thin man lay with blood on the front of his longshirt. A messy situation.

He decided to arrive in Blackwater without that particular load. The bog beyond the bridge abutment was large and full of deep holes.

God only knows how he did it all alone. Did he have a shovel in the cart?

Yes, there were shovels in his stock. Without handles. Did he pull out his knife and axe and make himself a shovel handle? No one knows.

A person who arrives in our mountain region may believe he has reached a vast wilderness. He may imagine he is invisible. The forest looks as if it could swallow everything up. And sometimes the marshes are vast and pathless.

But a person coming here is always seen.

Two shots had been fired and had rung out between the forest-covered hills.

It is worth noting, however, that the peddler and his cart did not arrive in Blackwater until a full twenty-four hours after those shots.

All that happened very long ago, and we cannot know anything about it with certainty. Not even that it was Morten Halvorsen, though that was what people said. Halvorsen did come across the mountain with a cart and set up shop. He became a wealthy man during the timber rush, during the first major presence of the companies in the village. He was the one who shot the Lapp, people said. But he laughed at them. He'd sure as hell never been so dirt poor that he traveled without a horse.

Yet people say that only he and one other person knew what had become of that Lapp.

The other one was the great grandfather of the boys out at Lubben. Eriksson at Lubben's father, the one they called the Squirrel. Supposedly he saw something. Some people even claim he saw Halvorsen digging.

The Lapp had a wife, the one who had appeared on the path for a moment, crying:

Did it hit? Did it hit?

But she never spoke of it. Ever. It was just as likely her husband had gotten lost in the mountains. Except that Eriksson from Lubben eventually dropped a hint or two about what his father had said. Just to the boys. But when their grandfather was dead, the oldest grandson at least claimed that the old man had known where Halvorsen buried the Lapp. And that he had set up a marker there.

Others, though, couldn't see anything at the spot but a rack built for drying peat.

Who's to say.

When I had heard that horrid old story about the peddler who shot the Lapp, I was stupid enough to go home and tell it to Myrtle who, of course, told it to Hillevi.

She was furious and gave me a dressing down. She asked if I was fool enough to believe Morten Halvorsen had crossed the mountain with a hand-cart. Without a horse.

Didn't I realize that those kinds of stories had always been told? Ever since the seventeen hundreds when the first settlers came. People just changed the names. She asked, scornfully I thought, if I'd heard that story at Jonetta's kitchen table. I said no. It was outside in the yard. She said she was relieved that at least Jonetta hadn't had to sit there listening when people passed on crazy slanderous tales about her own father.

Hillevi told me not to hang around up there. I should consider myself too good to sit at Jonetta's kitchen table and listen to Anund Larsson and other notorious liars. She held my arm tight and asked me if they drank spirits up at Aagot's. I said I'd never been given anything but coffee.

That calmed her down a little, and she told me I had to understand that I had grown up among normal people. She admitted that one thing and another had happened in our villages, things people would be better off not discussing. But such things didn't happen among people who led normal lives.

As we've always done, she said.

I recognized that.

Things weren't all that hygienic there, she would often say. Or:

That's not normal.

And then you knew.

Of course I didn't dare ask any more about that peddler, whoever he was, who shot the Lapp. But the story hasn't died out. The last time I heard it was last winter. It was during the fight over which village would get to keep its school. Lots of things resurfaced then.

So there was a lopped-off dog's paw in the wood box at Hillevi Klarin's, and she was tormented by thoughts about it. Her first impulses to toss it in the stove or run with it to Trond passed quickly.

She did dispose of it covertly, taking Sissla for a walk on a windy October night and throwing the paw out into the dark water from down behind the boathouse. Small choppy waves were breaking on the stones along the shore. A tremor shot through the dog's body when she threw the paw, but Sissla didn't rush out into the water to fetch it. She just sat looking up at Hillevi. With a gaze like a child's.

Hillevi thought: This all has to be over and done with before the baby is born. Everything has to be open and bright. Children should not have to look at their parents like that. Thank God she's only a dog.

She never found out who put that package on her stairs, but she knew whoever did it was telling her something. She also knew she had to respond. A conversation had been initiated.

It's hard to talk to someone whose language you do not fully comprehend.

She thought about dogs. It was the paw of a black dog. But there had been some white on it too at the very top. A black dog with white spots.

One dog immediately came to mind. One with white patches above the eyes, like a second pair of staring eyes.

She knew the person who had put the package on the stairs wanted her to remember that particular dog. All the more reason not to mention it to Trond. Because in that case the paw meant:

Get out of here.

It tallied with the fact that by moving to Blackwater she had come closer.

One afternoon she saw Vilhelm Eriksson from Lubben in the store. He didn't raise his eyes. Then she knew what shape her reaction would take. There was no need for anything but what was about to happen anyway. When the bans were read for Trond and her, the answer would be clear.

One extremely cold January day in the war year of 1917 Sooty and another gelding called Siback were straining to pull a sledge laden heavily with people, packs, and horse feed. Trond Halvorsen was driving. He was on the way to the home of his maternal grandfather at Lakahögen for his own wedding. Next to him sat Hillevi's cousin Tobias Hegger. Behind them were Halvorsen's sister Aagot and Hegger's sister, whose name was Sara.

Dolly was pulling a smaller sledge behind the big one. It was the same one in which Halvorsen had transported Hillevi ten months earlier on the journey from Lomsjö to Röbäck. Now she was holding the reins. Next to her was his older sister Jonetta.

They were all wearing wolfskin or doghide coats, and they were bundled up in sheepskins and reindeer hides. The guests had been lent soft Lapp shoes and woolen socks. Trond Halvorsen had on his bushy fox fur hat. Hillevi had heard Tobias say to Sara that he looked like Genghis Khan. She was glad his mood had improved and he could now see something romantic about being there, though Halvorsen was far from a bandit. He was a hardworking general store owner and forest worker who had now taken over both the consignments and the running of the store from his father. His father had kept the store during the first year of the war of course, when his son had been mobilized and stationed at the coast. Hillevi had some idea of the profits Morten Halvorsen had made during that first panicky war year when he had persuaded people who owned reindeer herds or forest land to buy up his stocks of rice, sugar, flour, coffee, and soap. Now Trond was left with the rationed goods and the shortages and seeing people's faces gradually grow more wan.

Because Trond was sometimes away inspecting the consignments, she had learned to drive the horses. He would go off loaded down with reindeer skins, birchbark for roof shingling, tubs of tar, and Lapp handicrafts. With wood grouse, black grouse, red grouse, and dried fish. With cheese, butter, and whey cheese. He would return from Östersund with whatever he could get his hands on beyond what the ration books would cover. Once there was a new product, macaroni. Hillevi stood behind the counter explaining how to prepare it by boiling it into a porridge with milk and flour. But don't serve it with sugar, she would say. That advice was easy to follow as they seldom had any sugar. Nowadays, even at the shopkeeper's, they sweetened their barley coffee with peppermint candies.

She had anticipated having plenty of time to work on her trousseau. She imagined sitting up late with her embroidery, monogramming sheets and towels as winter evenings fell. But it didn't work out that way. There was a rush at the store, a swirl of orders that had to be filled. She was afraid Trond would lose money otherwise. The hired help doled out rounded scoops and put a bit extra on the scale after the pans balanced. Aagot had probably once been more protective of her brother's interests, but when Hillevi moved in above the shop, she stopped caring. They didn't get along. No saying why. That's just how it was. Hillevi was relieved to have Jonetta in the sledge with her. She was just as dark as Aagot but not as stiff backed. She no longer had any teeth.

Halvorsen didn't like Hillevi hiring others to drive her when he wasn't there, even though her midwifery journeys were paid for by public funds. Early on, Haakon Iversen took her a couple of places. He had come from Fagerli many years ago and worked for Morten Halvorsen. He still looked after the stable and did the heavy chores when Halvorsen was away.

There was a storm just after All Saints', and the snow drifted heavily up against the stockroom door. Haakon had to shovel so they could get at the goods, and just then Hillevi was called out, so rather than ask Isak Pålsa, who had his hands full with the snowplowing, she got Haakon to harness the horse and took the reins herself. Good old Dolly could almost find her own way up to the woman in labor who had sent for Hillevi.

That January day Dolly had a ring of sleigh bells arching over her harness, and they rang out in tune with the bells jingling on Sooty and Siback. The sun was shining. The lake at Blackwater was a blinding white surface of snow. As they were crossing it, Tobias turned around and waved to Hillevi. He appeared to be in fine fettle now, and she was deeply grateful to him for the couple of difficult days he had just put in.

She had asked him to lance a carbuncle she didn't dare touch on the neck of an old lumberjack. It was as big as a dumpling.

Tobias agreed to see him at the guesthouse where he and Sara were staying. When the pus had all been drained from the boil, and his brown callused neck stitched, Verna Pålsa shouted from downstairs:

Alfressa's here!

Hillevi explained that a man named Alfredsson was having trouble with a body part she couldn't very well examine. It was probably venereal disease; he had worked on one of the ships that ran goods between Namsos and Bergen.

There's leprosy in Bergen too, she added.

When Tobias was done with Alfressa, he told Hillevi the fellow just needed to wash down there. Hillevi wasn't prepared to accept that diagnosis. She was deeply concerned because Alfressa, a loose-living man with a tightly cinched belt, would be going around among the girls with that open sore of his. She called him back in and asked Tobias to examine him more thoroughly.

It's a serious matter for the village if he has that kind of disease, she said. Take a close look.

Tobias did. He took a swig of brandy from his silver hip flask and asked Alfredsson to unbutton his fly again. He admitted it looked suspicious; a very small lesion but deep. He wasn't sure he had managed to persuade the man to make his way to a hospital because they hadn't understood much of each other's language.

You can leave that to me, said Hillevi.

After less than a quarter of an hour the next patient appeared with an infected and swollen thumb. He had stitched up an axe injury himself with thick cobbling thread but had failed to clean the wound properly. After him came a girl with runny eyes, a rash around her mouth, and lumps on her neck. Hillevi wanted Tobias to say if it was scrofulous and whether she needed a sanatorium. A young lad, not yet confirmed, arrived with swollen glands that might also very well be scrofulous. Hillevi had also encouraged a couple of women to stop by who wanted drops prescribed, as they put it, without saying why. One was expecting her eighteenth; the other had ten. Hillevi took Tobias out into the hall and asked him to talk to them about the suet and birch roots they had put inside to prevent painful prolapse. She wanted them to go to the hospital in Östersund for surgery and thought he could lend some authority to the idea. They didn't know he hadn't completed his medical training and was scared stiff. Of course he couldn't examine their genitals, but Hillevi described how the younger woman's womb had popped out of her vagina like a blue plum after her latest delivery because she had started carrying buckets of water and armloads of hay too soon. She asked him to give them a stern warning against inserting objects into their vaginas that might result in infection.

During the course of the following day and the day after that, as people appeared and waited patiently in the guesthouse tap room, Hillevi asked him at least to talk to the people he couldn't do anything for. He was to speak against homeopathic remedies, against the old men they called wise and the "helpers" who brought death and contagion to childbeds. He had never seen her so fierce. Particularly on the subject of one homeopathist named Lundström. She called him worse than the very worst, said his hands and trouser pockets were stuffed with money.

Tobias cut what he could cut and stitched what could be stitched. Otherwise he talked. He didn't think they understood what he said. And Hillevi could tell he was frightened.

She sat in the sledge beside the quiet, docile Jonetta, feeling this was the first time in months she had time to sit still and think. Looking back, she knew she had been scared too. But she wasn't afraid any more.

One day when she had been driving to a crown croft called Bend, she saw a shapeless creature wrapped in furs come down from the woods. She went rigid with fear, imagining it was a bear, and only afterward did she realize Dolly hadn't reared up or even shied. Whatever had been crouching up there on the slope, grazed to a stubble by the goats, headed straight for her and the trap she was driving. She cracked the reins against Dolly's back and got her trotting. Looking back at the furry creature plodding down toward the road she saw it was two-footed. That didn't exactly make her feel more confident.

He sat in the kitchen all afternoon and evening while she delivered the woman. His name was Egon Framlund. When Hillevi was all done, she lanced a little furuncle under his nose she didn't think looked very good. In the summer he lived in a hut that was actually a cave in the side of the cliff. In the winters he boarded at the croft and did some logging in the woods near Bend. He told her he was born in Sundsvall and used to be a sailor. He was something of a philosopher too.

When she told Trond how frightened she'd been when she first saw the man, he had a good laugh and told her Framlund was a harmless old geezer obsessed with stargazing. She learned that it's no use being afraid without a good reason.

In the lead sleigh Tobias raised his cap and twirled it in the air. He pointed at the lake with one of his big mittened hands: reindeer! She had to smile. He was like a child in a fairytale forest full of breathtaking sights. There were flashes when the hooves turned up swirls of snow. The sunshine was almost blinding in the cold air, intoxicating. The world became sparks and gold and a huge blue sky with darkening patches in the distance. On the ice way off by Mount Brannberg, near the cliffs, was a tiny herd of reindeer. Small as insects.

She thought about Trond being responsible for all of them in this cold weather, having to be sure the sledges would make it. What if a runner broke or a horse went lame in this resounding white solitude? They had worked together, counting up pelts, hides, and furs so there would be enough to keep everyone warm. She remembered their first journey together. Only ten months back she'd been sitting just as Sara was now, unaware and with no responsibility for the trip.

Sara hadn't allowed herself to be frightened like Tobias. She had quickly withdrawn to Hillevi's room to help with the last minute work on her bridal attire, still so incomplete. When she went out, she looked very much the tourist, staring off at the high peaks in Norway and saying she hoped she could come back some summer.

Hillevi had tried to prevent their coming up for the wedding. Uncle Carl and Aunt Eugénie had declined, although if truth be told she had never really invited any of the family. But Sara and Tobias got it into their heads that it would be a great adventure they were keen to undertake.

So they had to see the gray house where Trond and his sisters lived. Hillevi would have preferred for them to come up after their new house was built. Tobias surely realized she was pregnant too. She was starting to show, and her face was rounder. Trond had wanted them to be wed just three weeks after they became engaged; it was Hillevi who had drawn things out. She hadn't been able to bring herself to talk to Edvard. There was no question of his marrying them, but he would have to read the bans; it couldn't be helped.

In the end he had come to see her and find out why she'd left Röbäck. She didn't invite him into her room. Now she was the one being fussy. He noticed. Things were tense between them. Still she hadn't expected it to be quite so difficult.

They walked and talked in open view with Sissla between them on a leash. Hillevi had met Edvard for the first time at a hospital christening. She had felt subservient, no better than when she was training as a student nurse and had to wash bedpans. In those days students were not permitted to speak in the presence of a doctor or a man of the cloth.

She was wearing the big black hat she had brought with her from Uppsala. She'd ordered a new ostrich feather from Östersund and stitched it around the crown. She saw faces at windows, but she didn't turn back. The damage was already done in any case.

They strolled all the way down to the stream and across the bridge, turning around at the border guard's and walking back the same way, in full view of the village throughout.

When he removed his mitten and she saw his fine hand, she felt a pang. Looking at the fair hair under his Persian fur hat and at his finely shaven cheeks, she couldn't help remembering his timid embraces and his sense of shame.

Her nostalgia passed when he uttered one little word:

Pardon?

It came sharply and emphatically in reaction to her saying *t'shop* when talking about the store. Suddenly enraged, she felt determined to clear everything up.

Have you applied for the position after Reverend Norfjell? she asked.

He shook his head.

That was the main thing I wanted to tell you, Hillevi, he said. That it cannot be. I do not fit in here. I've prayed for guidance. I feel this is not my calling.

She did not disagree.

What will you do, Hillevi? he asked. When she didn't answer right away, he said eagerly, almost fiercely:

I am of the opinion that you ought to leave these parts, Hillevi. You have no reason to stay on!

His face went beet red. Or at least pink. She could have laughed if it hadn't been so painful for her. Hillevi this and Hillevi that. No familiarities any more. Not so much as my dear. Not my dear my dear dear, the way it had been when they were together.

Well, I'll be stayin' on, she said.

Excuse me?

He sounded nonplussed. Not so sharp any longer.

Edvard, you chuuuuump, she said with a sort of laugh.

Heavens, Hillevi, you certainly have adapted to local ways. Even your language.

When are you leaving? she asked, trying to sound calm again.

At Christmas.

So he won't have to read the bans for Trond and me after all, she thought. If we wait that long, quite a few people will laugh behind our backs. But I owe him that much. He's a gentleman after all. Inside and out. I don't wish him any harm.

He went off toward the guesthouse in his black overcoat. She stood watching him. Then she walked down toward the store.

There was sun on the water. It shone summer blue although it was late autumn with the wind blowing thin little gusts of snow off the Norwegian mountains. The snow melted as soon as it hit the water.

Haakon was loading reindeer pelts into a cart. The flesh sides were bluish white and streaked with blood. She heard Trond call out from the stockroom that he should count them and write down the number before he left. Two pointers were nosing about the load, but little Sissla was sitting on the steps waiting.

160

Hillevi stood for a few minutes letting the sun warm her face. Then she moved in the direction of the house. She thought she would rummage about and see if she could find a tablespoon of real beans to roast. She craved coffee.

Grateful to own it, she laid the hat with its ostrich feather on the kitchen settle. Oh, how she wanted a cup of coffee. While the stove was heating up and she was waiting for the water to simmer, she stood looking out the window at the blue lake. She thought about Edvard, about being finished with him.

She was going to marry a man who said wuz and figger instead of were and count.

When the horses had pulled the sledges up from the lake where it ran out into the border stream, they turned eastward to Lakahögen. They traveled through woods that were rocky and impassable in the summer but that now lay dormant and smooth under the blanket of snow. It was uphill the whole way. Morten Halvorsen had promised that the road would be plowed from Korpkälen. But what did promises and anticipation mean in this silence that would have pounded in their ears if it hadn't been for the jingling sleigh bells? Hillevi thought their ringing sounded drier now, the bells crackling and rustling in the cold. She kept thinking about Tobias. Sara had curled up like a child in her hides and put herself in the hands of others. She trusted the world in a way that would never abandon her although the validity of the feeling didn't actually extend far beyond Upper Castle Road in Uppsala. But didn't Tobias feel dizzy sitting there in the steam rising from the horses and all the jingling? From knowing nothing of the forests that gobbled up sledges, nothing of the village dogs panting in mile after mile of darkness?

Hillevi hadn't been to Lakahögen before either. But there were more connections than the roads linking the villages to each other, and she was already very familiar with the huge stretches of pine-covered land, rivers, and forest ridges running all the way up to the mountain marshes. In a way she knew them very well, having heard the tales of things that had happened there, of the people who lived there and what fates had befallen them. She knew they had just passed Isaac's tumble where a farmer from Greningen had a load of timber overturn on him. Jonetta pointed it out to her, and she also indicated the hawksnest pine on the ridge. Louse river, Klöst, Flärken, they were all markers in the whiteness. The streams ran from the north here, and she didn't know their names. But they surely had names, just as surely as people had given names to every little body of water and every single rise in the water-logged landscape, named them after bears they had seen and accidents that had happened with rifles, axes, or sledges heavy with loads of timber. Far below them was Lake Rössjön with its church, and beyond it Lake Boteln where Märta Karlsa's grandfather had gone through the thin spring ice with a wagonload. He hadn't been able to save the horse. There was the chapel out at the point where people said it had been foretold a church would stand and one day burn down. No one knew whether Ante's point had been named after the Lapp who had made the prediction or a man who had dug up a spruce root and discovered a vein of silver now exhausted but never forgotten.

Halvorsen stopped at a bend in the road as she had requested. That was so she, Sara, and Jonetta would be able to move out of sight and crouch down in the snow. They were stiff but otherwise merry; Sara's cheeks were aglow.

When Hillevi was peeing in the snow, squatting with her skirts hiked up, she felt the child inside her moving for the first time. Not a rolling motion or a kick. No, it was very gentle and at the same time perfectly distinct. A flutter of wings, she thought. A tiny bird. Like the movement of finches under the gables of the house on cold winter nights.

She pulled up her underpants and woolen leggings and returned to the sledge, drawing the hides tight around her. Sara was standing alongside, chattering away. Hillevi didn't answer her. It was clear she wanted to be on her own, so Sara walked over to the other sledge.

Hillevi felt at peace. Trond was over there, checking runners and harnesses. The horses were chomping in their feedbags. Everyone but Trond was chatting. He was looking at her.

She felt as if she were a wide bell covering the little being who was moving inside her. That was what it will be like, she thought. I didn't know. But now I do.

You and me.

And Trond over there keeping an eye on us. Checking that all is well. That he needn't worry about us.

He is thin and black haired and lively. And he is a hardworking man. He will never raise a hand to us. I know that. Before, I wouldn't ever have had such a thought. But I have them now. I've seen a great deal. I understand that things like that happened in Uppsala as well. But I didn't see them then.

He's looking at us now.

You and me.

There was a crown croft at Whitewater, built so the Lapps would have somewhere to take refuge when the weather got bad while they were moving or if they had to leave someone old or sick behind. The wedding party stopped there for a meal and to give the horses a break.

The couple who lived there were called Persson. He was a Lapp, and she was originally from Greningen. They were quite old. Their youngest was the only child still living at home; he would be confirmed in a year's time. They supposed they'd be all alone after that. The lad was sitting on a chair with the cat in his lap, looking down the whole time. A long fringe of hair hung over his face. Hillevi thought he might not be in as big a hurry to get away as they imagined.

There was only one room to the cabin. The hearth was built into the corner. Next to it was a chopping block and on the wall were fishnets, fox traps, snares, and birchbark packs.

They had barley meal gruel the woman made in an iron kettle on a tripod. She stirred it with a porridge ladle. Sara gaped at Hillevi when it became clear they were all meant to eat out of two wooden bowls and off a single flowered plate that were all passed around. The goats weren't milking, but there was aged cheese, marinated fish, and pork lard to put between rounds of bread the woman removed from a box. All Trond contributed was a bag of ground barley coffee, blended with some real roasted coffee beans.

Hillevi wondered what Tobias and Sara thought. She now knew Trond disliked people who were unable to accept hospitality and who insisted on eating the food they brought with them and otherwise flaunting their wealth. Not to mention people who showed their superiority by insisting on paying.

She also knew that Trond had unfinished business with old man Persa, who had sold Trond pelts on commission. There would surely be a tidy sum for Persa in the end. But the most important thing was that they left Whitewater without offending. Hillevi knew she had behaved improperly on other occasions. She still needed a buffer between herself and these people she really knew so little about.

The last ten kilometers they traveled in the dark, but the blackness of the sky was dotted with lights. Icicles in the heavens; cold fires that seemed to be breathing. Pieces of ice broke loose, as if from a sugar loaf, and fell into nothingness. You could see the Great Bear and Orion's Belt, although their contours were blurred by a thick swirl of less bright stars sprinkled across the firmament.

She thought about the gray creatures down on the lakes, the Big One who was hibernating and the eager Neckbiter lumbering about in the snow between the trees on his big flat paws. For Dolly's sake she worried about a green gleam of eyes that caught the erratic light of the lanterns. The little mare might take fright at a shadow that seemed to be crouching or the fluttering of light on a dead pine tree with a top that resembled claws and arms that seized. Dolly needed to feel through the reins that Hillevi was being vigilant, encouraging her to keep pace with the bigger horses.

When they got as far as the first houses in Lakahögen, she let herself feel how exhausted and stiff she was from the long drive.

The house was high up with a distant view of the white expanse of lake down below. There were lights in the windows. They had electric lighting from a little hydraulic generator that rattled in a waterfall. She had forewarned Tobias that, as she understood it, it was not a traditional homestead. It was said to be garishly decorated and have glassed-in verandas. But with the light gleaming behind colored glass, she thought it handsome. Her heart throbbed nervously at the thought of meeting the Laka King in person.

Trond's father had been to Blackwater to inspect his future daughter-in-law. He was a short stout man. It was he who now came out to welcome them, accompanied by the people who were going to stable the horses. They disentangled themselves from the various furs they'd been bundled up in and went into the study; the walls were covered with stuffed wood grouse and black grouse with fanned-out tails, and the floor was thick with animal hides. Reindeer and wolves lay side by side in the peace of death. Sara settled into the rocker, her feet on a little round beaver skin, very old and worn.

The little generator out in the cold winter stream produced a somewhat erratic light in the matte glass lamps. The ceiling fixture had a copper rim with a pattern of hammered leaves; the sofa was an oak frame with brown artificial leather upholstery. There was a tapestry above it in fluffy brown, green, and golden velvet portraying beer-drinking men in shorts and Tyrolean hats and a shelf with a whole row of pewter beer mugs.

Hillevi wasn't actually seeing these things herself; she was taking it all in through Sara and Tobias's eyes. She couldn't decide whether or not she ought to be embarrassed. It wasn't what Aunt Eugénie would have called elegant. But it was impressive: the big throw pillows with covers embroidered in stemstitch, the silver-plated serving pieces in the sideboard cupboard, the crystal vases, the gilded frame around the large photograph of Trond's late mother.

The old man known as the Laka King didn't come down that evening. He was resting up for the wedding, Morten Halvorsen said. But he had sent a gift for the bride.

Hillevi had to step forward and let Trond's father slip a ring on her finger. It was thick worked gold, set with a red gem. She was embarrassed at the thought that Tobias and Sara might be thinking her new family took the fact that she was obviously with child surprisingly lightly.

When they had eaten, she nearly fell asleep on the sofa. Her arms ached from holding them straight out almost all day; she had been afraid to relax the reins. She and Sara were to spend the night in a room upstairs. But her future father-in-law was still conversing with Tobias, and it was clear that he expected Jonetta, Aagot, Sara, and Hillevi to sit quietly on the sofa. He talked about railroad administration and the speed of steamboats, about the banking system in the province of Norrland, and about trade between Sweden and Norway. She couldn't imagine a way to break it off. There was a force in this dark brown room with its glittering silver that reminded her of the croft out at Tangen and the squat silhouette of Old Man Lubben against the gray dawn in the window, the last thing she wanted to think about right now.

Trond was seeing to the horses. When he came back in, he took her out onto the front steps with him. The air was sparkling and shimmering. There was a veil draped across the heavens that pulsed and rippled, then changed. For a long time white strands ran right down into the tops of the spruce trees. Then with a gentle puff they dissolved. They seemed to wander off, and were followed by translucent ripples. You could see the stars through them. The waves grew intensely green, then faded.

She was deeply moved by the sight, her first view of the Northern Lights.

It's a sign, said Trond.

She knew he meant for the two of them. But not signifying happiness. He meant that what they were about to do was solemn and significant.

In his day-to-day life he was a squirrel-quick man who scurried around the store between the syrup barrel and the box containing decks of playing cards. He even had that annoying pencil behind his ear she had hoped Tobias and Sara wouldn't notice. But he saw meanings that were far beyond their own lives. He had been raised listening to his father ranting about the future and his grandfather telling stories about the old days. He could see both coasts, the mountain you had to cross to get down to the western one and the river valleys and farming villages you had to cross to get down to the eastern one. She knew he was not especially religious. In church he would fall asleep or sit daydreaming about rationing. But he thought in biblical terms. Many people probably did. They considered their forefathers patriarchs.

One of them had come and dwelt in the plain of Mamre and set up a stone under a terebinth tree. Another had wandered to this place and carved his mark into the tallest pine.

They built roads nowadays and told stories about how someone who went before them had walked miles and miles across the mountain marshes to get to a station where he could catch the train for Östersund to do his compulsory courthouse duty. They were proud of things she had never heard of before coming north.

Now Trond was working hard, hoping to be able to invest in the construction of a hydropower plant without having to borrow from his father. And he said:

As soon as the road between Röbäck and Blackwater is done, I'll buy me a car.

He had shown Tobias the enormous parcels of forest land belonging to his father and grandfather. For endless miles the forest ran on, black and full of promise. He said there would be a lot of work for people. New roads would be built, and the villages would grow, develop into towns and municipalities.

Their getting married, like everything they did, was of great significance. The sky was aflame with it. He would soon be elected to the municipal council, she was certain.

Now she would finally have had something to write in the book with the red velvet cover her uncle and aunt had given her. She was marrying into a world of meanings.

But what she was experiencing didn't belong in that book.

Elated and at the same time deeply serious, she watched the curtains of light vanish over the trees. It's divided into parcels, she thought. The forest is parcels, and these parcels belong to my husband's grandfather. When Hillevi first came to Röbäck, it would not have occurred to her that specific individuals owned the forest. Now she thought about the roads that would be built through them.

They would write but not in any book. Their stories would come into being in the woods themselves. They would write them with the roads they built.

Once upon a time an old Lapp fell asleep on the shore of Lake Boteln. This was long before there was a chapel there. When he woke up, his eyes were gritty, and he seemed not to see what was around him. Which wasn't in fact much: moss and scrawny little evergreens. After a while he perked up, had something hot to drink, and then he sang.

Nananaa
Daesnie gerhkoe edtjh tjåadtjodh . . .
this is where the church will stand
here at this very place
where my body is
the candles burn na na . . .
when the candles go out
when the wicks smoke black
when it's cold
there will be blood in the church
blood and hair

maelie jih goelkh
aj ja ja ja blood and hair
and last of all the church will burn
yes, it'll burn in the end, the church
na na na nana
dihte buala . . .
burn
burn it will

No one ever told the Laka King what the Lapp sang. Perhaps someone should have.

Trond Halvorsen's father's good fortune was that he made the closely guarded daughter of the Laka King pregnant. She was dark complexioned, a head taller than her husband, and nearly ten years older. In the photograph that still hangs over the sideboard in the dining room, she is wearing the traditional silk shawl on her head, draped in a fashion that makes it look from the front like a turban. The sideboard is topped with a mirror framed in carved pine boughs and cones. Hillevi told me it came from the farm of Trond Halvorsen's grandfather in Lakahögen, which came to be known as Moneymount.

The previous owners had called it Sunnymount, but people soon made a joke of it when the Laka King moved in. He didn't care what people called it. He knew that in the long run money and parcels of forest land made for power and legitimacy.

I remember Morten Halvorsen. He wore riding breeches and green knee socks. He would produce a bag of candy from his trousers pocket, sticky from the warmth of his body. He fed children like squirrels. I was a bit scared of him when I was little. At first I was scared of everybody with pointy noses.

People often said of him that he was nothing on his own. But I don't think that was true because he must have been more aggressive in timber dealings than his father-in-law. Above all he was more mobile. He was the one who put the Laka King in touch with the Wifsta and Mon sawmills and others down at the coast.

The King preferred to sit still and wait for people to come to him. When he did travel, he only made unprofitable journeys up to the Lapp settlements.

Of course having herds of reindeer numbering in the hundreds and perhaps eventually in the thousands was a good thing, and it was important to be there when it was branding time. But his son-in-law no longer believed in the future of such easily stolen and disease-prone capital.

The woods are the way, he said. That's t'future, it is.

He mixed his languages as opposed to all the others, who were very careful to keep them apart. That made him ambiguous. I can recall Aagot frowning bitterly whenever she spoke of her father.

The Laka King had very old-fashioned ideas. The villages should be independent of the cities at the coast and of the towns down by the big lake, Storsjön. They should be self-sufficient. He never spoke any other language than the traditional local dialect. He talked about medieval King Sverre and eighteenth-century County Governor Örnsköld as if they had been contemporaries of his beloved King Oscar.

Most of his fur dealing had been with the Lapps on the Norwegian side. He bought his goods in Namsos, where they came in by ship from Trondheim and Bergen. He also ordered silver for the Lapps to work from goldsmiths in the coastal towns. He thought the dissolution of the union gravely injurious to Sweden and predicted his country would never again rise to its former glory. He believed the villainous clergy had tricked honest King Oscar into disaster.

Those things happened when he was getting older and slowing down. He also began to question the wisdom of his own rash youthful decision to convert the chapel into a tannery. Not that he hadn't bought it in a bona fide way from the state church. The authorities didn't want to go on maintaining that old chapel on the shore of Lake Boteln now that Röbäck had a village church of its own.

But many of the Lapp families' forefathers were buried by the chapel. The crosses and headstones were sinking into the moss there now, and the Lapps considered the foul-smelling tannery an insult to their dead. Still that hadn't prevented the younger ones from delivering loads of reindeer antlers to be ground into chips for the gluepots used in the former chapel. The old ones warned: cash and utility aren't the only things that matter. It was important to hold the dead in respect too.

Their dead were restless. Even the young people began to catch sight of them and to feel their clammy groping hands when they approached the tannery. The dead also puffed cold air and grasped at the legs of the lead deer in the herds, causing them to bolt. The Laka King decided to placate the dead and his conscience by turning the tannery back into a house of God. Vicious tongues said its day was past anyway, that even the old man's own son-in-law took his pelts to Östersund nowadays and got a better price for them there.

The King had all the smelly wooden paneling torn down and returned the building to its former glory with the help of the Lapps who remembered how it had looked. The walls had been white with streaks of blue. And so they were again. The pews and the altar were crafted by hand, and when it was all complete, he purchased an organ. The plaque in the vestibule read:

> *Efraim Efraimsson*
> *of Lakahögen*
> *restored and redonated*
> *this chapel*
> *Anno 1909*
> *Parish of Röbäck*
> *Constructed Anno 1783*
> *Matthew 23:19*

And so the state church, having failed to rid itself of the chapel after all, was forced to express its gratitude with an inauguration ceremony after the question had been debated in various committees all the way up to cathedral chapter level. Matthew 23:19 reads: *Ye fools and blind: for whether is greater, the gift, or the altar that sanctifieth the gift?*

It was hardly the restlessness of the dead that eventually made it impossible to decline the gift.

They say that when the Laka King heard that his daughter's son was going to marry a girl from Uppsala, he declared:

Girls from down that way are really grand, I'm told. But they don't make much in the way of wives.

Hillevi wished he would come downstairs so they could take each other's measure, eye to eye. She had no intention of lowering her gaze.

But he didn't come. All day sleighs full of wedding guests drove up. Doctor Nordin from Byvången, the man who didn't willingly get into a sledge even when a woman was bleeding to death in childbirth, came all the way.

So yes, she went around feeling annoyed. People poured in. This wedding was too big. In the fifth month things should be done more discreetly. But Trond and she hadn't been consulted. She did say she'd never wear Trond's mother's spectacle of a bridal crown, a wire frame strung full of paper flowers, beads, and silver clappers that needed polishing. But when the King found out, as he put it, that she'd jumped the gun, he had the crown packed back into its wrapping paper again. So she never actually found out whether he would have accepted her refusal.

She was going to wear a black silk dress. She would have preferred to wear white. White was in fashion, but no one seemed to care. Trond expected her to wear the dress starting the day before the wedding when they welcomed their guests. The next day a special woman who prepared brides would come to finish dressing her, putting on the train and the wax flowers.

As early as October she had gone out behind the boathouse and tossed her myrtle plant into the lake. She'd intended the myrtle for her bridal crown, but it had always been a pretty meager specimen. It never thrived, seeming to sense before Hillevi did that nothing would come of the match with Edvard Nolin.

The district police superintendent came and the farmers and sawmill owners from the towns. Now the Laka King's Lapp friends began to arrive. The most important ones were the Matke and Klemet clans. Their reindeer skin longshirts were buckled at the chest with decorative silver pins, and Klemet had rings on several of his fingers with little silver loops hanging from them that jangled when he moved his hands. Each of these men owned thousands of reindeer, and their wives had on heavy silver collars and high hats with colorful trim.

Their arrival seemed to signal to the King that it was time to come down. He was preceded by his son-in-law Morten Halvorsen and by a girl in black with a white apron who held the door for him.

Hillevi had seen him in a newspaper photograph Trond had saved. In it he was standing in a field in a wolfskin coat. The headline read RENOWNED VISITOR AT SAINT GREGORY FAIR. From the picture she imagined he would be enormous and dressed in local finery, but in through the door came a thin little gentleman in a frock coat.

He began by greeting the heads of the Klemet and Matke clans. They shouted strange words, pounded one another on the back, and shook hands for a long time and with much clanking of silver. It sounded like Bourregh! Bourregh! Then he cocked his head with its thin white crop of hair and gazed out over the company assembled in the dining room.

So where's t'bride? he asked.

People murmured. All eyes were on Hillevi, who had to step forward. To her annoyance she felt a blush rise to her cheeks. It was so unexpected and so idiotic it brought tears of shame to her eyes, and she had to look down. He took her extended hand in his little white mitt, and she curtseyed. Then he asked to see the other hand.

Got to see how that ring fits, he said. This was her opening to say it fit perfectly and was very beautiful and to thank him. But she had completely lost her good breeding and let him twist and turn her hand to display the ring to everyone. More murmuring. He patted her on the cheek and moved along to the Klemet and Matke women.

The younger ones giggled and blushed when he joked with them, asking if they had already fallen for the newfangled nonsense of stockings and garters. He raised their skirts and praised them when they proved to be wearing thin reindeer skin leggings. Sara stood next to them looking horrified.

They were married the next day by a young minister from Byvången who was visibly nervous. A small chest of drawers had been carried into the dining room to serve as the altar. Afterward the girls were quick to fold the lacy cloth back up and carry the chest out so there would be room for everyone to sit down to dinner. The dinner tables extended all the way out into the hall.

There was no woman of the house. The Laka King was the host, but it was his son-in-law who signaled to the fiddlers to play the toasting melody. People took their seats slowly and solemnly.

They were served reindeer tongue and aged goat cheese to go with the first schnapps. Then came a purée of Jerusalem artichokes with croutons served with sherry. After that, what they called the first platter. Huge cold poached char with consommé cubes was served at each table with tartar sauce and boiled almond potatoes. The Rhine wine was golden.

After this there was roast venison with glazed onions and gravy flavored with dried morels soaked in Madeira, cranberry jelly, and pickled rosehips. There were mashed potatoes made from another kind of potatoes more suitable for mashing. A kitchen mamsell kept an eye on the serving girls and answered Hillevi's questions about the various dishes. With the roast they drank a red wine that tasted deep and earthy.

Unexpectedly the venison roast was followed by bread and butter. Hillevi realized this must be an excuse for a second schnapps. Then came the fowl. Wood grouse was served at the top table and black grouse further down. There was more of the heavy red wine. The sauces were thick with grated liver from the fowl. She thought they should have strained it through cheesecloth.

More schnapps was served with the cheese that came next: pot cheeses and blue-green mould cheese, big chunks of aged Västerbotten, and soft reindeer cheese.

The dessert was a charlotte russe with a fluffy filling not of raspberries but cloudberries. There were almond cookies too and coffee and pastries. Last of all came the wedding cake, and Trond was asked to cut the first piece. Before he attacked the layers of cream, he lifted off the pink marzipan rose, handing it to Hillevi on a cake plate. He was rewarded with both applause and fiddle music.

There were speeches in the hot room. Afterward Hillevi recalled just as little of them as she recalled of the marriage ceremony itself. But she memorized the dinner. The next day she wrote down everything they'd been served in her black oilcloth notebook.

Two fiddlers led Trond and Hillevi into the study when it was time to begin the gift giving. It was extremely hot, and she was glad she no longer felt nauseous all the time. The room was full of black-clad guests holding the gifts they would soon present, stepping forward one by one. Tobias was called first. He was meant to represent the late parents of the bride as Morten Halvorsen said and perhaps believed. Tobias and Sara came forward carrying the serving pieces of the set of china from Hillevi's aunt and uncle. It was white with pink flowers and wavy gold edges. The rest of the set was in a crate at the foot of the gift table. Tobias carried the soup terrine, Sara the big platter. She burst into tears in the hot room, burying her face in Hillevi's white lace bosom.

I wish I could do what you're doing, she sniffled.

You'd never dare, Hillevi whispered into her hot ear.

Next Morten Halvorsen stepped forward promising them a new kitchen stove for the house they were building. He set a brand-new stove ring hook on the table to symbolize it. There was a round of applause, and the fiddlers played a tune. Hillevi wondered why they hadn't played anything after the china. Trond's father was followed by the Laka King himself. He had a piece of paper in his hand and cocked his head silently. Trond had to read it himself and tell everyone it was a certificate presenting them with Blackwater parcel 3:22. At this the fiddle music grew louder and even more boisterous, and people applauded. Everyone seemed to know what parcel it was. Trond whispered to Hillevi that it extended from the lake at Bend all the way up to the mountain woods.

Matke and Klemet each gave them two reindeer does to be the lead deer of their herds. The Lapp girls gave them hand-woven ribbons and their mothers little silver spoons with looped handles.

The minister kept a list. Trond had armed him with folio-sized sheets of lined paper folded back to make columns. He noted every gift and the name of the giver. Copper kettles and flowered china chamber basins were carried forward by people of whom Hillevi had never even heard. She understood, though, that it was just as much about business and connections as about family and good neighborly relations.

When all the gifts had been given, the minister brought over his lists, telling Hillevi there was one package he hadn't been able to write down because it was unopened.

She hadn't noticed it until he pointed it out. It was on the table and was about a foot long, wrapped in brown paper.

Just leave it, she said.

Her voice went so sharp she had to gloss it over. She took his lists and thanked him.

I'll open that package later, she said. You needn't worry about it, Reverend.

He showed her his draft announcement for the newspaper:

At Lakahögen on January 15 shopkeeper Trond Halvorsen was joined in holy matrimony at the home of his maternal grandfather, homesteader and lumber dealer Efraim Efraimsson, to midwife Miss Hillevi Klarin, daughter of the late sea captain Claes Klarin. The couple were married by Reverend J. Vallgren, and the wedding was followed by an excellent and copious dinner for more than eighty invited guests. The couple received a large number of presents, outstanding among which were an alabaster chandelier and a set of fine china.

There were a few errors in the text. Her father's name hadn't been Klarin, but that was nobody's business. She did, however, see to it that Trond's father was mentioned by name and that the excellent and copious were struck out. There was no point in provoking people in these days of scarcities. She had no idea why the china and the lamp were mentioned while the largest present, the parcel of forest land, was left out. Perhaps Trond's grandfather wanted it that way. She let it pass but told the young minister he could certainly put that the Reverend J. Vallgren also made a rousing speech to the bride and groom. He blushed. She took herself by surprise: here she stood appraising his writing and telling him what to strike out. She thought of Edvard. It would have been inconceivable. But something had changed. She couldn't actually remember anything about the wedding ceremony except the heat in the room and the creaking of leather when the guests shifted their feet in their tight boots. But it had done the trick.

She stood with her back to the gifts table chatting with the guests and receiving their congratulations. Behind her was that package, between a case of silver-plated spoons and a linen tablecloth rolled around a tube. When she found herself alone for a moment, she turned and snatched it up. She hoped no one would try to shake her hand while she held it behind her back. Her father-in-law clapped as a signal for the dancing to begin, and she took a couple of steps backward, dropping the package into the open fire so fast she was sure no one noticed. Trond put his arm around her waist and guided her back into the dining room for the bridal waltz.

Trond could hardly walk straight when they mounted the stairs to their bridal chamber, his grandparent's old bedroom, late that night. He was extremely happy and soused, though he didn't seem to feel sick, so she didn't worry about him throwing up. It would have been a shame to spoil the linen sheets with the wide lace edging.

There were the usual birchbark whisks and all kinds of other silly things under the covers. Down by the foot of the bed they found a corkscrew, the construction of which fascinated Trond. He fell asleep holding it. Outside the windows there were gunshots and loud men's voices.

She hadn't expected to be able to sleep at all, but in fact once the fire in the tile stove had died down enough for her to shut the damper, she was out like a light. It was still dark when she woke up, but her body could tell it was morning. Not wanting to take the risk of waking Trond by lighting a candle, she groped for her shawl and slippers. Cautiously she made her way down the stairs and across to the study. But she was too late. One of the kitchen girls was already up and was clearing the hearth.

Look what I found in the ashes, she said.

It was a sugar tong.

Hillevi said that if it was real silver, it would probably not be damaged very badly. They had a sensible little chat about how to best polish it up. But her heart was pounding.

She thought about the person who had put that package on her staircase. She had expected there to be more. One thing after another. But it wasn't necessary. He had already left his mark on her.

For four and sixteen and seven and two thirds
dumelee dumdum dum
for top and for length and for root so I've heard
dongeli dingdong dong

The log scaler comes in and measures and shouts
dumelee dumdum dum
and his clerk notes it down though I have my doubts
dongeli dingdong dong

He charges me extra for a high stump
dumelee dumdum dum
the scaler and cruiser should sure get the bump
dongeli dingdong dong

They've got all the tools and the power in their hands
dumelee dumdum dum
and fair is a word they just don't understand
dongeli dingdong dong

For two and fourteen and three and a third
dumelee dumdum dum
my profits are shrinking with every word
dongeli dingdong dong

I owe all my drivers for lodging and food
dumelee dumdum dum
though those men seem to think we're a slovenly brood
dongeli dingdong dong

To them a lumberjack's not worth a bean
dumelee dumdum dum
and the pay they cough up for our wood, it's so mean
dongeli dingdong dong

The days dark and chilly, our boots spring a leak
dumelee dumdum dum
The shopkeeper's greedy, our children grow weak.
dongeli dingdong dong

I heard someone sing that song the first weekend in August 1981 at the old timers' festival. People who had moved away from Blackwater came back and brought their children to visit. My uncle had been dead for many years. But they still sang his songs on stage.

Every single member of the local history society was dressed up as either a milkmaid or a lumberjack in a wide-brimmed hat. The men fried big pans of coalman's dumplings over an open fire with quite a lot of fuss. The women, who had prepared the meat filling and diced the pork, served them on paper plates for twenty crowns each.

And down there in the throng of locals and tourists stood an old man named Efraim Fransa giving us his version of our history.

Old Anund Larsson he never chopped down a tree, what I know, he shouted. And he didn't have himself a woman or any kids either. He was nothin' but a golldarned blabbermouth.

It's all about who manages to live the longest.

Now they're all dead, the old men who kept track of what was right and what was wrong in my uncle's songs. But people sing them all the same.

I allow they were right that he was never part of a logging team. But he had been to sea and worked the mines. It was neither shame nor poverty that drove him away from home. It was grief.

In July 1931, though, he had already been back for six or seven years and was a grown man. His grief was probably no less bitter, but he had grown hardened to the shame. And he made up songs. He stood on the stage at the dance pavilion out by the rifle range singing the one about the timber cruiser and the log scaler. Things were the same back then, except with more drinking and more voices.

What the hell do you know about logging? You've never chopped down a tree!

The air was thick with mosquitoes and ill will. Strangely enough people tend to love the songs but revile the person who made them up.

My uncle got mad of course; his anger came to a boil when he'd had some liquor off in the grove (the gathering being organized by the Good Templars, you had to sneak off to drink from your flask), and he swung himself back up onto the stage even though the music had already started, hushed the accordion and fiddle and shouted:

I'll give yez a song, I will! Now you're goin' to hear how the lumberjack got the young lads drunk and pulled the britches off 'em. You're all such great lumberjacks you are, and you want to hear about how strong you were and what huge trees you felled. And the clerk wants to hear about how fast he could scribble and the cruiser about how fair he was, and the shopkeeper wants to hear how he gave people work and how generous he was with his credit. And the wives want to hear how fine everything was in the old days and how hardworking everyone was before there were bicycles. But I'll give you sommat else now, I will. I'll give you the nasty stuff, he roared. I'll give you wolf bile. Wolf bile and fox farts and wolverine spew!

And he started singing to the same melody, and the only words I could make out were about a man out at Tangen who tortured his horses. Hillevi took me and Myrtle roughly by the hand and marched us off so fast the ground shook. Behind us we heard laughter and shouting, and I don't know what they were doing to Laula Anut.

My grandfather Mickel Larsson lost all his reindeer and with them his authority. In just a few years of harsh winters, when a layer of ice covered the reindeer lichen and the wolves decimated the herd like flashfire, he became a penniless man.

By the time Anund was old enough to work in the reindeer branding pens, his brand wasn't worth a thing, nor was my mother's. Their father no longer had any does that calved. Laula Anut had to take work as a deer hand for other, wealthier Lapps.

My grandfather was dead, and I was nearly grown up the first time I entered his *gåetie* up at the old spring and autumn grazing land at the foot of Mount Giela.

No one had told me I was born there. When I was little, I had no idea I even had an uncle. But he came back, and I met him on the bridge. After I discovered I could see him at Aunt Jonetta's, as Myrtle and I called her, I learned about where my grandfather had lived and where I was born.

Hillevi didn't approve of any of it. For that reason it took a long time for me to dare go up to the *gåetie*, or perhaps I should be calling it the hut. I guess it was a combination of the two. You crept in through a little entryway. There was a proper door with a timbered frame. By then it was just hanging on a single rusty hinge, but the pane of glass at the top was intact. The main area also had windows. It was a long narrow space that extended all the way back to the traditional tent-shaped structure made of peat. It had a plank floor and a little iron stove in the middle. A metal funnel ran up to the smoke hole at the top of the cone.

I had stood outside this *gåetie* many times. But in those days people frightened children with stories about ghosts; we were told the dead haunted abandoned huts. Grandfather's looked quite ordinary though. Outside the door was a barked sallow branch on which the old man had hooked his pails and buckets to dry. Hoping it wouldn't be too spooky in there, I hunched down and crept in. But just inside the door there was a dead fox on the floor, nothing but the bare bones left; his white teeth leered at me. I got no further that day.

When I finally dared to go all the way in, I was the same age my mother had been when she gave birth to me in there.

I saw the stove, red with rust. There was a margarine crate with a piece of oilcloth nailed to the top. A couple of other crates had been hung up as shelves. His pots and pans were still there, black-bottomed and dented. On the floor there were enamel mugs with big pitted spots exposing black metal. Mice and ermine had left droppings all over, and maybe they had knocked down the mugs and coffee cups too.

There were no tools or gear. I assumed my uncle had taken them in hand. I thought they hadn't had a table to eat on until I figured out that the wooden barrel lid leaning up against the wall had stood on the sawhorse by the fireplace and served as a table. There was no bed. When I was born, they had undoubtedly slept on reindeer skins laid on a soft pile of birch branches. But how could people sleep on a plank floor?

I knew nothing. I thought about the nursery where Myrtle and I had white beds. That made me scared of the whole thing. It was actually more pathetic than frightening, but I got scared and left.

My uncle said that when grandfather settled year round at the grazing land at the foot of Mount Giela, he only had a dozen or so reindeer left and could see no point in moving them to the calving land. The next winter was a cold snowy one, and the wolverines were greedy. But he didn't slaughter the last doe until the third year.

That was the end of it.

After that Mickel Larsson hunted and fished, and his daughter Ingir Kari had a little flock of goats to milk. So it goes.

D'you see the stags
their forest of antlers
huge crowns
many branches
swaying swaying
nanana na na na . . .
the does run at Giela
run on the mountainside
you see you see
how they glisten
glisten like silver
nananaaa
running running
at dusk they're running
nananana na na

No one had heard Mickel Larsson *yoik* except Laula Anut and then only when the old man didn't know he was listening. He sang to solace his heart. Beyond that he never showed any regrets about what he'd lost.

Anund was just a boy when he heard him, and he was afraid other people in the mountains might catch wind of the old man singing about reindeer that didn't exist.

That was how little I knew, he said afterward.

But in spite of feeling ashamed, he took after him. He couldn't help himself.

Sometimes I think my pa's *yoik* is still up there, Uncle Anund said. It's in the wind. When I lie in the moss hearing nothing but the silence and the wind, it sings. Nananana na na nanana na . . . There are his does running up to the calving land, running home, day and night into the wind, to get to a safe place. With an eagle circling overhead.

> *The calves dance*
> *snorting*
> *nanana na na*
> *but the eagle flies high*
> *waiting*
> *ajaj jaaaja*
> *his shadow follows the calf*

That frightened me because I had been abducted by an eagle myself. I thought of rough claws and of the ledge of a cliff spotted with droppings.

One December afternoon a few years before I was born, a couple of farm lads were out hunting hare. The dog was scouting a big area, and it was a long time before the lads shot anything. When they were ready to head home, they decided to take a shortcut past the tarn known as Lomtjärn.

After Bjekkertjärn they knew there was a steep section on the way down to Lomtjärn that would be difficult to negotiate. Those little round tarns are scattered along the rises to the east like steps on a tall staircase. Darkness was falling fast, so they decided to give it a try. It turned out to be much steeper than they had reckoned with, and they had to take off their skis and toss them down first, then clamber after bit by bit thigh deep in snow. Such bold feats would only be undertaken by extremely strong young men.

Well they made it down to the tarn and found themselves at the spot where the rock face is like a vertical wall and covered with thick icicles in the winter from flowing water that froze. Nowadays, with people going everywhere by snowmobile, it's become a tourist attraction. People spit out wads of snuff and leave beer cans, orange peels, and plastic hot dog packages there. But in those days it was a wonder of its kind.

The pillars of ice were gnarled and thick, hanging down toward the edge of the tarn, and when you came close, they were green and yellow. The boys kicked at the icicles of course, as boys do, and a few of them broke off and shattered. That was how they discovered the cave behind there, extending into the rock face. So they crawled in and found a slaughtered reindeer stag already butchered into manageable pieces.

They were smart enough to figure that a Lapp had been there and done it because the back, the legs, and the innards were already gone. The back and the marrow bones, the liver, and kidneys are precisely what a Lapp boils first they said to each other. The head with its delicacies, such as the corners of the mouth and the eyes, was waiting neatly at the entry to the cave along with the hooves and the heart. The ribs, shoulders, and legs were further in. Everything was covered with evergreen branches. They could see that whoever had done the butchering meant to come back and collect the rest before the wolverines and foxes got at it.

Afterward they claimed they had some idea of who the thief was and decided to give him a fright since he was known to be superstitious. Although they expected him to notice their tracks and be forewarned, they were lucky. A snowstorm blew up and lasted several days. It swept away every trace of them, and they imagined the thief would probably think the icicles they had kicked down had fallen in the storm.

They were also lucky that by the time the weather settled again, it was Sunday, and they could say they were going out to hunt hare again. They headed up toward Bjekkertjärn, taking a young Lapp lad along.

They hung around the cliffs up there for several hours, keeping an eye on the tarn. At dusk, just when they were about to give up and head back down, they saw a figure skiing across it and heading straight for the cave. They quickly hid above the icicles, with the Lapp lad in front. The idea was for him to frighten the thief by calling out in their own language. And he did. The minute the man down there, my grandfather Mickel Larsson, had disappeared into the cave, the boy started shouting he was hungry for meat and blood.

Give me meat or I'll rip your prick off! he shouted in a deep voice. I'll boil your balls in a pot and cut the breasts off your daughter and throw them in for good measure. Give me meat, reindeer thief!

Back then people used to frighten their children with stories about evil giants, but those tales would hardly have scared a crafty grown man like my grandfather. Still I can understand why he took off as fast as his legs would carry him. They caught up with him on the ice though, being fast skiers and much younger and stronger.

Afterward they showed people the heart and hooves he had stuffed under his longshirt. So it was clear they laid hands on him. There were three of them.

He never accused them of beating him up.

My uncle said this: there's nothing strange about a Lapp who's lost all his reindeer getting a craving for bone marrow and kidney fat. Others had stolen reindeer from him, which was part of his misfortune and his lost authority. But I know he would never have done it if my mamma had been alive.

If only he'd been sent to Härnösand, my uncle lamented. In prison he would have been able to atone for his guilt, if there was any guilt, and to see a bit of the world for once too. But they never reported him.

Instead, the air grew thick as the grease in a kitchen, heavy with rumors and lies. Soon there wasn't a lost mitten Mickel Larsson hadn't stolen. He stole out of people's food sheds, they said. He stole their nets out of the lake.

Being a reindeer hand for a rich Lapp was tough enough, said my uncle. But things were worse for a hired girl, who had to chop all the wood and the branches to cover the floor of the shelter. She carried the water and helped the woman of the household milk the does. She seldom got more than a coffee cup's worth out of them at every milking, but those precious drops were the basis of the cheese.

She had to milk both morning and evening and herd the does. She would wander behind the herd of deer as they grazed, and when they lay down for their sunrise rest, she would pull out her knitting needles, and again when they lay down to rest at noon and at twilight.

A doe, a calf, and a year's worth of clothing were what she could expect to be paid. Slaving with the wood would make her gnarled as a mountain birch and give her aches and pains and ugly knobs on her joints.

Grandfather, who was never again known as anything but Meat Mickel, would have said of course that this was the right life for a Lapp girl. What else was there? He knew it was difficult working for others, which was why he kept her at home as long as he could. He needed wood too, and his goats had to be milked.

But there was something about Ingir Kari that made her stand out among others. Verna Pålsa asked if she could come work at the guesthouse after her confirmation. The tourists would enjoy being served by a neatly dressed Lapp girl in the dining room, and Verna promised to buy her a new Lapp dress.

Why did she attract that kind of attention? I asked. Uncle Anund answered it was that she was so fine. Eventually I understood that he meant the same thing Hillevi meant when she said beautiful.

At first my grandfather had been reluctant. He had been against sending his children to school too since there was no longer any schoolhouse at the grazing land and the schoolchildren had to live down in the village. They learned farm folks' ways there and took on villagers' habits, he would say. But he was glad they learned some arithmetic. That would make it harder to cheat them.

It was the dress that settled the matter. A dress was a costly item. He let Ingir Kari work at the guesthouse. That was how she happened to go along with Verna up to Thor's Hole to serve the hunting party from Scotland.

Yes, they'd started coming again after the war. The admiral was dead and old Lord Bendam as well. The lord who led the hunting parties now had been there earlier too, but in those days he'd been nothing more than a lanky red-headed lad with knobby knees who had just learned to shoot a rifle. That was what Paul Annersa said anyway.

Why did he have to come back?

My grandfather probably asked himself that though there's no knowing for sure. Uncle Anund must certainly have thought about it with bitterness, at least to begin with, because he and his sister were very close.

What about her? No one knows. There's just a blank

Of course she's not in any of the photos from up there. None of the bearers and guides, wood choppers and drivers, or the ones who plucked the fowl and cleaned the fish and did the cooking and lit the fires and heated the bathwater were in the pictures. Myrtle and I used to examine the reflections in the windows in the timbered wall behind the huntin' gentlemen to see if we could even catch a glimpse of a face.

Myself, I can't be sorry he came back. It's hard to imagine I might not exist.

Myrtle saw things differently, I think. She imagined her unborn self as a soul looking for its home on earth. She would probably have preferred for that home to be the minister's house in Röbäck and for Edvard Nolin to have been her father. We used to rummage through Hillevi's drawers as children do, and we found a letter from Reverend Nolin to Hillevi. To this day I remember how it began: *My dear girl!*

That was why Myrtle looked longingly at Edvard Nolin's distinguished pale face on the photograph from Thor's Hole. Myrtle had a weakness for elegance and not without good reason. She had some of it herself in her long thin hands and narrow feet, for which she always had so much trouble finding shoes that fit.

I'm short, and these feet, they made Tore feel sorry for me when I was to be confirmed: the Good Lord sure broke off too big a chunk of clay for those clodhoppers of yours, he said. But it was mostly my boots, bought with room to grow in.

Elegance is so arbitrary I felt like saying to Myrtle. You were born with it and it's yours in spite of the fact that you didn't have the father of your dreams.

Look at me though, I wanted to say. I'm short and low-slung but wear shoes size eight and a half. It doesn't help that my lineage extends back to the times of King Arthur.

They say Aidan was a fairytale kingdom.

Once I asked my uncle where we came from on his side. But he said Lapps don't come from anywhere. They've always been here.

I stood by the stage listening to old man Fransa going on about Laula Anut or Anund Larsson as he called him. Claiming he didn't know anything about the things in his songs, claiming he'd never chopped down a tree. Then I went home.

I took the path over the hill instead of the road, and after some time I came out by Storflo marsh and passed the place where the shack on the shooting range once stood. Not a splinter of wood left there, not so much as a mound in the swampy ground.

The curlews called. An evening haze hung in the crowns of the spruces. In the distance I heard a voice coming out of the loudspeakers down where the festival was. Of course I couldn't make out the words. But I was reasonably sure the voice was talking about the old days since I knew that was what people really wanted to hear. They liked hearing how honest and hard working people used to be.

Your forefathers, they were. Just as greedy as you are.

You want to hear pretty things, you do.

But I'll give you wolf bile.

I'll give you wolf bile and fox farts and wolverine spew.

Elis woke up before the men that Sunday morning. He went out to piss; it was so cold he thought his spray might freeze to ice. When he got back into the cabin, he got the fire going. The old man they called Dongen had peered out of sticky eyes but went back to sleep when he saw Elis tending to the fire. Once it had come back to life, Elis too crept back under the hide that served as his cover to wait for daylight. It was bitterly cold, but not even the cold stopped the lice.

The cabin was large, well timbered, and insulated with moss. You could almost feel the warmth from the horses coming through the opening to the stable. He could hear their hooves stomping.

Light, light. Please, light. Then he remembered his promise to himself, and thought the words again, in Norwegian this time.

He pulled a paper bag out from under the straw. He'd flattened it with his knife. It was a large grayish sheet, not grease-stained at all. Please, some light now.

It struck him then that if he went and foddered the horses too, the old man would surely hear him and stay asleep for a while.

He fed Biggun first. They called him by another name. He looked different now that the light was beginning to creep in. It made his coat look fuller. Made it downy, softer. The light was a grooming brush, fluffing some surfaces and flattening others.

It was no surprise to him that Biggun looked different now that morning had come. Eyes saw things differently at different times. What did surprise him was that not everyone saw what he did. Most people seemed to see an object that represented the thing they were looking at. It was as if they were staring at the name itself.

He took up the pencil from where the driver, whose name was Moen, had left it. He was in charge of the logging ledger. No log scaler was going to cheat him. Luckily he used a lead pencil rather than a hard aniline pen. You couldn't get much life out of one of those. You wet the damn point, and all you got was an uneven purple smear as toxic in color as it was in taste. But the soft pencil obeyed him. The pencil lines were fuzzier on the rough side of the bag, but that pleased him. He'd use that side first.

The men were sleeping hard after a night of drinking. They never drank on weekdays, but yesterday had been Saturday. At some point Moen had had to separate two of the young men. One now had a swollen lip that was puffed right up over his teeth.

Elis had meant to start by drawing Biggun, but somehow the pencil sketched out the edge of that fat lip all on its own. His nose. The roughness of the bag made it easy to draw the whiskers and the lines at the corners of the eyelids hanging heavily in his drunken boyish sleep. Little bubbles came out of the side of his mouth. His knitted cap had slipped over his forehead. They all slept with their caps pulled tightly down.

The roughness proved to be so well suited to all the things in the cabin that he quickly committed everything in sight to paper. He'd meant to do Biggun, but he hadn't gotten there yet. Instead he drew the skillet on the iron grating over the fire. It had a rough black layer of encrusted fat on the outside and was half-full of congealed grayish drippings. He noted that he'd started drawing it as he thought it would be rather than as it was.

I thought the surface was completely flat. But I'll be damned; it's coagulated in a sharp wave. Somebody must have bumped the pan just as it was hardening.

He went on to draw the piece of burlap stuffed in a cracked window pane. The rough paper helped him there too, but it was hard to bring out the pattern of the weave, the interlaced strands. He began to regret wasting the paper on things he hadn't mastered. He could have done Biggun without so much rubbing out and smearing.

But there was something altogether too easy about horses, their hindquarters and necks. He'd drawn too many damn horses. His eyes were really alert this morning. Noticed the roughhewn stones of the fireplace behind the shelf. Gray but not the same gray as the pencil lead. And sooty. Soot on everything, especially the wooden funnel leading up to the central smoke hole. A piece of pork was lying in the trash on the floor. Had the rats gone completely blind? Frozen to death more likely. The rosy streaks of meat in that bit of pork with its thick yellowish fat. If someone like the Laka King got butchered—well not him, he's not fat—but, say, the doctor from Byvången, someone with a real belly on him; if you chopped up a belly like that the pork on it would look like it had been packed in Chicago. And he'd squeal like a pig in a slaughterhouse too.

He worked over the whole thing one more time: the heavy vest and the work shirt hanging at the fireplace, the seven sooty coffeepots, his own in particular, so dented. Little sparks of fire shot out onto the paper leaving flakes of soot. The boy they called Nils's lad had dropped his harmonica onto the trash: he was sleeping with a homespun shirt rolled under his head. Instead of a piller. But it would be pretty damn strange if anyone had a real pillow up here, strange indeed. And the skillet with its layers of fat, frozen in time, broken up and then congealed during the fight or earlier while they were singing. I came so damn close to getting it wrong, not seeing the ripple on the surface.

The surface cracked.

When he heard that thought, he realized he'd stopped concentrating again and was thinking in dialect or Swedish or whatever it was, that language he'd have to wipe out of his mind if he was going to live in this country where not a single damned soul knew him.

Damn, he thought again, hearing how he had to pronounce the *a* differently. Daemn, daemn. You kind of had to open your trap wider.

Then the boss woke up.

The men on the logging team weren't bad. No one had raised a hand to him. The Swedish fellow from Värmland had grabbed at the fly of Elis's trousers when he was drunk and got a grip that was painful in spite of the thick homespun cloth. He'd grabbed his aching balls and said the time had come to show them if he was a real man. But then Moen said he'd already proved he was, and that had been the end of it. They'd all laughed at him of course.

But the odd thing was he hadn't proved it yet. Though the fellow from Värmland didn't know it.

They were decent men all right. No one here would give him a slap in the face or a blow across the neck because of a paper bag. No one would call him a worthless damn lout no good for anything but wasting paper. And yet his habitual caution made him want to keep his drawing to himself.

The old man they called Dongen went through his morning rituals, scratching his whiskers and spitting on the floor. Then he lit his pipe. One by one the others woke up and went out for a piss, all but the driver who went to the horses first. The cold air came rushing in, icy and metallic, and as always the first words were about the door: shut the goddamn door! That was the Värmlander. As soon as he was up Elis was on his guard.

The lad with the swollen lip reeled outside, but by the time he came back in his legs seemed to have steadied. Everybody had a laugh at his expense, but he didn't notice. He dropped back down onto his berth and was soon out like a light again.

They put their coffee pots on the fire. The wood and water were in; Elis had got both before he sat down to draw so he could take advantage of the morning light until the others were up. The bucket was near the fireplace and only had a thin layer of ice on it now.

When Bendik and he had left the farm they'd each been given a coffee pot. Elis's was so battered the lumberjacks joked that it must have been through the San Francisco earthquake.

They didn't run away; Bendik hadn't wanted to. Elis pretended he'd started remembering where he came from, at least vaguely. Someplace up in the woods around Namsos, he said. By a river. He thought he'd be able to find his way back.

Had they believed him? Maybe. At least they never took him to the parish minister for an interrogation. And they had let Bendik leave too. Though not until he had served his whole contract.

In Fossmoen they met up with a team of lumberjacks. The driver was one man short, and he hired Bendik. Elis was part of the bargain, just as he'd hoped.

But Bendik had second thoughts. That evening when the men were drinking at the inn before heading off with the horses for the next six or eight weeks, he started talking about going to sea again, about wanting to ship out on a whaler. Toward morning, when Elis woke up, he was gone. Elis suspected he'd headed back home and not down to Namsos. Bendik called it home although it wasn't where he was born. He'd said several times that evening how good they treated him back home. Kind 'uns he'd called them. After the loggers gave him a shot of liquor, he was close to tears. They laughed at him and called him the whalin' lad. His body was fully grown, but like a child, he wanted everyone to be nice. Elis was both embarrassed and amused.

He was taken aback, to say the least, to find Bendik gone. He'd slept too soundly. After their long trek, sleep had outwitted his fox instincts, and Bendik had crept out of bed without waking him. He knew at once that without Bendik there would be no place for him on the logging team.

So before dawn he snuck off too.

Nevertheless, a couple days later he found himself on his way up to the logging area. He figured that if he got all the way up, they wouldn't turn him away, and he could say he and Bendik had got separated. I thought he was here, he planned to say.

He almost didn't make it. His provisions ran out on the long trek. He really didn't want to start stealing again because someone might recognize him later if the loggers sent him to get milk and things from the farms. If they let him stay. If he made it at all.

He had been given detailed directions, but everything seemed blurry and looked the same. Roads that should have been there weren't; whole farmsteads were missing, maybe buried in snow. It was so quiet you could hear a pin drop, and there was no chimney smoke. Once he saw a cat in the middle of all the damn snow and realized there must be a farm nearby. He followed a branch of the river with steep forested cliffs on one side. The jagged black spruces were heavy with snow. Once in a while the crust of the snow had been scratched by a wing or marked by paws under a spruce; otherwise it was dead white and shadowless.

The light would soon go blue as dusk fell. The relentless darkness under the spruces would soon be apparent. He felt like a kitten being swallowed by the bag.

Then he heard a clanging. And he remembered that if you heard a bell ringing in your right ear, someone was going to die.

It was difficult to say if it was his right ear. So he stuck his finger into the left one. He could still hear the ringing.

If he was going to die, it would surely be that night. There was no one here to die but him.

The ringing grew sharper and louder, and as it grew closer, he realized it was nothing but sleigh bells. Ashamed about having fallen prey to a superstition, he pulled his mitten right back on and went from being Elis Eriksson to *I dunno.*

The sledge was driven not by a man but a boy of maybe nine and pulled by a fat old mare. The boy had round cheeks under his leather cap. He was sitting with a hide covering him from his middle down to his boots, and someone else had clearly tucked it around him. There were tubs and casks on the sledge, some bedded down in straw.

Had it been a man, he would have asked. As it was, Elis just jumped up and crouched behind the boy.

I'll be a ridin' withya, he said, wondering if he sounded right. He'd been walking alone for far too long thinking to himself. But it didn't matter. He wasn't afraid of this driver. He was nothing but a kid they'd sent to take provisions to a team of loggers because there wasn't a man free.

The boy was talkative. But it was no use asking him the way; he had no idea. The horse was the one that knew.

At first the boy chattered; then he suddenly went silent. Out of fear in both cases.

Yes, he was afraid.

Are you scairt of t'wolf? Elis asked, not bothering much about how he sounded. But he must've said it wrong; the boy didn't understand.

Wolves, said Elis. Is ya feared of 'em?

The boy shook his head. They'd sent him out with an old reliable mare and a set of bells on her to keep him company or to scare off wolves. But wolves would have kept their distance from a noisy load with a big horse anyway. Still maybe it made the boy feel safer.

He was tucked in and well fed and ruddy cheeked and must have felt quite important. He was the kind of kid people fussed over. A future farmer. But now he was scared.

Of me, Elis thought.

Actually he thought more about it afterward, once he got there. He thought a lot more about it a few weeks later when the Värmlander turned up. Though a bit of mischief did run through his mind on the sledge. Because the lad was so lovingly tucked in and so chubby. And because of all the food he had in the wagon. No doubt there was pork and dumplin's and dark bread and cheese and one thing and another. He wouldn't be able to stop Elis from prying off a lid. He could stuff his mouth full of pork and leer at the boy.

But he didn't. Soon they stopped talking too. There was no point since the damn kid didn't have the foggiest notion where they were going, what the lakes were called, or how long the way was. The mare knew. But all she could do was plod on.

Toward evening they came to a farm, and she turned in, pulling the sledge almost to the stable door. The dogs started barking and people came out.

Elis sensed they weren't overjoyed to see him there. But they gave him the same porridge and bread with pork drippings as the boy. He didn't bother with his *I dunno* since they didn't ask his name. He said he was headed up to a logging area and that the team driver was Holger Holgersen. They recognized the name and treated him better afterward.

He had to share the space alongside the stable with a fellow who wasn't quite right in the head. The boy was lodged inside, tucked in under hides and bedclothes.

When they left the next morning, he seemed less intimidated by Elis, but they didn't talk much anyway. Elis had a description of where he should hop off to hike up to the logging area. He saw how the lad brightened up when he said they were there. Thanks, Elis had planned to say. For t'ride. But he didn't. Something about that chubby face provoked him.

Though he didn't really think about that until the Värmlander arrived.

The first time Elis came into the cabin it was evening and warm inside, and he got a whiff of the rotting trash under the table and around the fireplace.

The cabin was timbered and held the heat well, and he soon stopped noticing the smell. They were good men. They let him stay. Not surprisingly they called Bendik a pile of shit for having signed on and then run off. It raised Elis in their estimation.

His arms were thin, and his back small and bony. But he could help the log loader clear the snow from the strip roads.

In the end not much came of that either, which was a good thing since he didn't really have the strength and his cough was far too bad. He became their jack-of-all-trades. One day he helped strip bark. It was difficult in the cold. Another day he helped the load binder or whatever he was called up here. Rather than use a wrong word he said nothing. They accepted his not knowing who he was or where he came from. In fact it amused them. They would chew it over in the evenings as they filed their saws and sharpened their barking tools or mended their trousers. He was sick and tired of his own eternal *dunnos* though, and of sounding like an idiot. So he started saying he remembered this and that. That one thing and another was coming back to him. He said it so often it gave him a name. Comeback, the Värmlander called him, and the others copied him. Elis didn't like the name, but it was better than nothing.

So now he was Comeback, whose job it was to give the horses water and chop the wood and keep the hole in the ice open and pull up the buckets of water so everything was more or less like at home. But better. The cabin was a place he actually liked. A real nice 'un.

Yes, that was how he felt, in his ignorance. He helped the boss man Dongen keep the road passable, poured water to ice it down so the provisions sledge could get through, or shoveled scoops from the anthill to make the slopes less slippery. Where it was steep and narrow he put out markers along the edges. He ate pork from the barrel and hardtack. To begin with, his hunger made him so greedy he would lick his finger and pick up every single crumb from the rough tabletop.

The Värmlander had heard down in Fossmoen they were one man short. He was a big feller. He could drop eighteen trunks a day, and he drove up the pace of the whole team, which pleased the driver.

Everyone was pleased. Except Elis. But he couldn't have said what the trouble was. He wasn't sure himself. Just that he was on his guard.

The Värmlander's eyes followed him everywhere. Sometimes he looked amused. As if they shared a secret. Elis thought he'd figured out he was Swedish and a runaway. That made him even more silent.

He had met men from Värmland before. They would come up to Blackwater as log drivers for the floating and sometimes stay the winter on a logging team. This man was really good. But he still seemed to feel that he had to prove his strength and toughness over and over, even about little things.

The others were always ready for a laugh. He would take Holger Holgersen's knife, the one he'd just used to scrape out a horseshoe, and cut himself a piece of pork, stuffing it right into his mouth. But Elis didn't laugh, and their eyes met. There was a black gleam. Though the fellow was actually blue-eyed and had dark hair, straight as a Lapp's. On the rare occasions when he took his cap off, it stood out in all directions.

That night after the boys had been fighting and Moen and Holgersen separated them, when some of the men were already snoring in their bunks, the Värmlander had grabbed Elis again. By the neck. His head was lolling from side to side, and what came out of his mouth was probably supposed to be a song.

Now sin, well it's blacker
than charcoal so dark

His grip tightened.

the soul how it flutters
like wings of a lark

That was when the boy on the sledge came back to Elis's mind and what had amused him so much at the time: seeing the flutter of fear in his eyes.

Yes, m'lad, said the Värmlander in a tone of voice that contrasted with the hold on his neck. His voice was slurry as if he were crying. But when Moen passed by he tipped back and fell asleep.

Although it was Sunday, they were still working half a day. It wasn't the driver's idea; it was Moen's. The younger fellows were eager to finish up and get back down to the settled areas. There wasn't much left in the pork tub, and one of the men lost a whole work day if they had to go down and replenish their stores. They hadn't sent Elis the last time; Holgersen said he was coughing too much.

So that Sunday morning all of them picked up their tools and headed out except the Värmlander, who wanted to sleep a couple more hours. He was extremely hung over, and besides, he was such a good worker he would fell as much as the others even if he came out later. So no one objected.

Dongen had said it was wrong to work at churchgoing time. To no avail.

Old fellows tend to be against everything that isn't done as it always has been. But he turned out to be right.

Elis heard Holgersen hollering for him. There wasn't the sound of a single axe or saw. Nothing but the shrill voice of the driver shouting in the woods.

When Elis made his way there in the deep snow, he saw Dongen bent over the poor devil who'd had his lip split the night before. As if that hadn't been enough.

It must have been a deep wound because he was ashen and staring straight up. Probably didn't want to see how bad it was. Dongen had cut away his trouser leg so he could hold the edges together, but the blood was seeping out. He was chewing out the lad for not having gone around to the other side of the trunk before chopping off the branches. Elis could see how all the branches had been cut on the one side and concluded the younger man must have been feeling too lazy and hung over to go around. And so it had happened. The axe caught him just below the knee, and the wound slanted all the way down his calf.

Holgersen shouted to Elis to run to the hut and get the cobbling needle and thread. He'd have to stitch the wound before they could move him.

Elis tried to take a shortcut but found himself in very deep snow that was extremely difficult to walk through. He quickly developed a pain in his side and was coughing so hard he thought he'd choke. It had been a bad decision to take the shortcut, so he trudged back to the strip road, where he crouched down to catch his breath and regain his strength. He felt so worthless, useless to the team. Until then he had managed to hold the thought at bay, but now he couldn't: there was something wrong in his chest.

When he got to the cabin, he remembered to be cautious, tiptoeing silently past the Värmlander in his bunk. He grabbed the cloth bag of sewing things from Dongen's berth and stuck it under his sweater. But on his way out the straw rustled, and he was caught.

Those damned arms of yours are thin as matchsticks, said the Värmlander, pinching hard. Don't you have any bones in your body? Let me have a feel.

He held his upper arm tight with one hand, groping and digging lower down with the other. When he was about to rip open the fly of his trousers, Elis pitched the top of his body back. The Värmlander tried to sit up but slammed his head on the top bunk and lost his grip on Elis's arm. Elis tried to get over to the door, but the man, hardened to pain, was on top of him almost at once. This time he didn't hold him down but threw him right across the room toward the fireplace. Elis's hip bone slammed against the side of the cast-iron cooking surface, and his hand and arm slid through the embers and ashes.

You filthy little shit.

His voice was thick, almost like it had been the previous night. Elis hade slipped down to the earth floor and was hunched by the fireplace. This was the moment to say there had been an accident and he had to rush out to take Dongen the needle and thread because he was holding the edges of a wound together as the blood streamed out of it.

But he couldn't. Everything but his own Swedish dialect had gone up in smoke. There wasn't a word of Norwegian left, not a single one. He was scared. Pure and simple. And that fear was in his own language, so all he could do was keep his mouth shut.

You're nothing, said the Värmlander.

He was standing over by the door. His hair was tousled and unruly, he hadn't pulled on his cap. Legs wide apart, he stood there in nothing but his underwear and wool socks with lumpy darns in them. Elis saw everything very clearly. His black whiskers. His puffy eyelids.

Nothing. You know that? You think you're so special. With your damn drawings. But you're nothing. In Bergen a man can buy a kid like you for one crown and use him as he pleases. Behind a woodpile. Or in a doorway, wherever. There are lots like you there. You know that? That's where you'll end up. And you know it, I s'pose, though you try to put on airs.

Elis felt calm in a way as long as the man was talking. But when he moved toward him, he curled up tight. He's reeling, he thought. It's not just a hangover. He's drunk. Unsteady and drunk. He must have stowed a bottle in his berth.

He's a troll was his next thought. I'll poke out his eyes with the needle.

But he never got at him. The Värmlander shuffled across the floor toward the fireplace. First he pulled Elis to his feet and gave him two hard blows to the head. Things went dark but not completely. Then he pulled down his underpants and, holding Elis by the nape of the neck, thrust his face to his cock, which reeked of old cheese and filth.

I'll give you a whole crown's worth, he said, shoving Elis toward the table. The stump of rope belting his pants broke as soon as he tugged at it. Elis felt the rough boards of the table against his face. Then something burst in his bottom. At first he thought the man was pushing the handle of a tool up his behind. Yes, he imagined a gouge and thought: As long as he doesn't twist it. But then he realized what it was. Every thrust was as explosive as the first. He couldn't scream because there was a hand around his neck pressing his face down.

The Värmlander shuddered a few times and finally dropped his full weight onto Elis's back. Elis felt him withdraw, heard him stagger to his berth.

He knew he had to get out of there now, but he couldn't move. If I lift my head up, I'll pass out.

My behind hurts bad.

He could tell that even before he moved. But only inside. He thought: If I could've talked. But that might only have made things worse. A Swede and a runaway.

He was lying face down. I'm so dizzy the world's spinning.

If he moved he'd puke. He knew he still possessed one thing though. One single thing.

He heard the cork plop out of the bottle in the berth.

Oh kid, kid, the Värmlander moaned from deep in the straw and his bed of hides. If you only knew.

His voice broke with emotion. Now there was nothing but his mushy weeping.

Elis snuck out. Not until he was outside did he dare knot the rope around his trousers. He had managed to get the needle and thread anyway. And that one single thing:

You don't know who I am.

Nobody knows.

Hillevi devoted the end of her pregnancy, when she was very heavy, to arranging the nursery. She organized things and arranged them. The set of white furniture Trond had ordered consisted of a crib, a chest of drawers, and a child's table with two little chairs. She put shirts with lacy edges and cloth diapers and swaddling blankets into the drawers, feeling at peace. It was nice not having to work in the store. She enjoyed being alone; if it had been up to her, she would have just stayed inside behind the door to her room. At those times she felt calm. The very next day, however, she might find herself sitting there having dark thoughts about stillborn and deformed babies. She'd had those thoughts earlier too, had wept stormily on Trond's shoulder. But at the very end she withdrew, needing to grapple in solitude with being buffeted between fear and longing.

She had continued to work in the store and as a midwife through the first and second trimesters. Precisely three months before the baby was due, the new midwife came to Röbäck. She was from Härnösand, the daughter of a customs official, and quite a lot older than Hillevi. She got a room with a kitchen on the ground floor of the parish hall, an office in the garret, a storage shed, and four hundred crowns worth of repairs. According to Märta Karsa, she was quite pushy.

She was certainly anything but bashful when she arrived on a bright early summer day to deliver Hillevi, who was sweaty and in the opening phase of her labor. When the examination was over and it was clear that the cervix was three fingers dilated, that brassy woman marched straight into the nursery. Hillevi heard her pulling out drawers. Of course all she just wanted was to locate the baby clothes, but her way of commenting and praising made Hillevi both furious and ashamed.

That was the way she herself must have behaved.

At least everything was ready. Hillevi had been sewing little shirts of fine white cotton and edging them with English stitching. The diapers were made of the same fabric. She had made little undershirts and thin blankets of white piqué. She had used heavier twill for the swaddling. There were navel bandages and baby soap and a container of talcum powder.

Now that the relentless course of events had begun, however, she recalled all her preparations as if they had been a child's irresponsible and self-important game.

Afterward she couldn't remember much about the delivery. She had intended to be in control, say when she was ready for her enema and discuss what else was needed. But there she lay, red and sweaty in heavy labor. Once the really painful contractions started, everything else was a blur. Afterward she recalled drinking a cognac and egg toddy. She also had a vague memory of a saline solution enema, but she wasn't certain she'd actually had it.

Oh yes she had because she remembered telling that woman for God's sake to keep Halvorsen out of the room while it was happening.

That woman became Ester as the hours passed. Her name was Ester Spjut. And she had firm hands. In the expulsion phase, when it hurt worse than anything and felt heavy as a load of timber—or like she was trying to hold back a load of fifteen tons that was sliding down a steep slippery slope—she actually liked the woman. Because she understood.

Look me in the eye, said Ester Spjut in her resolute voice. Look me in the eye, Mrs. Halvorsen. Now round your back ma'am. Round, round. Arms out now—well done! You know all about it—rounding your back helps. Good, Mrs. Halvorsen. You're doing fine. It'll all be over soon. Just look me in the eye now, please. Chin to chest! That's it. And again. You can do it again. Yes, yes, yes . . . you're pushing just fine. Once again now. Chin, that's right. Push! Yes, now!

At last, with exhaustion and a sense of relief that felt like a deep fall, Hillevi saw those strong white hands holding a body covered with vernix and streaks of blood, a body that looked much smaller than it had felt. When the midwife had bathed it and held it out to her, she could see the disproportionately large scrotum and the penis and knew it was a boy before she said it.

A fine healthy boy. Hillevi counted his fingers when he was in her arms, a bundle of white piqué and fine cotton. When Ester Spjut brought her coffee and a slice of bread with cheese, she thought: I'll count his toes later. And then she fell asleep.

Undress, said the doctor without looking up from the slide he was smearing. There was a stink from his mouth sour as the scrapings from a pipe. Under his white coat he was wearing a three piece suit and a shirt with a starched collar, yellow at the neckline. His suit was brown striped, his tie black and thin and crooked.

Undress!

Elis didn't move, and the doctor stared at him. He had little hairs in his nostrils and red hair on the backs of his rough hands and below the middle knuckle.

Get a move on, he said.

So Elis undressed.

Underwear too, said the doctor.

He should have run away. As soon as the logging driver said you've got consumption, he should have bundled his belongings and left. That very night. If he'd had any sense. He could have tried to find another logging team. He'd get better as soon as summer came around. In the winter a person was always sick.

Instead, he got taken to the doctor's. Moen went in with him, and there was an awful lot of talk. Moen talked about his cough. Then Elis and the doctor were alone.

I don't got consumption, he said. He wanted to say he had just taken a cold, but his mind got stuck and couldn't remember how to say it in Norwegian.

Can you see this lung spot? the doctor asked. He was so close Ellis smelled the stink of tobacco from his mouth again.

Here at the top of the X-ray. That's tuberculosis. Do you know the meaning of the word?

Elis said nothing.

Consumption, said the doctor.

The nurse came in and told him to lie down. She gave him a thermometer. He was confused and just lay still not looking up. She told him to stick it in.

Right up the unmentionable, said the doctor, walking over to the stretcher where Elis was lying. Elis could feel his bottom burning. Two obedient buttocks and an obedient asshole, that was what the doctor wanted. But Elis didn't move. So the nurse stuck the glass rod up his behind. In that very place. By then the doctor had left. He'd gone into the next room and was sitting at his desk. He couldn't see up Elis's ass from there.

How old are you? he asked when he returned.

Dunno.

Twelve?

Older, Elis thought.

Twelve? asked the doctor, smelling of black pipe again.

That settled it. Twelve. But inside he was older.

What's your name?

Dunno that either.

Did you run away?

They said the sanatorium was called Open Spaces. He got to take the train. Grabbing hold of the iron gate to climb on, the palm of his hand got black. He found himself standing on a kind of porch with an iron fence. The three of them went through a door; it reeked of piss. They opened another and he saw lots of people on wooden benches. So this was what it was like on a train. But he was old enough to recognize every experience: the train smelled of meeting-house. People sitting all over the place, the ceiling vaulted and yellowing.

Everyone sat silently looking at Elis and the two other new passengers. Then the locomotive tooted and started to puff and rumble. He saw white smoke out the window and the stationhouse was drawn backward as if on wheels. There was a dragon's head on the ridge of the roof, and for a little while it looked as if the smoke were coming out of its jaws. Then the smoke dispersed and familiar black forest appeared outside. He wondered if there could be any animals around the tracks. They probably fled the tooting and the stench.

He held on so as not to tumble. Some people slid aside to make room for them on a bench. Packed like salted fish in a barrel, they sat there with the train car rumbling. It smelled of coal. Everything rattled and creaked. The sides of the mountains were shaggy with trees so high you couldn't see the tops. Later in the afternoon he saw a blue fjord. There was a boat with a brown sail. It was a cutter, said the man sitting next to him. The lady was opposite him. The doctor had instructed them both to keep an eye on him until they were all the way there.

He's a runaway, he'd said. Don't let him out of your sight.

So the man in the jaunty cap accompanied him to the end of the car when he said he needed to pee and stood smirking outside the door of the train privy. Difficult to say whether he was embarrassed or pleased with himself.

Elis couldn't pee in there. He remembered the time he and his father had caught a fox in a trap the shape of a little house. Or a train privy. The fox kept still, crouching down. His eyes were yellow and staring. Until he got clubbed on the head.

The hole was porcelain and streaked brown from shit. Down below the ground rushed past. The train was moving too fast, he couldn't hop off. When it stopped at a station, he was quick to open the privy door. But the man was still standing there.

The tubercle is a deadly bacterium. The doctor had said that outright. So they were sending him to the sanatorium. You went there to die. He didn't say that. But Elis had never heard of anybody coming back from one.

The man in the cap spoke of the sanatorium as if he were going to stay at a guesthouse. He'd been there before, and he told Elis about the food and about girls there. He said he had a squeezebox. The woman said nothing. When she coughed there was a little red stuff in her handkerchief. She folded it in carefully, perhaps thinking they hadn't seen it. For a long time she pretended to be sleeping, but Elis saw that she was crying. The man saw it too. He whispered that she had three children back home. The youngest wasn't a year old yet.

Elis wished he would shut up. But he kept on talking about his squeezebox and about everything you could do at the sanatorium. He said there was a lounge with a piano and a fireplace. They'd light fires, and people would sit by the lounge fireplace and enjoy themselves.

What a load of shit.

Elis knew he would end up sitting by the wall at that place. He'd sit still and go gray in the face and die there.

He was bathed in a basement by a big-boned woman in a yellow oilcloth apron. She deloused him, and then she weighed him. After that he was taken to see the doctor, who rapped on his back and listened. He put a wooden funnel to Elis's skin and listened through the other end.

Exxxxhale, he said.

This was a different kind of doctor. He didn't mess about with your ass. He was thinner too, and he didn't shout. Elis undressed.

Cough! You can cough louder than that . . . coooough!

The nurse stayed in the room the whole time. She was smooth and white. Between her shoes and the hem of her skirt, her legs looked painted. You couldn't tell she had on white hose; they didn't sag at all.

The doctor pulled out a sheet of paper and told him the first doctor said he had swollen glands. He could see them on the X ray too: the glands at the base of his lungs were spotted and enlarged. He said Elis was going to have to stay in bed. Elis remembered what Old Man Lubben had said when his mother had taken to her bed: The bed'll consume you. He thought maybe that was why they called it consumption. He knew he was going to die if they made him stay in bed; his features would go gray and then vanish. Better to sit by the wall then. Until that point he hadn't said anything except that he didn't know his name and that he didn't have consumption. But now he said he didn't want to be put to bed.

You're worn out, said the doctor.

It was settled. They took him up several flights of stairs to the very top of the building and gave him a nightshirt. He was dizzy and paid no attention to who was looking after him. But afterward, lying in a hard white iron bed with no straw in the mattress to make yourself a hollow in, he realized he should have had a good look at the outside of the building. It felt large as a church, or even bigger. Everything had happened too fast.

There were eight beds in the ward, nearly all made up but empty. There was a strong smell. And the expanse, this churchlike enormity all the way up to the ceiling, it sang like an organ inside him. It sang of death. Yes, it howled. He had to shut his eyes tight and lay as still as if he had already packed it in. Way off down the ward he could hear someone coughing long and hard, a professional cough. He realized the old man who was his grandfather had been right: a bed is a dangerous place. You can get stuck in a bed with your cough and your spitting blood and your gray mucus. A man's got to work himself healthy. Or else he'll be goin' to hell. Direct.

After some time people came in; two of them had beds near his. Before getting into them, they stood over him and asked his name and where he came from. He didn't want to say Comeback; it sounded dumb. He now understood that a person cannot live without a name. But he didn't know what to say his was. So he just told them he'd come from Grong, which was true in a way because that was where he'd been to the doctor.

Then he shut his eyes and thought that if they believed he was really sick, they would leave him in peace. And so they did for a while. Then one of them couldn't contain himself any longer. It was the younger one; he was probably just sixteen or seventeen. He asked if Elis was going to be collapsed. Since he didn't understand what that meant, Elis didn't answer. Then the other one said he'd had his right lung collapsed.

And this feller's been double collapsed, he said, pointing to the man who'd gotten into the next bed.

He went on to say he might have to get burned as well because his lung had grown into his pleura and couldn't be collapsed.

Collapsed. Burned. Elis pretended to be asleep; it was all he could figure out to do. But his heart was throbbing; his chest felt like it might burst, and his mouth had gone all dry.

The young one had said his name was Arild. The other one was called Harald Flakkstad. He was a lumberjack, thirty years old, with a wife and three children. Arild told him that.

Elis soon realized that at this place people told each other just about everything. Preferably everything. He had never in his life heard so much needless talk. True, the men on the logging team would talk in the evenings when they sat by the fireplace filing their saws and mending their trouser bottoms and sock heels. But not like this. This was sick people's talk, nervous and disjointed. Arild's face went blotchy when he talked.

Elis pretended to be asleep for quite a long while. When he opened his eyes, he just had to ask:

What's that smell?

They said there was no smell. Later he found out it was camphor. And Lysol of course, said Flakkstad. After a while Elis asked why the beds were so hard. Arild told him he was lying on a box spring. He must have been able to tell Elis didn't know what that was because he began to explain officiously: The bed's got a mattress on springs. Elis realized this must be fine as all get out. He decided not to ask about the bedbugs, why he hadn't seen any, why not a single one had dropped down from the ceiling.

At first he ate almost nothing because it made him nauseous. That was a terrible shame because he'd never seen food like this before. Rich and filling. But the minute he put a forkful in his mouth it seemed like sawdust, and his stomach turned. Just as well really. It would cost less that way; they could hardly charge him for food he wasn't eating. Not if they were honest. He asked Arild about that and was surprised to hear that the sanatorium didn't cost anything. Elis didn't believe it. He couldn't say why without revealing that he remembered some things. But of course you have to pay, he thought. At some point anyway.

After three days they gave him clothes. He thought they were letting him get up, but he was only going to see the doctor and get a haircut. The nurse brought in clothes that weren't his, a double-breasted lined suit coat. It was made of black serge and so were the trousers and the vest. She gave him a shirt too, and socks, and suspenders that buttoned onto the pants. He was told to take his spitter cup along, the little one. The doctor wanted a sample to examine the bacteria. He took the lidded spitter cup they'd given him. Not much bigger than a snuff box.

His hair was cut in the basement. The bath attendant started with a pair of scissors and moved on to a little bladed machine that cut right down to the scalp. She rubbed in some more gray salve and made him sit there for a while. Then she washed what little stubble was left and dabbed at his scalp with sabadilla vinegar.

This time he was shown into a different examining room. The doctor was sitting behind a desk. He put his pencil down, removed his glasses, and regarded Elis. Then he slid the book in front of him in Elis's direction, turning it around for him to read.

Patient's full name and occupation:
For children: Father's name and occupation
Year of birth (Month, date).

He asked whether anything had come back to him.

Nope.

Nothing at all?

No, not a thing.

The doctor was silent. He had picked up his pencil again and sat fiddling with it. He was a tall thin man. Leaning over the desk, he appeared stooped. He had straggly black hair brushed forward. Elis had never seen a man who brushed his hair down toward his forehead before and thought he'd probably forgotten to brush it when he got up. The doctor had an aquiline nose and small blue eyes set close together. He pointed out the window with his pencil, asking Elis if he knew what kind of trees they were out there. There were no leaves on them yet, but they were clearly not ashes or rowans. And they weren't birches. Elis could truthfully answer that he didn't know, which was a relief.

The doctor got up and fetched a book. He opened it and pointed to a page.

Can you read this?

Yes.

Let's hear it.

He pointed with the pencil.

One characteristic of this epidemic is that it almost exclusively afflicts children. Treatment of this illness, with its extremely rapid course, has not been particularly effective owing to long distances. My efforts have often been restricted to establishing the cause of death and supplying medicine for possible future outbreaks.

He couldn't. That second word was nothing but a pile of letters that seemed to have collapsed on each other in no particular order. Then he saw the words *of this* and *have often been* and, toward the end, *efforts*. But of course he couldn't just read words out of context, that would be too stupid. So he shook his head. The doctor shut the book and sat considering for a few minutes. Then he asked:

Can you tell me the name of the king?

Haakon, said Elis.

The doctor nodded.

Do you know how old you are?

Twelve.

Are you sure?

Naah.

Do you recall anything from the past?

Elis shook his head. But then he said he remembered a river. He'd told the men on the logging team that he'd been born by a river.

Are you sure?

Yes.

Being born by a river felt safe because there was no river in Blackwater. He had never seen one before crossing over to the Norwegian side. But then he was ashamed because the doctor was a kind man.

He sighed and said Elis had to have a name. They had to be able to call him something, and he had to put his name on the medical records, in which they kept track of his bacteria count and temperature. So would he please tell them what he wanted to be called.

Elis was so taken aback he was silent for a long time. The doctor displayed no impatience, just sat looking at him, rolling the pencil between his fingertips again.

In the end Elis said maybe he could be called Elias. If that would be all right. Then the doctor asked something he didn't understand, a long string of words. That frightened him. Things like that always frightened him. The doctor might notice he only understood the language mamma and Aunt

Bäret spoke. He might think Elis had never been to school. But after a few minutes the doctor asked:

Why?

Then he understood. But it wasn't easy to come up with an explanation. In the end he said he'd been thinking of Elias in the Bible.

The one who rode up to heaven in a chariot of fire pulled by fiery horses? The prophet.

Yes, said Elis.

So the doctor wrote in his name and said they'd have to give him the last name of Elv, the Norwegian word for river, since that was all he remembered, not his father's name or the name of the farm he was born on. He also wrote that Elias Elv was twelve years old. As someone who was fourteen going on fifteen, he was indignant about becoming a child again. He didn't object though because it was good too. No one would imagine a twelve-year-old had been through so much.

They went into the examining room, and the doctor told him to take off his jacket and shirt. He listened to his chest again and asked him to cough. Once he got started he couldn't stop. But the doctor paid no attention because he'd caught sight of the scar on Elis's scalp. His fingers probed it very thoroughly. Finally he rolled a little distance away. There were wheels on his chair. For a long while he sat contemplating him without saying anything. His nose, his cheeks, the skin under his eyes—everything on his longish face was saggy. Elis was pulling his shirt on when the question came:

Did you run away from home?

He didn't answer, didn't even look up. He suddenly felt an aversion to telling the doctor an outright lie. There was total silence again.

If you ran away from home because you've been beaten and abused, the doctor finally said, you can tell me about it.

Elis kept quiet and put on his jacket and buttoned it up without looking at him. The doctor rolled away and started busying himself with the spit sample over at a counter with glass tubes in wooden holders. Without turning around, he said Elis would have to stay in bed for at least two weeks. After that they'd see. If his temperature went down.

Meanwhile you can think about your life story, he said. Then maybe you'll have something to tell me when we meet again.

Back in bed he asked for a book to read. He was really afraid to ask for anything at all, mostly because he might have to pay for it. But he had to take the risk.

The nurse, a younger one now, just a student nurse, a cheerful girl with thick black hair in a wide braid pinned up into a bun, came back with a Bible. He saw Arild and Flakkstad's surprise, but he didn't care what they thought. The main thing was that they got the idea he knew how to read.

The doctor would pass by he knew. Every day he walked through the ward with a whole crowd of nurses, talking to the patients and inspecting the papers in the metal frames above the heads of their beds. Their fevers were charted on them in red. You could see your temperature creep up and then go down a mark or two before it crept up again.

Elis read and read. He didn't plan to put the Bible away when the doctor arrived. Perhaps he'd be asked to read a passage out loud. In that case it seemed likely he'd ask him to read about Elias the prophet. He searched for him. He had to be somewhere. Elis felt feverish, but it was from eagerness and fear that the doctor would come before he'd found the prophet. Toward evening he located the passage: the time God took Elijah up into heaven by a whirlwind, this is what happened.

Elijah!

Now he was a goner. Elias was the wrong name, at least in Norwegian. That must have been Swedish, in which case he'd given himself away.

When the doctor came the next morning, he didn't dare show the Bible. He'd put it into the cupboard where his spittle cup and slippers were kept. All he could hope was that the doctor would forget what Elis had said about the prophet.

He went back to it though for want of anything better to do. And because they left him in peace with their questions when he was reading. Arild and Flakkstad had respect for the Sacred Book. It threw them completely. He didn't mind a bit if they thought he'd been saved. He didn't give a damn.

There was a man called Elisha too. He tarried on earth when Elijah went up to heaven and dropped his mantle as he rose. He took up Elijah's mantle and then went around helping people. There was a boy who got a headache and died. But his mother called out to Elisha, the one who had tarried on earth. And then came the amazing part:

> *And when Elisha was come into the house, behold, the child was dead, and laid upon his bed. He went in therefore, and shut the door upon them twain, and prayed unto the LORD. And he went up, and lay upon the child, and put his mouth upon his mouth, and his eyes upon his eyes, and his hands upon his hands: and stretched himself upon the child; and the flesh of the child waxed warm. Then he returned, and walked in the house to and fro; and went up, and stretched himself upon him: and the child sneezed seven times, and the child opened his eyes.*

Tore claimed that when he was three or four he'd been pulled through the looped root of a tree to cure an illness. I never believed it; he was such a big talker. I remember him at the kitchen table with the coffee thermos. He could drink it to the dregs in a couple of hours; his teeth were stained from all that coffee. Next to his cup he had lined up his pills. He always put them on one of the stripes in the oilcloth. His cigarettes and lighter were also at hand on another stripe. He was quite pedantic.

Being pulled under that root, he said, was his first memory. His second was when Dolly foaled; pappa Halvorsen told him the filly would be his own horse and it was up to him alone to give her a name. In his amazement he couldn't come up with one. Hillevi told him that if he went back out and looked at her again, he'd know her name. And she was right, said Tore. Standing there in the dim light listening to the muffled trampling of Dolly's shuffling hooves, he saw the gleam of his filly-foal's eye reflected in the stable window and knew her name was Ruby. But I was much older then, he said. That was way after the root thing.

They had started by rowing across the lake. It must have been early in the morning since it was misty. He sat next to Hillevi on the aft thwart; an old woman was rowing. He was wrapped in a blanket, gray with blue stripes.

He remembered walking uphill in the woods. The huge spruces on either side of the path frightened him. They were old trees with gnarled gray-needled branches hanging down. Higher up there were "witches' bundles," branches that had clumped together.

They passed by a tumbledown hut built into the rock face. That scared him too. It must have been the Squirrel's hut he realized later. Finally they came to a huge spruce tree with a thick root resembling the shaggy arm of a giant. It shot up over the ground in a loop, so probably the earth under it had been dug out. The soil looked cleared, and there were neither moss nor blueberry sprigs. He remembered screaming when they pulled him through the root. Hillevi had been implacable. The old woman stood on one side, and she stood on the other. Mamma pushed, and the old lady pulled, he said.

It must have been in the twenties, by which time everybody had separators and iron stoves and meat grinders and pedal sewing machines at home. Blackwater had electricity from the falls. Not just that little generator running current up to the guesthouse but a real hydropower plant supplying the whole village. I don't believe people still thought their children could be cured by being pulled through a looped root in those days. Certainly not Hillevi.

There's something amazing about stories though, even ones that aren't true. I can see Hillevi with her son close beside her in the mist. Hear the pull of the oars. See the old woman rowing. They're all completely silent. And the black water's sucking at the oar blades.

The moment he put the Bible away Arild was hanging over him asking whether the doctor had said where he'd be going afterward.

Correctional or orphanage?

He answered *Dunno* and shut his eyes tight. But he was so jittery inside he had to look up and ask:

Correctional? What's that?

Thus he found out there were homes where runaways got sent. Arild was standing over him. His face looked like it was falling off. His eyes were runny; the skin around them sagged.

Elis felt like giving him a slap across the face, but he was lying on his back and too weak. Just as weak as that blabbermouth with his saggy skin falling off. He was gray all over. Not gray as a wolf or homespun trousers, not like a stone foundation or the bugs that lived under the chopping block. No, gray as the little bit of spittle on the bottom of a spitter cup.

He was one of the people who couldn't pull his weight, who had to be dressed and fed by others. He ate and drank and went to the washroom and cleaned himself up like a girl. Fussed with various parts of his body. Spent half the day lying in bed, the remainder resting.

A consumption patient.

A heap of gray bones with flappy skin and a chest that squealed like a leaky accordion. A person who would never work again. And with a stream of babble running out of his trap like phlegm from a cough. He wanted to explain everything to Elis.

From the washroom window he had pointed out a little building at the back of the sanatorium. The window was high up; you had to climb up onto a ledge to see. The building down there was white with a black roof and no windows. That was where they laid out the bodies of the dead. He said they carried them out at night shrouded in black. But some of them only appeared to be dead.

He looked excited when he was describing that. It was the same when he talked about correctional institutions and orphanages. Elis heard his voice, the endless stream, but shut his eyes tight and said nothing. He was not a child and was not going to be sent to a home. If only that gray shit knew. He was in for worse than correctional unless he kept his mouth locked up tight. It was lucky they thought he was twelve. A twelve-year-old was a child and hadn't done anything. Not that kind of thing. The kind you got sent to correctional for.

Now he knew he really had consumption. It was true. He was done for. Soon he would be stiff as a ramrod and dead.

He didn't know what dying was like. The result was that you were dead of course. People were afraid of your ghost. You lay in the same place the whole time. Mamma, she was in the churchyard at Röbäck. When she was buried, the minister called the church the sail and the churchyard with its white fence the ship. You could imagine that ship would sail right out into the lake, he said. And on judgment day it would sail out into eternity with all the dead aboard.

There was no being certain Reverend Norfjell had believed all that. He said things that sounded nice. Now he was dead himself, after being bed-ridden from a stroke. As far as Elis knew, it was no different for a minister than for a calf.

The dead rotted. Their eyes glazed over, and in the end they were nothing but mud. The hair fell off their flesh. Everything dissolved.

A person with consumption rotted while he was still alive. From the inside out.

Lungs are like blisters, Arild had said. Full of gray sticky goop.

Soon it would all be over. He'd be a goner himself. That explained the ringing in his right ear, though he'd been foolish enough to believe he was going to die that very evening.

The consumption was everywhere in his body. It was like a lamp burning in his chest. Soon he'd be done for. You died when the fire in your chest went out.

In the morning they told him he really ought to be in the children's ward. But they were keeping him on because the doctor had said he had *entered puberty*. That scared him and he didn't dare ask what it meant. He wondered if the collapsing and burning came after that. He didn't want to ask Arild either, though he felt less aversion to him. And he wasn't all that angry with him. Arild was nothing.

For a long time he lay there thinking about being nothing. Then the black-haired one came and told him to eat up his gruel. She was the student nurse; they were told to call her Miss Aagot. He thought about the shopkeeper's daughter back home who had the same name and who was dark haired too. She asked if he had read the day's activities in the corridor. He didn't know what she meant. They were typed out, she said, and he ought to familiarize himself. He'd learn what he would be able to do in a couple of weeks when he no longer had to be in bed. Things would be different then, she said. He'd be able to go to school with the children and maybe walk around the grounds. Won't that be fun? she asked, encouraging him to hurry up and get well so he could be out of bed.

This long speech gave him lots to think about.

First, she had told him to read the day's activities. So she had noticed that he could read. Maybe she'd tell the doctor. Second, she'd talked about playing and having fun. The directress, the nurses, and the woman who'd bathed him were all reticent. They gave orders; that was all.

Use the spittoon for your phlegm!

Wash your hands!

By now he knew no one whipped you if you didn't obey, but it still seemed wisest to do as they said. There was something stern and frightening about them. The black-haired one was different though. She spoke to Elis as if to a child.

Would he end up in the children's ward after all?

Today was the first day he was Elias Elv. That was better than being nothing. But he wasn't sure it was better than being no one. He was Elias Elv, twelve years old, and he was to sit up in bed and eat oat flour gruel with prunes.

These were his tasks: eat, piss, shit, wash himself with a washcloth, and brush his feet with a brush. And rest. This was Elias Elv's work.

His life story, long or short.

He was ashamed and shut his eyes tight again. If only he had paper and pencil now that he was alone. But he just had the damned Bible that made the others imagine he was a believer. He was never completely alone of course. At the far end of the ward lay two others who weren't allowed to get dressed and walk about either. They made noises.

Wheezing and moaning. Coughing and panting. Heavy breathing. Creaking. Snot and muck.

Then he started to cough himself. It tore at his chest, and black spots swirled before his eyes. Afterward he was almost as sweaty as at night.

The ward had whitewashed walls. Hanging between the windows was a picture of Jesus dressed in white and standing in a green meadow with his arms outstretched. He was surrounded by flowers, and the sky was blue. That was the only painting. Otherwise there were the eight beds, the bedside tables, and a larger table between the windows. There were two rib-backed chairs at the table, a little red checkered cloth across it, and a potted plant with big leaves on top. A potted plant. He made himself think it in Norwegian. Mustn't forget. He mustn't forget to always use the Norwegian words for these everyday objects.

There were light clouds in the sky, trails of white pipe smoke interspersed with blue. And treetops. Spruces. Pines. Birches.

Whispering. Murmuring.

A dripping sound from over there. Then a loud stream into the piss bottle. Drip, drip, drip. Creak, creak. Moan. Cough, cough, cough, cough. Sigh. And in the distance footsteps on the linoleum. And voices. Even though it was rest time and supposed to be quiet.

He got up and walked to the window. Now he could see whole trees. It wasn't a forest, just a line of trees running down the slope. Fields with a little snow left in the furrows. A glimmer of blue water. Was it the sea? And just below a graveled yard with a flagpole. Like at the minister's in Röbäck.

He heard footsteps approaching and got back into bed just in time. When they came in, he picked up his Bible and started to read. This time he didn't lie around looking for a passage. He started from the beginning. It said:

In the beginning God created the heaven and the earth. And the earth was without form, and void; and darkness was upon the face of the deep. And the Spirit of God moved upon the face of the waters. And God said: "Let there be light!" And there was light.

That was the kind of stuff teachers and ministers believed. Or at least said they did. Serine believed it too. God and Jesus. She believed Jesus saw everything they did.

Even what the old man does? Elis had asked. She thought so.

Will he get eternal damnation for it?

She shook her head.

All will be forgiven, she said.

That was her faith.

But the rib that turned into a woman and the serpent who offered them the fruit, you can't possibly believe in that, can you? he wondered silently. Serine was seeing to the cows and the ewes. As soon as she came in he would ask her out loud. He saw her face in his mind. That was when he woke up in a fit of sheer terror.

That was the worst thing about the sickness and being in bed: you couldn't hold your thoughts at bay. They took you hostage. There was a darkness you had to be sure not even to nudge, or it would engulf you forever.

Do you want to hear how death and madness come into our lives?

No, no, he didn't want to hear. He didn't want to think about things like that. And so he had to read about the serpent who was the wiliest of all the animals and about Cain who went at his brother Abel and murdered him.

The Flood was the first thing he read about that made any sense. Except where it said Noah was six hundred years old when the Flood came; that had to be wrong. But the rest. They were wise to build themselves an ark before the water covered all the houses on the farm and inundated the fields.

He thought about what it was like when the snowmelt was upon them back home, when it peaked. Some years the warm weather came so late that the snow down in the woods and up on the mountains all melted at once. The water came rushing down the brooks and streams and rivers into the lake at Lubben, and it rose all the way up over the far field. It wasn't difficult to imagine what it would be like if the water never stopped pouring down the mountainsides and the rain just went on forever, if the real Flood came. The lake would rise and rise with every passing day. The cows and the ewes and the pig would be swimming about in the water seeking dry land to crawl up onto. In that case it would be pretty sensible to get the animals into an ark and float until hell passed over.

Reading about Noah made him think of his grandfather, whose life history he knew as well as if it had been a Bible story. His ares and his hectares, his years and his money. All the children and grandchildren of Erik Eriksson from Lubben could reel it off better and faster than the story of Adam and Eve. His wife's name was Eve too for that matter. He sometimes talked about her as Ava but mainly as the ol' woman.

Sometimes he would get drunk. Not often admittedly. But now and then a bottle appeared on the table, and he was in fine fettle. If you wanted to call it that. That was when he talked, and they all had to listen to what he had to say.

'Cuz this was how it was, he would begin.

And then he told them, the same way every time, about how Tangen was nothing but a landholding until he built the house he named after himself, Lubben.

He arrived in 1887 with a wife, three children, and a cow. Elis's father Vilhelm was the oldest child, born in 1880. The youngest was their daughter Anna, six weeks old at the time.

Erik Eriksson had spent five hundred crowns on four ares of land from the state. One are was a thirty-second of an acre. How much was an acre?

He interrogated them. Woe be unto anyone who gave a wrong answer or was too frightened to answer at all. Because back home at Lubben this was their Bible, the book of Genesis in which Eriksson himself was God, Adam, and Noah. And Job for that matter. But that part came later.

He arrived in the spring and started by building a hut out of a couple dozen boards. But the first few nights the only shelter for all five was their baking board, and all summer and well into autumn his wife did the cooking over an outdoor fire built over a few slate slabs.

In June he cleared a plot of land. The ground out there at Tangen was stony and difficult to work. Later in the summer they dried enough hay to get one cow through the winter. In autumn-summer he made a log cowshed and stable, splitting and carving the wood for a ceiling. The boards that had been the hut became the walls for the interior of the cowshed, into which the family moved along with the cow. He put out fishnets in October when the char spawned; they got through the winter months on salt fish.

That winter Eriksson earned three hundred crowns from logging. When spring came he plowed; in the summer he gathered sedgegrass and argued with the neighbor about who could gather the grass from which bogs. That was the beginning of a stubborn enmity that lasted as long as he lived. He gathered hay from the ungrazed pasture land and brought home leaves and rowan bark. By that time they had enough winter fodder for two cows and a mare who would foal.

The second summer he built the homestead and fenced in the acreage. He asked his children and grandchildren how many fathoms of fence posts he had mounted. They were supposed to jump up and answer:

Ninehundredfifty!

If they didn't, they were in for a good hiding.

The next winter he did more logging, and in the spring some timber floating. He plowed more land with a harrow and a plow he borrowed in the village.

By 1909 he had cultivated two and a half hectares of arable land.

How many acres is that? he would ask when he made it as far as this significant date. And you answered:

Five!

Eriksson now had a good barn with boxes for the animals and a muck hole, a privy, outbuildings, and two hay sheds in the far pastures.

What was the total number of loads of stone he had removed from his farmland by cart?

Sixthousand!

He had a horse, two cows and three heifers, eleven goats, eight ewes, and a whole battery of laying hens. He sold four hundred crowns worth of butter, cheese, and potatoes a year. He had brought eleven children into the world, of whom nine had survived. All was quite well. Although the barley seldom ripened.

But what happened next?

The land parceling act.

And how was his labor rewarded?

He was in debt.

How deep in debt?

Now you withdrew into a corner if you knew what was good for you. But you had to answer:

The money owed was calculated at three thousand crowns. A homesteader's loan application was filed and was rejected by the Agricultural Society.

That was Lubben's story. The old man was deeply, incurably bitter. He did not appeal to God or the Agricultural Society. He did not rend his garments nor did he strew ashes in his hair. Instead, he beat them.

Listening to the old man, you could imagine he'd been like Adam out there at Tangen, that he'd come from nowhere. But he had actually arrived with five hundred crowns, a wife and three children, a cow, an axe, a saw, pots and pans, and a baking board. And he'd really only come from the other side of the lake. Aunt Bäret knew. She was the one who helped them after mamma died. The old man claimed she went around to other farms gossiping. And people definitely told tales. Although she came from Jolet, she knew a lot about Eriksson out at Lubben. He himself never talked about the hut at the foot of Mount Brannberg or about his father, the man known as the Squirrel.

Aunt Bäret said the Squirrel had been a man of the woods from beginning to end. He never so much as dug himself a potato patch, living only on what the forest could provide. She had seen him once when she was young in a homespun shirt and an otter fur cap. His belt was pulled tight so he could fill the bulge of his shirt with fowl and squirrels. His trousers had no fly, just a drop seat, and he wore soft moose hide shoes with heels made from the antlers.

He and his Lapp woman lived in a peat-roofed lean-to he built into the rock face. He never married her. They ate almost nothing but wild birds they salted, dried, and smoked. Now and then he would shoot a moose but not often. He owned a rifle and was so miserly about his lead bullets he would pick them out of the animals he shot and remold them. He could skin a squirrel as easily as pulling a sock off his own foot. He'd hang squirrel stomachs to dry on the wall behind the roughhewn stone fireplace. They were white and full of seeds. Then he'd fry the seedy stomachs over the coals and eat them as a delicacy.

The old man fished too, and the fat from the char was what put some flesh on their bones. He pulled up the burbots that hovered motionless at the bottom of the lake. His old woman was partial to their liver. He would salt their entrails and boil up a porridgelike mess of it.

Of the children born in that cabin, only Erik survived. He was short of stature and very strong. No one expected him to be much of a man since he'd done nothing but chase after squirrels and ermines until after he was confirmed. But he was the one in the family who snared birds and set traps and clamps and who rowed across to the village with feathers and down, with dried fowl, with squirrel, ermine, and otter furs, trading them for the things they needed. His father had been satisfied with salt, flour, and gunpowder. But Erik had a hankering for more than the simplest bartered goods. There was large scale logging nowadays, and lumberjacks and team drivers were paid in cash. Once he'd been confirmed, he joined a logging team every winter. He was reticent and ill tempered, but his physical strength won him respect.

His father and mother died the same cold winter. He found them stiff as boards in the cabin when he came skiing across the lake with provisions. He was inclined to believe they'd just given up, he told Pål Isaksa, whose team he was on that winter. Though he didn't understand why. There had been fatty pork left in the barrel.

People in the village talked about their deaths. They speculated that the Squirrel had died of a stroke, and when the woman who was Erik's mother was left alone, it wasn't so strange that she let the fire go cold.

A man with no fire is a dead man, the Squirrel had said when he was alive.

Erik spent the winters logging and continued to snare wild fowl and trap animals for their fur. After the hay was gathered, he pulled up stumps from felled trees and burned tar piles on the far side of the lake. He never indulged, saving every penny he earned. When he had accumulated four hundred and eighty crowns, he borrowed twenty from Pål Isaksa and purchased those four ares out at Tangen. He married a thirty-year-old woman from Skinnarviken by whom he had already fathered three children.

Elis thought for a while about all this. He'd never really considered it before.

He'd lain with her and violated her up at Skinnarviken, he thought. Maybe in a hay shed, and they had three children. Their names were Vilhelm, Isak, and Anna. When Erik had taken Eva to be his lawful wife, there were nine more children. One was called Halvar anyway. Another was Assar. And one was named Berit.

And Vilhelm fathered Elis.

And Elis fathered a daughter. A little girl.

His father and his father before him laid hands on him, so he ran away.

Elias!

He heard shuffling footsteps running down the corridor; he heard Arild shouting. He entered the room in the homespun outer garments they had to wear for resting out on the veranda. He hadn't taken off the straw shoes, and his hood was pulled up. He was waving the local paper.

Elias! Read this! It's about you!

Sister Aagot came running after Arild, instructing him to lower his voice and get right back out to his cot on the veranda.

It's rest hour!

She took him by the arm and marched him out. But he managed to heave the newspaper onto Elis's bed.

He was extremely frightened. The only people who got written up in the paper were thieves and people who went bankrupt. His old man used to say they'd got themselves a spot in the dailies. You could tell he thought it served them right.

The Bible was on Elis's chest, the newspaper down by his feet. Sister Aagot came back.

Did you read it?

He shook his head, and she picked the paper up and read in her clear girlish voice:

A lad who appears to be about twelve and in an advanced stage of tuberculosis has been admitted to Open Spaces sanatorium, where efforts are now being made to discover his origins. The lad is suffering from amnesia and is unable to say who he is or where he is from. He is emaciated and has a scar on the back of his head assumed to be the result of a serious accident. Beyond that, he has no particular distinguishing features but is tall and lean in stature, with blue eyes and fair hair. Please contact senior physician Odd Arnesen, Open Spaces, with any information.

Oh, Elias, I'll bet you'll get your family back now, she said when she had finished and folded the paper.

Yes, he was in danger, no doubt about it.

For several days he lay there waiting for the doctor to come through the door saying:

Now I know who you are.

He read the Bible to keep from thinking about things he could not influence. Finally his two weeks came to an end, and the nurse told him he could get up and get dressed and join in the schoolwork. The doctor still hadn't said anything, and Elis had read all the way up to the part where Saul is angry with Jonathan. He intended to read the whole Bible from beginning to end; he knew there were people who had done so. But nothing came of it once he was allowed up.

Sometimes he would read in the evening anyway but at random, mainly the bits he liked. The best story of all was the one where Elisha brought the child back to life, and it sneezed seven times. He knew how that felt. He had held the body of the little girl against his own skin and warmed her in the same way as the prophet. He had saved her life.

The spring night was cold in spite of the heat from the wood-burning stove. There were sharp sounds outside. At first it sounded like barking dogs. But what kind of dog would be barking out on the lake? Later Hillevi thought it might be the flapping wings of the bird of death.

The rain slashed down the window pane at a slant. Sometimes when the weather froze up, there was a snow flurry. The night wasn't pitch black. She could discern Mount Brannberg when the showers let up.

The place where you meet your death is your death space. Most people know when they get there.

She had, of course, heard a lot of nonsense since she arrived here. Especially about illness. Superstitious talk.

But that lake outside her window was certainly a death space. She knew many people met their death there.

In here there was her baby. His wheezy breathing. The smell of his infected throat. The sickly hot dryness of his skin. He barked like a saw hacking at dry wood.

Hillevi stood with her forehead to the window pane, listening to the sounds from his throat as he suffered. She wished she could open the airing pane and let in a gust of damp air. But she didn't dare.

His death space. He was hacking his way toward death.

The thought came sneaking up on her, then monopolized what was left of the night unlike any other fear she had ever known. Previously fright had curled inside her like a live animal. But this terror was freezing cold. Behind her his windpipe continued to rattle. She walked back to his crib.

It was the third day since the doctor had been there. That evening when she had swabbed the child's throat with potassium chlorate as she had been doing four times each day, she thought it looked better. He had actually eaten a little, late in the evening. Wheat flour gruel with butter and sugar. For a few minutes he had sat up in bed, playing fumblingly with a string of empty thread spools. After some time they both fell asleep, her on a mattress Trond had carried into the nursery.

She woke to his moaning and immediately recognized respiratory distress. She thought his lips were blue, though it was difficult to tell in the dim lamplight. His little body was laboring, and he wheezed every time he inhaled.

His windpipe will rattle. That was how the doctor described it. Tore had reached that stage now, sounding like a hacksaw. Exactly like a saw. She propped him up and thought it helped a little. She could feel the struggle for every breath inside his tiny rib cage. He wasn't getting the air he needed. He wasn't getting any rest. The saw hacked on. Hacking.

His pulse was a hundred and thirty now and erratic. He was like a different person. The stench. And the hissing. This wasn't him. This person didn't even have a name.

Her child was little Tore. His scent was of flower petals; he was gurgly and always cheerful. He could say pappa and Siback and Dolly. And Backy for Blacky. Had a horsewhip of his very own, and he drove an upside-down kitchen chair. Her child looked like something out of a picture book, with blond curly hair, a pinafore, and a longshirt.

This one was different. This one was a troll.

No, these were just sick fancies in the pallid gray light. For an instant they overshadowed reason and memory as the winter morning broke. The moment she touched his body her fingertips recognized him. His thinness. His fragile rib cage. His hair, damp now, with its soft cowlick at the neck where he was not yet sticky with perspiration. This was him.

His windpipe rattled on. The saw continued to hack. His body never got any rest. It was slack, his face blue and pale. Early in the morning Trond stood in the doorway weeping openly.

Anger simmered inside her. She was furious with God, and with Edvard. It was like strong coffee from real beans; it was what kept her going. Tore, her child, dwelt in the vale of shadows where no one could reach him. Hillevi touched his hot cheeks, felt their dryness, felt his blazing heat.

There was a terrible smell from his mouth. His lips had once been flower petals. Now they were coated with yellow mucus that dried to a membrane in his throat and on the roof of his mouth. She swabbed him again, scraping away all the odorous gunk she could.

That morning when she stood in the shop talking to her cousin Tobias on the telephone, the customers stared. She could hear how shrill her voice sounded. She was shouting too. He tried to calm her down; her son wasn't undernourished; he would weather the crisis.

When she got out into the blinding March sun in the yard, the old woman was there. She knew very well who she was but had never exchanged a word with that woman. Sorpa-Lisa.

People said she could drive out evil. She soaked moldy bread and laid it on wounds.

To Hillevi she said:

I heard he was poorly. Sounds like the strangler. It often follows on.

Hillevi didn't answer.

Sitting by his bed at night, she would read her medical textbook when Trond wasn't there. She knew the words by heart; they had become a kind of obsession. *The closer to death, the weaker the inhalations.*

She tried to wake him, but he was beyond reach.

The boy pulled through. But when he returned from the other side he brought along a farewell gift. It was croup. "Crupp" the villagers pronounced it. What the old woman with the dirty hands called the strangler.

He wasn't the only one. That spring-winter of 1919 a diphtheria epidemic struck Blackwater, Skinnarviken, and Röbäck. Nine children died in three weeks. Raging with fever and incoherent, they died of dehydration or their hearts seized up or they were no longer able to breathe when the mucus on their tonsils blocked the windpipe.

Hillevi, usually helpful when there was illness, did not visit anyone during the epidemic. She had always believed that if you kept your house neat and clean, used spitters, and regularly covered the contents of the privy with lime, you could keep infection out.

Diphtheria was a frightening word though. It had scared her into staying at home. She felt she was breaking faith, and she was, betraying her confidence in cleanliness. By staying away from homes where there was contagion, she was admitting that the blight of illness could also make its way into well-kept houses.

Still she had refused to believe it at first when the fever lit up her child's cheeks. Then hate possessed her. She knew how the infection had come in. Drops of saliva. Sneezes. Fingers that had just been rubbing a nose. Unwashed hands.

Sticky intimacy.

The workers were pulling down the barricades that separated them from the higher estates, trying to achieve equality by dragging the upper classes down to their level. During the war many people feared there would be a revolution; Sara had sent a letter describing the machine guns mounted on the roofs of the buildings around the royal palace in Stockholm. In Blackwater the poor were not revolutionaries. Here a different kind of equality frightened her. The kind that trickled in. The sticky kind you caught by inhaling the air others had exhaled.

It was so confined here. People were too close together. Particularly in the store. Constantly bumping and rubbing against other bodies and clothes. She had to empty the spittoon every evening and clean it. And some people didn't even use it; real men spit wherever they pleased.

She circulated information about how every kitchen should have a spitter but without much response. The loyal Verna Pålsa had had one of her sons make her one, but when visitors came, she shoved it in under the kitchen settle so no one would think she'd got high-falutin' ideas.

When children's hands had been on the counter, it had to be wiped clean. And the scales: children loved to play with the bird's beaks that showed when the scale pans weighed even. She polished the door handle. When she swept the floor, the dust whirled up, dragged in on their boots from other floors where no one had put out a spittoon.

Her hate frightened Trond. He didn't know what to say or how to divert and subdue her fury. He mumbled that they were all in the same boat.

The same boat.

That boat was the bitter dregs at the bottom of the cup she had to drain.

She often thought about God during this time and about his mercy. Edvard Nolin's face came to mind, his modulated voice. That was how the last spark of that particular ember died out. It was ashes now. Ashes.

They said the sickness migrated with the Lapps from Norway. Hillevi didn't believe it. In that case it would have begun when the Lapps came down from the mountains. Late summer that was so damp and autumn when things decayed were the right time for epidemics. But this one came in wintry March. It came out of hell. And the doctor came from Byvången, spouting powerless words. *Exantem* he called the redness and the bumps. On the second day he examined her child's tongue, gums, and throat—extremely swollen and red—his runny nose, his sticky eyes.

Hillevi said his temperature that evening had not been much over normal. But the doctor shook his head, reminding her of an old badger. She felt almost physically ill when he told her he'd been out at Tangen where there were three sick children in the same family. He said *prognosis pessima* about the youngest one.

He was in his element, instructing her to try to remove all the *excoriations*. Because Hillevi had training, he assumed she would understand. Being called to the shopkeeper's livened him up. He probably anticipated a good dinner, perhaps a cognac with his coffee and a nightcap before the long sledge journey across the slush on the lakes.

But he had to go to the guesthouse if he wanted a meal. Hillevi didn't leave her spot next to Tore's bed. Downstairs, Trond ate what he could find, standing at the kitchen sink.

Tore was asleep. When they woke him to be examined or swabbed, he fell right back into his torpor as soon as it was done.

The doctor had left a bottle labeled *Sol. chlor. ferrio. spir.* She was to give the boy eight drops in a large glass of water four times a day. She stared at the label. Didn't believe it would have any effect and felt nothing but dull deep despair. Edvard came to mind again: despair was sinful, the most cardinal sin of all he had said.

She knew that she couldn't have endured having Edvard by her side now praying, if this had been his child.

Instead of a prayer, what went around in her mind was *sol chlor ferrio spir, sol chlor ferrio spir, sol chlor ferrio spir*. It was driving her insane, but she

231

couldn't get it out of her head. She touched the skin on the boy's neck, hot and damp. She slept for a few minutes now and then, her head dropping forward.

In the morning, so early Trond had just opened the shop, that awful woman was standing there again. Like death personified.

She was looking up at their windows. Biding her time. Was she daft enough to imagine that Hillevi Halvorsen, a trained midwife, would ask for help from a blood-stemmer and layer on of hands? A woman whose dirty fingernails had been in people's bleeding genitals and passed along childbed fever to newly delivered mothers?

Hillevi had spoken matter-of-factly with others about her, and when that hadn't helped, she had shouted, trying to root out of their heads any belief in that ignorant woman and her tricks.

She also shrouded the dead. She'd poured water over a row of seven corpses and gave it to the sick to drink.

She stood out there that wet morning for a long time. Hillevi hoped her boots were leaky. Let her die.

Let her die and Tore live.

That afternoon he was slack and blue, but the wheezing had stopped. He breathed in short superficial gasps. Trond sat with him while Hillevi went to phone her cousin Tobias.

Can't you come up? she shouted. You could operate, do a tracheotomy!

The old woman was there again, standing by the syrup barrel.

He'll have weathered the crisis before I could get there, Tobias said.

Out in the yard she met Sorpa-Lisa face to face and did something she would never be able to understand. She invited the old woman in for coffee.

She had a strong odor but not a bad one. Hillevi poured out the grounds and made a fresh pot. When they had their cups in front of them, she asked:

I s'pose there's nothing we can do?

The old woman drank her coffee so hot it must have cracked her teeth.

It's a difficult sickness, she said. *Stuore namma.*

She took her time, slurping, dunking a rusk and sucking in its warm doughy taste before she spoke again.

Yes, it's got a big name, the strangler.

Hillevi knew that only dangerous diseases, real epidemics, had big names. Smallpox had one. And typhus.

My mother called it bull neck. That was their name for it, up where she came from.

Hillevi had heard that Sorpa-Lisa's family migrated from up north with their reindeer herd. On account of the authorities of course. They'd blasted away their lake.

So it came to be called bull neck. Swelling sickness. Your throat closes up. It comes from the ground. We call it the strangler too. Yes, it has a big name. *Stuore namma*, it can strangle children.

She slurped her coffee again, dunking a sweet roll. She had married a villager named Ante Jonsa, and she kept a flock of goats. She hadn't lived in a *gåetie* among her own kind for a long time. Hillevi could see now that Sorpa-Lisa wasn't as dirty as she'd imagined.

In the old days there were lots of sicknesses in the ground, she said, that came from below and took the children. When there was a sickness, all the children got it.

This spring it's almost like the old days again, she said. No one has any other sickness, and the doctor can't do a thing. This sickness comes from the ground, and everybody gets it. Drinking tar-water doesn't help either. If a sickness wants to get in through the door, it will, no matter what. Even if people burn tar. They think it'll scare away the strangler. But *stuore namma* isn't put off, not by any stink or any doctor.

She was quiet for a while and then started in on everyday subjects, one thing and another. Aagot who had gone off to America although she was only seventeen. Jonetta who was going to marry a Lapp, the price of lamp kerosene, twenty-seven *öre* a liter. That was a lot of money for a poor Lapp woman, she said. Hillevi realized she was getting down to business at hand as she saw it. Hillevi hadn't mentioned it of course. God forbid.

Sorpa-Lisa wanted cash. Maybe not now. But later. If the boy lived. That was certainly the point of her talk about the price of kerosene. It was difficult to know what she was thinking though. You could never catch her eye. Gray headscarf. Knitted sweater. Homespun skirt, striped kitchen apron, sooty on the front. Lapp boots, all wet from the road. She probably wasn't as old as she looked. She'd been a child when her family came wandering from the dynamited lake and calving lands. Hillevi knew the new Lapps had arrived some thirty years ago.

Can you give me a lock of hair? she asked.

Hillevi must have looked confused.

The boy's.

Trond would never need to know the old woman had been there. He surely wondered, of course, why Hillevi came into the room with a little pair of scissors from her instrument bag and cut a lock of the child's hair. But she didn't explain. He could think what he liked.

Sorpa-Lisa was silent after Hillevi gave her the folded piece of paper with the lock of hair in it. She turned it around, unfolded it. Then she took the wisp of hair between the thumb and forefinger of her left hand. She put the paper in her apron pocket and left without a word.

They said she gathered the last saliva out of the mouths of the dead.

The next morning his fever broke. All night it had raged. His breathing was labored, and he was weaker and weaker with every bout. She tried to get fluids into him, but his sick suffering little body rejected everything she offered.

That morning she sat leaning against the white ribs of his crib. Drowsy and exhausted, she felt the warm sun and heard a great tit chirping in the birch outside the gable window. When she straightened up, the sun fell on the child's face. Her first impulse was to shade it. Then he opened his eyes. She could see right away they looked different, and his forehead was cool to the touch. He was making little movements with his lips; she realized he was dehydrated and thirsty. The water had been standing all night and needed to be replaced. But she didn't dare to wait, just raised the cup to his parched lips. And he took a sip.

He lay in the sunlight gazing at her. Blue, blue were his eyes. She began to cry. Not sobbing or spasmodic gasps like the worst nights. The tears just streamed down her cheeks, and he looked at her. They were both perfectly silent.

But outside the window the great tit had worked up to exultation with his two simple tones, and she had to smile. She was sure Tore was listening too, though he didn't know what it was. It hadn't yet been spring when he fell ill; the birds hadn't started singing on cold spring-winter mornings.

Do you hear that? she asked.

His mouth was moving again. There was a little gurgle. She was quite sure he said tittering she told Trond later.

I definitely heard titter. Loud and clear.

Trond wiped his hands on his work apron and went upstairs with her. He stood with his head cocked, looking at Tore's face, at his alert blue eyes. Without turning to Hillevi he put his hand on her shoulder and squeezed it hard, hard. She saw the tears in his eyes and Tore's smile.

Lucky you've got your shop cap on so he recognizes his pappa, Hillevi whispered.

It was the first playful thing either of them had said for weeks. She had believed they would never joke again. The great tit went on chirping; her child gurgled. She smelled that nasty stench from his mouth. His tonsils were yellow and coated from the horrible bacteria.

Now he was going to get better. She knew it.

The nursery would never be the same again. It had white wallpaper with pink stripes and bouquets of forget-me-nots, a picture of mother and child in a gold oval frame, and two cross-stitched dogs. Pink and white rag rugs on the floor and white nursery furniture. But it didn't help. She could never get over having seen his death space there that night. Never again would she dare let him sleep there alone. She had to be able to hear him breathing at night. The white room would stand empty.

Some women said you should never ready a room for a child you were carrying; it was bad luck. As a midwife she had spoken quite sharply to people who neglected to prepare. But when she was pregnant herself, she grew afraid. Although she held superstition and omens in contempt, she said they could always take in foster children if something went wrong. That was her formula against disaster.

Years later, when in a way her fears were realized, she wasn't surprised. There's something to it, she thought, fate. Invisible and lying in wait. Maybe listening.

A lament, that's what I'm singing. Someone has to sing it. But silently. No one goes up into the mountains to sing their sorrows to the wet clouds any more.

My mother was just a girl, barely full-grown. I find it strange to think about that now that I'm old. They gave her long stockings and a corset with garter straps at the guesthouse and instructed her to wear them when she was serving at Thor's Hole. No trousers, no. No leggings of fine thin reindeer skin under her skirt.

The grief is inside me. Oh ah oh for the grief.

No one sits at Aagot's kitchen table any more singing about the wounds to their hearts. But the kitchen table is still there, the same one. The house belongs to a doctor from Byvången now, but he only stays there when he's not working. He looks sad sometimes. But he doesn't sing.

Once he showed me an old coat he'd found in the loft. It's probably still hanging there. It was of black broadcloth and made for a slim woman. Inside it was lined with spotted ermine fur. It wasn't Aagot Fagerli's as he thought. Aagot's coats were American made.

He's a nice man. I should have told him the coat had been Jonetta's. That her Antaris had actually trapped the ermines. Tjietskie was his word for the little creatures.

But I didn't say anything. I didn't feel like hearing the doctor gasp in astonishment or pronounce judgment on the past.

He's put in underfloor heating. In the basement a heat exchanger rumbles. Does he know the house is full of little people who can't be seen? Has he heard them tiptoeing and whispering at night?

In spring-winter 1923 Ingir Kari Larsson died at the sanatorium in Ström-sund. Hillevi heard about it from Vera Pålsa at the guesthouse. It upset them both, not least because Ingir Kari, although she hadn't been married, had a daughter who wasn't even three years old.

Even the minister spoke to Hillevi of his concerns about Ingir Kari. He was worried about her grave.

Jon Vallgren succeeded Norfjell as minister. He'd risen rapidly with a stint of good luck beginning the day he was asked to replace the local minister at that big wedding in Lakahögen. That was in 1917; his superior had a gallstone attack after a wedding in Kloven. Vallgren had been extremely nervous, but Hillevi Klarin, who became Mrs. Halvorsen the shopkeeper's wife that day, had helped him over the worst of it. Since then he had always appreciated her advice.

He told her Ingir Kari's brother Anund Larsson had had all manner of ideas about her funeral. To begin with, he had wanted her to be buried in the Lapp dress Verna Pålsson had given her, though this had been out of the question since she had already been shrouded at the sanatorium. They couldn't be expected to open the coffin after so long and change the clothing on the corpse. He'd have to accept that.

What was more, Reverend Vallgren had told him, he ought to bear in mind that the dress was worth a tidy sum. It would be better for them to sell it and use the money to feed and clothe the motherless child.

Next Anund Larsson wanted to sing at his sister's funeral. Sing solo, if Mrs. Halvorsen knew what he meant.

He had, of course, turned the offer down as tactfully as he could. But Lars-son wouldn't take no for an answer. He said he'd no intention whatsoever of *yoiking* if that was what the minister was afraid of. He submitted a written document to Vallgren, a song he had written in Swedish to the memory of his sister: it was deeply felt. This was what he was planning to sing. It was difficult to dissuade him; meandering about alone up in the mountains, he had obviously become a bit obsessed by the thought.

Well, in the end he had to see it was impossible. The funeral was held. The bodies of four other destitute individuals were committed to earth at the same time. Mickel Larsson, the girl's father, did not attend. He said he didn't have any suitable clothes for a funeral. Anund didn't either for that matter, but someone who had been confirmed at the same time lent him a suit.

He turned up again shortly after, this time with a photograph of his sister in a little oval frame with convex glass. He wanted it set into a wooden cross he had made to mark her grave. He also wanted a stone slab on the ground over the coffin engraved with his poem so that people could read it.

Reverend Vallgren explained that it was strictly forbidden to have images of the dead on their graves. It was unchristian. But people did it in Norway, said Anund Larsson. Wasn't Norway a Christian land?

His grief had certainly not made him humble. He showed the minister the poem too, neatly written out and under glass. It read:

As pink as the petals upon a rose
Was always your blushing cheek
In the innocent joy of youth you chose
A hope-filled future to seek.

Perfumed roses will mark your grave
The wind will whisper its song
I'll wander in sorrow now far, far away
Life's journey feels toilsome and long.

Hillevi thought the poem was beautiful, though she didn't say so to the minister. She realized he considered it devoid of Christian hope and thus unsuitable for a gravestone. But it actually reminded her of Anund's sister, of how she had looked.

Some people are born beautiful, though it's unusual. Emaciation and ring-worm and scrofula did their work on the children when they were growing up around here. But strangely enough not on Ingir Kari Larsson.

She was born to beauty. It was entirely unexpected, like stumbling over a ghost orchid shot through with green and finely grained in a spot where, year after year, only sedgegrass and moss have been.

She had black hair and brown eyes that gleamed golden in bright sun-light. Fine-limbed. Erect. That was unusual among her people. Most of them developed rickets in childhood.

When Ingir Kari was buried, it was too late in the spring to travel by sledge and almost impossible to make it up into the mountains on foot with the rushing spring snowmelt. But Hillevi made up her mind to go up to the settlement where Mickel Larsson lived and see how they were managing to look after the child. She knew there was no one up there but the girl's grandfather and her young uncle.

Although Hillevi was no longer the local midwife but only helped out when needed, she felt some responsibility for the children she had delivered. She hadn't helped Ingir Kari's little girl into the world though. No one had sent for the midwife when she was born.

When she arrived, she was tired and longing for coffee, but there was no one in sight. A flock of goats grazing around the *gåetie* came bounding toward her and crowded around. There was a dog tied to a birch with a rope, barking hoarsely. A hard wind was blowing off the mountain heath, and to get out of it, she sat down on a log in a woodpile by an open shelter. It was still so cold up there on Mount Giela that the sorrel leaves growing under the birches were red, and big patches of snow remained here and there. The marsh was yellow and waterlogged, recovering from the winter.

Exhausted after her long uphill trek, Hillevi dozed off. She awoke to find a child, a little girl, standing there staring. She could see the girl was Ingir Kari's daughter and reached out a cautious hand as if calling to a cat or a puppy. But the girl backed off, and when Hillevi stood up, she ran and hid behind the hut.

That was when Hillevi realized the little girl might never have seen anyone who looked like her before, a creature in rubber boots and an oilcloth hat.

She removed the hat and approached the hut cautiously. A little gray smoke was trickling out between the logs that formed the cone at the top, and there was a strong smell. This must be Meat Mickel's smokehouse. Who knew what he smoked in there.

The dog just kept on barking, though more hoarsely, shifting from warning to rage when Hillevi circled the shelter slowly, capturing the little girl in her arms. She reeked of smoke and was half-naked in the chilly spring wind. Severely undernourished. Covered with ugly sores. They looked like dog bites.

She had the most improbable red hair and blue eyes. Her face was contorted when she screamed. She was terrified. Hillevi rocked her, talking softly. She didn't seem to understand.

Sitting there rocking and humming softly, with the girl flailing and hollering, Hillevi realized she was being observed again. Mickel Larsson was standing by the smokehouse watching them.

She could tell instantly it was going to be a contest of wills, but she figured she could win him over with words. She failed. She did give the old man a piece of her mind about how the little girl looked, about how she hardly had a thing on in spite of the cold. First he listened. For a long time. Stood there, bowlegged, in a longshirt stiff with dirt and leather leggings black with age and grease and soot. On his head he had an old black leather cap, slick with wear. His face was wrinkled and weather-beaten. Her thought was that he hadn't exactly aged since she saw him up at Thor's Hole that summer long ago. He was just darker.

When she had said her piece, including that she intended to see to it that the little girl was taken down to the village and properly cared for and furthermore she was asking herself whether such flagrant neglect shouldn't be reported, the old man began to speak.

Yo, yo, yo, he said. At least that was how it sounded when she tried to imitate him afterward. She was dead tired by the time she got home. She'd met her match in the talking department, Trond laughed. He knew Mickel Larsson.

Oh, that man, said Hillevi. He sure gave me a song and dance. But now he's going to dance to a different tune. I'm reporting this to the police. It's child abuse. Neglect, pure and simple.

It's the younger one who makes up songs, said Trond. But the old man can talk a blue streak.

Hillevi started by discussing the matter with the chairman of the municipal council, feeling he should see the sorry state of things with his own eyes before she reported it to the police. He went up there with two other local officials, and Mickel fed them the same cock and bull story. But as opposed to Hillevi, they weren't sure what to believe.

They stood at the foot of Mount Giela pointing at a particular ledge in the rock face, assessing the distance. They lifted the little girl up, holding her like a big fish whose weight they were trying to gauge.

Could be, they said when they came down.

Hillevi was shocked that they were even willing to consider Mickel Larsson's pack of lies. That little girl needed their help right away. A man who was a bold-faced liar, a drunk, and a reindeer thief shouldn't be the legal guardian of a child.

But they just talked and talked, and then the local paper got wind of it. Sometimes lies have wings. She could hardly believe her eyes when one day Mickel Larsson and his son Anund were elevated to the status of heroes.

LAPP GIRL ABDUCTED BY EAGLE, Trond read when the post office truck had delivered the paper.

This has gone too far now, Hillevi said.

Little Risten, only three years old, was playing in front of her Grandpa Mickel Larsson's hut when an eagle swooped down from the sky and seized her with its hard talons. Her grandfather watched in horror as the eagle took flight, carrying the little girl in the direction of the mountain heaths at Munsen. Larsson loaded his old rifle but did not dare shoot at the eagle for fear of injuring his little granddaughter. He fired right up into the air to scare the bird. The result was that the eagle changed directions, flying toward Mount Giela. Another shot into the air, and the eagle dropped its prey! At that point neither Mickel Larsson nor his son Anund believed they would ever see the little girl again. The camp was in mourning when they headed up the mountain to search for her body.

Spare me, said Hillevi. But Trond just shifted the wad of snuff under his lip and went on:

They searched for two days and nights; Mickel Larsson was ready to give up. But then his son Anund pointed eagerly, indicating a ledge in the rock face. Imagine his father's astonishment when a couple of hours later his son descended with little Risten in his arms. She had deep scratches from the eagle's talons and was tired and hungry, but she was alive! There was celebration in the hut that evening, and little Risten, whose real name is Kristin Larsson, fell securely asleep in the home of her maternal grandfather wrapped in reindeer skins.

That damned scoundrel, Hillevi said. It was the only time Trond ever heard her swear.

When she went back to get the neglected child, she was accompanied by the chairman of the poor relief board. This time Mickel Larsson mostly kept silent. He was clearly good at that too. Hillevi tried to strike a conciliatory note.

It can't be easy to care for a child with no womenfolk in the shelter, she said.

They had some ground beans with them, which made him congenial enough to light a little fire under the coffeepot. By the time he had a cup of hot coffee in his hands, he was saying it was just as well Risten was taken down to the village.

Why's that? Hillevi asked, astonished to find him conceding so easily.

She's not a full-blood Lapp, he said. Not really.

Taking her away, they discovered she was strong-willed. She screamed until the shelter and the barking dog were out of sight and earshot. The old man had disappeared.

She was physically strong too, despite being undernourished, as Hillevi found while bathing and delousing her. The sores had healed but left nasty scars. She put her to bed in the empty nursery. Unfortunately the pretty room frightened her, particularly the picture of mother and child. At first Hillevi thought it must be that she'd never seen a picture before. So she took them all down, but the little girl started screaming again in her loud shrill voice. Hillevi carried the pictures in and out until it became clear the girl only wanted the ones with the cross-stitched dogs to stay.

She's certainly got a mind of her own, Hillevi said to Trond when the girl had finally fallen asleep.

She was clearly afraid to sleep alone, so Hillevi sat with her until she finally dropped off, her face swollen and red after tantrums and tears. In the morning Hillevi found her curled up on the floor in the far corner of the room. She'd moved there with her blanket and pillow, and when Hillevi lifted the blanket, she found Sissla sleeping beside her.

That spring Trond's grandfather was to turn eighty. He'd been very sickly for a couple of years though and was slowly wasting away. Late one April evening Morten Halvorsen phoned to say they'd better come right up if they wanted to see him alive one last time. Trond wasn't sure they could get through; the roads were going so muddy.

He's working the edge of the sheet, said Morten.

That was a clear sign he didn't have much time left, so trusting to God, they set off in the sledge the very next morning.

Morten had been telling the truth. The old man's hand was ashen, the skin translucent. His fingernails had grown long during his illness. It was the claw of a bird of prey working the sheet, picking at the wide lace edging.

He was stronger than they'd thought. Like the many clocks in the house, his old heart went on ticking in the silence. Sometimes he raised his wan eyes and looked at Trond, who leaned forward and called his grandfather by name. A moment later he would drift off again.

There was tension in the air up there at Lakahögen, though the old man didn't notice it. The local shopkeeper went bust while they were there. Morten Halvorsen and his father had some timber dealings with him, and Trond suspected that the bankruptcy would affect Morten as well.

Morten seemed not to want to face either bankruptcy or death, and he left in spite of the bad roads, saying he had to pick up a car he'd bought in Östersund. They expected him back in a few days, but instead he telephoned from the inn at Lomsjö. He'd crashed the car but wasn't hurt. He'd get a ride home with a wagoner who was coming that way.

Tension, tension. The old white fingers picked and picked. But did he have any idea what was going on around him? Trond called out his name softly, but the only response was a fluttering of the eyelids. In the end Trond had to go back and see to the store. Hillevi was left with the old man; she nursed him for nearly two weeks. His thin body had terrible bedsores that were beginning to get infected. She sent for an inflatable rubber ring to put under his meager buttocks but was afraid it would be all over before the ring arrived.

She had never been parted from Tore before. He plays with the Lapp girl and is much noisier than he ever was on his own, Jonetta reported on the telephone. Hillevi was a little disappointed he didn't seem to miss her. He'd only been unhappy for an hour or so, according to Jonetta.

Efraim Efraimsson died one May morning when the meadow was full of thrushes migrating north. Hillevi had help washing him and laying him out in a cold room. They agreed on a coffin Trond ordered from Östersund. Morten Halvorsen, who had lived under the same roof as the old man, was strangely withdrawn, and she wondered how much money he had lost in the shopkeeper's bankruptcy.

She had to travel home the long way around, riding with passing wagoners. What with the spring snowmelt, the roads through the woods down to Blackwater weren't passable. Trond came and collected both her and the wreck of his father's automobile at Lomsjö.

The innkeeper's wife set them a table in the dining room, where they were the only guests. Loud voices filtered through from the taproom along with gusts of tobacco smoke and hot air from the stove every time the innkeeper's wife came through the door. Things hadn't changed. But Hillevi felt it was a whole lifetime ago that she was there, freezing cold and hiding her chamber pot behind the curtains.

Trond had also applied to the Royal Swedish Government that year for permission to change his own and his family's name to the Swedish spelling, Halvarsson. The application had been granted, and he had just picked up the new stationary for the store. He had a sheet to show Hillevi at dinner. The header said *Trond Halvarsson* in big embossed letters. Under it, in print resembling fine script:

We stock:

Groceries, Provisions
Dry goods,
Woolens, and Notions
etc.

There was a line with *Mr.* followed by a dotted line for the name and a line with *Debit*. Trond left the sheet on the white gravy-spotted tablecloth, so of course the innkeeper's wife had to take a peek. She called it ever so grand, and heaven only knew how much implicit criticism that remark contained.

She had already made Trond uncomfortable with her lighthearted report about his father's car accident. She told them people were calling the spot where he went off the road Halvorsen's Flip. Well, of course they would make fun of him, but that wasn't really fair. The car hadn't actually overturned; it had just slid right off the road into a potato patch. Of course they would have loved to see Morten go bust just like the shopkeeper in Lakahögen.

But *Halvarsson* wasn't in nearly as much trouble as Halvorsen. Trond's position would be very stable once his grandfather's estate was settled. Hillevi felt they'd come a long way from flips and other even more incriminating rumors. A new era was beginning and not only for themselves. There was finally a real road from Röbäck to Blackwater, so it was no longer necessary to row across the lake with goods and the mail during the months you couldn't go through the woods by sledge. Morten had been furious about his car going off the road, saying he'd never sit behind the wheel again as long as he lived. Trond was going to take it over so he could get to town quickly and easily for goods. And he would be able to take passengers too. It had both a cab and space for goods. At home a post office was set up down by the bridge.

Now travelers would pass through more often; they'd use the new road, maybe come by car, and the world would be a different place. Less confined. Freer and more open. Perhaps even cleaner. Disease, slander, and old ingrown hostility would be things of the past.

Trond wasn't equally enthusiastic. He said sorrowfully that a great many other things had passed with the Laka King, his grandfather. He couldn't really pinpoint though what those things were.

In bed that night he put his mouth to her neck, his arms around her waist, and pulled her bottom close. He lay there and talked to her about his grandfather and the long trips they had taken together when he was a little lad. In those days they'd ride behind a team of domesticated reindeer with Trond wrapped in layer upon layer of furs. The stars shone above them, and the northern lights rippled and fluttered in the sky. He thought they were at the center of the world.

I imagined my grandpa had power over everything, he whispered. It sure did seem that way.

The Laka King had known people who moved easily between the two seas. Now Trond would be able to travel by car to whichever of the coasts he pleased in a few hours. But it wasn't the same kind of ease.

Tore was nearly four now, and he still slept in the long narrow closet by their bedroom. It had a diamond-shaped window and a ceiling that slanted sharply under the eaves. Hillevi left the door ajar at night to hear him breathing. Now and then Trond would go and close it, quietly but very firmly. Those nights he didn't have the least little grain of snuff on his teeth either, and she blushed in spite of being married.

Ingir Kari Larsson's little girl slept in the nursery now. Unfortunately Jonetta, who had looked after the children when Hillevi was away, had let her have Sissla in bed with her. It was, she said, the only way to get her to stay there. Now she was no longer afraid of the bed, but she refused to sleep without the dog beside her.

With her blue eyes and her red hair, she didn't look like a Lapp; she looked like a troll. A changeling. And what a temper she had! She insisted on being called Risten in spite of Hillevi telling her it wasn't a real name, that her name was really Kristin.

From the beginning she hadn't known a single word of their language. She went around calling Laula Anut, by which they guessed she meant Anund Larsson. Hillevi thought laula must mean uncle, but Verna Pålsa said that it didn't and that it was probably just baby talk.

Jonetta, who was now married to that Lapp of hers, said she'd been told Laula meant sing.

Perhaps the little girl had said that to her uncle: laula Anut! Sing, Anund! Or perhaps she'd called him Singing Anund. It didn't really make any difference now that Anund Larsson had gone off to Norway. Who knew what he was up to there. And the old man on the mountainside wasn't likely to ask for her back. He never came down any more. Trond said he'd lost heart.

Hillevi felt strongly that Kristin Larsson should be put up for adoption and found a good home. In early summer a childless couple from Östersund came to look at her, a well-to-do customs official and his wife. These solid people sat in the dining room drinking coffee and observing the children at play. But when they were on their third cup, the woman said she thought the girl seemed terribly Lappish, and the customs official nodded in agreement. Hillevi spoke before she could think:

But she's not! Not really!

She was ashamed when she realized she was spreading Meat Mickel's made-up story. But she was infuriated. Who did these people think they were? What gave them the right to come into the shopkeeper's home and inspect the merchandise, twisting and turning and then saying she wasn't what they had in mind? In front of the child no less. And she was no fool.

Attentive and quick, she had already picked up quite a lot of their language. She wasn't exactly a beautiful child. Neither was Tore for that matter, though for a long time Hillevi insisted he was cute.

Mr. and Mrs. Customs Official left without making a definite decision, saying they'd be in touch. Hillevi didn't believe a word of it, and indeed they never heard from them again. Trond thought they should phone and ask, but she refused. Later in the summer the chairman of the poor relief board said a homesteader from Byvången and his wife were keen to come and have a look at the girl.

Trond came in from the shop to tell her, and for a long while they sat quietly looking at each other across the kitchen table.

It was awfully unpleasant the last time, Hillevi finally said.

Shall we put them off?

Yes, good idea.

And one thing's for sure, she said. That little girl's brought us good luck.

She gave him a veiled look, and Trond asked innocently:

How so?

Month after month she had been disappointed. She hung her sanitary napkins out to dry down by the boathouse when she did the washing because she didn't want anyone to see them from up at the shop. It wasn't just that she was embarrassed about that kind of laundry. The worst part was that they were tangible evidence of her failure to become pregnant again. They had made it visible every single month for all these years. Her first pregnancy had taken her completely by surprise, so she'd been sure it would be easy in the future as well, maybe even far too easy. But it hadn't happened. Not until now.

We're going to have another baby, she said. I think the girl must have something to do with it. Taking in a foster child can have that effect. It's well known.

Then we'd better hang onto her, said Trond with a smile.

How many people remember Jonetta? She lived in the house now known as the doctor's. Before, it was the teacher's. And before that, Aagot Fagerli's.

But Jonetta's father bought that little house for her, and at the age of thirty she could finally marry Nisj Anta. Anders Nilsson as they said down here. His real name was Antaris.

You might say she finally dared; her old grandfather had been against the match, not because her betrothed was a Lapp but because he was penniless. Once the Laka King became sick and powerless, her father decided to intervene. Antaris and Jonetta had been together for years of course, but covertly, and people had laughed at Morten Halvorsen behind his back because of it. Now he gave them permission to tie the knot on one condition: he didn't want Jonetta to live the life of a nomadic reindeer herder. And when Fransa's widow died, he bought them the house up by the ridge.

Antaris said at once that the house was no good; it might even be dangerous. Morten thought he was just full of crazy Lapp notions. But Antaris insisted there be a reading for the house. Jonetta, embarrassed, said all right if he insisted, but he didn't have to tell people about it.

I learned all this from Hillevi. However peculiar it may sound, she was there when one of the Lapp wise men came from Norway and read for the house.

And here comes the weird part.

Jonetta only had six years in that house by the ridge. She lived long enough to plant the rosebushes the doctor takes such pride in. She planted Arctic root and yellow stonecrop and baby's breath in the cracks between the rocks on the steep hillside. And the yellow globeflowers that blooms in the spring. It was as if she wanted to bring the mountain down to the village for Antaris's sake. She even tried growing angelica, but it never took root.

Not until a full year after Jonetta's death did Antaris explain how he had found out the house was a dangerous place.

The first time he came there was in October. A trace of early snow lay on the sloping meadow. In those days it wasn't tufted and overgrown but kept in check by grazing animals and scythes. He walked up the long hill glancing as he reached the top in the direction of the cowshed. A woman was standing there. She had her back to him but looked over her shoulder once. He couldn't tell what she was doing.

It was all very odd. The woman wasn't anybody he recognized. She was handsome, he said, tall and thin. For a moment he'd even thought it might be his sister-in-law Aagot Halvorsen, the one who'd gone to America when she was just seventeen.

He started to approach her, but she walked away. She just glanced at him and headed up the ridge. He wasn't pleased; the house was Jonetta's legal property after all. If the woman wanted something, she should tell him what. But she just walked off, faster and faster. He strode after her, his steps longer than hers but not as quick. Strangely, it didn't occur to him to call out; it was as if something was keeping him silent. A kind of fear he said. Actually.

They passed the privy, which was falling down, and the widow's rubbish dump where her false teeth lay grimacing. He thought perhaps the woman was a relative of the late widow, someone who had come to see if there was anything left to collect.

He picked up speed, but the woman began to shrink. He was so mystified he just stood stock still, watching as she grew smaller and smaller, soon the size of a doll. As she swayed along the path, he began to realize what he had met up with. Then he didn't dare keep on following her. He was right: when she got up to the top of the slope, she changed shape.

She turned into a grouse hen, he said.

The woman who had shrunk to doll size and then become a grouse slipped in among the trees and vanished. Antaris went back down, not bothering to look for her tracks in the newly fallen snow. He knew the only tracks he would see were his own.

Gufihtar, he said she was called. Anywhere she turns up is a place to stay away from, he said.

Well, be that as it may, that house certainly didn't bring happiness. It didn't help that Antaris built a barn down by the road and tried in every possible way to become a farmer and a permanent settler. They had summer grazing land for their livestock on the other side of the lake, and Jonetta rowed over twice a day in summer to do the milking. By that time she was already tired and worn and her skin had started to go brown. She lost all her strength, and then she died.

I asked Doctor Torbjörnsson about her illness. Did he think it could have had anything to do with the house? I didn't dare say anything about dead people who haunted houses where they had lived, but I asked if she could have fallen ill from dampness in the walls. Or if there could even have been some poison in the wallpaper.

He said he didn't know. But he asked me a lot of questions about what Jonetta had been like before she died: he said it sounded as if it could have been a rare condition affecting the adrenal glands.

The doctor gave me a lift home after Myrtle's funeral. When we got to the shop, he asked if I really felt like going down to the house all alone.

Why don't you come up with me? he asked. At least for a while.

I knew I'd have to go back to my solitude sooner or later, but I was happy to postpone it for a while.

I stayed at Torbjörnsson's until evening. We watched the seven-thirty news and he made tea and we ate the leftover sandwiches from the funeral reception. I'd brought them back with me. We talked about Myrtle's illness and about things from long ago—Jonetta and all that. But he knew so little, he said.

In spite of being district physician for many years and piecing together all the stories I've heard about people and their illnesses. Because they're also the stories of their lives, he added. Of our lives.

He couldn't say either why Myrtle had had to die.

They did everything they could for her, he said. You can rest assured of that, Risten.

I suppose so. She had chemotherapy up there at the hospital in Umeå and radiation. But none of it helped. And of course I do know: our lives on earth are only brief loans.

Aagot came home from America the year Jonetta died. She bought the house from Antaris Nilsson who wouldn't have gone on living there for anything, understandably enough. What's more difficult to understand is why Aagot, who had lived in a big house in Boston and been housekeeper in a wealthy family, would settle down in a tiny cottage with nothing but a kitchen and bedroom. More than half the room the doctor now uses as a living room was a baking shed in those days, unheated when it wasn't in use.

Everything is so different now, although the timbered frame is still there and the windows are in the same place. Under the eaves, of course, the great tits and other little songbirds still huddle up on cold winter nights as they always have. There are still bats in the attic. An ermine has its den under the stone wall by the slope; I've seen him when I've been sitting at the kitchen table that was the teacher's before it became the doctor's. White in the winter, so only the black tip of his tail and his eyes are visible against the snow, brown in the summer with a creamy bib. I suppose he's a descendent of the ermines who scurried across the snow up here when I was a child.

Hillevi and her cousin Tobias were sitting at the kitchen table gazing out across the lake. The water was still. On the other side dusk had already swallowed Mount Brannberg. The dark mountains grew even darker.

Two whooper swans were floating softly, almost as if they were asleep, although they hadn't yet tucked their beaks under their wings. Their reflections were broken up by a red band from the western sky.

Tobias drank the last of the coffee in his cup, setting it in the saucer so carefully she realized he felt it would be a shame to break the silence.

Time stands still here, he said.

The bird-hunting season ended, and he returned to Uppsala, but she would always remember this. She would really make an effort to sit by herself for a few minutes every day at dusk. He had called it letting the dark fall on your mind. But it was difficult to find the time.

She received a letter from him.

Do you remember that Alpine glow we watched from your kitchen window? Do you still sit there in the twilight taking it in? What a lovely habit—letting night come slowly down over your spirit while the mountains on the Norwegian side glow like the iron in a forge! Those views! The purity in that air I imbibed so greedily! You breathe it every day, Hillevi, I envy you! I walk around here inhaling carbolic acid. You live your life among those robust and honest men who for a couple of carefree weeks taught me the art of living. If only I could apply it here!

The water was just as black now but with a film of new ice over it, trembling when the wind rose. The sky grew dark earlier. In the west the glow paled and was quickly extinguished. There was a thin sparse coating of snow on the mountaintops.

Now she could no longer see the glow of the light in the ice. Perhaps the thin layer would crack if the wind picked up early in the morning. It wasn't yet really autumn-winter.

Time did not stand still.

He was wrong.

Time is a rushing stream, she thought. We roll in and tumble down headlong like logs being floated downstream.

She lit the kerosene lamp. The electric light came on so suddenly and was so brutal. Upstairs the children were running across the plank floor. Myrtle whooped with laughter. Hillevi heard Sissla padding down the stairs; she was getting old and no longer appreciated noisy play.

I must speak with Trond, Hillevi thought. But she didn't know if she dared. When she brought up subjects he didn't think were any of her business, he met them with a grim silence. Particularly if they were things she had heard in the village.

This time she had no choice though. This has to do with me too, she thought. Though he doesn't know it.

She got the embers to flare up and set the pot of water for their porridge on the stove.

He didn't come in until after nine. By that time she and the children had eaten, so she put out bread and some cold meat for him. He was pale with exhaustion.

He lay down on the kitchen settle to read the paper. Hillevi was heating dishwater in the pot, clearing the plates while it warmed up. The children were asleep. Now, she thought. I have to. For the children's sake as well. She said:

I heard you've lent Vilhelm Eriksson the money for two horses.

She was standing with her back to him and heard the newspaper rustle. He was silent for a few minutes.

I'll be damned, he said.

What?

The things people know.

I heard it at the guesthouse. It started with Bäret I think. But is it true? And that he hasn't been paying it off?

True enough, he said.

For the last five years!

The first one, he said. The second's only from a year back.

It was quiet for a while, and she thought: Now he won't say any more about it. But then she heard as the paper rustled:

Vilhelm's had such damn bad luck with his horses.

It sounded almost like an apology.

How much interest are you charging?

Three percent. If you must know.

He was angry. But she couldn't turn back now.

Your father charges seven!

The silence from the settle was so compact she didn't dare pursue the matter further. At least not at the moment. So she washed and dried the dishes and went upstairs and checked on the children. All three were asleep.

By the time she got back down, he was sleeping too, with the newspaper over his face, but her footsteps woke him.

Dozed off, he mumbled.

She knew he wanted to drop the subject, but there was no going back now. She had no choice; she had to get it out.

Vilhelm Eriksson's in debt for horse feed and provisions too. And tools! Since last year. What's going to happen? Will you let him keep buying on credit? What about the things he needs for this winter?

Well, they marked off his felling areas today. He'll never be able to pay us if he can't do the logging.

She knew that the teams had started parceling out the work. The logging drivers had picked their teams, and now the parcels were being numbered and lots drawn. Then they would decide where the strip roads would go and start clearing the undergrowth.

Whose team is he going work on? Surely he'll not drive one of his own?

Oh yes, I imagine he'll have to. It's the only way he can possibly turn a profit. And the family's big enough to make up a team now, Eriksson and his boys. We'll see how it goes.

They're nothing but youngsters!

Not the two oldest ones. Gudmund's twenty-two I think. And Jon's twenty.

The younger ones have helped with the floating before; they've cleared the banks for at least the last couple of years.

For half what a grown man gets.

He said nothing, picked up the paper.

You'll never see that money again, she said.

Although it was impossible to say any more about it right then, she was burning with the urge to press him. Still she didn't dare to bring it up again for some time. One afternoon Trond came into the kitchen with the man from Värmland who was his log scaler. They sat discussing the various parcels. Hillevi was at the stove clearing the coffee through a fish skin when she heard Vilhelm Eriksson's name.

That bastard, said the scaler. You shouldn't have stopped me, Halvarsson.

I think it was best. You mustn't fight when you're out marking the trees. Save your fights for Saturday nights.

Well, he was lying about me falsifying the measuring lists.

He wasn't talking about you.

That was all they said about it. But the minute the scaler said thank you for the coffee, picked up his documents, and left, Hillevi asked:

Was it you Eriksson was accusing? Of falsifying the lists?

Mmmm, something along those lines.

She saw his agitation.

Well, that has to be the last straw, she said.

But he didn't answer. She stood there with the fish skin filter in her hand.

Trond was the kind of man who, when he heard any bad talk about himself, turned it inwards and just clammed up.

She was quite sure he was ransacking his own mind. He might even be searching for some confirmation. But he was unlikely to find any this time: he was not a cheat. In the end his anger surfaced. She could feel it too. It didn't just flare up and die. Trond was a man who bore a grudge. He never forgot things that wounded him deeply.

This became clear one afternoon when Vilhelm Eriksson came into the store. Trond turned his back on him, took his coat off its peg, and went out.

Eriksson just stood there at the counter and then turned to Hillevi, although with distaste she could tell. He started listing what he needed, provisions for his men in the woods. He began with the pork.

She listened without saying anything. When he had finished his list, concluding with a lumber-marking pen and two iron wedges, he said:

Our Gudmund'll collect it all tomorrow.

I'm not sure that's going to be possible, Hillevi said. Just talking with him almost made her short of breath. She had always avoided the men from Lubben when they came into the store. Vilhelm had aged during the years that had passed since she had really looked him in the eye that once. He made her think of a wolf.

I'm not sure we're giving credit any more, she said. I'll have to ask Halvarsson.

Weak-kneed she turned around and started arranging the dry goods shelf. Only then did she realize they were alone in the shop. She heard him breathing heavily; then he spat out a wad of snuff. When he had slammed the door behind him, she sat down on a barrel. Her heart was pounding.

That evening there wasn't a calm moment until they were in bed. But then she said it:

I want you to demand payment on those loans and for everything he's bought on credit the last two years. This has gone too far.

Everyone thinks the Norwegian doesn't care about anything. He's an old loner, that's for sure. Says he doesn't give a good golldarn what people are up to nowadays. But with me he sometimes talks about the past. At those times I realize he's curious about this place he's ended up in. Allowed himself to end up in.

You could have lived in Italy, I say when he curses the winter. Or the Bahamas. You could afford it.

He just scowls.

The water is playful today. Little waves, sunlight gleaming. At least the earth is green and is still holding us up I think. Then I turn the radio off.

All the layers of the air, the cold ones and the warm ones, the dry ones and the damp ones, the deep stretches of cold water in the lakes, the glimmering surface, the mountains and the marshes with their patches of sunlight, their little quilts of gold, all of them are friendly toward us today. The gentle morning light, the darkness that is to come, that will inevitably come, and dawn and dusk and leaf and grass and woods, and the animals who wander there, today it's all lively and friendly. The earth holds us up, and we walk upon it easily.

But I know that the earth is a threat to us as well.

Cold and hunger can catch up with us. We can be pulled down by the quicksand in a bog. A knife can slip. Held by the wrong hand, it can stab. We can bleed to death.

We fall ill; we experience deeply traumatic events. It certainly isn't easy to talk about them or about how it was to give birth to children, to bleed and suffer to be delivered of them.

But we each live our story, however difficult it may be. That is the only thing a person can do.

Others respond to our story. I told him that: nothing is truly lived or experienced until we have told someone about it and heard responses to our story.

He just glared at me. A mocking stare. I was eager, excited about this thought of mine, and said in my opinion there's something about people's stories that can't be wiped out, even when memory fails and physical objects are gone.

Something found in stories and only in stories, I added.

Aha, he said. And I thought you were religious.

He went on mocking me. At first he sounded serious enough, but it turned out he was being sarcastic. His voice went harsh as he told me what lies stories are, how everyone lies to make himself seem better. We all do it when we talk about ourselves; it's inevitable. The memories we recount with such dead certainty are nothing but fragile snippets that disintegrate the moment words touch them. Words transform them instantly into lies.

A person is alone in the world. Has nothing in common with others. Nothing but this talk, the stream of lies flowing out of our mouths.

Then he sat silent for a long time, seeming tired and deep in his own thoughts. I boiled a little coffee for us. Although he came from somewhere else and has been all over the world, he prefers his coffee the way we make it, boiled. When we'd had some and he'd perked up and looked less ashen, he asked about Lubben and about the people who'd lived out there in the old days. At the far end of the point, at Tangen.

That was the Erikssons, I said. We called the grandfather Old Man Lubben. He came to a dreadful end.

How so?

I said I'd tell him the whole story, from beginning to end.

From the beginnin', he jeered. What do you know about that?

I know that the Erikssons were deeply in debt at the shop, I said. And there were loans for horses too. My foster father'd lent them money. But in the end things went too far.

Vilhelm Eriksson had some bad luck. Or whatever you might call it. He took his lads with him as a logging team to keep the profits in the family. He'd had two rough years, and his debts just kept growing. Now he had to make up for it all. But the boys were too young and not strong enough. No matter how hard they tried, they couldn't keep pace with the logging, the competition, or the fight for cubic feet.

It was cold that winter, which made it difficult to bark the trees. All evergreen trunks had to be barked, and the Eriksson's parcels out by the border stream and up on the ridge were covered with pine.

Old Man Lubben went along and did some logging or driving when he could. But he couldn't put in full working days because he had to look after the livestock at home. There was no woman in the household that winter. Bäret was in Skuruvatn tending her mother, bedridden with consumption.

The boys worked hard, trying to be grown men. But the day the timber cruiser stood there on the ice with the counting board in left hand, punching a hole in the paper for every tree trunk, the truth was revealed. It had all gone to hell.

Two women spoke up for the Erikssons. First there was Aagot, who swished in wearing one of her coats from America. She said she was just stopping by. Because she'd never stopped by before, Hillevi suspected ulterior motives. But she couldn't understand what made Aagot go out of her way for Vilhelm Eriksson.

What're the folks out at Lubben to you? Hillevi asked her outright.

Of course she didn't answer. She just sat on the couch in the front room with a coffee cup from their finest china in front of her and looked around. Her gaze was like that of an estate administrator. The gramophone made her smile. Hard to know why. Was it not big and American enough? Or too showy for a village like this?

They'd never gotten along. Aagot had nagged her father until he gave her the money for a ticket to America so she wouldn't have to be Hillevi's housemaid. That was how she put it. They had Norwegian relatives in Boston, so Morten Halvorsen had allowed her to go. She started out lending a hand at her aunt's guesthouse; later she was taken on as a housekeeper in a well-to-do family. Everyone was surprised when she came back home and moved into the house that had been her sister's.

The kitchen table up there was the same one. It seemed to attract the same kind of people too. There was always somebody having coffee, just as in Jonetta's day. Aagot didn't do much; there was no need. She had the money she'd inherited when her grandfather died, and oddly enough she received money from the U.S. Every single month. This was the subject of a great deal of gossip, which started down at the post office of course. But Aagot had mastered the art of keeping her mouth shut when she chose.

Trond, who had taken the name of Halvarsson, wanted Aagot to take it too. But instead she applied to have her name changed to Fagerli after the village where her family came from. To people from out of town she always said she was of Norwegian farming stock. But she was also the granddaughter of the Laka King, and everybody knew it. In that respect taking a new name didn't help.

She'll probably get married anyhow, said Hillevi.

But it was difficult to imagine Aagot marrying anybody from the village. It wasn't just her hats or the coats with the machine-stitched buttonholes. There was something about her whole persona. She behaved in a way Hillevi would never have dared to. Like gentry. And at the same time she socialized with people Antaris Nilsson had dragged in. People the mild-mannered Jonetta

259

had never dared give a piece of her mind. She's being drawn down toward her origins after all, Hillevi thought, though she didn't say it to Trond.

She rejected Aagot's appeal in any case. Trond couldn't go on feeding the Erikssons from Lubben out of charity, year after year.

But what about the boys? asked Aagot.

The boys were naturally a problem. The poor always had so many children. She said Vilhelm would just have to get a job elsewhere. Like other people did.

Work? Other than in the forest? asked Aagot. What kind of work could he do?

That's not my problem, or yours either.

Aagot didn't appear to have the slightest idea of all Hillevi had done over the years. In addition to visiting the sick. Food baskets when times were hardest. Hand-me-downs. Free medicine.

Women came to Hillevi with their aches and pains, for some drops to ease them. One said she was out of breath all the time; another felt nauseous from the moment she got out of bed and all morning long. No one wanted to admit to exhaustion. Better to say some unidentified illness was making your head spin. She knew their symptoms now and the words they used for them. And she also knew that the real names of those conditions were malnutrition and overwork. She couldn't help them enough. Even if we gave away everything we have, she thought, what good would it do?

And it wouldn't be right.

Still Hillevi felt bitter that no one had told Aagot she gave people food and old clothes and medicine. It was embarrassing to have to say it herself. But on the defensive she said she'd helped a lot of people over the years.

Not the people out at Lubben, Aagot replied.

The second woman was Bäret. She came after Trond had finally decided and had talked to Vilhelm Eriksson. There she stood in the kitchen, wrapped in shawls and with her leather cap pulled down over her forehead, looking more or less the same as she had the first time Hillevi set eyes on her in the dim shop.

Speak with Halvarsson, said Hillevi. He manages his own affairs.

Mrs. Halvarsson had something to do with this *affair* if you ask me.

She had a particular way of saying the word. And she just kept on standing there. Hillevi didn't know what to do. So she turned her back to her and started filleting salted herring on some newspaper. It seemed Bäret stood there forever; it was so quiet she could hear her breathing through her open mouth. If only the children had been around. But Tore and Risten were at school, and Myrtle was playing quietly up in the bedroom.

Bäret finally left. Hillevi's knees buckled under her when the door finally shut. She sat down at the kitchen table, head in hands. Her fingers smelled of herring. She would have liked to have a good cry, but she couldn't. Then she heard the front door open again, and she got quickly up and smoothed her hair thinking with annoyance now my hair's going to smell of herring, to boot. Everything was going wrong, big things and small. When she turned around, Gudmund Eriksson was standing in the kitchen doorway. He didn't remove his cap.

What do you want? If you've come for your aunt, she's already left.

He didn't answer. She looked out through the window with a view of the shop and the road; she could see Bäret sitting in the wagon out there.

What is it?

My pa told me to send word to you, he said.

I've no say in this. Halvarsson's already spoken with him.

We know. But my old man said to have a word with you. Alone.

I can't do anything.

He was tall like all the boys from Lubben. Fair and coarse. His half-lowered eyes never left her face.

My old man says you'd best beware, he said. He told me to tell you that.

Is that a threat?

He sneered.

Foureyes'll catch up with you in the end, he said. My old man said to tell you.

Then he turned on the heel of his heavy work boot and left.

She found it upsetting not to know what he had meant. She couldn't ask Trond when he came in. When it came to the people out at Lubben, she couldn't say anything now.

She didn't know of anyone called Foureyes. They had all kinds of strange names for people. Quickie and Ohno. There was even somebody so thin they called him Kindling. But she'd never heard of Foureyes.

Later the same week she and Verna Pålsa were baking, and standing by the oven in the baking shed, with Verna rolling and herself putting the bread in and taking it out, she said as if in passing:

Foureyes, do you know who that is?

Verna didn't have the slightest.

Where'd you hear it?

I can't even remember, said Hillevi.

The girls were with them, rolling their own bread down at the end of the table. Risten said:

Foureyes is a dog.

Oh? said Verna. Whose dog is that?

I dunno. But my uncle says there are dogs with four eyes. They're called *Njieljien Tjalmege*. That means Foureyes, Uncle said. The way we talk.

Verna laughed.

That girl! she said to Hillevi. She doesn't miss a trick. Do you speak up like that in front of the schoolmistress too?

Nope, said Risten.

Trond was forty now and not always so cheerful. When she showed him Tobias's letter, he did laugh, though it sounded a little bitter. Sometimes Hillevi worried about him.

You're getting thin, she said. Not unwell, are you?

Consumption had claimed three lives out at Tangen that autumn.

Hell no, said Trond. I'm strong as a horse.

Hillevi thought it must be the logrolling association that was worrying him. He'd taken over his father's holdings in it. When they decided to broaden the portion of the river used for floating, Morten Halvorsen pulled out. Too costly, he said. But the truth was that he was abandoning his timber dealings more and more, selling out.

He's speculatin', Trond said. Suddenly it's all stocks and shares.

I mebbe ought to do some of that speculatin' meself. At least it doesn't take any work.

She couldn't tell if he was serious. His comment was unlike him, almost too caustic to be ironic.

You've got too much on your mind, she said.

Money's a stern master, he said. It sure doesn't make a man carefree. It's a real educator, I'll tell you.

Bitter words like those upset her.

Well, I don't think it's the money exactly, she said. I think it's the responsibility. You've got responsibility for the people here. Seeing to it that they have work and can make a living.

Well, everything's going to hell for the Erikssons now. And I certainly seem to be responsible for that.

You know what? she asked. You don't need to take responsibility for people like them. The best thing would be for them to leave this place.

But Ville and I were at school together.

He has to be at least five years older than you. You went to school with everybody.

This battle of words was actually unnecessary. She knew he'd made up his mind. The Erikssons' place was up for executive auction. But she pretended not to know since she'd heard it in the village.

It dragged on. Forever, she thought. But finally the day came, a Saturday in January. People went, as they did whenever something was going on. A preacher or an auctioneer, it was all the same to them.

She hadn't intended to go. But alone in the kitchen it suddenly struck her that Trond probably planned to bid for and buy Lubben. And who knew what would happen then? Decent man that he was, he would probably find it difficult to evict the Erikssons. He'd be likely to let them rent it or give them a long lease on both house and land. And what would be the point then?

So she headed out there after all. She had to dress the children warmly and take them along since the girl who helped her had asked for the day off. It's not like we have an auction around here every week, she'd said. But in fact there were auctions altogether too often nowadays.

It was a cold day with a clear blue sky. The children waddled ahead of her like baby chicks wrapped in shawls and scarves. The narrow track down to Lubben had been trampled down by horses and people.

She had only been there that once. Never again. Most of the time she didn't give the place a thought. She was afraid of Vilhelm Eriksson but had never imagined what he could do to her.

Or she to him.

He'd had a dog with a white patch above each eye. They'd looked like eyes. Foureyes. That dog had been dead for years now. No one knew that better than she did.

Walking down to Lubben in the sledge ruts, avoiding the horse droppings and keeping the children moving, though they were chatting and babbling and wanting to make all kinds of detours, the whole thing was completely unreal.

She started thinking about the girl, Serine Halvdansdatter. About whether she was still alive.

There were lots of sledges; the horses stood eating out of their feedbags. Someone was walking toward them leading a cow.

Imagine taking a poor confused cow out in the cold.

Let it be over soon.

The cabin was so small, smaller than she remembered it. People going in and out. Carrying in snow on their boots. Two of Eriksson's boys had climbed up into an empty sledge and sat there watching people carting off their things. They must have been about thirteen or fourteen but were so thin they looked much younger. Emaciated in fact.

What could anyone do beyond giving people jobs? The socialists, who were mostly found among the lumberjacks, said it was greed, pure and simple, that was behind everything. Whatever the bosses did, they did out of avarice and with evil intent. That was why their own plan was to take what the bosses owned away from them: the forest from the forest owners and the factories from the factory owners.

But that wasn't right.

You can't take what people own from them. Even Uncle Carl had said that in his day.

Those had been hard times too, though she hadn't known it. Well, of course she did know about the general strike of 1909.

She had believed that if people just got work and behaved themselves everything would be all right. But then came the hard times, a worldwide plague. How could it be cured?

People were carting things off that until moments ago had been the Erikssons' household possessions. A butter churn. A wall clock. They looked as if they had got some real bargains, but they probably had more or less the same things at home already. That old Norwegian churn of Mamma's, the clock ticking on the wall. An old woman came dragging a cover made from an animal hide. That was foolhardy; these children's mother had died of TB. Still it was more than ten years ago, maybe twelve. People's memories were short.

She could tell that the chattels auction was over; the tools had been sold as had the livestock, the sledges, and the wagons. The people who were planning to bid on the homestead itself had gathered inside. Trond must be in there.

Gudmund came out into the doorway and glared. Of course there were only men inside; she ought to have left. Although she had come to talk to Trond, she absolutely did not want to go in through that door. Never again. So she sent Risten in to ask Uncle Halvarsson to come out.

He appeared in the doorway, Risten pulling him by the hand.

Could I talk to you for a moment, please? Hillevi asked.

The bidding's about to begin.

His face was blank.

I need to tell you something, she said, although a lot of people were staring now. She knew what they were thinking: we can see who wears the pants in that family

It's important, she said softly.

So he took a few steps aside with her. She saw Jon over by the cowshed, an insolent look on his face. Neither Vilhelm nor the Old Man were in sight though. She took one last look at the door, standing ajar, thinking I will never have to see this place again.

Go have a look at the horses, she said to Myrtle and Tore, who had started clinging to Trond. Pappa and I have something to discuss.

Risten did as she was told, taking the other two with her. She could tell by the tone of voice when something was serious. She had a good head on her shoulders and always looked after Myrtle, who was timid and withdrawn. Shy, people said. It was good for her to be with someone who was plucky and assertive. Risten had carried Myrtle all over for as long as she could. Now she was too big, but she always held her by the hand when they were out. Tore traipsed behind. Hillevi wished he would make friends with the other boys at school, but they bullied him. They called him American Piggy. He paid a price for having a father who sold pork.

When the children had gone over to the horses, she took Trond by the arm and walked a little way with him.

I don't think you should bid on Lubben, she said.

He didn't answer. She knew she had embarrassed him by asking him to come out. This undoubtedly made him even angrier. If only he would say something!

I've never poked my nose into your affairs, she said.

I should hope not, he said, so sarcastically she was taken aback.

No, I know. You do your job, and I do mine. But this time I'm asking you to listen to me.

He said nothing.

I don't want you to bid on Lubben. It would be bad for us.

Bad for us? What the hell do you mean? Business is business, period. You were the one who told me to get my money back.

Never mind about that, she said. Do as I say this once. Don't bid on Lubben.

His tongue roamed under his top lip. He spit at his feet, a yellowish wad. He was usually discreet with his snuff when she was around. This didn't bode well.

He left her and went back in. Hillevi collected the children and headed home without looking back.

A few days later she heard in the shop that a timber dealer from Lomsjö had won the bidding for Lubben. She never dared ask Trond if he had bid and given up when the price went too high or if he had never bid at all. She knew he didn't want to talk about it.

The horses were big and steamy. People were dragging covers and chairs. There was a mutt tied to a wagon, hoarse from barking all day. When an old man started untying the rope, the dog bit his hand.

That man had bought the cart, I said, and wanted to drive it home of course. But the dog wasn't about to let him take anything from the farm.

The Norwegian just laughed at me. He didn't think I could possibly re-member any of it.

So you think I'm lying?

He laughed again.

You're fabulating, he said.

But I remember it all. I was nine years old. Then one night the store burned down.

Misfortune pounded on the door. Afterward I never found out whose fist did the banging. It was after midnight and we were all deep in sleep. For a few seconds the pounding rang out in the dark, meaningless. Then I became aware of the smell of the dog and the dampness of the bedding. We heard heavy, hurried footsteps, and I knew where I was. It was our stairs somebody was running down.

Mamma! Myrtle cried.

A gleam of light flickered against the wall and her face. She was crying, screaming, and we huddled holding hands in bed, with Sissla there too. Then Hillevi came running, and Trond shouted from downstairs:

Hillevi, my britches!

She left us instantly but the sound of his voice was comforting in its ordinariness. He wouldn't call for his trousers if we were all about to die. Sissla jumped off the bed and ran down the stairs barking hoarsely.

Hillevi came running back up when she'd taken Trond his trousers. She brought Tore in and told him to get into the bed with us too.

The shop's on fire, she said, and we could see she was crying. You just stay inside.

Then she vanished back down with a shawl around her shoulders. We sat still, Myrtle and I, holding each other's hands tight. We were cold and our palms were sweaty.

If the shop burns down, there'll be no food for us, said Tore. Nobody in the whole village will have anything to eat.

I told him not to be a fool.

Myrtle said, Now we'll be poor.

She was only five years old going on six. But she was more sensible and more of a thinker than Tore, who already went to school.

I told them to put on their sweaters and socks and take their blankets down with them. I knew the kitchen would be cold and no grownup would have time to light the stove.

We climbed up on the kitchen counter by the window, where we could see the shop. Huge flames leapt toward the night sky; we heard them roar. There were lots of men running around in the snow; the fire illuminated their black clothing. We wrapped ourselves in the blankets and sat watching as they started pouring buckets of water straight in through the windows. Trond was running around with his nightshirt hanging out of his trousers. He was the only bright one, in white. Soon Hillevi brought out his overcoat and his fur cap and then he too became black.

It was a cold night. Twenty-six below Hillevi said afterward. We watched the whole shop burn down. The flames were like those you can see in a huge boiler, not like the ones we used to draw with our yellow and red crayons. The fire was that special color only fire can be, with lots of different hues at the top of the flames, bright blue as bluing and the same green as tarnished brass candlesticks. We saw coal-black flakes of ash float down on the snow, so fragile they broke to pieces when they landed. Sparks sprayed up from a spot that had been black a moment earlier. We heard the kerosene kegs explode, and when the windowpanes shattered we saw the shards of glass rain down onto the snow, which was growing blacker and blacker. Men ran back and forth with buckets. There were so many people now they formed a human chain down to the lake where Trond had broken up a hole in the ice. Haakon eventually arrived with Sooty harnessed to a wagon containing the fire hoses that were stored west of the bridge. But nothing helped.

We sat on that counter for hours. In the end we were stiff despite the blankets we'd wrapped ourselves up in. Our noses were cold. Myrtle wept almost the whole time.

But afterward we weren't poor.

That night Erik Eriksson from Lubben crossed the lake. At least that's what most people thought afterward. His tracks led from the boathouse below the shop out along the south shore and Mount Brannberg. But in the flurry of activity that followed the fire, no one had time to trace them.

Milder days arrived. New snow sifted down over the soot around the burned-down shop. The deep tracks in the crusted surface of the snow on the lake began to thaw, only to be covered with new snow.

A couple days after the auction, Vilhelm Eriksson and his two eldest sons

Gudmund and Jon had left the village. They went looking for work in Norway. The younger boys went to Jolet with their Aunt Bäret; their mother's relations had promised them a roof over their heads for a while. But jobs would still have to be found for them, and that wouldn't be easy.

Nobody knew what had become of the old man.

One Sunday morning a young fellow who lived out at Tangen, whose name incidentally was Nilsson though people called him Jo Nisja, was skiing across Blackwater Lake to see if any grouse cocks were roosting at the tops of the spruce trees on the other side. Nobody ever heard any shots fired though, and he was back within a couple of hours.

He'd discovered Old Man Lubben in the ramshackle hut where people said he'd been born. The corpse was stiff as a board. The people who skied out to collect it said his heavy knitted vest had reeked of kerosene.

When I told all this to the tall thin old fellow they call the Norwegian, he sat quietly for a long time, and I thought he'd lost interest in hearing about things that happened so long ago. But I guess he was just thinking because after a while he asked:

Were you afeard of 'im?

I nodded.

I think we all were.

All the children?

No, everybody.

Is that so, he commented, stirring the dregs in his coffee cup absentmindedly. I poured him the last of what was in the thermos, but he didn't seem to notice this third cup. He sat gazing out across the lake that Old Man Lubben had crossed so long ago.

I s'pose we're all afeared of the truly poor, he said.

A poor man wants something we aren't prepared to give away. We try material possessions. We give him clothing, money, and food.

But he wants something else.

Get yourself bathed and deloused, we say to a man who has nothing. Learn to speak correctly. Clean your teeth and see to it that your trap doesn't stink. Do that and then we'll see.

But a poor man wants something from us without having to give anything back. He's that shameless.

Give me it, he insists.

You'll have to get rid of that rash on your face first, we say. And the nits in your scalp and the lice in the seams of your clothes. Get rid of the piss stink in your bedding and we'll see. I also want to hear you speak and speak properly.

But the poor man doesn't give a damn about what we want. He's not prepared to give anything in return. Underlying his complacency, beneath his hardness, beneath his whining and cringing is a taunting demand:

I want what you have.

Give me your humanity.

After they'd found Old Man Lubben at the foot of Mount Brannberg, the cold that had killed him returned with a vengeance. Tears turned to ice if you stayed outside too long. Hoarfrost no longer formed on the charred beams in the pile of ashes that had once been the shop. Everything was desolate and frozen, and the children stared out the kitchen window at the pitch-black rubble from the fire.

Hillevi was too exhausted to talk with them. She could just barely manage to get through her chores. When night came and it got even colder, she could hear the walls groan. She lay cocooned behind spruce logs with moss between the cracks, behind insulation and wallpaper. To her this shield against death seemed pretty damned thin.

Sleep eluded her. Her body stung and ached with fatigue, but darkness brought no relief. There was no one she could talk to, even if she'd wanted to. Trond was ever solicitous. But she was too worn out for his comfort or his explanations. She wouldn't have believed a word of it anyway.

She thought about Erik Eriksson, about his being dead. That dragged her up out of bed with a shawl around her shoulders, forcing her down to the kitchen to light the fire. It was just as well to warm things up a little since she couldn't sleep anyway. She stood listening to the crackling of the spruce kindling, imagining she was standing looking into the cabin out at Lubben. It must be empty and icy cold now.

She realized almost everything in the world is beyond our thoughts. But it's still there. Somewhere there was Serine Halvdansdatter, whom she'd tried not to think about for years. For that matter she might even be dead.

The boys were there. She didn't even know the youngest ones' names.

Outside the window the lake lay under a moon that resembled the sun-bleached skull of some beast. It looked evil. She saw the jagged black spruces on Mount Brannberg and thought about Erik Eriksson again.

When Myrtle woke up, the first thing she did was scurry to the window and gape at what was left of the store. There was just a little rectangle, as if nothing but an old outbuilding had ever been there. Tears rose in her eyes when she gazed at what had once been syrup and knitted caps and horsewhips and sweets. Each day she remembered something else that had been there, in what was now nothing but a mess of ashes. Hillevi had tried to comfort her. But after she heard about Eriksson lying there in that hut frozen to death, she had no patience with Myrtle's whining. She scolded her sharply, saying it wasn't exactly a national disaster that some flour, sugar, and snuff burned up.

At least Pappa still has his ledgers, she said. They're under the settle seat in the front room.

Of course Myrtle couldn't know what the cash book and the receipts and expenses ledger were, and Hillevi couldn't be bothered to explain. Risten had the patience however. She lifted the child down off the kitchen counter and deposited her on the settle next to Sissla. She gave her a cup of cocoa and told her there was no need to be unhappy.

But we're poor now, Myrtle sobbed.

Oh no we're not. Uncle Halvarsson still has his books where it says how much people owe, she said. And insurance too. He'll be getting money in the mail. Then he'll build a new store. So we aren't poor at all. You just drink up your chocolate.

At which Hillevi burst out:

No, some people never come out poor! Whatever happens they don't. It's just plain impossible for some people to come out poor!

She saw the children's startled expressions and could hear very well how shrill her voice sounded. She pulled her apron up over her face and slammed headlong into the closed front room door. Behind her she heard Myrtle gasp, give a little hiccough, and then start wailing again. Louder and louder.

Hillevi continued into the front room. Her head hurt. How stupid to bang her forehead on the door on top of everything else. Not to mention shouting at the children like a fishwife.

They just don't understand. They think everything we do is right!

The front room was dim and gray in the January morning light. Her deceased mother-in-law stared down at her from a portrait in a gray satin turban and a high-necked black dress with a heavy gold brooch over the lace inset. The crystal vases and silver-plated trays the girl had polished at Christmas gleamed on the sideboard.

She could hear Myrtle crying in the kitchen and Risten's efforts to comfort her with small talk. Hillevi remembered one time when she herself had sobbed so hard her whole body was shuddering. It had had something to do with Edvard—a christening at the hospital when he had just nodded at her as if she were a stranger. Not so much as a look or slight squeeze of her hand to indicate that they belonged together. His face had been tense, his handshake formal. That had been such a tragedy she'd gone to pieces and cried uncontrollably when she got home. Afterward she'd been all shaky, her breath nothing but gasps and sighs. The next time she saw him though, she was so ashamed of her own behavior that she hadn't brought it up.

Actually, her sobs had been nothing to be ashamed of. They had been wiser than she. But now that she really needed to cry she couldn't. She was caught up by her own emptiness and contempt.

Contempt was a feeling she found difficult to admit to. Wasn't she a kind-hearted person who saw the good in everyone? She was the understanding one, always ready to help.

Still what was all that kindheartedness, deep down, but a way of demonstrating that she knew best? Underneath it was a craving for power. And wasn't that actually a kind of contempt?

Well, whatever it was, it turned inward. There was no end to the feeling. *But as for me my feet had almost slipped . . .* Was that from a hymn? Leading straight down into the darkness. She wasn't thinking. She was seeing: rope and knife.

She just sat there on the couch in the unheated front room, getting colder and colder, unable to make herself go back to the children.

It was Sunday so the two older ones weren't even going off to school. She would be stuck with them all day. The worst thing wasn't Myrtle's tears and fears; it was Risten's face, wise beyond her years. She heard Trond come downstairs, heard their soft voices. Finally he came to her. He held her rigid body in his arms.

They decided Hillevi should go to Uppsala. She needed to get away. That was what Trond had said she wrote to her aunt. And it was as good a turn of phrase as any. She kept it close to her on the journey like a handbag: *I need to get away.* And Aagot will surely be able to manage the children with the girl to help her. I'll be able to sleep once I get there, she thought. And if I can just get some sleep everything will be different.

She hadn't been to Uppsala once in all these years. It was a long trip, and she'd always had so much to do. The shop mainly. And the children. When Uncle Carl died, Myrtle had only been a month old. She had missed both Sara's and Tobias's weddings.

Now she was of no use to her children. A mother who shouted was not a good mother. That Sunday morning, if not before, she had realized it was likely to end with her striking one of those soft childish faces that had always been so trusting. They looked out of kilter to her, like clocks that had been roughly jolted.

Getting away was more like going home. Uppsala felt familiar and welcoming despite all the years that had passed. Of course nowadays there were lots of cars. But horseshoes still clattered against the cobblestones, and the river water rushed by. The cathedral was still standing like a red stone rock face. Its shadows were cold and reminded her of Sunday mornings, going to church and sitting still in icy pews. She recognized the cries of the rooks and the noise in the air when the great flocks settled on the steeple for the night.

This is where I should have lived, she thought. A perfectly ordinary life. Here we understand and protect one another.

She protected Aunt Eugénie by pretending not to notice how far down in the world she'd come. It was most obvious when they sat in the drawing room that also had to serve both as sitting and a dining room. Her aunt had been forced to economize since her uncle hadn't exactly left his finances in good order. Tobias said they'd been living beyond their means for years. Now Aunt Eugénie was living in a one-bedroom flat at 7 Iron Bridge Road.

It was a strange feeling to watch her serve coffee from a silver-plated pot. There was something wanting and faded about her home now that it was no longer suffused with the scent of Uncle Carl's cigars, now that the heavy solid silver and most of the dark paintings were gone. Hillevi, to whom they had sent a gold necklace when Tore was born and a bracelet when Myrtle came along, experienced the strange sensation of being better off than her Aunt Eugénie. Hillevi's hats, made by one of the milliners in Östersund, were more fashionable than hers. To tell the truth, her aunt's were nothing but old worn-out bonnets. She still had one from the prewar days.

Aunt Eugénie boasted about a neighbor who was a baron, a certain Herr Monch, a proper-looking elderly gentleman whose ageing black overcoat shifted in shades of gray. His hat was worn with brushing. A few days later Hillevi realized that he lived in the garret, in lodgings intended for a student. Early in the mornings he would come tripping across the courtyard with a package wrapped in newsprint, taking it into the privy.

She couldn't sleep here either. It was no better. Her body no longer felt solid. It was like loose mesh. Cold weather and strong emotions swept right through it and caused the mesh to tremble. By five in the morning she would be sitting at the kitchen window gazing down into the courtyard, hoping her aunt wouldn't realize she'd been awake for hours. She was ashamed of her insomnia. She wouldn't hold up much longer and was tempted to ask for some bromide. For the first time she also began to wonder why her aunt had taken bromide for as long as she could remember. Even in the old days when they still had their silver cutlery and Uncle Carl slept by her side in their mahogany twin beds, Hillevi had carefully shaken the pills out of a brown glass bottle for her. They were little gray balls rolled in stag's horn powder. She was afraid of them now.

The time around sunrise and the following hour or two were the only time of day she felt more or less alive. She was alone then and felt less pressure to bear up. She did not need to smile, talk, or most importantly, try to fall asleep. The baron, to whose proximity her aunt clung in her reduced circumstances, crossed the courtyard quickly on his short legs. His newsprint-wrapped package, probably containing his bowel movement, dangled from a loop on his index finger. It would have been beneath his dignity to cross the courtyard carrying a chamber pot. Instead, early in the morning he pranced across with his packet. It was a farce. Her aunt's life was a kind of masquerade as well. The words *pauvres honteux* crossed Hillevi's mind along with the thought that the cup of poverty contained the dregs of shame even for those who were not starving.

Tobias finally saw how things were and brought her some sleeping powders in neatly folded packets from the hospital pharmacy. She enjoyed clinical sleep for four nights, battling the hangover for the same number of days. Then she decided to try to get through the nights without the powders but found herself in the same vicious circle of aching dry insomnia as before. Still her days were better. Looking back, she felt as if she had spent four days and nights drunk and numb.

As the days and even the weeks passed, the familiarity of Uppsala began to be a thorn in her side. She was impatient with her kin. She wanted their love but not their understanding, vast and treacherous as a marsh. She recalled the words *spiritual guidance*. She had heard Edvard Nolin use them, but she was bitterly aware of what kind of guidance that was: *leave unto God all that you, in your human frailty, cannot help.*

But God was the pale yellow skull of a beast. He stared at her out of his empty sockets at night.

During the day her own eyes were merciless. She saw her sister-in-law's fatigue after four childbirths in five years; how hollow, gray, and wilted her girlish face had become. She noticed the beet stain on the white tablecloth. Could smell when Sara was having her monthlies. Her desperate childlessness reeked. Listened to the clock in her aunt's silent parlor: one tick closer to death, and then another.

Some time in the second week of March she said goodbye. Trond would be going in to Östersund for the Saint Gregory fair, and she had decided to ride home with him.

At home she could no longer sit in the kitchen in the mornings when she couldn't sleep because the settle, the table, the sideboard, and the chairs had all been carried out and stored in an outbuilding. The kitchen was full of kegs and barrels. Until the new shop was built they were selling staple items from their kitchen and heavier goods from a shed Trond had cleared out. The hall smelled of kerosene, the larder of salt herring, and the kitchen itself of soft soap, dried fish, and coffee. Risten missed the lovely drawers from the shop. Their little girl was still beside herself with anxiety. Why was Myrtle so afraid of becoming poor while Risten, who knew true deprivation, wasn't? Is there a seed of anxiety inside some people at birth just waiting to sprout?

At any rate Risten was able to distract Myrtle and eventually to make her laugh. Now she was trying to teach her to read the names on the washing powder packages: Lux Flakes and Persil.

And high time too, she said. Who'd ever know you were nearly six years old? Let me tell you how I learned to read. One day I met my uncle outside the shop, and when he heard I was going to start school in the autumn, he told me we'd probably have "A" for homework the first day. That's what we had in the Lapp school, he said. I was bewildered as could be, having no idea what "A" was for. But I went home with a head full of "A." We wuz all real excited about startin' school and learnin' a thing or two. Though my pa said the only thing you learned in school was how to behave like a farm kid. All the learning he'd got was about Jesus from a confirmation pastor. He'd never been much for readin'. He did say it was a good thing to be able to do sums though, so's they wouldn't be able to go on cheatin' us Lapp folks.

Once my Uncle Anut told me that, I started thinking about "A," with "B" and "C" added in. I had one of those ABC books with the rooster on it, you know. I'd learned almost all the letters in it. And I'd worked out it wasn't enough to know that "K" stood for kitchen since it stood for Kristen as well. And that there were lots of words. I asked Hillevi for some others, and she said kindling. But she was always in such a hurry. You go out and play now, she'd say.

She had a shelf with books on it, but they were too hard for me. When I went looking for "K" words in the shop I found plenty though. And I didn't even have to ask anybody. You just had to open the drawers and see what was inside. Then you'd know it said kidney beans or kerosene or kale or knives. There was one with keys too.

So I started all over again and wrote it all down, even right off the tins.

Almonds, Aniline, Anise
Anchovies
Bay leaves, Barley, Biscuits
Baked beans, Baking soda, Binder twine, Broadcloth
Borax

There's a good word for you.

Risten wrote as she spoke. She had an aniline pen and a piece of graph paper. Myrtle stared.

Camphor, Coffee surrogate, Cinnamon
Currants, Calumet

Uncle Halvorsson gave me a pen and a piece of paper and every single day I wrote down my words from the shop. I kept a list now; he said that was the right way. In the morning I'd look in my ABC to see what letter I was supposed to be on that day. Some days I did two I was so caught up in it.

Damask
Dark chocolate
Dates

No muddle. I mean like gelatin, salt, tobacco, vitriol, ink, bay leaves, marjoram, licorice, figs, pigs, carded wool, pepper, candles, and brushes. That's just one big muddle.

Now she could hear Myrtle squealing with giggles. She'd forgotten her poverty.

Like I said, here's how you should do it.

Reddle
Raisins
Rutabagas

That's right, you get it.

Hartshorn
Hog casings
Horseradish

Tapioca
Tartaric acid
Tobacco

Sugar
Soap
Starch
Sardines
Snuff

Syrup
Salpeter
Quicksilver

That one's your very hardest letter. It's called kee-you.

The smells in the kitchen soon merged into one big cloud that began to resemble the smell of the old store. But it wasn't exactly a cheery place to be. The entire village came and went in their kitchen, and they couldn't even keep the floor clean from one evening to the next. There was no way Hillevi could go downstairs and sit on a sack of sugar or a keg of syrup and wait for the others to wake up. So she decided to start walking instead.

It was March now, nearly spring. The light glared in her eyes no matter whether it was a cloudy day with snowdrifts or the first hint of spring in the air. She had a pair of solid boots made for her by the cobbler who lived and worked in what used to be the inn. If she kept them well greased, the water from the melting snow didn't seep into the leather. Early in the mornings it was still below freezing of course, and what would later be slush crunched under her feet.

The first morning she walked along the road toward the sparsely settled and more distant area west of the bridge. She stood watching the turbines in the rapids for a few minutes, how their rotations were sometimes out of synch. Another poor fish must be stuck people would say when their electric lights flickered erratically.

The spruce trees looked black the way they always did when the snow was thawing. She saw two staring eyes and realized it was a marten. A second later he was gone. She could still feel his black gaze, hard as glass, as if it lingered on in the big spruces. Sissla hadn't noticed. She plodded along on legs that were slight in relation to her body, old and unhappy about being dragged out into the cold morning and the crunching snow.

Hillevi passed the house that had once belonged to the border rider, now dead. There was finally somebody living there again. It had stayed empty because people claimed it was haunted. Now the new customs official and his family had moved in, and he assured everyone he had not yet heard a single groan except for his mother's when she leaned over to lace her boots.

The hose house, as they called the fire station, was on the other side of the road. It was a hexagonal building, a communal facility. She recalled the pride of the men on inauguration day when the water from Black Reed stream had shot straight up out of the hoses. But when the shop caught fire, the water they produced was vaporized before it ever even hit the flames.

Those dawn mornings in early March when she walked the misery out of her body and seldom met a soul, she gained insight into the village. She realized that putting out fires might not be the real point of the hoses. That would have been an insane thought in the light of day of course, or if she had said it aloud. Nevertheless, there was something to it.

The hose house. The shooting range out by the river. The dance pavilion nearby. The post office on the ground floor of Elsa Fransa's house. The telephone switchboard at the inn. The power generator. The cables that drew the cattle ferry across to the summer pastures on the south side. Yes, even the paths and the roads, that special spruce tree you could seek shelter under, and the trails the herders made through the woods when taking the animals to pasture, all this was shared by everyone. It was the precise opposite of burnt-down buildings, stolen reindeer and fetuses buried in dunghills.

Long ago this had all been leasehold land where the farmers from Lomsjö fished and cut the wild grass to dry for fodder. They would row up here with their farmhands in October when the char spawned to put out fishnets. They would trap grouse and shoot partridge in the mating season and pick pails and pails of cloudberries. The land was far from unexplored when the first settlers came. People had been bringing their cattle up here to common pasture lands in the summers for a very long time. This forest was full of invisible agreements among people.

The farmers from Jolet were the first to use the grazing land up here. Röbäck parish had belonged to Norway back then, as had all of Jämtland in the days when King Sverre and his armed men made their way up from Värmland through the virgin forest. Risten's Uncle Anund figured the king must have ridden right through this very village on his way down to the wealthy Namsos valley to demand that he be reinstated on the throne. The youngest of his soldiers had drunk their mugs to the dregs here before their fast ships had hurried them on across Blackwater Lake with rows of oarsmen, and the king on sheepskin bolsters according to Anund. King Sverre's soldiers, the birchlegs, had passed right by Antaris Nilsson's cabin, he claimed. On hazy days you could still catch a glimpse of them occasionally. Their birchbark shin protectors gleamed in the mist between the trees.

Pure springs whose water brings good health. Sacrificial sites in the mountains. Moose pits. Pasture paths. They were all agreements in a language etched into the very earth.

She knew the first settlers had arrived in the 1760s. There were two families: one had claimed the hillside overlooking the inlet, the other the point out at Tangen. The only remaining trace of them was a big hay shed. People claimed they had had fallen out with each other about which family had the right to harvest the grass in the marshland for fodder. The very first summer they had cut the few precious blades of grass with the bent scythe they called a sickle. When the hay dried they had stored it in their newly built sheds. But in the autumn when the nights grew dark, one of the settlers set fire to the other's shed. Their goats couldn't survive the winter without hay, so that family had to move on.

The women had encouraged the feud, people said. But she didn't believe that. She thought they would have needed one another. The wives should have known the value of neighbors better than anyone. They'd have needed a neighbor to turn to if their fire went out. Or to get a little starter for a new batch of cultured milk. Not to mention the looms. It took four hands to string a loom, didn't it? And where else would she get some sourdough when her own bowl was scraped bare?

Every morning Hillevi walked away from what she regarded as the heart of the village. But she knew that to the people who lived farther out, where existence was more tenuous, the store was a treacherous place to which you sent your kids so you wouldn't have to show your own face. The shop was where you had to pay up. The ledger with the brown marbleized cover contained the truth about all your shortcomings.

One morning she made it all the way out to the edge of the village where a man called Gran lived. The little house wasn't visible from the road; there was a dangerous bog in between. He butchered and skinned animals for a living. She'd seen his kids but never his wife. People said that he threw the animal remains into the marsh and that a man from Lakakroken had supposedly disappeared that way too.

There were folks who preferred to be out on the fringes. Were they as terrible as some made out? Perhaps they simply belonged more to the forest and the marsh than the village.

She didn't walk out Tangen way. Not until one morning when she actually met another person on the road. It was Kalle Persa with his white beard and green-edged moustache. He was always as kind as could be, completely belying the story of the ill-tempered northerner. That day he offered her a perch. He'd laid nets under the ice and had just been to check on them. So she walked with him, and he gave her a big perch wrapped in used paper from the shop, and she took it home.

That was how she happened to end up out near Tangen after all. One very clear morning she went back again. She saw a gray shape scurrying along the slippery path to a privy after which people and settlements were behind her. The path was unplowed. Finally she got close enough to Lubben to see the cabin and the cowshed.

She never had the same kind of thoughts later in the day that she had on those morning peregrinations. Later the kitchen buzzed with chatter and everything the customers needed that was no longer in stock. She had to do her cooking in the little space there was, lay the table in the front room, and wash the children's stockings and underwear during the brief respites when there were no customers in her house. She detested having to do her chores in front of all those curious eyes. But there was no choice. Her insomnia and the cramped conditions tried her patience, but she hadn't been vicious with the children again. Now at least she got a couple of hours' sleep in the early part of the night.

She had sworn to herself she'd never go back to Lubben. But her feet led her there. She went in the morning darkness. There was hardly a glimpse of dawn above the woods.

Her body drew her. It was as if, against all better judgment, she was being pulled toward another body. But this had nothing to do with warmth. This was just forgotten pain wanting to surface again. Pain that was far too old was pulling her through the frozen slush without her really understanding why.

When she arrived, the daybreak had turned the snow blue. The buildings looked dark and heavy. Only gradually did the grayness of the timber emerge.

They had been empty for over two months now.

To what end?

To give me peace of mind, she thought. But it failed.

She began to realize that peace of mind was not something a person could achieve single-handedly. I should have told Trond, she thought. But no matter what, she knew she would have been deprived of the precious gifts of sleep at night and a cheerful heart. Oblivion and bustle and distraction. Quick thoughts instead of this heavy ravenlike circling around death and darkness. As if around a carcass.

She walked over to the cowshed door, opened it a crack, and felt the cold air inside exude its pungent odor. Not exactly life. Neither the warmth of cattle nor the wooly scent of sheep.

There was a great deal of snow. No one had shoveled or plowed. She had to forge her way through, making deep boot tracks. Anyone coming out here before it snowed again would wonder. But she no longer bothered about what people might say. Besides, everyone already knew the shopkeeper's wife wandered aimlessly in the early mornings. Let them think whatever they pleased.

Now the day was growing lighter, but behind the window all was black. She removed her mitten, exploring the thin bubbly glass with her index finger. Just a single pane of glass to keep out the cold. It must have been freezing in there even when the stove was lit. Cold draughts along the floor. The little ones must have spent almost all winter behind the doors of the cupboard beds. Where the TB bacteria thrived.

She remembered that the first time she had been out here she had come from the schoolhouse, where she'd been vaccinating children against smallpox. In those days she had been full of her calling, her training. She thought she had arrived as a gift to this distant parish and recalled clearly how proud she felt as she signed her name in the guest ledger of the inn at Lomsjö. Not to mention when she'd torn down the note someone had posted on the wall at the shop warning people of the dangers of vaccination. She'd carried that strong sense of purpose with her out to Lubben just as she'd carried her medicines, instruments, and clean towels in the birchbark rucksack.

All of it was scattered to the winds out here.

You don't need to take responsibility for people like them.

Did Trond remember her saying that? Probably, just as clearly as she did.

What did he think of her deep down?

She tried the door to the cabin and, as she had expected, found it unlocked. It was just about as bright or as dim as it had been the first time she stepped inside. Though that time it was evening and dusk was falling.

It was empty. Sold off and scattered. But the cupboard bed was still there, with the doors shut. She forced herself to open them and look at the empty bed frame. Then she walked straight across the uneven floor and opened the door to the back room.

How long had the girl been standing there? Had they sent her out there when they saw the meddling midwife approaching? Or had she been banished from their sight earlier?

She'd been standing here in the cold. The fetus's head had been too big for her narrow ricket-damaged pelvis. The baby.

It was a baby. A living child.

Whose beside Serine's?

She should have reported it. Then at least the girl would have been helped. But instead she had decided to spare Vilhelm and the boy named Elis. Though her real reason was to protect herself.

Well, I wanted to marry Edvard Nolin, she thought, so desperately I would have done anything to avoid getting mixed up in a courtroom trial.

She walked back more quickly than she had come.

On her way back from Lubben she knew exactly what she was going to do. She'd go home and make the coffee and take Trond a cup in bed. Then she'd talk to him before the children woke up.

I feel so terrible about all this, she would say. I feel as if I was the one who drove the Eriksson boys away from Lubben. Vilhelm and Jon and Gudmund too of course. But I think most about the boys. I'm not getting much sleep. I don't know if things will ever be all right again.

He would set his cup down and look her right in the eye.

I feel like I was the one who drove Erik Eriksson to set the store on fire and then walk out, she would say. Yes, to walk out on the ice.

And she would go on to say the words a person could hardly utter: to kill himself.

Because that was what he had done.

She knew Trond so well she thought she could imagine what he'd answer. That the old man had had plenty of disappointments. But that I was probably right anyway. Except on one point.

It wasn't only your fault. We were both responsible.

And then she would tell him about the thing they weren't both responsible for. About Lubben. About what happened there in 1916 as winter was turning to spring.

But she had been out longer than any other morning, and so Trond was up when she got home and had been dressed for ages. And he wasn't even alone. His father was down from Lakahögen on business and had spent the night at the inn. Morten Halvorsen had been drinking and playing whist until two in the morning. He reeked of cigar smoke and wasn't wearing his starched collar. She guessed it had got dirty during the night.

And it doesn't even bother me, she thought, realizing she was becoming a different person.

No, not a different person. You were always the same person as long as you lived. But shirts without collars were problems you came to take less seriously. Spots on vests and tablecloths. Gossip. Judgments.

There was a world of thoughts she had known nothing about. But you have to be sleepless at night to think them. They were out there. The forest itself thought them but always before people were up and about and had started slip-sliding their way toward privy and cowshed. The water and the trembling ray of dawn in the current thought them. Strangely enough they could also be thought here, right in the middle of all the chatter and the rattling of the coffee grinder. She hadn't known that.

In the midst of all the talk, while she was standing there lifting cookies out of a painted metal tin and placing them on a silver-plated tray with a lace doily in honor of her temporarily collarless father-in-law, she thought:

No, I will never tell Trond about what happened at Lubben.

They'd probably talk about the auction, and she might even tell him she felt bad about it. But she wouldn't tell about the baby. Or the icy water.

There are things you have to keep to yourself. She looked at Trond and his father having their coffee in the sitting room. The children had come down now and were clambering all over them. Morten Halvorsen pulled a paper cone of candy out of his pocket. They were all stuck together, and Tore was pulling them apart with not-quite-clean fingers.

Sometimes you have to shield yourself against those who understand you.

The next morning when she went out the temperature had fallen way below freezing. The moon was flat and spotted, a cracked plate the sky seemed to be trying to penetrate. Instead of walking on the road she went down to the boathouse. She stood there for a while, contemplating taking her skis. But then she stepped out onto the snow-crusted lake and knew the snow would bear her.

It didn't bear him, she thought. He walked out in the dark. The sky was clear and starry that night.

So she started walking in what were no longer his tracks. When she was right out in the middle of the lake, fear seized her. Her old ordinary self warned her what do you think you're doing?

But it was too late now.

The forest on the mountainside formed a vast rounded blackness sloping down to the edge of the frozen lake like a huge animal hide. The sky seemed more enormous than ever before. Even the Norwegian mountains bowed to it. She walked for a long time, knowing that she was no more than a poor little hare out at the wrong time of day, struggling through the whiteness on little legs. When she got closer to the south shore of the lake, it began to open up to her, very gradually and in an everyday way. Despite the height of the tall spruces, they were somehow on the same scale as she.

Not until that moment did she consider how difficult, possibly even impossible, it would be to make her way through deep snowdrifts and over the hard crusted surface up to the hut in the shadow of Mount Brannberg. But almost immediately she found a ski track made by a bird hunter. It was frozen hard and led her right to it, making her feel she had been destined to come there.

The snow hadn't fallen evenly on the shingled roof, and it had caved in. How had he even got inside this shambles of semi-rotten logs and boards?

There was a door, though it was no longer on its hinges. It was heavy. She tried to push it aside with her hands and arms, but in the end she had to put most of her body under it and throw all her weight into shoving. It dropped into the snow with a dull thud. Now the hut was open.

The stone hearth was made of slate slabs, large and small, that had shifted every spring when the snow melted. The stove was gone. What remained was a bed frame on short sturdy pine legs.

No kitchen utensils. Not so much as a frayed garment—just this bed of roughhewn logs. The light was forcing its way in, as the mosses and lichens had.

This was where he had lain down.

His life ended alongside a rough rock face.

His last deed before crossing the lake was evil. Surely he had wished the consequences would be more evil still. That it would be our undoing. That our children would suffer. That Trond and I would be at our wits' end with their hunger.

To die in such deep cold was probably not quite like going to sleep. It was different. What it was she would never know. Not even here.

The lice.

She found herself thinking about them. How they must have crawled away. They scurried out of his hair and across his cold brow, abandoning him.

When she was back outside, the disk of the moon was even paler. Like bone.

The skull of a beast?

A God with no charity, with no mercy. Who let life end in cold and evil.

She was tired, walking slowly toward home. The warmth of the rising sun was melting the crust on the snow. No doubt she would sink down time and again before she managed to cross the lake.

She retraced her own footsteps with great difficulty. The sky was white. It was so huge she couldn't bear it. The thought came to her, not all at once but gradually:

What if I am meant to be eyes for the great blind beast?

They said there was more light in the world than darkness.

They showed Elis their canvases from Normandy and Provence; one of them held up a painting made in Algiers.

Look at the light, they said. The vastness of it.

Not even on summer nights do we have such light. We're in the wrong place. We happen to live on the periphery of the world. We're sitting in one of its shadowy corners. When it's winter here our fingertips crack, and we get cold sores and headaches. You should go down to France, Elv, they told him. You'll see when you get there: the light in the world is more vast than the darkness.

But that wasn't true. It just wasn't right, what they said.

He looked at their paintings. As artists they weren't bad. And so the shadow weighed more than the light. It was smaller. But it had been compressed and gone black.

The sharper the light the blacker the shadow.

They talked. But they didn't paint badly. He watched what they did and paid no attention to their talk.

At the first sanatorium, the one called Open Spaces, Senior Physician Odd Arnesen gave him a box of paints and some brushes. The first thing he painted was for the doctor's wife; he decorated a window shade with two grouse surrounded by dwarf birch branches bursting into leaf. He was particularly successful with the grouse breasts. Later they gave him the leftover bits and pieces of wood from a building project. He acquired a bottle of turpentine, and the matron reluctantly relinquished a few white rags. For a whole autumn and winter he painted on those bits of wood. In May a charity presented him with a real *panneau*. The doctor, who had arranged it, came up to his garret studio to see how he was faring with the valuable gift. His comment was that the painting would surely be very nice once Elis started using all the colors in the box, not just mixing the black and white into shades of gray.

Elis, who was preoccupied with the problem of light at the time, suddenly felt almost contemptuous of kind Doctor Arnesen. He was shocked that the doctor had been unable to discern the colors.

That night he lay awake until nearly four o'clock, his muscles aching. He coughed more and more as the night wore on, disturbing the others. A nurse came tiptoeing in and administered some Dover's powder and a camphor pill for the sweating. What was keeping him awake though was what Arnesen had said to him.

Back in Lubben they'd beaten him for his dabbling. At the logging camp in the woods near Namsos, they'd praised his ability to draw such damn real horses and wood grouse. Arnesen's words were the first criticism he had ever received. Suddenly he was strongly aware of something he'd only sensed before: other people did not see the way he did. Sometimes he didn't think they could see at all.

The problems he was working on in those days resembled mathematical ones. Problem, of course, was a schoolmarmish word. Just like spiritual agony. But the problems he posed for himself had solutions. With hard work he would find them. At Open Spaces he worked on becoming familiar with weak light. Although he had been very close to drowning in them, he didn't yet know there was a term for "nuances."

In a combination of fury and fear after Arnesen's visit, he began to invoke what was under the haze of snow he had put so much effort into painting: it came out as soft blue-green and thickened into the edge of a forest. Carefully he allowed the hole to deepen. It was even more difficult to extract the figure; it was so difficult to suggest in a painting that a snow flurry, a fog, the water in a lake, or a distant forest could also be a creature, a human being. The result was either something entirely invisible or this; when the doctor came back, he still thought Elis was at some preliminary stage. He still didn't see the snow haze or the hole in the ice with its black water. What he saw was a spring in the woods. He saw a girl standing looking down into the water as if into an enormous eye.

You see nothing.

He allowed himself to think that again the next time Arnesen came up and stood close to him, talking kindly.

You know nothing.

The changes he'd made were trickery, pure and simple, and they won him a great deal of praise from the doctor.

He had turned the painting into a nude dairymaid getting ready to bathe in a tarn of black water. Two of her goats lay watching. Of the rest of the flock the painting only suggested one rear end and two cleft hooves. He figured the imagination of the viewer could fill out the landscape beyond the edges of the canvas.

Even in those days though he himself knew there was nothing beyond the frame of a painting. So he also knew he had duped Arnesen.

He had been extra attentive to the girl's pile of clothes, the dog that was guarding it, and the birchbark pack hanging from a branch. Later they made him put the clothes back on the girl, which required a lot of work on the body and the spot where the clothes had been lying. Well, why would she have wanted to bathe in an ice cold tarn anyway? With these modifications the painting was approved and hung over the mantelpiece in the big dayroom. They inaugurated it as part of an evening's entertainment. A woman sang a song out of Bjørnstierne Bjørnson's *Arne*. Elis expected her to sound like a braying fox. Most singers did. But as he listened, something inside him shattered. It happened when she sang:

> *I must get away—far, far away*
> *beyond the high mountains . . .*
> *Away from all this, so dull, so stuffy and cramped!*

Trembling with emotion, he suddenly understood about that kind of music. It shot into him and took up permanent residence. At that very moment he also realized how phony and ingratiating and bungled his painting was. He had to get away. Far, far away . . .

And away he got but only as far as the next sanatorium at Vefsn where, in a long period of apathy, he didn't touch the paint box. He did sketch though. That was when he developed his interest in the human skeleton, which wasn't strange, surrounded as he was by emaciated bony bodies. He began with his own hands, which he knew so well he could see the furrows between the tendons growing deeper with every passing day. Over the knuckles the skin stretched tight. He began to wonder how skin pulled over hipbones and started sketching in the washroom. Most people didn't mind. He began to see how consumption chiseled out the skeletons of men and boys; he developed a truly gifted sketching hand. He didn't feel much of anything. It wasn't his business to feel. His business was to see.

That spring he coughed up foamy red-streaked mucus; he was painfully aware of his own skeleton. When the cough strained and pulled at him, he thought his bones would burst right through the skin. He had to throw his arms around himself and hold on tight.

He was sent from Vefsn to a nursing home at Brønnøysund. That meant there was no hope. Only hopeless cases got sent to nursing homes. The ones who were responding to treatment remained at the sanatorium. But he continued to draw with a feverish intensity, possessed by an idea: someone has to see this.

Looking around at the others withdrawn into themselves, he began to think he and the doctor were the only ones who could see. The doctor ate. The doctor was strong and healthy. So Elis started eating again. Each bite turned to sawdust, went fuzzy, swelled up and stuck to the roof of his mouth. But he forced it down to have the energy to draw, and after some time his condition improved, and they sent him to Trondheim. They collapsed his lung there, after which he had to rest for a long time so it could heal. His skeleton became less conspicuous. But he knew it was there. Inside him there was a hard dead man.

That was why the art books weren't the first ones he looked at when they allowed him to go out and to the library. He studied anatomy from pictures in medical textbooks. Next he discovered the library of the Museum of Arts and Crafts. It was warm, and there were floor-to-ceiling bookshelves. He felt protected from the autumn rain and the raw cold. But it may still have been too much outdoor walking for him along the canal down at the harbor, sketching the sailing ships and small motorized cargo boats along the piers. He warmed up at the cafés, where he sketched other cold people slowly imbibing their coffee.

He probably ought to have kept out of the raw air and fog down there. Just when he thought the consumption was completely cured, his fever rose again, and his test results came back positive. This time they sent him to Kristiania, where he was eventually declared noninfectious. At that point he believed he had spit out his dependence once and for all and snapped the lid shut. Now he was going to work: lift demijohns in an apothecary's yard and freight at the station. Mix dough at a bakery. Sweep tavern floors with damp sawdust. Whatever the hell he could find.

But in this city, dense with civilization and pleasures, there was not much work to be had. Hands, eager to toil, quickly grabbed every broom, sledge-hammer, and stonecrusher. He found lodgings with a carpenter he'd become acquainted with when the new wing of the sanatorium was being built; he shared a room there with an apprentice. The carpenter's wife made his meals for a price, but he soon had to move because his room and board and the laundry she did for him cost him everything he earned. He ended up in a room down by Pipervika. There were eight of them sharing it, and they slept in shifts. Meals were mostly soup at the automat or workingmen's canteens so he would have money for drawing paper, charcoal, and pencils, and to sit at cafés, which beyond the evening drawing classes he attended, were the only places he could sketch. Luckily for him one of the waitresses—her name was Ester—began passing him wrapped sandwiches on the sly and letting him sleep in the room she shared with two other girls during the day while they were at work. He bought canvas and paints and started painting up there in the minimal light that came from the north.

So he spent his nights at cafés while the girls slept and worked at a bakery from late night through the early morning hours. He ate so many sweet buns his digestive system was a sticky mass, but together with the leftovers Ester brought home from the café, he got the nutrition he needed. He felt better and hardly even noticed he had slipped back into dependence.

Every two months he had to go up to Grefsemoen to provide a saliva sample for microscopic testing. The day he got the all clear he heard himself asking the doctor who had helped him get into the evening art classes if there wasn't a job for him up there. They already had plenty of people with collapsed lungs doing their lifting and running their errands and sweeping their floors though. He even lowered himself to asking if he could empty the spitter cups and run them in the sterilization machine. But they said no; they couldn't risk using a former patient for that job.

What he'd actually been after was the hospital food, and he did manage to get a brief job in the storeroom, long enough to put some flesh on his bones. However, since the trip down to his classes was both time consuming and expensive, he didn't really mind when the job ended. After two weeks of semistarvation he was taken on by an apothecary. The doctor had pulled a few strings. He kept that job a long time and had no idea that he smelled like an apothecary himself when he arrived at his sketching classes. His work consisted mainly of carrying open demijohns of various liquids in from the yard and pouring them into smaller glasses and receptacles. It was impossible not to spill on yourself now and then, and the hours he spent in rooms full of fumes quickly shut down his own sense of smell.

Once he realized the smell had permeated his clothes and his skin, he began to detest it. Smelling like some damn serpent, slithering and poisonous. Smelling of morgue and embalming fluid.

Ester said afterward that he had smelled of mulled wine and mentholated oil. But he didn't believe her.

After a while she had begun to set stricter rules for his being in the room; he could no longer come and go as he pleased. She no longer shared the room with those two other girls, and he couldn't figure out how she could afford the rent on her own. But all shall be revealed—preferably under a microscope. When he realized she'd given him the clap, he stopped going there altogether.

They called him the Asphalt Boiler because he was trying to prove what he knew about darkness. He did it on the very first large canvas he could afford to stretch. By then he had been accepted as a student of Alexander Vold's, and spent the mornings with eleven others painting at the Vold studio, five flights up in a house on Queens Street. Vold said of his anatomy that it was exceptional. His understanding of color was excellent. He was making great progress on perspective. But:

Refinement, Elv!

In that respect he was far behind. He was also youngest at the studio.

In the beginning the words whirled meaningless when he sat with the others at Kaffistova, the art café, listening to their talk about artists who worked in oil. And French miniaturists. He knew nothing. They spoke of the double standard. The masses. The femme fatale. He didn't find it difficult to keep silent.

In May 1925 the Kaffistova group had a joint exhibition. They called themselves "The New Generation." Elis had two paintings in the show. He sold one.

He watched it happen, trying to make himself invisible against the wall at the contemporary art gallery. Vold, his teacher, caught sight of him and motioned him over. But it was the professor from the Art Academy who introduced him:

Here he is, Elias Elv, the artist!

The professor was wearing a tan spring overcoat. The shipowner's widow who had bought his painting was dressed in gray. In the cleavage exposed under her coat there was a rise like the breast of a bird that had been attacked by an owl, but it was silk and pearls rather than blood and guts. She extended three slender fingers and spoke. It lasted for four minutes; his answers were monosyllabic, after which he was alone with Vold and the professor, who told him the widow owned a van Gogh and two Seurats.

He very seldom thought about Old Man Lubben, but now he found himself doing so. He imagined saying I's sold me a painting for five hundred crowns. Picture of a mare by a fence.

He knew what the old man would answer.

The only painting you're any good for is waiting to be done on that fence out there.

The professor said, pointing to Elis's canvas, that an interplay of volumes did not necessarily have to counteract closure and weight. He said he experienced it as contradictory motion, a tension between the barrels on the wagon and the horse, a balance of forces. A volatile equilibrium, and yet a balance. Not a statuesque heaviness.

It has potential.

The professor had lit a cigar and waved it in the direction of the fence. Vold seemed to be afraid Elias was going to let it go to his head. He countered:

But refinement, Elv, refinement! The young criticize the shortcomings of acknowledged masters. Yet they lack refinement.

And ideals, the professor added.

He extended his cigar case toward Elis, who accepted one but then didn't know what to do with it. Light it? No. Put it in his pocket. Too subservient. So he held it. And the professor went on.

You think you can go straight to Cézanne and Matisse! Don't ever forget the steps along the way!

When it was all over, he needed to get outside. The awnings were flapping in the spring wind. He had a feeling someone was following him, so he sneaked into an automat and poked a twenty-five *öre* coin into the slot. With a cup of coffee in his hand he saw that it was Miss Blumenthal. She was outside the window, bouncing up and down. He went on drinking his coffee, which was hot but tasted as if it had been filtered through a leaky shoe. He needed to be alone.

She came in of course.

I knew it! she exulted.

When he first came to Kristiania, he had studied with her for a few months. She gave lessons to ladies who painted in water colors. Her confidence in him had been unfailing, and she had retained him as a nonpaying pupil when the women's society stopped subsidizing his lessons. Her old violet plush hat, her shoes wobbling inside her galoshes, her much too long coat—all of it was of course just as absurd as the value painting she taught. But he was more comfortable with her than with the art professor. Right then, though, all he really wanted was to be alone. Because there was only one thing on his mind. The Østensjø School.

She had flat dark-brown eyes like a Pekinese lapdog. There was nothing he found more difficult to understand than eyes. Tears appeared now in Miss Blumenthal's. Tears covered the hard eyeball with fluid.

My dear young man, she said. I have always believed in you.

Then she left. She had a slight limp.

He was alone.

For several days the sky had had a heavy gray-green tone, and the rain had seldom stopped dripping through the blue treetops in the Castle Park. They made him think of the edges of fish gills, sieves for water and oxygen. His shoes were falling apart in the wet, the toes being soaked through; he'd had no potential, two Norwegian crowns in cash, and no jacket. But now he had sold the horse by the fence and had a cigar to smoke afterward. Like a livestock trader.

He was exhausted; he had to pull himself together. He found himself on a bench up in the Castle Park in the muted green light under the trees, a good antidote to all the frenzy.

At that very moment a dog came ambling down the gravel path, sidling along as dogs do. He was big and burly with a black coat.

Actually Elis shouldn't be drawing dogs. Or horses. He shouldn't be drawing any animals at all. But it's like an erection. It just comes over you.

And so he pulled a pencil and little sketchbook out of his inside pocket and began to draw the movement of the rambling dog. He was male. His scrotum was shiny; his organ hung heavy in its hairy pouch.

What are you looking for, you old fox? he thought.

But he wasn't after a bitch. Food was uppermost, which was sensible. He sniffed around the benches to see if anyone had been sitting there unwrapping a sandwich.

The ribcage. Elis knew the skeleton of both man and wolf now. He took great pleasure in developing the skin and the muscle mass with the point of his pencil now that he knew all about skeletons. He'd drawn lots of them at the natural history museum. At the Academy they drew from plaster models.

There's something fishy about plaster, he said to the dog.

You'd never sink your teeth into plaster.

The dog had found a sunny spot between two lindens. The grass was dry. The buzzing in the air of little winged creatures who wore their chitinous skeletons on the outside. He'd found the stored up sunlight, and it was spreading through his stiff limbs. Bones. A swollen foot pad that needed very thorough licking.

Ah well, we all have our troubles.

A muscle attachment is like a knee or a wrist; it reveals the amateur in the draftsman. You and I in the sun, you ragged wolf. We weren't born yesterday, neither of us. You lick a moment's pleasure; otherwise you're a professional. You know the backyard of every tavern and which ones have bins that fill to overflowing before the garbage man can get there.

The thigh, the bone at the hip joint. That's how it hangs together. That's how you were constructed to make your way in this world.

Now I'm sketching your scarred nose, your pointy ears, and your dusty tail. And then we go our separate ways, ragged wolf.

By the time he slipped the thin paper sketchbook back into his pocket, the urgency had passed. It had come over him suddenly when he saw the dog. Now he could devote himself to pleasant five-hundred-crowns-thoughts.

A mural commission.

The competition for the Østensjø School.

Now he could afford to participate.

How many others would there be?

He knew he was not the only one who harbored delusions of grandeur. Wanting to paint on a large scale and preferably al fresco. Wet dreams. All of them were hungering for vast walls to paint on.

He could copy Alf Rolfsen's frescoes from the telegraph building in his sleep. Sweet Jesus how he longed for clarity. Structure. Logic. No fumbling for feelings. To reveal the principle. The one in accordance with which even a dog's carcass was constructed. Revold sure as hell shouldn't have painted the apotheosis of labor on the walls of the Bergen Stock Exchange. It should have been the apotheosis of expediency.

The difficulties of sidling through life.

He had found the logic of structure in Picasso reproductions, especially the abstract ones in which reality was pieced together in accordance with principles he had also seen in the work of Raphael. The professor wasn't entirely wrong when it came to refinement.

Reality had also been painted al fresco during the High Renaissance. The smell of wet plaster contained the vapor of creation.

He had attended night school drawing classes for months that became years; he had learned to poke and fiddle until he succeeded in producing the effect of light. Then it became intolerable. The caution and humility he had learned there disgusted him for the rest of his life. A tentative hand constantly awaiting praise and approval before going on. Like value painting. The ingratiating triumph of sentiment.

No, he would dare to be great. Use color to construct volume. Al fresco. Smell the wet scent of his instincts. Be God.

He didn't go back to the art gallery that day, and he didn't go for the drink they'd arranged to meet at Kaffistova for after the exhibition closed. He didn't go to Dagmar's either; he just returned to his lodgings in the garret above the bakery. There he pulled out his trunk and the scraps of papers with sketches of Serine and the horses. He spread them out on the bed and the floor and sat staring at them in the light filtering in from the north that May evening. Biting a thumbnail and seeing, truly.

When he was still at Grefsemoens Public Sanatorium, spitting into a cup with a lid, he had realized that he had to be careful not to develop a reputation as an animal painter. Once you were classified, it stuck.

You might be a landscape artist. Or a flower painter. Or a horse painter for that matter, the destiny that threatened his own talent.

Even a long time back, at the logging camp in the woods near Namsos, he had known he mustn't fall for the praise he got for drawing the hindquarters of horses.

Still what he wanted to paint on the wall of the gymnasium at Østensjø School was Serine and the horses. He didn't stop to consider. He had always known I need to do this on the grand scale.

His first sketches had been done with charcoal from the stove on inside-out paper bags. Because he hadn't had any fixative, they were blurry.

In those days he hadn't known the word motif. He had never seen Serine meet up with horses in the woods. But he used to run into them himself on the slopes of Mount Brannberg across the lake. They came thundering down the path to the south pastures. Some forty mares and geldings.

In the winter they pulled twelve- or thirteen-ton loads of timber.

Sledges that slipped and slid on the icy surface. Chains and heavy duty harnesses squealing.

Cold and iron.

Now they'd put the cold behind them and forgotten it, as well as the screeching of the iron and the loud shouts and the gusts of frost in their nostrils. They no longer remembered winter. Summer had settled into their large bodies for good. And they themselves had taken on eternal life.

He thought they smelled like bolete fungus or milfoil flowers or like a spice drawer at the store. When he patted one of their ungroomed hindquarters, the sound under his hand was like laughter. They were always glad to see people; there was nothing more exhilarated than a herd of horses in the woods when they encountered a human being. They were eagerly inquisitive, frolicking and friendly, prodding you with their soft muzzles, turning nice hindquarters toward you and farting airily. A rear hoof gave a random kick, too close for comfort to a human skull, fragile as a glass carafe. (They knew it, they knew it.)

He had drawn Serine with those horses in the woods, the massive, excited herd. Sketched the scene in both pencil and charcoal. At the time he hadn't known why, but now that he had begun to structure his work and to use color he had some idea. The volume that was Serine was translucent as paper against the mass that was a horse. But there was still space!

In those days he had thought naturalistically. Thirty-five horses contrasting against a slender girl's body. Cézanne, with his bathers, could have filled a canvas ambitiously.

In the sketches that he now started making there were never more than eight horses. He didn't count them until long after the function of each was clearly established. He chose them carefully and by color from memory. Isak Pålsa's roan with the gray dapples freckled across her long lovely muzzle. She had pale yellow eyelashes. Blacky, the shopkeeper's stallion, heavy with latent power. The long hair bearding his hooves, the red highlights. The long fringe over the eyes of the shopkeeper's mare Dolly. How she tossed that mane. A real woman. Two Norwegian *döles*, lots of black in their short-sheared manes and hooves, so dark and shiny they looked polished. His old man's mare whose brown hindquarters gleamed in shades of fox-red. Her stallion foal, almost black, shadowed with blue from the trees, rearing with nervous energy or possibly with fear. The big light-brown mare Albin Gabrielsa had bought at the Saint Gregory fair in town. She made him think about the slaves of antiquity he had read about at Open Spaces: waiting drearily to be sold again. Not a hope but perhaps an extended longing, insistent and calm at the same time: let it not be too hard. Let there be food. Over there. At the next place. At the next master's.

When he saw the Munch with the girl's head on the pillow, he realized that as long as a decade ago he had been on the right track. Back then it had made him think of coming; the sweet, intense pleasure of knowing: not all that damned refinement and book learning. There's something else to it. Something I *have*.

But this didn't happen very often.

He had to paint that scene on the grand scale; he had always known it. It ought to be done on plaster that was still wet, in the scent of creation, though of course that wouldn't be possible in reality, not at the Østensjø School. But still! Whole tins of paint and large brushes. Not cracked tubes squeezed empty. Not frantically scraping out the last little dabs of paint wondering if it would be enough for one stupid little sparrow.

The wall of the gymnasium was 8.5 x 3.5 meters. He got all the information the very next day. He would paint in casein. He would start by making a sketch for the drawing he planned to submit; he was still far from ready to make a full-scale drawing. Far from mixing colors. And from painting without being able to make changes. What terrifying ecstasy that must be!

For the moment he went on working on Serine and the horses with pencil on paper. He drew lines and angles and wrote himself detailed notes regarding color. In the midst of all the fussy detail he knew that he was completing the preparations for the painting of a lifetime. Once he was there, at the wall, he would just work his way from one solution to the next, solving the problems he was now describing to himself. The figure of Serine surrounded by the horses would reflect how it felt to discover them.

The huge joy of horse.

Of an exhausted body being healed by warmth and drowsiness and grass, tall and juicy, and night light. That enormous summer joy only a horse could feel.

But the oats and the trough.

The wall of the stable to keep out the cold and the wolf.

The dependence.

For years he himself had lived in kindly nourishing dependence. And with the chains and harnesses of the discipline of the sanatorium. He had been dependent ever since the Norwegian Women's Heath Protection Society had given him a Bible because the nurses thought he was a pietist. Dependent on Arnesen, the senior physician. On matrons and doctors and librarians. On Miss Rebecca Blumenthal. On Dagmar Ellefsen.

Getting to know educated women was stimulating but made him nervous. Lovely nails, deep thoughts, brushed hair. But you had to have an upper secondary degree, or at the very least a secondary one, if you wanted to get between those legs in their mercerized cotton stockings, into their well-kept and seldom-visited secret places. He was there by special dispensation. And restful it wasn't. At every instant something was demanded of him, preferably words.

Dagmar Ellefsen gave him the use of her studio during the summer when she was painting up north and for the weeks she spent in Paris every year.

And then there was Ester.

When the widow of the shipping company owner had paid the five hundred crowns for the horse by the fence, he thought of her right away. He wondered if she was so established by now that she got free medical examinations. Did they still have to get their books stamped to show they were noncontagious? He tried to remember what they had talked about the last time he saw her. Was it just small talk? He must have said something about how she was certain to come to grief sooner or later. He recalled that she'd assured him, then or before, that only proper gentlemen came to her, heads of families and young students. Educated people. Almost like friends. Polite and never more than a little drunk.

Now you can still pick and choose, he had thought. Because, surprisingly Ester—known to the gentlemen as Kitty—had all her teeth. I got my good teeth from my pa, she said. He had such strong teeth he could bite right through cobbler's thread.

Yellow-gold was her hair, frizzy from the misty air, and her eyes were dark. A shepherdess lost in the mist of the street lights. But she had come to the capital from Stavanger, where she had packed sardines at the cannery. The stink of it! No, she preferred gentlemen's cologne and clean undergarments. Theirs really are; you should see. But he didn't like her talking about it.

She had lent him money for paint, and he had been clear and cold as if he were standing with his feet in an ice cellar when he took it from her. He thought about financial circulation in society: his brushes would paint the cadmium yellow and Verona green she'd been able to buy for him thanks to her intercourse with those solid gentlemen friends, canvases that hopefully would be bought by those same gentlemen, who would thus pay for them twice. He had nothing against that.

But this.

With the hundred-crown bills in his inside pocket he went down to the part of town known as Vika on the slope above Pipervika harbor, between the piers at Aker brygge and Akershus castle. The moment he saw the ram-shackle houses and lopsided fences, he was overcome with shame. Damn, how different it felt to be among these people when he had money in his pocket. Their semistarvation, life without vests and pocket watches had made them immune to all finer feelings.

He couldn't find her, and it was driving him mad. At the café where she had worked they didn't even recognize her name, though it wasn't as if years had passed. Only months. He shouted his question to a man in a blue workingman's apron who was sweeping damp sawdust on the floor, but he just shook his head, dismissing him as an idiot.

Was she at a sanatorium? She might even be one of the syphillitics in a hospital ward with twenty beds. He walked down to the harbor and stared into the water.

In the end he got hold of her by pure coincidence. A couple of weeks later in a dairy shop on Majorstuveien he was served by a girl who one of the waitresses Ester had shared a room with in the early days. She told him she knew where Ester was living, but he must on no account go there. He was relieved to know that she was living somewhere. But what had become of her?

He went back to Majorstuveien three times before she said Ester had agreed to meet him at the café at the east railway station. Far from Vika in other words. How odd, he said. Her girlfriend replied that she didn't want to be recognized.

They were to meet early one morning. When he arrived, she was already seated at a table, her hat pulled way down on her forehead. Well, that was the fashion. She was carrying a basket, looking like a housewife on her way to the butcher's for soup bones. She explained that it was out of decency and caution they were meeting far from dirty run-down Vika because she still lived there.

While she sucked in the hot coffee between her front teeth in the way he recognized from the hustle and bustle of her waitressing days, she told him she had done well for herself.

She was strong of course. But she'd also been lucky. Her case of the clap had been cured, and one day she had been picked up by a thin man with a droopy black moustache. They had met in a poorly lit café; she had mistaken him for a gentleman. Outside under the streetlights she could see his celluloid collar and preknotted necktie. She wanted to back out; she had enough shame not to take money from her own kind. When he asked about her price, she said he'd made a mistake. He was embarrassed. All he really wanted was a little company, he told her, and a few minutes of human conversation; she shouldn't imagine anything else. She invited him up for a glass of wine: they sat in her room without touching, in mutual respect.

He was a master stonemason, a widower with two little children. When it turned out he could support her, Kitty fell for him like a ton of bricks. They were married now. As soon as Ester started looking after his children, their scabby scalps and painful diaper rashes healed right up. Being a stonemason, he had one too many every now and then. But not too often, and he never raised a hand to her.

She'd been lucky all right, he thought. Not least at microbial level. Which, as he knew, was where a person needs luck most.

She wouldn't take Elis's money.

It was summer. They traveled to northern Norway, to Normandy, and to Provence. They painted at Sognefjord and Hardangervidda. The roads were dusty. Elis was extremely careful about dust. He knew what swirled up in it.

He had been collapsed and burned. But he still had all his ribs. He had survived. He didn't talk like people from Jolet any more, just gave a general impression of coming from somewhere up north. His speech was refined now. Almost, and except when he was down at Vika.

Basically, of course, he lacked refinement. But still he knew more than his café mates about some things. They were radical. He wasn't particularly. During the stevedore's strike in 1923 almost all of them had taken temporary work down at the harbor. Many of them needed the money for paint and the rent. They didn't seem to understand the consequences of breaking a picket line.

Sometimes he got a whiff of bedclothes from their radicalism too. It was incredible how important their sex life was to them. It was quite a while before he became refined enough to realize he had missed the entire previous century.

His grandfather's father, the one known as the Squirrel, had come straight out of the pioneering homesteaders' era. Elis didn't imagine his view of sex had been much different from that of County Governor Örnsköld with his silk suit and powdered wig. In the picture their schoolmistress had shown them, Örnsköld, benefactor of Jämtland, had been holding a slender fine caliber rifle. That was what made Elis realize he was a human being, the same as the Squirrel.

The bohemian crowd debated problems and elucidated them, while wholesalers and merchants, rooted in a nineteenth century the Squirrel never experienced, made girls stand on their hands at Christmas with lit candles in their exposed parts.

There were medical students among the men who gathered at the café. They performed postmortems on streetwalkers and compiled statistics. But Elis kept his counsel, thinking if everything went according to the statistics I would be dead and Ester would be an abused woman, an outcast. But she takes her basket to the market to buy soup bones, and I am entering the competition for the Østensjø School mural.

Elis sold the horse by the fence in the middle of May. When he had worked on Serine and the horses for three and a half months, he submitted his drawing to the competition. On the twenty-seventh of September his teacher Vold came up to his lodgings to tell him the jury had awarded the commission to someone called Bjarne Ness.

He stood in the doorway watching Elis's face. There was no getting away. Can't believe I didn't slam him flat to the ground, he thought afterward.

Vold had come up because Elis was so young. He understood that much. Young is foolish.

Had he thought Elis would do himself in?

Who did you say? he asked after some time. He was so shocked the name had passed him by.

Bjarne Ness.

That consumptive, Elis thought. That puny consumptive shit.

Afterward he wasn't quite sure whether he had said it aloud. If so, he didn't know what language he had used. Not since his old man whammed him from behind when he was standing by the stove at Lubben had he been caught so badly off guard.

The entries for the competition were on display. Vold asked what he thought of Bjarne Ness's sketch. He said he hadn't seen it. He hadn't been to the exhibit.

Vold would never be able to understand that: that the other submissions had been of no significance to him. But they had nothing at all to do with it. Bjarne Ness and whatever the hell their names were. For him it was between himself and the wall of the gymnasium at Østensjø School. That was all.

Not people.

Himself and the wall.

Vold suggested they go to the exhibit. He might find it enlightening. Elis asked what he was supposed to learn. To paint like Bjarne Ness?

Vold left. Late that afternoon when the retching and the wild uproar in his stomach and digestive system had settled, Elis went down to the hall after all. It was so painful his jaws ached. There was nothing cerebral about it. His whole body was in pain.

There were more people than horses in Ness's drawing. Was that the lesson? One horse. Just one. It was wearing a wig like a lady on stage and had empty eye sockets. A Picasso horsehead. He had made the forequarters disappear by putting in a figure, someone leading the horse. That kind of thing exposes a painter, Elis thought.

He found Vold at his side. Sneaking up on him like a shadow. Elis wanted looking after. He was dependent, wasn't he? And so young.

He asked Vold without looking at him what he was supposed to learn, and his voice almost cracked.

Vold spoke of the dynamic interplay of forces between the bodies in the picture. How the boy in front of the horse was pulling that heavy volume across the diagonal. And the statuesque posture of the conqueror. The tranquility in it.

The Return of the Conqueror was the title of the picture. The loser, thought Elis, looking at Serine with the horses.

Now he knew what he was doing there: learning how their minds worked. In terms of painting he had nothing to learn from Bjarne Ness.

He couldn't see much when he got out into the street. For once he was staring into himself. A sensation of grayness and steep cliffs. That's what it's like, he thought. Although you all pretend it's not.

No, he would never understand them. He felt nothing but hate.

They were inconsistent. Their jaws were constantly flapping, and their eyes, wide open at first, narrowed to slits later on. Why?

He found himself heading instinctively for Vika. The afternoon had darkened. Wet paper and leaves stuck to his shoes. In the cafés the lamps were lit, revealing the tops of heads. The faces were turned downward toward the shadows. He saw a mask of a woman's face, a chiseled mouth. He knew that she thought she was smiling and that everyone who saw her thought so too.

At that moment he felt a wave of longing for a sanatorium. Any sanatorium. He had nothing against a regimen of activities that determined what he was supposed to do, hour by hour. The only thing he had longed for then was to be truly alone. But he never had to put his energy into understanding endless talking and affected facial expressions. Because the dying never put on an act. Once he was allowed up and around, he had been able to avoid the others who were on their feet. After some time he became known as the fellow who painted. That put a stop to their questions.

Late that evening he was having something to eat in a café, fish cakes and fried potatoes. Outside the window he saw a black dog nosing around. Sometimes it vanished out of sight, but then it would come back. It must have known this was a good place to find scraps.

The neighborhood was empty. The cobblestones were shiny from the rain. Wooly yellow light seemed to be hanging from the street lights on their sagging wires. Men and women scurried by, shadows passing quickly across the picture. They could have been cardboard figures. The people playing cards in the café and the tired waitress resting her behind on the counter looked equally unreal. It was a picture. A memory of life. Something remote.

He recalled other occasions when he had seen the café and the street this way. Emptied of life except for a brewer's horse or a few sparrows on a nearly shadowless Sunday street.

Now there was this dog.

He was almost certain it was the same one he'd seen that day in May when he had sold the horse by the fence and was sitting in the Castle Park smoking a cigar. Stiffness had set into the tender spot in his front paw. He had a little limp now.

Elis set three twenty-five *öre* coins on the table and dumped what was left of the fish and potatoes into his newspaper.

Nearly two weeks later he turned up at Dagmar's. He had spent most of the interim among the tumbledown houses in Vika, walking the streets and narrow alleys while the autumn went rough and sour. Being in her heated rooms made him feel feverish.

Coming here *now*? Where have you been?

He couldn't say I came because I started thinking about you. Now. Today. She would, of course, reverse it: why hadn't he been thinking about her before?

He didn't know. And he was damned sure no one else knew either why a person started to think about something—or didn't.

Dagmar thought about him constantly. He'd assumed it was an act of will, but perhaps it was more like with him and the dog.

He didn't, of course, know why he had been following a dog for nearly two weeks. In the beginning he had let him slip away in the evenings and gone looking for him again in the mornings. After a while he figured out the dog spent the nights in an open wagon shed, and he started enticing him up to his garret lodgings instead.

He wasn't a wild dog or even a tame dog gone wild. But he had lost the hand that fed him. Some old haulier who had died, Elis imagined.

Dagmar and the dog intimidated each other. Both were restrained. The dog crouched, ears pulled back. Dagmar did her best not to look at him. But the hot room brought out his strong smell.

She wondered what Elis was laughing at, but he refused to explain. Piano, plush, palm, drapery, oriental rug, rattan furniture, rocking chair, easel, paintings, teacart. These were words. They weren't what the dog saw.

What's he called? Dagmar asked uncertainly.

Until then he hadn't had a name. Now he got one:

Roughpaw.

The mural commission didn't go to you.

He was overcome with rage and got up. The dog rushed quickly to the door, but the curtain in front of it scared him.

Elias!

She took him by the arm; the dog snarled. She pulled her hand away quickly, backing up until she bumped the rocker. She stood behind it and started going on about how unhappy and upset she knew he must be. That was what had kept him away.

Don't give me that kind of crap, he thought, examining the canvas she had on the easel. She was working on two lemons surrounded by apples on a platter. He thought: What about painting them in the horse shit out on the street instead or in a chamber pot full of piss.

She asked him if there had been a jury citation. He said the only citation he had heard was from a woman standing in front of Bjarne Ness's submission. She'd said he had a sense of empathy.

Aha. And what did they say about your submission?

Cheap, disgusting. Product of a deranged mind.

That's not true Elias.

She started making tea. The dog lay by the door. His strong odor filled the room. Dagmar chatted on, arranging cardamom rusks on a fancy enameled plate, black with yellow roses, and for a moment Elis felt truly deranged.

I have no sense of empathy, he said. Clearly.

Oh yes you do, she said comfortingly. To be a painter you have to be able to identify with others.

The hell you do!

The dog was back on its feet, poised. Dagmar asked Elis to make him lie down.

The day you understand that there is reality—beyond feelings and words and facial expressions—you'll be able to paint too.

He hadn't actually intended to say that out loud. But it came out.

I don't give a good God damn about your identification with a banana and a couple of lemons.

There is no banana, Dagmar said softly.

He was always saying the wrong thing. On this rattan sofa with its cloth bolsters he heard himself saying piss, crotch, cunt, dick, and groin. She called the material chintz. Whatever. In any case there were lilacs on it.

If only she had said, why are you being nasty, Elias? But she continued to bandage his sprained and swollen self-esteem. Wanting to nurse away the inflammation. Wanting him to paint more lemons and fewer horses. Humility and a sense of empathy—those were the characteristics she believed a painter required.

Your little fucking lemon is only masquerading as a lemon, he said. Just as you're masquerading as a person.

Am I not a person then?

No. How could you be? Umber blouse. Burgundy necklace. And coffee-brown skirt, a huge field of coffee-brown with violet patches of cloud. Your face a yellow surface with some violet-brown holes.

Change your clothes or undress and pose for Vold's sketching from life class and you'll see you aren't a person. You'll hear it too. You are ratios. You are tensions between surfaces. You are the difference between the bearing and that which is borne.

What about that young waitress then? The one from Vika.

Hadn't he painted her with compassion? Her effort to unload everything her body had borne as she rested on her right foot and leg. That arching line—wasn't there empathy in that? And the detail, so precise. The high-topped shoes, holes cut out for her toes and heels where the pressure was worst. He had painted the bearer, revealing everything she had ever borne, although at that very moment there was nothing in her hands.

Of course you have compassion, Elias. But you don't want to acknowl-edge it.

I suppose I have a certain ability to observe. That's different. And one helluva lot better. To see is not to pity.

But you communicate empathy. You show someone who has borne bur-dens. Every line of her body contains the burdens she has borne.

She has borne the weight of men too, Elis thought. Then he couldn't stop himself from saying it. That she had borne the weight of the wholesaler, the ship owner, and the professor from the Art Academy. When they stood in front of the painting experiencing that empathy she was going on about, they saw the same bodily lines she did. They saw her hips, her breasts under the bib of her white apron, the black cloth straining. The nostrils of the wholesaler trembled in anticipation of that line: he knew the smell of her perspiration; he wanted to pry her legs apart, and he knew he could for no more than it cost him to have his laundry done.

Oh how he identified with that bearing line. He saw pride in it, the pride of a woman in her body. I have borne the weight of a wholesaler, I have. I have felt the wholesaler's balls swell. A clean, proper gentleman. Linen underwear! Real gentry. A big thing for me, poor girl. A big thing when it's inside me too—that wholesaler's a real man. And afterward, with his cigar dangling from the corner of his mouth, when he's found his collar button and knotted his necktie, he stuck some bills under the doily on the chest of drawers.

That's a woman's pride, and a wholesaler at an exhibition can identify with it. He has a sense of empathy, he does. Arrogant empathy—he can stuff it right into the bodice of reality. And of course I agree that he gets it from my painting. Without it he's nothing but a piece of raw flesh in clean underwear. He needs art. That's why we make art, so wholesalers can feel a bit of empathy; to make their sense of empathy swell.

And so Bjarne Ness wins the prize for being able to identify with how a young man feels on the back of a horse.

Dagmar said that his girl with the horses did not lack that empathy he held in such contempt. But she found it a frightening picture. It probably wasn't at all suitable for a boys' gymnasium. She could imagine though that if the girl were to see it she would identify with the image.

I don't want to hear another word about her from you, he commanded, and the dog raised its head.

Dagmar sighed and said she knew he would have liked to paint a different kind of picture. Clear and logical. He replied that those pictures were already being painted. But not here.

You want to go to Paris.

She said this in a tone of resignation.

Not Paris, he thought. But Berlin. Where the Blue Rider awaits me.

That evening he walked by the harbor with the dog. This city, the name of which was now Oslo, was becoming a major metropolitan area with regular ferry connections to Copenhagen, Amsterdam, Bordeaux, Hamburg, Hull, London, and Stettin.

He'd get himself a seaman's card.

He wanted to tell the black dog about Franz Marc, another man who was good at painting horses. There are lots of horse painters he wanted to tell him. Egedius. Degas. They don't have to conceal the forequarters behind another figure, one they are competent to paint.

But Franz Marc was the greatest. He understood how horses were built. He understood how alone they were with themselves.

Elis sat down on a bollard, inhaling the scent of the sea at night. The dog padded behind him on the wooden pier. The water was gleaming, constantly in motion.

We are alive. We are moving side by side.

Franz Marc was still alive when I lived at Lubben. But one day he rode off. Could it have been the same day I ran away from home? He rode until he came to a grove of trees. That was where it happened. The horse?

The horse probably stood under the tree for a while before going off to find dependence again. To find solitude in the darkness of the manger.

It was in March 1916. Blood dripped from Franz Marc's temple. Of all the men who died at Verdun he was spared death in the muck. He never reeked. But they extinguished his eyes.

There is no longer anyone who can see what he saw.

Elis looked at one of the big boats. There were lights behind portholes. That must mean some people didn't go ashore.

You're going to be on your own again, he said to the dog. But you'll probably be fine.

As if the dog understood his words, he started to move in the direction of the harbor warehouses. He ambled off. After a while he vanished into the shadows.

When Myrtle and I were children, we saw wolves on the lake. We would glimpse them, gray shadows on the ice. They moved quickly and were rapidly absorbed into the dusk. The only time of day we ever saw them was at twilight. It would be nearly dark inside; we would be waiting for Hillevi to light the lamp over the kitchen table so we could draw. But she always put it off as long as possible; she loved to sit and look out. Her sewing, almost always darning, would drop into her lap, but she was never the one to see them first.

Look, said Myrtle. There they are now.

We would walk over to the window and look out, exhaling circles of mist onto the glass. Hillevi told us not to wipe the window with our hands; it streaked the glass.

It was difficult to count them, but the grownups said there were seven or eight wolves running in a pack near the villages during those years.

Wolves, Myrtle whispered. We can't go out now, can we?

But when daylight came, we could go out of course. Wolves were timid. All the grownups said so. They were sly but cowardly. Myrtle, though, found it difficult to forget the story she'd heard her pappa tell. When he was a child, big packs roamed around up at Skinnarviken. They were bold, going right up close to the houses. One day a boy came inside saying he'd seen a large dog out by the stone cellar; it wasn't a dog he recognized. His mother was so scared her heart seized up, and after that the children were kept indoors, even down here in Blackwater.

Hillevi recalled the winter of 1918 when there had been so many wolves the Lapps lost almost all their reindeer. Over the next few years they tried to keep watch over the does when they were calving, the few that were left. But a wolf was like poison or fire. In the end all the reindeer-herding Lapps had to move away from these parts.

My Uncle Anund returned, as I've already explained. He came and went. Because there was no more work for him here, no reindeer owners who needed a hand during the branding.

When he was a half-grown lad, fourteen or fifteen I think, he went on a wolf hunt around Skinnarviken and up to Mount Giela, the area now called Bear Mountain on the maps, with two young men from the Matke clan. They were paid by the day at a rate set by the local council. They hunted on skis when the crust on the snow was so thin it didn't hold up under the wolves any longer. It was sharp as glass and cut the legs of the animals when they went through. The men hunted the pack, urging them on hour after hour.

Through many a valley
across many a marsh
until the air tasted of blood
and their eyes went dim

my uncle hummed softly, *ajajaja jaaa* he sang; they urged the wolf on until his life forces were extinguished, gave him a taste of his own evil *ajajajaaa*, his own hate to eat. Like vomit he had to gobble it all up, his own blood dancing before his eyes until he turned around and glared, and then Matke's son Nisja, or maybe it was Johanni, struck him a blow on the muzzle with his pole. That was all it took; he was already half-dead.

After that Uncle Anund, who was behind them, had the job of skinning the wolf. The other two rushed on, pursuing the rest of the pack. He often got quite far behind, he admitted, because the two of them were great skiers.

But even after the reindeer-herding Lapps had left, villagers wanted to kill the wolves. They baited traps with pieces of meat laced with strychnine. But my uncle told me that our people would poison lumps of reindeer fat. Wolves gobble that fat without a moment's hesitation; they're as crazy about reindeer fat as the Lapps. In that way they're similar.

Everyone participated in hunting down the wolves, if not with poison and sharp ammunition and shards of glass, then in their thoughts. Everyone but Kalle Persa, the fisherman, who was such a gentle soul he would only kill fish.

313

There was a certain bone you could take from the thigh of a moose; people called it the "wolf bone." If you stretched it tight and concealed it in the bait, the wolf would gobble it up, and then the sharp bone, keen as a newly-honed knife, would pop open in his stomach or throat. Apparently people had a lot to be vindictive about.

In 1929 a wolf crossed the ice at Blackwater. He came from the slopes on Mount Brannberg and crept up unseen alongside the Storflo marsh, although he left tracks of course. Probably he wandered on toward Skinnarviken and from there up into the mountain woods. This was in January; very few people saw him. Those who did figured he was a male looking for a mate.

By then it had been a very long time since anyone had seen a wolf in Röbäck parish. There was general agreement that this was probably the last survivor. He would be difficult to entice with a piece of poisoned meat now that he had gone up into the mountains.

A couple of young men went to Aagot Fagerli's to ask my Uncle Anund Larsson's whereabouts. When he was out of work, he often spent time at her kitchen table. He made ends meet as a songwriter and performer, playing and singing at parties and celebrations. He had sent for an accordion from Åhlén & Holm and got some of the logrollers to teach him the fingerings. That day he was in Skuruvasslia for a wedding. They told Aagot they needed his help tracking the lone wolf. Some lumberjacks had seen his tracks up by Bend.

My uncle sent word not to count on him. Down in the shop people quoted what he told the wolf hunters:

There's no point. You might as well spin around and slap yourself on the jaw.

Those were strange words, and most of them were soon lost, yet I still sometimes hear people say "'There's no point,' as Anund Larsson said," though they don't even know who he was.

The hunters went off without him and located the tracks, but they never caught up with the wolf. The next weekend when there was some new snow, they decided to try again though, and in the new snow on one of the tarns below Bend they saw his tracks, so enormous the men were stunned. There had been no thaw to make the paw marks spread either. This was simply one helluva beast.

They continued to pursue him, and when they finally caught sight of him, they fired. But the shot didn't put him down. All they saw was drops of blood in the snow. He had first moved quickly off to the side, then stood still. There was a puddle at the spot. But he was no longer there, and anyway it was getting dark.

The next day was a Monday, and they had to be back at the logging camp. So Sunday evening they went up to Aagot Fagerli's again. Anund Larsson was there this time, and they asked if he would track down the injured wolf for them.

That was a request he couldn't turn down. It wasn't as though he had any pressing commitments. So he headed out and was gone for three days and nights. I don't know where he slept. Perhaps the people at Bend put him up. Or maybe he made a fire in my grandfather's old shelter. The third day at dusk he caught up with the wolf. He didn't have a rifle with him. He did it the old way.

I heard at the store that my uncle was back. So I hurried up to Aagot's and there he was on the kitchen settle. He'd left his cap by the door. His hair was all matted, and there were black streaks of dried sweat on his forehead. His eyelids were so swollen I could barely see his eyes, and his skin was rough and red under his whiskers. He was holding the coffee cup in both hands as if he would never be warm enough again. Aagot had put so much wood in the stove it was humming. I'd thought he would be pleased.

Aren't you going to sing now, Laula Anut? I asked.

Oh, singin' . . .

It sounded as if he didn't even know what that the word meant. When he spoke, his lips were stiff.

Leave your Uncle Anund be. Can't you see he's tired? Aagot said.

I asked again though. Wouldn't he sing the song for a dead wolf? A *vuolle*, a lament for the wolf, the kind he had told me about but never sung himself. He had only heard others, important old men, real wolf hunters and great singers, for whom he had the utmost respect. When he was a lad he had never killed a wolf himself. When the points of his skis touched the yellow and gray matted fur of the still-warm body, he'd been frightened that it might start moving again, that there might still be a bit of life in it.

315

Before he dared touch the body of the wolf with his ski pole, he removed the knife from his belt. He said he'd felt nauseous with fear. *Tjöes*, was his word for it. My uncle was different from other men in that way: he didn't mind telling you when he'd been scared or unhappy.

No, he didn't sing.

He told me the songs were in the wind. But he could no longer hear them.

The lake water is velvety in autumn-summer. Rowing is like stirring veal stock that's just starting to thicken. It's a lingering, leisurely season. The leaves at the tops of the dwarf birches are already aflame in yellow and burning red. A snow flurry dotted the mountain bog overnight. But down here the heat has been stored up in rock slabs and steaming anthills.

Bluebells. Yellow tufts of birdsfoot trefoil in the clefts of the rocks. Lousewort, almost withered now, brown straggly stems. Hillevi was rowing so close to the shore she could see the plants pushing up through the cracks in the slate along the shore. She could even see the bilberry and lingonberry plants a little higher up, and she thought it looked like a promising year for berries.

Sunday morning, church service time. But no church bells could be heard from this lake. Trond was sitting reluctantly in a pew in Röbäck; he had to attend a council meeting afterward. He'd taken the children along to play with Märta Karlsa's. Tore wanted to see their filly-foal. Hillevi had a loin of salted pork soaking in milk back home. She was planning to roast it, stuffed with prunes and spiced with ginger, and have it ready when they came home.

On an impulse she rowed into the little bay by the pasture lands. She would live to regret that urge deeply, regret giving in to that kind of spontaneous summer whim, when you could just take the rowboat out for a while on a Sunday. Maybe she wanted to see whether the goldeneye chicks had survived, the fourteen she had seen swimming along behind their mother the last time she was out.

When the bottom of the boat scraped against the stones, she had another impulse: might there be some red bartsia still in bloom in the shady area above the boat landing? A bouquet for the Sunday dinner table. That tiny crystal vase that had belonged to Efraim Efraimsson and a clean cloth, she was thinking, and if only the village had a proper communal mangle with marble slabs. The only mangle up here was a wooden one with twin rollers. You made do.

No red bartsia. But a bird rose in fright from among the alders, a gentle fluttering sound; big but not a bird of prey. What has such large, soft wings?

She must have been walking along looking down, looking for cat's-foot and wild thyme. The pasture land around the hut, so neatly grazed down in Jonetta's day, was starting to go wild. There was no grazing livestock here any more, but she had an urge to call out the soft names she remembered: Lady Ewe, Moo Cow. Blackear! Curlycoat! Kiddies, my little ones! She was still smiling to herself when she caught sight of Aagot. Completely unexpectedly.

Her stately white nudity.

Hillevi had no idea her black hair was so long it reached down below her waist. She never cut it. Nothing stylish for Aagot; she still wore her outdated coats from America. Such a big bottom. She hadn't imagined that either. Aagot, who had been slender as a reed in her youth.

There was a zinc tub on the front steps and next to it a sooty steaming pot of hot water. Her hair was wet. That was why it hung so black down her back, and lay so flat at the top of her head. She took a scoop of hot water and stirred it into the tub. Then she ladled some over herself. It ran through her hair, down her back. But why in heaven's name didn't she bend over?

On the contrary.

She turned around as she ladled the next scoop over her head, water dripping down her breasts, with their big dark brown nipples, and smiled.

Then her face stiffened.

Hillevi wasn't the person she had expected to see when she'd heard footsteps. The water ran between the planks of the dark ageing steps, the soapy fuzz sought out the cracks, and the water in the pot continued to steam. Aagot's face went rigid.

Tobias had appeared from behind the cookhouse. He was carrying two pails of water from the lake. He was the person Aagot had been expecting. Hillevi had time to see his smile and to watch it stick like cardboard to his face under his wide terrified eyes. She turned and fled back to the boat.

She was swallowing her tears as the oars rang out and the boat scraped roughly against the stones on the bottom because she would have preferred to vanish into a silence so total they could have believed they'd been dreaming.

As she rowed across the lake and around the point at Tangen, her head came to be filled with things people had said about Aagot and Tobias. Little innuendos she hadn't understood at the time. But her memory had stored them. Viciously they snapped out of safe-keeping:

That'll please Aagot, won't it?

Hildur Pålsa when Hillevi told her Tobias was coming up for the fowl hunting season. And as long ago as last year a voice—whose?—at the store:

Well, he's got his reasons.

She didn't know how she would ever be able to look him in the eye again. Or sit at the dinner table with him, passing the prune-stuffed loin of pork. She thought about her sister-in-law Margit, the mother of his four children. And a fifth on the way.

Every word he'd ever said about the fine healthy life up here, about how much he missed it when he walked the streets of Uppsala longing for the evening skies and the murmuring brooks and the mountain views, took on new meaning. Now she knew what he meant about that murmuring and those skies. There were dirty words for it.

The kitchen clock showed just past one when she got home. She had a few hours to herself. Unless Tobias got it into his head to come over and talk to her. Talk it out.

No. She would never say a word to him about Aagot. About what they were doing. She'd lock herself in the bedroom if he came.

There was no encounter that evening; Tobias didn't come back. He left on the early bus without saying good-bye to her.

Wonder what took him off early? Maybe an emergency at the hospital Trond speculated. But there hadn't been a phone call to the store.

She said nothing. She should have. But she had a dream about Tobias that night, in which he was depraved as an ape and behaved shamelessly. In public. It was a sickening dream.

She started sleeping badly again. Waking up in the middle of the night thinking about how, many years ago, she would sneak into his room when he was at the hospital and take Georg Kress's *Human Sexuality* down from the shelf, how she would settle in on the floor behind his armchair to read it, telling herself it was part of her education.

Once he'd left a shirt on his bed. She had picked it up, pressing it to her face. Yes, she had smelled it.

What is it, Hillevi? Trond asked, covering her hand with his own. She shook her head, and he must have decided it wasn't important. He had a lot on his mind because of the store. She was left in peace.

The worst part was remembering the sight itself.

Aagot, white and glistening with water. Between her thighs and all the way up her stomach there was dense curly black hair. How could a person look like that? Hillevi had shaved women prior to hospital surgery, but she had never seen anything like it. A patch of black animal fur, distinct and sharply outlined.

And the stretch marks.

Aagot had those white streaks on her abdomen that reveal that a woman has been heavily pregnant and carried the baby to term.

This was a secret Hillevi didn't want to know, a secret Aagot had presented to Tobias, her lover, in the bright sunshine and streaming water.

She tried getting used to words like that.

And she saw the sight over and over again. It became like a curse branded in her mind: that white body, silvery under the stream of water. Dark brown nipples hardening and rising out of the areolas.

But she got through the week and thought she was over it. It was ages until the next time Tobias was supposed to come up, if he ever came again. She wasn't worried about facing Aagot. They'd always kept their distance and would surely be able to put up a front now too.

On Saturday afternoon when Trond had shut the store he came in as usual and asked her for some hot water to shave. She'd already heated it, and now she poured it into the white china bowl, adding cold water from the copper tub. He angled his shaving mirror up over the window that opened onto the lake to get the right light and honed his razor on the leather strap. The girls were drawing at the kitchen table. Trond brought them white wrapping paper, and they drew on the rough side. When that side was full of princesses and brides with diadems, trains, and ribbons, they turned it over and continued on the shiny side, which was more difficult.

320

Trond had a badger hair shaving brush with which he worked up a lather. When his cheeks were soapy white he grinned at the girls, who shouted: Sambo!

Hillevi had never understood why, but she had to join in the laughter.

Could I please set the table? she asked, trying to squeeze the coffee cups in between the sheets of drawing paper. The razor was making a lovely scratching sound on Trond's cheeks. He rinsed his face, wiping off the remains of the lather by his nostrils. Hillevi lifted away the bowl of water with its foam and floating whiskers.

It was just an ordinary Saturday, so he didn't put on any aftershave. But when he was dry and smooth cheeked, he turned around and asked:

Got a shaving kiss for Pappa, now?

Those words brought it back to her full force. Not as grief or anxiety but as pain. She ached inside.

It wasn't the first time she had found herself upset when Myrtle, slender and with kissable lips, rose up like the angel on a bookmark and put her pursed lips to Trond's cheek. When the girls were smaller, Kristin had always lifted Myrtle up to her father. Hillevi's heart had gone out to the fatherless child. Trond didn't mean to be cruel, but blood is thicker than water and men can be thoughtless.

What she felt now was different.

She remembered how it was before the children came along, when that shaving kiss was no little girl's kiss but her own lips gliding down his newly shaven cheek seeking his mouth. In those days he still washed with soft soap, and the skin of his neck had that wonderful smell. His white Saturday shirt held the scents of ash lye and lake water. All that came back to her now, even the memory of the first time she saw him shaving up at Thor's Hole. His narrow waist, its leather belt tightly cinched with its loose end dangling, the whiteness of his shirt in the summer evening.

She left the room.

The chatter of the children's voices was only remotely audible up in the bedroom. She remembered other things: how he had stood by the bed, naked. Taken her hand and guided it to that spot in a natural way. She had closed it over his scrotum, felt its weight. It was dark, shadowy blue like his whiskers.

That had been during their early days, in the room above the old shop. They had nothing to worry about—she couldn't get any more pregnant than she already was. If anyone had seen them, or even had any idea what they were up to, it would have all seemed shameful.

Now she saw Aagot again and bare-chested Tobias. She had never known Tobias had black hair on his chest. Not as thick as Trond's. What seemed like naked shamelessness when she caught sight of them had been private, their own secret world.

They too had been in that kind of bell jar of intimacy Hillevi had once known long ago. She recalled it in hues of brown and blue, with a warmth for which she had no words. But Trond had sometimes whispered words. In Norwegian. It was easy to guess why. During his bachelor years he had traveled back and forth to Namsos to buy goods. Slept away, as people called it.

She didn't want him to have sown any wild oats.

She had never told him about Edvard Nolin, about how far they had gone. But he had undoubtedly guessed. He had nothing to fear from those comparisons men were so keen to make, and he surely knew it. She remembered the jokes the others up at Thor's Hole had made about Edvard, and her own hot, confused thoughts: *earthbound lust!* Now she could laugh about it.

But not about what she had lost. How had that happened?

Children's illnesses of course, sleepless nights. The door ajar. And the exhaustion. Not least his. After the fire his tiredness weighed even more heavily on him.

But there was something else as well. A kind of awkwardness that had crept up on them.

When he came to her now, it was gently and affectionately, his body groping for hers in the dark. It could just as easily be a good night peck and a pat on the cheek as anything else.

When it did happen, it was quiet. Sometimes almost without moving.

We wouldn't want an afterthought taking us by surprise.

No, no, a mid-life baby would be awkward. She was over forty now besides.

She knew though that fundamentally something else had robbed her of Trond's eagerness. His passion, to put it simply.

He'd become afraid of it, and so had she.

For an excellent reason.

Love turns into affection and caring if you have the good fortune to find a kind husband.

But the heat burns out. In the long run it cannot continue. Not for people settled into a neat orderly way of life.

She didn't know what to call it, even in her mind. *It.* That terrible hunger for someone's skin, for his breath and his smell. The madness that led a young woman, although she was secretly betrothed, to make love with a man she barely knew under a spruce tree.

Lucky, Hillevi. You were lucky, that was all. Because it could just as easily have ended badly. He might have preferred to pay, as he had put it. Or even denied his role. In which case she would have been a single mother now. She began to wonder what she would have written when applying for a position. Told them about the child? Or let it come as a surprise to the parish council? Been driven out? Possibly tolerated. Sullied and gossiped about.

She heard his footsteps on the stairs. When he came in, he sat down on the edge of the bed.

I thought it was coffee time.

She nodded. Suddenly she found herself telling him about Aagot and Tobias, about their shame. They went downstairs afterward, to the children.

But at night the sight of Aagot's white body came back to her.

The time has come. It's Röbäck or Blackwater. Of course the decision's really already been made. But a person has to take sides. If you live in Blackwater and aren't on the same side as the local councilors, you'd better stay indoors. It's unthinkable to go into the store and say: I think, meself, there's somethin' to be said for havin' the school in Röbäck; it's more central. The kids wouldn't have to travel so far.

Oh no.

Now they mean business; it's in or out the window or before you know it, you'll be trapped: Röbäck or Blackwater. Norway or Sweden. Wifsta or Mon.

It's hard to believe, but the loggers would argue and even come to blows just because they were felling for different companies. The youngest and drunkest ones would at least. And not many years ago people were like cats and dogs about Sweden's joining the EU. I've heard there was more than one fistfight over how to vote on that one too.

Us or them.

National Unity or the Resistance, the Norwegian snickered, when I brought it up. Yes, they've certainly had their axes to grind on the other side of the border too. Though he claims most people would actually have chosen to lie as low as genuflecting lice.

Windows and doors, windows and doors,
go in and out the windows and doors
as we have done before.

"You can tell she's a Blacky," they said about me, but I rarely had to take sides. The time they tried to force me to, they must have thought they finally had me.

We used to play in the schoolyard like this: standing two by two, opposite each other holding hands, our arms arched to make a bridge. And then, if you didn't want to be trapped, you had to say what you were for. They would ask: lingonberries or blueberries. Buns or biscuits. Dogs or cats at worst. But that was too harmless for Margit Annersa. I could tell there was trouble brewing when I saw all the others huddled around Margit. When it was my turn to pick between windows and doors, Margit hissed:

Lapp or Swede?

She thought she had me.

Swede! I said.

She wouldn't let me through; her arms snapped shut like a huge rat trap.

I'm every bit as much a Swedish citizen as you, I said.

That's what Trond had taught me to say if anybody started in about the Lapps. She hissed, and the game came to a halt. Everybody dropped their arms, and her partner Ingalill stood there chewing on her mitten.

One day I would take the other side. But that was far in the future. I was the foster child of the shopkeepers, and that of course gave rise to some envy. There was even talk of my being included in their wills. A foster child, people grumbled, didn't deserve to reap the benefits. Ah well, they had no need to worry on that account.

Many people must have thought deep down that in spite of my having been so lucky, I took the other side, whether it was rich or poor, villager or Lapp. Because they told me the kind of things they would never have told Myrtle. They didn't think I would pass it on at home.

And I didn't.

Because just imagine if Hillevi and Trond had heard what they sang about Morten Halvorsen when he died. After Ivar Kreuger's empire collapsed and he killed himself in Paris, Morten didn't live much longer. He'd gone bottom up too with all those stocks and shares of his, and in the winter of '33 his kidneys failed. I heard the song up at Aagot Fagerli's. My uncle wasn't the first one to sing it, but they said he'd made it up. He looked a little discomfited when Helge Jonasson started in:

Before the crash, before he died,
Morten had a single friend,
a profiteer who skinned our hides
and left us for ourselves to fend.

Morton offered explanations,
blamed hardships on the powers-that-be;
for loggers' kids starvation rations
the one to blame in fact was he.

At that point Uncle Anund grabbed Helge's guitar (he could play anything he got his hands on) and started singing himself:

Let us not deride the dead;
no bitterness should linger on.
Instead, recall with fear and dread,
mortality, our common bond.

At his grave we raise a toast,
not to praise but to relate
the story's moral, now exposed:
that cruelty in time breeds hate.

I'm sitting here with Myrtle's songbook in front of me. She wrote in her lovely even hand in pencil so she could erase things and change them. Some people would sing a verse one way, others another. Sometimes they couldn't remember either. Gone, they'd say, trying to hum the words back to mind. If they failed, Myrtle would leave the page blank, and it's easy to see where she filled things in afterward.

I have a rose for every thorn
a diadem of gold . . .

There are a lot of lovely songs in Myrtle's songbook. But no dirty ones and none like the one about Morten Halvorsen and the crash. All the more peculiar that she once sang something that made me so ashamed and upset. She didn't have the slightest idea what she was doing.

The matter she sang about I had never mentioned to a soul. I didn't pass along spiteful stories.

Myrtle had a guitar, a chord book, and a pretty soprano voice. Although I wasn't much of a singer, I could learn the alto parts. We sang Swedish folk songs about coming back home and picking wildflowers at midsummer . . .

Pick, pick, pick, pick would be my part.

It was Christmas eve. We had new dresses. Myrtle's was red velvet; mine was green. In those days people thought green was the best color for redheads.

You'll outgrow it, I expect, Hillevi said about my red hair. I did.

We were sitting in the dining room, and the candles were lit in the tree. Everyone was keeping a close eye on the flickering flames of course. Since the store burned down, we had become very cautious. So when Myrtle picked up her guitar and strummed a couple of chords, Hillevi suggested we blow out the candles on the tree. And that was quite right. Once Myrtle started singing, you threw caution to the wind.

We had a plate of rolled wafers and sugar cookies on the table, and we still had coffee in our cups. The dog we had in those days, a pointer called Karr, was lying in the kitchen, whining softly behind the door. He was accustomed to being with us. But his smell was so strong he wasn't allowed in the front room.

Sissla never reeked like him, said Hillevi.

Trond poured some arrack for Aagot, Hillevi, and himself. Yes, Aagot was there, though she didn't usually spend much time at our house. Things were strained between the sisters-in-law. But it was Christmas, and Christmas is a family time. Ours was a very small family now. Tore, who was seventeen, the same age as me, didn't get any arrack. He didn't object, but I wondered what he was thinking. I knew he had started drinking. More than a little.

Myrtle and I sang *Silent Night*. Sometimes when I looked at Hillevi's face when I was young—not a child but a young woman—I could sense she had feelings she didn't show and that they were sometimes painful. On the outside adults were always sensible and proper. Always knew everything. They dismissed pain with "chin up" and exhaustion by citing duty. But when Myrtle sang, the expression on Hillevi's face made me anxious, even when she actually looked happy. I sensed that somehow happiness is also pain. I had no idea at all of why though and just wished Hillevi's face would go back to normal.

Perhaps Myrtle felt the same way. Because when she had sung *Lo, How a Rose E'er Blooming* (which went too high for me), she struck a few faster chords and started singing *Run Little Willy* softly. Hillevi tried to hush her as usual, having taken it into her head that there was something off-color about *Little Willy*. But she always gave Trond a merry look when she heard it. Myrtle moved along to a ballad, and this was it:

She was dark, a lovely flower,
embellishing the garden bower,
the rich man's home she too adorned.
She could work and she could sing
she could do most anything,
the fairest maiden ever born.

That was awful but so far only for me.

Sing something else now, I said. How about *O Little Star of Bethlehem*?

But she just rolled her eyes and went on. Myrtle could sometimes, you see, add a vibrato to her lovely voice, the kind they call a maid's tremble. When she sang like that, everybody knew she was making fun both of the song and of the kind of people who would sing it. When she got to in Boston town, I didn't dare to look up for the longest time. But Aagot looked indifferent, helped herself to a rolled wafer from the plate and nibbled at it. She smiled, and so did Hillevi, when the wealthy consul's heart began to pound for the lovely serving girl because his wife was sick abed.

He was wealthy; he had money
handsome house and voice like honey

And so the serving girl fell for him. Well, she must at least have been a kitchen maid, said Hillevi, and I felt my cheeks burning. But Myrtle was unstoppable.

Her beauty drew him like a flame
he fell in love, and who can blame
the heart for passionate pursuit?

When she got to *Clandestine love would soon bear fruit*, Hillevi did try to hush

Myrtle because she was only fourteen. But soon the story got so exciting they forgot their misgivings.

> *From prying eyes it was her scheme*
> *to hide the child, she never dreamed*
> *her sorrow too would be appeased.*
> *But still their story didn't end*
> *in sad lament—he made amends,*
> *his castle had an heir, his worries eased.*

Castle? asked Hillevi. And Aagot described, without blinking an eye, the huge mansions of the wealthy in Boston and how some of them had turrets and towers. Myrtle finished the verses about the money the kitchen maid was paid to abandon her child to the rich man and his bedridden wife. And then, of course, there was

> *Yet her heart went on repenting*
> *and her grief was unrelenting*
> *That her only child she'd sold*

and beautiful closing chords and vibrato, and then at last she was done. But I didn't dare look up out of fear Aagot was sitting there staring at me.

Trond and Hillevi began discussing whether you could really say she had sold her child. Hillevi maintained that she had made her choice in the child's best interest. Imagine how he would be raised, what a future was in store—and what an inheritance! It was a whole different life from being an out-of-wedlock baby to a maid who had been given her walking papers. Aagot said nothing, just sat with her black eyebrows raised. They were thin and looked penciled. Hillevi said she plucked them. She was looking at me the whole time.

It was awful.

I couldn't keep it to myself. When Myrtle and I had gone to bed, I started telling her in a whisper that in the village people said Aagot had sold her baby to her employer in Boston, that the money she got from America every month was from him, and that the song was really about her.

Aunt Aagot? I heard Myrtle whisper in the dark.

She was quiet for some time. Then she said:

Why would they say that?

And suddenly I understood it myself and was deeply ashamed. I could have answered her if I'd been able to break the silence in the room with the white furniture:

Because she's so beautiful.

Death reposes on empty plates.

Tore would say things like that at dinner with a full platter of meatballs on the table. It just wasn't right. Hillevi worried about him. She could see it upset Trond too.

Took down eight trunks today, said Tore. But that's hardly what you'd call bringing home the bacon.

Oh, she couldn't stand it, his not realizing what he was saying.

It's hardly a joking matter, she said softly.

He had been meant to get a higher education, but it didn't work out. He was unhappy away from home during the first year of upper secondary and moved back from Östersund when it was over.

I was no one there, you know, he said honestly.

It would have been better to let him go on helping out at the store. But Trond said that because he and Myrtle would inherit the parcels of forest land one day, he needed to have done some logging. Otherwise he'd never learn to deal with the drivers and would be incapable of managing forest holdings. He'd be cheated. He was over twenty now, full grown and strong, and he had to get some experience.

If only he had joined a good team.

One morning Hillevi opened the door and thought the dead Vilhelm Eriksson was standing outside the store. She did a double take, stepping back into the kitchen in surprise. Their girl stared at her. She realized she must be very pale.

Hillevi was always quick to dismiss all talk of ghosts. The girls who had helped in the kitchen when the children were younger had been told off in no uncertain terms if they started telling stories about people who knocked from inside their coffins or about headless night wanderers in the village. So one look at the face of the girl made her regain her composure. She knew who she had seen. Even as a boy Gudmund Eriksson had resembled his father.

She'd heard that he and Jon had come back, bringing their father's ashes from America in an iron urn with a pattern of lilies etched into it. People gossiped.

Only poor folk, Hillevi said dismissively, would cart an urn of ashes across the sea. And that long costly journey.

But Trond said they didn't seem to be completely penniless any more. They'd come home with some money saved up. How had they saved it? Nobody ever found out.

Then came the second shock. They hadn't returned just to bury their father in Röbäck churchyard. Gudmund had brought a wife and children with him. She was Swedish, or at least of Swedish descent. Just as reclusive as that wife of Vilhelm's from Jolet had been. People said she'd never come to the store either.

They bought a piece of land from the company, not out at Tangen as might have been expected but high on the slope overlooking the store. They built there in the light spring evenings and long into the nights. During the day they rolled timber, and by the time winter came Gudmund had bought a horse and organized a logging team.

They became the best team. However that happened. Which was another reason it was crazy to make Tore a member of it. He had no experience working in the forest, and he was also quite heavy and clumsy. She feared the worst. But Tore seemed to enjoy the company of the lumberjacks, and when he came home for supper, he imitated them:

Why's a man born into this misery? Shirt sagging over my chest and teeth chattering half the year.

With a gleam in his eye and a piece of pork on his fork. Oh no, Tore.

Timber driving means constant fighting. That one was true at least. But: a person's a slave to the sawmill owners from cradle to grave. He shouldn't have said that kind of thing. People frowned. The worst part was that he took their glaring as praise. He was a born imitator and sounded just like the log scaler when he hollered:

C'mon over here you fat ass and have a look; tell me if this isn't one a gorgeous bottom! You deserve a kick in the pants for it. Not even three inches across with the bark on.

But he should never have mimicked the scaler's comments about him. Not *fat ass*.

It stuck.

As did the throat clearing.

There was a man they called Wolf Spider because he was thin and had spindly legs and carried his rucksack just like the female spider carries her eggs. He had a way of clearing his throat: hurrmhrrhrr . . . Tore mimicked him to general mirth. The man didn't realize it himself. He said: hurrmhrr . . . hrr . . . And a few minutes later Tore went hurrmhrrhrr . . . And they went along hurrmmhrring all day. To start with, the loggers were doubled over their saws with laughter.

But in the end that stuck too. Hillevi felt like crying when she heard him hurrmmhrring at home all evening long. It was Myrtle who found the word.

A nervous tic, she called it.

The lake was still frozen over. But in some places a gap several arms' lengths wide had opened up between ice and shore; they had to jump across to get out to the timber. It was a tableau: silent black figures in fur caps. But she knew that the log scaler was out there shouting the dimensions to the timber cruiser who was driving the point of his pencil incontestably as the loggers cursed and grumbled.

Timber driving means constant fighting; that was as true an adage as you could find, and she wondered uncomfortably why Tore had to be out there with them. Wouldn't just the driver have been enough? No one would try to cheat Gudmund Eriksson, would they?

The store was crowded for a while around suppertime, and by the time she came back in the men were no longer there. It wouldn't be long until the ice would start to groan in a spring storm, and then it would crack so the timber crashed down and piled up in the black water to be floated down to the river.

Tore didn't come in for supper. She set a bowl upside down over the potatoes and returned the pork to the frying pan. Trond had driven to Östersund.

After the meal Haakon Iversen had gone up to his room above the stable for the night. The girls were far away. That evening Hillevi sat crocheting with their letters in front of her. She reread the one about Queen Street and the pedestrian bridge in Katrineholm, about the cinema there, and how the girls were going folk dancing. Shaking the homespun, as Kristin wrote. Sometimes her tone made a mother anxious.

Around nine there was a pounding at the door. She could hear right away that something was wrong. She recognized that ominous battering. The fear that goes straight to a person's fist and makes the door throb like a wooden heart.

One of the Annersa boys, not confirmed yet. He was apparently working as assistant to Wolf Spider on Gudmund Eriksson's team, helping him clear strip roads.

He said Tore was lying on the ice.

Drunk, she thought, as they made their way out there. The boy had told her she'd better take the horse and sledge. She didn't wake Haakon. She was ashamed. They had a little mare again, a dappled one they called Silver Pearl; the two of them got along well. The lad helped her to rig up the little sledge. They didn't say a word as they went.

She helped Silver Pearl cross the wet area at the shore and the stones in another shallow spot where the ice had melted. A good way out onto the ice the boy pointed toward the pile of timber, saying he was over that way. Behind, he said. Then he tried to jump off the sledge and run home. But she grabbed him by the nape of his neck. Without help she would never get Tore onto the sledge, assuming he couldn't stand on his own two feet.

The sledge creaked on; Pearl's hooves scrunched and crunched over the crisp top layer. Hillevi pulled her to in front of the timber; it looked black. There was silence, and in the dim light no tracks were visible in the snow. She knew there must be lots of footprints and piles of horse droppings. But the gray spring night had settled over it all now. The black fringe of spruces on the south side was silent and motionless. The lake and the thick heavy air kept their counsel.

At that very moment she had a powerful feeing of déja vu, such a strong sense of recognition that for a moment she was tossed about in time as if in a wild stream in which the current was unfamiliar. And yet it was so quiet.

Everything was so familiar. The hour, the dim light. The wetness and the horse scent. She knew Tore was lying there dead: on his back with rigid arms grasping the air.

Then there were two sounds at once. The lad gave a sob, and Silver Pearl tossed her head and exhaled a puff between her soft lips. Hillevi told the boy he needn't be afraid and he could just sit in the sledge for the moment.

She walked over to the timber and found him easily. He wasn't lying at all as she had imagined. He was on his side. He'd lost his cap. She never had to feel for a pulse at his throat; she could hear he was breathing.

When Hillevi was very young she had believed that a mother and her child were originally the same being. She ought to have remembered it every time she heard Aunt Eugénie's shrill voice cry to Sara:

But I'm your *moooo-ther*!

She hadn't. She found it unpleasant. Sensed that her aunt was wrong, that what she was referring to could no longer be a circulatory system and shared membranes, although that was how it sounded when her voice trembled. To a fifteen-year-old being a mother had its meaning in the social sense. Conventions, memories, and emotions linked mother and child. But not blood.

She had an insight during her midwifery training. The first placenta she ever saw was on a dissection table. The blood vessels of mother and baby were interwoven. A brilliant and complex dependence, a fine intertwining and binding together. She was able to examine this miracle with pincers under the magnifying lenses of the microscope. The nutrient uptake vessels of the fetus lay interposed with the vessels of the mother. And yet you could trace them one by one, individually. The child was an independent being from beginning to end.

She wished she had had an afterbirth to demonstrate this to every single girl who trembled when her mother's voice quivered its peculiar message: you are mine and you will never be free.

But nowadays she knew it was the mother who was never free.

Tore'd taken a beating. A pretty rough working over. No broken bones, but his face was swollen and one of his eyes was shut tight, embedded in dark blue tissue and fluid. His hands and feet were, of course, chilled down more than the rest of his body. He couldn't have been lying there very long though, and she knew how to get his circulation going. They didn't seem to have knocked him unconscious. He was just drunk.

He reeked of strong liquor. His swollen face was unshaven. That flower petal skin. There was clotted blood in his soft hair. Her memories were intertwined with everything that made up his body and his manner and his voice.

At first she had a wild desire not to let them get away with it. She would make Trond go to the police. But just as quickly she knew how meaningless that would be. No one would have seen a thing. The lad who came to get her had claimed he'd gone back down to the ice to look for a knife he'd lost. That was how he was supposed to have caught sight of Tore. A lie of course. No one would look for a knife in the dark. He'd been sent to get her. They didn't dare leave Tore alone on the ice to freeze to death. They knew the limits, and they must have been more sober than he was.

She wondered if they'd also waited to beat him up until an evening they knew Trond was away.

He came to after a few hours. His blue eyes looked at her for a few seconds; then he started snoring again. She'd set up a makeshift bed on the kitchen settle because she wasn't strong enough to get him up the stairs. He was too big and heavy.

She wondered if he would stop his throat clearing and joking about empty plates now. I could have told you how to live, she thought. In fact that's all I've ever done.

The kitchen clock ticked.

After some time he looked at her again with his blue gaze. He smiled softly, his lips swollen and cracked. She could tell he was still drunk enough not to feel anything. But he would no doubt be in pain soon enough.

They're like homing pigeons.

That's what Hillevi used to say about her children. She meant they came back. Whenever you sent them off, they would eventually find their way back.

Myrtle was like Tore in that way: she had come back too. The room she rented in town was too lonely. That was why a few years later they decided to send us to Katrineholm together, to a private school for older students. Hillevi was determined for Myrtle to finish school. Until that time I had helped in the store, but now I was to go along so Myrtle wouldn't be lonely. Cure her of her homesickness and see to it that she stuck to her books. I attended the same school but in the home economics program in a building that had once been a vocational seminary.

Myrtle wept. But it passed. I had a ball from beginning to end.

That was the kind of word we learned there.

And ones like jazzy.

To begin with we only went folk dancing. We did line dances on the wooden floor and hopped and sang ginger and horseradish fa la la. After a while I started going dancing at the public park with the girls from my program. I was four years older than Myrtle after all. We started smoking cigarettes and having our hair curled at the beauty salon. Some evenings I waited tables at private parties and in better homes to fill up the holes in my budget. Silk stockings and permanents were expensive.

But I wasn't stupid, and I noticed how hot it got when we danced in our line singing I have a fellow back home on the farm. So in the end I took Myrtle along to the real dances too. But we never told Hillevi.

And Myrtle was ever so cautious.

In Katrineholm there were lots of people from up north. None of us distinguished between Jämtland and Lapland and Härjedalen and Ångermanland. We were all just from up north, where people talked about the lean years and knitted socks and sent us care packages.

I met a boy from Vännäs. He owned a single pair of trousers, two shirts, a slipover, and a jacket. The overcoat was his uncle's, like his fur hat. He was ashamed of it.

He had very cold lips and hands. There was a gap between the top edge of my stockings and the elastic of my underpants. I could feel his cold fingers on my skin, his hunger.

We had nowhere indoors to be.

There was a place called Gustaf Robert's woods. Tall spruces and a few benches. I may be an old woman now, but when I smell cigarette smoke out in the cold air, I still sometimes get that feeling, the feeling of giving in, that soft pleasure.

People were like homing pigeons in those days. There was a place on earth they wanted to return to.

Today people are different. And here everything is silent, so much quieter than it used to be.

We were always coming and going.

And people were coming home all the time. People came by bus to Röbäck and Blackwater, to Träske, Kloven, and Skinnarviken. There were lumber merchants and preachers and homoeopathists and men selling ladies' garments and hats.

In the spring the boys would say: our fellin's done for this year. Put those axes away! The logs'll be a rollin' soon! Then the logrollers would arrive, mainly from Värmland. I had a crush on one of them, though I never spoke to him. His name was Fryklund, and he leapt from log to log like a cat. Quick as the water sprite, the old men said. When he came into the store, I felt faint.

The Norwegian must come from someplace too. And he's old enough to be the homing pigeon kind.

But he just sits here and sulks.

There he is now, making his way up the hill with the *Östersund Post* under his arm. I wonder if he ever gets any mail. He's tall and stooped and thin. Not exactly pigeonlike. But I suppose he comes from somewhere too. When he walks up the hill and in among the little spruce trees, he looks more like an old billy goat than anything else. Where do you want to be buried? I feel like asking him. But I'm embarrassed to be so straightforward.

Wherever are you going
you poor old gray goat?

He'll probably end up in the Röbäck churchyard too.

Elis would never have dared go to Gerhard Rosch's art gallery on Friedrich-strasse during his first year in Berlin. That year he didn't own an overcoat, and when he was desperate, he would mask the dirt on his paper collars with a line of white zinc. He was taken there the first time by Erling Christensen, and when he came back alone, the owner didn't remember his name.

The friend of Herrn Architekten Christensen, he said to his wife. She sat in a little room at the back of the large store, a mink stole over her shoulders. Later Elis learned she suffered from rheumatism. She was, said Herr Rosch, my wife, née Sebba.

Gerhard Rosch was correct to a fault and quite solemn. That his wife's maiden name had been Sebba was something he said much later. By that time the cuffs of his suit jacket were as threadbare as Elis's had been. His wife Valdy was still wearing her mink stole.

Dearest God please make me blind
so everything will seem just fine.

Where do these things come from? He must have heard it, but at first he couldn't remember where. He felt like saying it when he noticed that the silk lining of Frau Rosch's cape was tattered to shreds. But he knew that was the kind of thing you should be careful about.

Herr Rosch had three watercolors by Franz Marc. Elis saw them the first time he visited the gallery. He turned away in the middle of the introduction Erling was making, with his thin spring coat thrown across his shoulders, with the nonchalance so typical of his clique and for that matter of his class. Herr Rosch had a well-constructed web, Erling had told him. When he pulled a string gently for a young artist, the big spiders came crawling. The experts and the collectors. Elis would probably have stood there waiting, hat in hand and feet close together in his cracked but well-polished boots, if it hadn't been for the three watercolors. He walked straight over to them.

The first was of a hardy blue horse in a mountain landscape with trees hovering like flowers. The second was three slender horses in pleasing motion. They were hibiscus pink with violet manes. Behind them hills in yellow, misty blue and turquoise. Blue-black cliffs.

Erling came up behind him.

Isn't this kind of thing a bit like cream cakes? he asked.

No.

Well, it certainly is a long shot from everything primitive. And he's flirting with abstraction.

It was correct that in the third watercolor, which was the best one too, the bright yellow horse shapes were overdone and showed a tendency toward the abstract. And yet the roundness of the necks and the huge hindquarters were *horse*, with a timeless scent of stable, of powerful timber pulling, of innocence and solitude.

He craved those three watercolors. By the time Herr Rosch had accepted four of his paintings on commission he had decided to tell him to hold onto the payment if he sold them. Elis hoped to build up his credit that way so he could eventually acquire the Marc watercolors.

Of course it didn't turn out that way. His life was changing, he needed a summer suit and shirts with turndown collars. Dress shoes. A soft hat.

This was because people saw him now. In the past the point had often been not to be seen. To look just like everybody else at the Royal Library, also known as "the Commode." To keep your vest buttoned. Hair short at the neck. Your round-brimmed hat brushed all the way down to the hard-as-nails felt bottom. And yet not to give in to the all-consuming dissolution of poverty. The intoxication of starvation. The feverish hallucinations. To stay on course. Better to die than put one's vest in hock. Go to the library to keep warm because one lived in a ramshackle building where the wallpaper went moldy and the dissolving wooden walls flaked like oatmeal when you pounded in a nail. Except for the cockroaches, longhorn beetles, bedbugs, and sinewy cats, his closest neighbors had been an ageing prostitute with a retarded daughter; a Galician tailor; a "doctor" whose patients were primarily young women who were either unflinching or dissolved in tears; and a stock boy with whom Elis played chess.

Sitting at the library was also educational. The King's Commode brought him refinement.

And now life was changing. There was money in spurts, like when you let yourself come on a girl's stomach. He and Erling Christensen had become acquainted at Alexander Vold's art school. Erling, however, had long since abandoned painting to study architecture in Hamburg, where his father, who was in the shipping business, had contacts. Here in Berlin, in soft-as-silk camel's hair, he was his own man at last. He was ambitious. He stayed solid as Essen steel when splatter painting came into fashion. It pleased him to be the benefactor of a countryman from the provinces.

Consider this noble young savage, he would say to the girls.

Take a good look.

Or shut your eyes. He even smells primitive.

The black suit Elis had purchased secondhand probably smelled of naphthalene.

These were girls who expected a camellia or an orchid corsage from Schmidt's the florist when you collected them for an evening's battle. It had its price.

Although he was never able to purchase the watercolors, he went and checked on them. The art dealer always received him courteously, kindly. Sharp-eyed Valdy Rosch sat in the room at the back calculating on her abacus. Her strawberry blonde hair lay in stiff waves. Her thin lips smiled gently when she saw him. Occasionally she invited him to stay for a cup of tea.

Herr Rosch told him that for the moment the spirit of the collectors was basically cautious. Expressionism, cubism, futurism; they had invested heavily and with no hesitation in those styles. But they weren't very enthusiastic about the pure trickery they thought painters were up to at present. Macabre balls, concerts with monkeys and vacuum cleaners, evening readings where artists chopped their work to pieces or poured unmentionable fluids upon them while the prophets of the day read newly composed manifestos. Such things age quickly. There wasn't much in it for an art dealer either. Therefore, said Herr Rosch, there is more than a negligible interest in people like yourself,

Herr Elv (he pronounced it *elf*): born illustrators, true painters. Artists who stick to their own form of expression.

Elis was embarrassed when Erling boasted of him as primitive, feeling as if he were still wearing a stiff black suit from the Jew who sold secondhand. But with Herr Rosch it was different. Except that it didn't generate much profit. He painted up a storm but barely made enough to keep himself fed in his new suit. Sometimes he would go alone to Pschorr Haus at Potsdamer Platz or other simple eateries just because they served large portions. Sausages, veal shank, trotters in their own fat, and heavy sauerkraut. Piles of Austrian *knödel*. Königsberger *Klops*, and other kinds of saucy meatballs swimming in gravy pearled with fat. He thought of the tuberculosis as if it were one of those wild emaciated cats that rubbed around his legs in the Kreuzberg tenement where he rented a room. Those fiendish memories had to be appeased.

In Berlin he recognized nothing when he first arrived. The throngs of people distorted his picture of the world. True, he had hardly known that he had one before. He had thought the world was the world. With mountains and oceans at the edges. But here: was the sky even sky and the rain rain? He went to the Tiergarten, dragging his thin-soled shoes through the grass. It seemed so rough and matted. Could have been factory produced. The smell of gas and garbage, of beer, of thick human filth, of fumes in the underground rail system, coffee beans roasting, dog piss, and pit coal penetrated his dreams at night. He tried to recognize something. Anything. But around him the city turned, its streets spokes, burning and flickering with human faces. The wheel of Ixion.

The refinement for which he had the Commode to thank didn't help. He had seen blood on the street but did not know how it got there.

Back in Oslo it had been made clear to him that you didn't travel to Berlin without addresses and contacts. He had one single one, a girl called Irma. He'd met her at the cafés, seen her dance at parties at artists' studios. She was a dancer. Not a ballet dancer. The kind of dancing she did she had learned in Berlin, where she had returned when she realized that Oslo, which was still the old Kristiania in many ways with its rigid, extremely provincial bourgeoisie, was not yet ready for her dancing. Or even for expressionism.

Irma was nowhere to be found. He tried to trace her to a cabaret and to a department store where she had modeled. That was where her tracks vanished.

Sometimes when skinny women pressed close to him on the street, he would wonder if she was out there in the flicker of the street lights. He tried to conjure up a better fate for her: some rich fellow had noticed her at the department store. She was a real looker. Maybe she was in the pictures now.

The streets clattered and screeched and squealed in his brain when he tried to sleep. The people were as impatient as bedbugs. He shut his eyes tight. One night when he had insomnia and was out wandering the streets he heard a body fall with a heavy thud into the River Spree. He had glimpsed Home Guard uniforms down at the harbor and had forced himself to continue walking normally, indifferently, like a person who had heard nothing and seen nothing. After turning the corner he began to run; he ran until his lungs ached, and he found a café to slip into. He couldn't sleep that night either. He was afraid.

He thought about his grandfather. The Old Man. And about his own father, who hadn't been a bit better. But now there was not any specific face he knew was the one to keep an eye on so you'd know when you were safe. There were too many. Though the fellow he saw on the steps that night and who scared him half out of his wits was probably just as frightened as he was.

While saving up to leave Norway, he had dreamt of a solitary existence in Berlin. The end of all that humiliating dependence. A place where no one would try to find out who he really was.

You don't know who I am.

When he realized no one really did know though, literally not a single one of the millions of people in that huge wheel, terror seized him.

At that moment of abandonment his memory produced an address.

He had come to Germany by boat, working his way over as a mess waiter. When the boat had passed Bremerhavn and was creeping up the Weser, past small towns with homes that looked like dolls' houses, he stood on deck telling the chief machine engineer his plans for Berlin. He was a decent man. His sister was married and lived in Berlin, where her German husband was a printer. He mentioned the address, and it sank straight into the strange oblivion that is one huge reservoir, inaccessible to either willpower or intention. When the terror came over him, when the wheel of Ixion swung at night with its fluttering faces and he was half insane with the solitude he had so hotly desired just six months before, it finally surfaced. He could hardly believe it was true. It was as if someone had touched him.

And stranger still, *Sieger und Sohn Druckerei* was no more than a couple of blocks from the tenement where he lived.

Karl Sieger was one of the few who had something to come back to after the war. His right leg had been badly injured by a grenade. It was amputated at a hospital at the front, and he had walked on a strapped-on wooden leg ever since. He also had something to offer the young Norwegian woman with whom he had fallen in love: a printing house, a petit bourgeois life in a Berlin neighborhood with a milk store on the corner, a textile shop, a bakery, and a local branch library.

They had met when each of them was on an outing: he with his brass band, she with her world traveler of a brother who was a ship's engineer on a Norwegian cruise vessel that had been rerouted to Rügen. Since then she had had no one to speak Norwegian with, and she was hungry for stories from the town she still called Kristiania.

Needless to say they didn't have a job for Elis. The printing house was very old. They produced wrappers for wedding and funeral sweets, songbooks, poorly illustrated dream books, and handbooks in fortune telling. Their most lucrative business was in colored woodcuts from old blocks: the infant Jesus with lambs and doves, girls sitting looking dreamily out the window, cheerful craftsmen wielding a plane or a trowel. There were verses under the pictures, printed in the old, difficult-to-read but dearly beloved Gothic script. A carpenter sat with his foot on the floor, his muscular leg tensed, leaning forward with all his weight on the jointer plane. He appeared to be singing something like *Carpenters are wise and clever, making things that last forever.* And the smith's occupation was also an essential one: *See the blacksmiths at their bellows; we require those cheerful fellows; both in wartime and at peace, our need for them will just increase.* These bright verses with their idealism from a guild society reminiscent of times past seemed comical to Elis. But Karl Sieger made it clear to him that they were anything but. Craftsmen's trades were gaining status again. Had he not heard of the National Socialists? He gave him flyers to read. There wasn't much about trades in those particular ones, more about Bolshevism. Karl also confided that there was a rumor the party wasn't satisfied with the quality of the printing his firm was providing.

They thought the emblem was too heavy. The district head was threatening to order his flyers and brochures from a different printer.

Karl didn't see what the problem was. He thought it looked solid. But Elis immediately knew what they wanted. He had a nose for that kind of thing: a kind of modern elegance based on tradition. Look, this is what they want. An iron cross with bent arms. He drew it to show what he meant. Elegance. Austerity. A sense of focus the old blocks would never render. So he made a new printing plate for the swastika.

That was how he got himself hired. Old Grünbaum almost lost his job over it. There was a horrible moment when Elis realized—him or me. He was old and thin and supported a daughter with an out-of-wedlock child who was now an unemployed youth of sixteen.

The wheel of Ixion. It flickered. The human spokes branched out. You or me?

That time the swinging wheel spared them both. Elis had the ideas and images that brought them business. They were both kept on, Elis as an illustrator and tinter. Herr Grünbaum took Karl's hands and wept.

Elis went to Die Neue Welt, a huge beer hall where men, mainly workers, drank and listened to the new political upstart who was originally Austrian. He found him parodic.

A long time passed before he heard Adolf Hitler again. By that time he had met Erling Christensen and no longer sat in backstreet cafés and beer halls. He had even been to the Theatre im Westen, the Scala, and the Wintergarten. Erling, who moved in a circle where everyone mocked everything, took him along to the university student union. When Elis heard the man's voice, he thought at first it couldn't be the same person he'd heard at Die Neue Welt. He was soft spoken and responsive to the crowd. Erling didn't comment afterward, and they didn't go on to a bar, just went their separate ways. He needed to be alone.

Ah well, the solemnity would pass of course. Elis recognized that from home. Every time an itinerant preacher came around, the whole village turned religious. After three weeks he was forgotten and everything went back to normal. No chapel was ever built in Blackwater because on an everyday basis the villagers were more drawn to common sense than to the metaphysical.

Soon Erling was back at the Papagei mocking almost everything again.

345

They played Negro jazz there and made mixed drinks with Bols and Polish vodka. He and Elis also went to cheaper bars patronized by working girls, where they drank razzle-dazzles mixed from unlabelled bottles of crude alcohol and sweet thick black currant syrup. Elis moved out of Kreuzberg, didn't look in at the Siegers' so often in the evenings, but continued to work at the printing house until the architectural firm where Erling was employed started taking him on regularly to do wall commissions. The first one was in a newly built villa in Grunewald. *Funktionalizmus*. The owners wanted a painted vineyard to cover one of the dining room walls.

Although he still couldn't make his income extend to the Franz Marc watercolors, they had become an obsession. He had come to Berlin because of Franz Marc. He hadn't known what a thing of the past expressionism was. It infuriated him that everything happened so fast. Wasn't a good painter a good painter regardless of how the wheel of time swung? Erling Christensen smiled.

You're nothing but a kid, he said. A young wonderfully raw man of the forest from the periphery of the habitable world. But for that very reason, the future belongs to you.

No, Erling didn't know who he was. And that was just as well. Elis went off to Friedrichstrasse to ask Herr Rosch to hold the watercolors for a while longer. But they were no longer on the wall where they had hung.

You didn't sell them!

No, he had moved them for safekeeping.

Gerhard Rosch seemed secretive. Damn it, he may not be reliable after all, Elis thought.

I can offer you the 1916 edition of *Der blaue Reiter*, the art dealer said.

So Elis left with the expressionist calendar edited by Franz Marc. Rosch didn't charge him for it.

I won't be able to keep them anyway was Rosch's perplexing comment.

The next week Elis received a sizeable payment from Erling's architecture firm, and he went to Friedrichstrasse to offer Gerhard Rosch a down payment. He had an unpleasant feeling that now they were the ones who didn't trust him.

I'm not asking you to give me the watercolors now. I just want to put some money down so I can be sure you will hold them for me.

Gerhard Rosch sat looking down. It was hot in the little room at the back of the shop. The light was weak because Valdy Rosch had pulled the curtains. Elis had had tea. He didn't like it. It was virtually tasteless. Frau Rosch served Italian almond biscotti. The curtains were English chintz. The walls were covered with little paintings, perhaps Valdy Rosch's own favorites. Mostly landscapes. Nineteenth century. Some quite early. Italian villages on mountain slopes. Ocean bays. Cliffs in Switzerland or Austria. The multitude made him nervous. The cramming.

Frau Rosch suddenly said:

My husband moved the Marc watercolors down to the cellar. We can't have them up here.

I don't understand.

The only thing Elis could imagine was that they'd found out the paintings were stolen property but didn't want him to know.

We've had a visit from a storm trooper, Frau Rosch said.

Valdy!

She held up her hand with its slender fingers to her husband and went on:

You must consider the matter carefully, Herr Elv. Do you really want to buy those watercolors? I am not even certain they would allow us to sell them. In any case we will have to bide our time.

Elis didn't know what to say. He wondered how the storm trooper had behaved. Had he ranted and raved? Been violent? He felt like making a comment about the uneducated but bit his tongue. Refinement, he thought. There are people who lack it everywhere.

Did he shout? he asked cautiously.

Herr Rosch nodded.

They certainly had, when Elis considered the matter, any number of things for sale that the new regime termed depraved and perverse. And of course they had brought in tidy sums. Gerhard Rosch's long nose had a talent for sniffing out good art. Frau Rosch had a real hand with the abacus.

There were two things he didn't understand. Why wasn't good art simply good. Once and for all. I can tell when it is good. It doesn't require many words. No theory of art and not a lot of political philosophy. It's *good*. Gerhard Rosch knows that too.

The second thing: Jews.

They were sitting next to each other. They seemed to be about the same height, but the man was dark and thickset. Frau Valdy was strawberry blonde and bony. They're Jews, he thought. Obviously.

But what's that? He thought about the tailor he knew. An entirely different kind of person.

Thinking about it upset him. It was the same feeling he had had when the people he socialized with in Kristiania had talked about their sex life. They were so radical they rushed straight into the biology of it.

The zoology of it.

For God's sake.

They were sticky arguments. They clung to whoever was being discussed. The trash. The Jew.

Herr Rosch, he said. I expect to be able to purchase those watercolors. And I thank you very much for the tea. *Vielen Dank, gnädige Frau Rosch! Auf wiedersehen.*

He felt like saying: bear up. It will be over soon. But of course he didn't say it. With Rosch, the art dealer, he was on formal terms.

Erling Christensen was convinced things would soon blow over. The excesses, that is. And yet Elis didn't really feel like telling him about the storm trooper who had—most likely—raided Gerhard Rosch's art gallery. At the architecture firm they scoffed loudly at the new men, at their strutting in uniforms, at the nationalistic blather. In short, the excesses. However, according to Erling, a revolution was actually necessary. Germany had to rise up out of the humiliation of the shameful peace of Versailles. If young people weren't endowed with ideals and confidence in the future, the Bolsheviks would take over, and it would be like Russia. He had shown Elis photos from the Ukraine: the corpses of people who had died of starvation on the streets.

The revolution had arrived, although not in the way one expected revolutions to begin. The National Socialists had won an astonishing landslide victory.

The will of the people, said Erling. The good German people.

He had signed on with the party quite a while ago, taking on various assignments for the district offices. There was a flurry around Erling Christensen like the wind in your hair when you rode in his Deutsche Kraftvagn convertible. But he was the same sarcastic jester he had always been. *The good German people.* Impossible to know if he was mocking.

Everyone at the firm of architects, with the possible exception of the secretaries, constantly made fun of the propaganda. The slogans flew around the room. And sometimes when they were all standing there studying the blueprints for a bathhouse, fat Aron Klein might have to leave for an appointment with a client.

Ah! Erling would sigh. Alone at last!

His way of talking was a parody of propaganda clichés. And his jokes were naturally much funnier the closer they came to the really sensitive subjects. Even the secretaries listened, giggling and blushing. And there were risks associated with making fun of propaganda too. Herr Christensen was priceless. You never knew what he would say next.

He was long legged and elegant. Probably exhausted from overwork, but he got through on phenidrine. *Well, only just this once!* At a time when everything, everything had to get done!

It's only this once
It won't come again . . .

No, there was nothing like Erling's humming, his laughter, his heels clattering down the stairs to capture the flurry and the wind in one's hair that was the future. Everything was possible.

They rode in his DKW. Elis toured Germany. He also traveled alone on trains to decorate the walls of bathhouses, gymnasiums, schools. But it was more fun gadding about with Erling. Late one Saturday night in August, they had driven out to a Bavarian veterans' meeting. The party officials called the place Valhalla. It wasn't actually a place at all, just farmland with wheat fields smelling of dung in the night air, groves of pine trees with a scent of balsamic turpentine, and a sandy patch on which the old storm troopers had erected their tents. The campfires glowed, and the veterans sang: *Sacred beacon, gather our youth!* Erling and he had never laughed as much as they laughed that night. At their drunken revelries, their superannuated enthusiasm.

Philistines in uniform! whispered Erling, choking with laughter. The old men reeled around the fires, bellowing like ruttish bulls.

The next morning when Erling and Elis left in the DKW, they had the top down and were singing:

Sacred beacon, gather our youth!
That courage may grow
by the flickering flame!

The uniformed philistines were supposed to continue on Sunday with athletics, but many of them were sleeping it off in the wheat fields. Erling and Elis hadn't overdone it since Elis was expected to be back at work on Monday morning decorating the canteen wall in a textile factory.

The new men wanted lots of murals, large and bright. Throngs of people. Horses tossing their manes. He sometimes thought he was doing a good job of painting à la Bjarne Ness, the one with that goddamned *Conqueror*. But Ness hadn't been a bad painter after all, and Elis was having one helluva fine time. Making money too.

He hadn't given the Marc watercolors so much as a passing thought in the last couple of years. But one morning he was sitting in his bright new apartment—a bedroom, a kitchenette, and a large studio with a skylight—having a cup of coffee before getting down to work on a large preparatory drawing. He was hunting for his pencil sketch when the blue rider surfaced. There were a few other things having to do with Franz Marc in that pile as well. A catalog. Cassirer's facsimile edition of the sketchbook.

He thought about Cassirer being a Jewish name. That made him uncomfortable. It must mean cashier. Like Frau Rosch at her abacus. He knew that Marc had been at least half Jewish. Half—a quarter—an eighth? Those absurd but adhering terms. Yes, *sticky.*

Erling Christensen laughed at them.

Don't take it so hard, he said. It's all an invention of the bureaucrats.

But on the street, said Elis.

My dear Nordic innocent, there is no doubt that a great many things take place on the street that should not. But what can you expect? All the out-of-work thugs who were robbing people in the name of Bolshevism just a few years ago are now being taken in hand by the youth movements. It takes time to civilize them.

Herr Grünbaum's grandson Erich now got up early in the mornings to participate in athletic exercise and parades. Elis assumed he would have been in prison now if he had kept to his old ways. Herr Grünbaum was grateful. The neighborhood was also neat and tidy. That was something in any case.

They never spoke for long about the political situation, he and Erling. There wasn't time. He had touched on the matter of the Jews once, the last time he had been to Rosch's art gallery. He had been very upset afterward.

But look around, said Erling. Is not our dear friend Aron Klein a Jew? We are working at top level, responsible directly to the *Generalbauinspektor* now. And you see Aron is included. Aron is one of our best and most sought-after architects. And who was the Olympic hope of Germany? Who threw the javelin like a Teutonic Amazon? A little Jew-girl! We are in a completely different situation now than during those frenzied early years. Good Lord, Elias, don't sit there *drooping*. You look like Aron Klein. Grouchy and pasty. I swear to you he'll be around the firm until the end of time. Ever dissatisfied.

Aron Klein was black haired and almost pathologically fat. He moved slowly. Erling was right about his often looking discontented.

Elis recalled a poster now. Little girls on a bathing beach. A sign: FÜR JUDEN VERBOTEN. And that collective sigh of relief he had once heard Erling mimic when Aron Klein left the room: *Here we are, alone at last!*

People can joke about anything, Erling said.

The Jews who had conspired with Bolshevik Russia were all gone from Germany now, he said. The loan sharks too. The goal has been achieved. And you will have noticed that the boycotting of Jewish shops never really got off the ground. They'll shuffle around here until Armageddon. What the leaders are preoccupied with now is foreign policy.

Dearest God please make me blind
so everything will seem just fine!

It just popped up. But it went wrong. The wrong kind of mockery. Erling gave him a cold stare.

Where do you get that kind of thing from? he asked. Your friend Herr Rosch?

But it had passed over quickly. He was very enthusiastic about Elis's drawing.

You're an ignorant animal, you gifted shit. No analysis. Zero knowledge of history. You musicians and artists. You live in a world of your own. But what fantastic characters you make. You really *see*. This fellow from your home tract in Norway—well, I assume that's where you got him from—is divine. Aryan beauty. What is he, a fisherman? A crofter? Oh yes, Elias. You talk all kinds of bull. But you are such a great fucking genius I forgive you. Look at him. The Northerner. A fisherman chieftain with the pure profile of Echnathon.

Akhenaten, he corrected. He was so wound up he had started speaking Norwegian. Otherwise they mainly spoke German together nowadays. Erling had married a banker's daughter. Aryan in spite of the profession, he had laughed.

Elis didn't acknowledge his comments about the profile. The man was his father Vilhelm.

His pa. Gudmund. Jon. Even Old Man Lubben himself. They turned up now and then. They fit in.

The pure profile of Akhenaten.

It wasn't a joke.

Erling said Elis *saw*. Truly saw.

But what do I see?

He leafed through the folders in front of him. Franz Marc wrote that the European eye had poisoned and maimed the world. That is why I dream of a new Europe.

So did Erling. But he probably didn't mean the same thing Franz Marc had meant.

Just take life as it comes, Elias, Erling had said. It's stronger than you are in any case. Sail right into the wind! No cowardice and no whining—face the storm!

Herculean, he said. That was Herculean thinking.

Who the hell was he? Elis looked Hercules up the next time he was at the Commode. But it didn't do him much good. He felt ignorant. If he had met Franz Marc, he thought, they wouldn't have been able to have a real conversation, just a lot of café banter and mockery. He had too many gaps to conceal. But when he saw Marc's paintings he knew what he meant. He decided to go back to Herr Rosch and make him an offer for the watercolors. Gerhard Rosch ought to be open to negotiation now. Unless he was too frightened. That was an uncomfortable thought. But new regulations kept being announced.

When he got to Friedrichstrasse, although it was the middle of the day, the metal blinds at Gerhard Rosch's art gallery were down. Elis went into the pastry shop on the corner and asked. The girl behind the counter didn't know anything about the Rosches, not even who they were. He convinced her to go and ask the owner's wife.

They must have moved, she said.

Where? Do you know?

She just shrugged her shoulders awkwardly; he was outraged. She was a proper German Frau with a potato nose, a bust like a loaf of bread, and an enormous bottom. She looked absurd when she tried to shrug her shoulders. Had she learned that at operetta performances?

Do you have an address register?

The damnable woman shook her head.

Things went just as badly at the tobacconist's. The owner, an old war invalid, of course had a register and he leafed through it skillfully with one hand. But Gerhard Rosch wasn't listed.

What do you want with him? he asked.

It was beginning to remind him of a game of chess. Although Elis was just an ignorant gaping Northerner out in the great big world, he was not a fool when it came to chess. He knew when a move had been made that would prove much later in the game to have been decisive. A shabby tobacconist would not ask that question of a well-dressed man unless the moves were not going according to plan. So Elis answered:

He owes me money.

And yes, that changed things!

Ask the Herschels. Greengrocers on the corner. I'm sure they keep track of each other. You must get what he owes you.

Elis found the shop, but it was closed too. The windows were covered with paper. But the tobacconist had sounded sure they were there. Elis pounded for a long time, and when a woman finally opened the door, he could tell she was afraid although she was trying to look nonchalant. Behind her in the dim interior he glimpsed a small thin man in a black felt skullcap. No dissimulation there; he looked like a dog, and he was anticipating a beating. Frau Herschel, who was sweaty and fat, said she didn't know where the Rosches had gone.

Aren't they still living in their apartment? she queried.

Do you have the address?

She shook her head. She probably did. The shop smelled of earth and mold, but there were no vegetables. Not so much as a crate of potatoes.

Instead of continuing to interrogate the surly woman, he said a polite thank you and farewell. He saw her combination of relief and amazement. And he wasn't even wearing his NSDAP pin. He actually only wore it when he had to. He took it out when they were going to show drawings to the leaders at the GBI offices or when he traveled to a new place for a commission. It was a formality, Erling had told him. Party membership wasn't even compulsory if you were employed directly by the *Generalbauinspektor*. But it facilitated contacts.

He didn't know what to do next. His mind was blocked. He was always in a hurry when he was out: on the run, had appointments. That was how he felt now too. But inside him a clock had stopped. His whole body was suffused with a long drawn-out feeling of extended time. If he had stepped out onto the street, he would have been run over. The wheel of Ixion would have turned right on top of me, he thought. I would never have been fast enough to escape.

He found himself at a standstill in front of a butcher's shop. Pork rind scrubbed white. Bacon streaked pink. Dark succulent beef roasts, their surfaces gleaming. It all looked extremely neat and delectable. Except for one thing: a black clot of blood in a pig's ear.

He crossed the street to a bar and had a double cognac. There was no whisky any more. Cigarettes tasted like shit. He ordered another cognac and tried to strike up a conversation with the bartender, who was polishing glasses with a bleached and mangled towel. Asked about the packet of cigarettes he had just purchased, whether Timms were what used to be Times. The damned man just shrugged his shoulders. Elis felt the pull; he could see the wheel swinging. Talk, smoke, booze. None of it helped one damned bit. And the people everyone was talking about, the people he had never seen at the hotels, the swimming pools, the office, or even at the Papagei, those original Aryans, the German people, *Das Volk*, had started shrugging their shoulders. Like the French. Didn't know that Timms had ever been Times. Didn't know that the wheel was spinning them.

Drinking wouldn't make it go away. It was spinning, revolving fast.

Ixion, you are spinning in blood.

Of course these are exaggerations, he thought. I see in images. That makes it absurd. But significant. That's my talent. *It.* I have it and without it I'd be—scraping the bark from trees?

No, I'd be dead.

Damn that pig's ear. Now all he could see was blood. Women's blood on spread thighs, the clotted blood sliding. Why he saw those things he didn't know. He saw the backs of heads, skulls. Clots of blood in graying hair. He saw clothing: gray-brown wool drenched in blood.

Even when he was little he had had inner visions that were clear and distinct and full of details. Often they came to him when he was falling asleep. He thought he must be sick in the head. At the same time he took pleasure in evoking them. In allowing himself to slip into that visionary state.

They were not memories. He had visions of things he could never possibly have seen. He had painted the vineyard on the wall of the Grunewald villa more or less on the basis of one of those childhood visions. He didn't know where it came from. But he no longer thought of it as a sickness.

I ought to be painting now. Because I can see things; I am somewhere between intoxication and nausea. My painting would be full of significance. The greater the light, the sharper and blacker the shadow. I'd like to paint everything I've seen since I arrived. Out of tightly compressed darkness, sharp as a knife, one figure at a time. One. And another. And another.

Lift them off the wheel of Ixion and affix them, imbued with clarity and significance. See. Not take pity. Truly see.

In the end it wasn't difficult to get hold of the Rosches' address. Erling had it. But Elis had been reluctant to ask him. He finally pulled himself together to do so at the Papagei after a few drinks; the girls were quarrelling, and the orchestra was playing Viennese waltzes. That's what was played all the time nowadays. No nigger music and no pimps around to make sure the girls weren't wasting their time.

Ordnung muss sein, said Erling sarcastically.

Speaking of which, do you know where Rosch lives?

Speaking of what?

Nothing. Where does he live?

Peppermint tea! one of the girls shouted. They were talking about how to treat a urinary tract infection; their speech was already slurred.

What do you want from Rosch?

He owes me money.

It just popped out. Landed with an unintended splash. He wished the girls would change the subject. They weren't attractive.

Oh shit, said Erling. You must get it back before he clears out.

Clears out?

Like Klein, said Erling. He's in New York now. There are two kinds. The ones who want to sit and sigh in the synagogue go to Palestine. The ones who are drawn toward capitalism end up in the U.S. Don't let him spend your money on his passage.

Elis went to the Rosches' apartment the very next day, but no one opened when he rang the bell. Why did he have the feeling there was someone in there anyway? The artificial silence when he peered through the letter slot. As if the murmuring and ticking and creaking you would normally hear in a city apartment were being held back.

That was his imagination of course. But unpleasant nonetheless.

He went home and wrote a letter: *Sehr geehrter Herr Rosch!*

Two days later and at the hour specified in the letter he rang the bell, but no one opened that time either. The nameplate was gone. A week later a letter arrived from Gerhard Rosch saying they had moved but Elis's letter had been forwarded. He gave Elis the new address.

Kreuzberg. Unbelievable. Not far from the tenement he had lived in himself. Straight from Wilhelmstrasse to poverty. While he had hastened in the other direction, toward the finer parts of town, to Alexanderplatz to have his residence permit renewed.

Poverty was the chapped, drafty, stained state that as a child he had believed to be natural. The slightly nasty smell in the corners. It didn't suit Valdy Rosch. She was still wearing her cape, though it was worn thin.

I waited too long, Elis thought. But why did I come here at all? He said to himself that people are more appealing when they are poor. Easier to deal with. But he would still have preferred them to be as before. The only familiar objects were an Italian landscape and an ocean bay, two very small oils in thick frames he recalled from Frau Rosch's cubbyhole office. Everything else had been sold at compulsory auction. That is, everything that was left after the raid. Which hadn't been much.

Raid?

We had invested heavily, Herr Elv. Do you recall my Otto Dixes? My Kandinsky? The painters of Franz Marc's generation. The blue rider group, you know.

Did they confiscate the watercolors?

No, naturally not. I saw to it that they were in safekeeping. You've paid three hundred marks after all. You have an option to purchase them. But I don't know if you'll be able to get them out.

Out?

Gerhard Rosch looked down at his hands. He looked embarrassed. There was no question about what he had meant. Out of the country.

Let me pay you another three hundred. No, two hundred. That's all I have on me.

It's not so easy to get at them now.

Accept Herr Elv's money, Gerhard, said Valdy Rosch in her cashier's tone of voice.

He was so deeply distressed that it was a great relief to get away. Afterward, he thought he should have asked them more questions. If they weren't allowed to have the gallery open any more, what were they living on?

Out of the country, Herr Rosch had said.

Did they intend to leave? And in that case, did they have any money? Would they be able to get exit visas?

He had found it too awkward to ask. They had always lived in different worlds. Questions didn't roll naturally off the tongue. When he was with them, he was always afraid of saying something inappropriate and awkward, even now when Gerhard Rosch's jacket sleeves were frayed at the edges rather than his own.

I don't even like them very much, he thought. I have always felt uncomfortable in their company. Particularly now. When I gave Gerhard Rosch the two hundred marks without getting a receipt, both he and I were ashamed. It's just as well we don't meet again.

He would have liked to be on his own now and just paint. But he had a deadline, had to submit a full-scale drawing on cardboard within a week. When he got back from the Rosches', it looked vapid and flat.

He was overcome by the urge to paint in oil. After pacing his studio for a while, he turned the cardboard sketch to the wall and started tacking a canvas to a frame. The soft hammering sound restored his confidence. Once he had begun to paint he stopped thinking. Was unable to think, did not need to. Erling Christensen had been right. Ignorant as a beast. No analysis. So just keep on going. He painted all week.

He knew he'd missed the deadline, but he was unable to stop painting and turn the cardboard back around. So he asked for a reprieve. After a couple of days he tacked a new canvas. He didn't see anyone but the tobacconist and the girls where he ate. In the evenings his mind was completely blank, and he could hardly wait for morning to come. He drank at night to dull the ennui. But not very much. He was too eager to get back to work, and he worked best from early in the morning until noon.

In the end Erling came up to see him, concerned at not having heard anything.

I got stuck on that sketch, Elis said. Don't know what the hell the problem is.

Erling turned the large piece of cardboard around. He had to agree that it didn't seem to be shaping up very well.

I've painted too many people walking into the wind, said Elis. Their hair and their skirts blowing. And mural painting is getting so damn dry and dull. I used to have al fresco dreams once upon a time.

But this stuff you're doing in oil, what the hell is it? Caricatures?

Don't you recognize this lady? Elis asked, pointing at the canvas on the easel. She was a little woman with matchstick-legs protruding from her galoshes. She wore a violet hat with a drooping bow. Her eyes were like black shiny buttons.

Sie ist aber komisch—ne?

358

But Erling shrugged his shoulders. He didn't find her particularly comical. And why should he recognize her?

I thought you might have seen her around Oslo, said Elis. She was quite a character. Her name was Miss Blumenthal. She ran a painting school in those days. In fact, maybe she still does.

And what are those wavy lines?

Well, in a way they're a gate. And a fence. Ironwork from the Drammen Road. As I recall it, you know.

But what about the red swirls inside it? Is that supposed to be some kind of plant?

Shit, no. that's her circulatory system.

In the fence?

He ignored the question, saying that he had recently become interested in blood and circulation.

I used to do skeletons. I learned to draw from the inside out. Remember?

This isn't going anywhere, Erling said, turning his back to the canvas.

But he was wrong. Miss Rebecca Blumenthal was good. She looked at Elis with those Pekinese eyes of hers.

My dear young man, she said.

He said he didn't think he was ever going to be able to submit a drawing for this competition. Erling Christensen was upset of course, said he was letting them down.

I'm just a painter, said Elis. I paint what I see. Not what I want. And oh, yes, I paint what amuses me too. And that little old lady amuses me.

I can't see anything funny about that painting. It's equivocal and disagreeable.

I've heard that one before, said Elis. Cheap, disgusting. Product of a deranged mind.

All right, all right, said Erling, as if to a child.

And every single one of these canvases is a portrait. Almost every one anyway. From memory. The war invalid is a tobacconist on Friedrichstrasse. That young man is named Grünbaum.

Erling stared at Erich Grünbaum, who had a hungry doglike face and a saggy brown uniform.

The old man in the skullcap is a greengrocer. Or was. Can you see how he has locked his face and shut it up tight?

Dearest God please make me dumb
so to Dachau I won't come.

There was silence for a while.

Do you socialize with people like that? Erling asked. People who say that kind of thing?

No, you and I heard that in—what the hell was it called? That place they said was Valhalla. Don't you remember?

No.

Jesus Christ, Erling, don't you remember that veteran's meeting in Bavaria?

Oh yeah, said Erling. But you can't have heard anything like that there. Out of the question.

But I did, I'm telling you! Late that night. From a man reeling out into the wheat field. One of those total boozers who was stomping around the campfire bellowing Sacred beacon. Remember?

Sacred beacon, gather our youth!
That courage may grow
by the flickering flame!

Erling actually started to laugh. And responded softly in Norwegian.

They were already losers.

The storm troopers, losers? He found that difficult to believe.

Would you like a cognac?

Erling actually looked at his wristwatch before saying yes. *Ordnung muss sein.* He was a married man now after all. Seldom went to the Papagei. He found it too rowdy.

Those old storm troopers, he said. The ones who went around selling copies of the *Angriff* and paving the way for the revolution. Now they're quite taboo.

Think so? They had already outlived their time when we sat snickering at them, hadn't they? The intellectuals were in now. *We need minds!* And they came of course, wagging their tails behind them. Bringing their analyses and their knowledge.

Erling took a long look at him.

You don't count yourself among the intellectuals, do you? he asked.

You have frequently pointed out that I am not one.

But you can be a damned snake in the grass, that's for sure.

He had suddenly begun to laugh, and they raised their glasses. Elis thought: This is a conversation straight out of our youth. When we sat and chatted at the cafés or had our great visions up at Vold's. Particularly after Vold had gone home. That was why it seemed so harmless. Forgotten tomorrow. Yes, it was quite simply right out of the Norwegian days. He was pleased about that. Erling and he shouldn't part at odds. Because he wasn't ungrateful in fact.

That was when he realized he intended to take off.

Perhaps the drink was starting to go to his head. In any case he brought out two of the other canvases he had painted in the last few weeks. He wanted to show Erling that he trusted him.

Look, he said. This is a portrait.

What the hell? It's just a dog, said Erling.

Yeah, these are old ideas, you know. There are hardly any new ones. Gainsborough. He did dog portraits. Pomeranian Bitch and Pup.

But yours is nothing but a mutt, said Erling.

Right, a real son of a bitch. Black and filthy. I knew him. And here's that little girl from Tannenberg. Remember her?

No.

She modeled one day when I was working on the auditorium mural.

The girl had been rosy and round cheeked. A chubby hand holding a teddy bear. At the time he had put her at the far edge of a group. Now she was alone, and he had put in a rat on a treadmill instead of the teddy.

Are you out of your mind?

That's realism, said Elis. Solid realism. Have you seen Otto Dix? And you know of course there are rats, rats with wheels and rats with motors. They have rough coats. Glued onto sheet metal. You wind them up with a key on the side.

But they don't have that symbol.

Maybe not. But the symbol can be found on children's balls and play tanks. And even on my mouthwash.

I would advise you to remove the emblem, Erling said softly.

And that low tone of voice was virtually a pledge; this and other matters would be forgotten when they had parted forever. He didn't know what to say. In the end it flew out of him:

I'm off to Paris, I think.

Erling said nothing.

Don't you want to see a bit of the world yourself? Elis asked, doing his best not to look Erling in the eye.

I'm married now. I have citizenship. I can't just take off at a moment's notice.

Whatever. Myself, I think I need to see Paris before war breaks out, said Elis.

You're scared.

Yes.

Amazing. It was as easy as that to say it. When he said it, his pa and Jon and Gudmund sank into the wall. Even the Old Man vanished. None of them said a word.

The first time I was in Jonetta's house I was six years old. I went on my own because I had heard in the shop that my Uncle Anund Larsson was there. And he was too, sitting on the kitchen settle.

It's a good thing you've come, Risten, he said, because I've been up at our old camp and seen something I think you would have liked to see, would have given your life to see.

I wondered what that might be.

You try and guess, he said. He was a little critter, I'll tell you that. No bigger than an ermine.

That made Jonetta laugh, and she said that in the old days they had been bigger, almost like people. I couldn't guess at all, and I felt foolish and a little unhappy. So Laula Anut lifted me up onto the settle and Jonetta gave me milky coffee and rusks to dunk.

When I got home, I didn't tell Hillevi I'd seen my uncle. I don't know why I kept it to myself. But I couldn't resist asking about the gnomes. She just laughed.

There's no such thing as gnomes, she said. They were just something people believed in in the old days before there was electric light. In those days people saw all kinds of things in the corners.

But my uncle had told me you could see them in broad daylight and quite clearly. And I'd known it before: lots of people didn't dare to go into a pasture hut in the autumn in case the gnomes had already moved in for the winter. There was that one my uncle saw in his father's abandoned *gåetie*. He had stepped right back out, hasped the door and left.

They may be little people, but they aren't harmless, and they want to be left in peace, he said.

They had white cows and little goats with gold bands around their necks, he'd told me. And they loved to dress colorfully. They carried silver around and buried it.

And incidentally they had dog eyes.

I knew the little people had abandoned the villages, which was probably why Hillevi thought they didn't exist. My uncle said they just moved as far as they could from anyplace there was electricity. They lived way up in the woods on the mountains now. They were on Mount Giela, in the birch woods so high up that only a few spruces appear among the birches, and they had been there for two hundred if not four hundred years.

Up there no one counts the centuries; the little people certainly don't, my uncle said.

They no longer wore the colorful garb with shiny buttons that older people talked about. They were small and gray now. In the past they had been the size of children, now they were no bigger than ermines.

Laula Anut was one of the few who knew what their lives were like nowadays. They mainly lived under the roots of trees and in windfalls covered with green moss. They made burrows there and lined them with soft things: tussocks and reindeer hair and grouse down. They still had their cows and their goats, but the animals were smaller too and so gray it was hard to catch a glimpse of them. You mistook them for wisps of mist in the marsh.

But you can hear their bells ring, he said. And you can hear the elves call their cows. It's just too bad the streams murmur so loud; their noise drowns out the sounds.

But some people still thought you might encounter them and should watch out not to trample on them or get in their way.

If you do go wrong and stumble over them, you must be quick to apologize, said Laula Anut, though saying they're sorry is something people generally have trouble doing nowadays.

Some people said the problem was that so many people had come up from Värmland and other parts, what with the log rolling and timber transports. And a lot of them ended up being carried down with broken legs too. Plenty of others got their axe edges nicked and holes slashed in their britches. They called it having a spell of bad luck. But they'd really got in the little people's way.

People like that would be sitting around their campfires and would toss the hot coffee grinds right out of the coffee pot when they were done. Without saying:

Have a care!

They wouldn't move over, even if they heard a very clear knocking sound at the spot where they'd decided to sit down. And they insisted on making their fires wherever they happened to choose no mater now much ash and smoke got in their eyes, instead of moving a little way themselves. That's the kind of people they were.

Before long they'll be the only kind, said Laula Anut.

In the autumn when the rowans on the mountainside are as red as a flash fire and the birches and ashes are bright yellow, the little people sometimes dress up in their finery again, although they are otherwise so careful not to be seen. They love colorful things and can't resist imitating when they see a blue jay for instance. So father gnome gets himself a fine black and blue striped coat with a row of white buttons. His cows wander with silver bells and shiny red bands. And his little wife wears beaded sedgegrass shoelaces.

I'm sure that's how it really is.

I think when I married Nila I was wishing to be up there. I wanted to be among the kind of people who still said "Have a care!" when they had to use things that were hot and sharp. They weren't reckless with fire and axes the way the other kind were.

I knew nothing about how harsh the mountains were. No one knew people would one day try to take control over that harshness, nor how insidiously it would manage to get the better of them anyway.

Much, much later, I wanted to say Have a care! to my son Klemens. Have a care! my boy because human beings are also fragile—as fragile as the stream and the moss and the grouse.

Can you hear the cackling of the grouse cock up there in the mountain bog?

He's not mocking you because you got lost. No, don't believe it. But he may be saying: move over. Leave me in peace up here.

Although Hillevi came from Uppsala and had grown up with a telephone and a water closet, she probably knew better than I did what it could be like up in the mountains. She had delivered lots of women up there. When I told her that Nils Klementsson and I had become engaged up at Aagot's and wanted to be married as soon as possible, I saw deep anxiety cloud her eyes.

Sometimes I have wondered if a look of anxiety isn't the real mark of motherhood. To see it gives you a guilty conscience: I knew that very well in spite of her just being my foster mother. And yet I was glad to see it. It meant she was anxious about me as if I had been her own child.

The evening I told her she didn't say very much. Then I went off with Nila to meet his parents and be up there for the calf branding. We'd get married when we came back down. The timing was good, between the branding and the slaughter. It wouldn't have been possible if everything had still been like the old days. But now Trond would be able to pick us up in the car at Langvasslia. The road between Sweden and Norway was supposed to be finished and inaugurated by then.

When we returned to Langvasslia after a long time in the mountains, there was a letter from Hillevi waiting; it had been there for quite a while. She had put weeks of thought into it; you could tell from the date. It is unlike anything else in her handwriting. I have set it out here, alongside the letters she sent to the address where we boarded in Katrineholm and the letters she wrote me during the war. They were all full of her worries of course. When we were at that school, she wrote about our going out in stockings that were too thin and not eating right. During the war years her worries were deeper, but she had to be cautious about what she wrote, so I got good at reading between the lines.

This one says, in her lovely even script:

Blackwater, July 2, 1939

Dear Kristin, my dear girl!

You are so much in my thoughts these days, up there in the mountains at Skårefjäll, trying out your new life. And truly, I do wish you would let trying it out suffice for now. I can see you before me, sitting here in the kitchen telling me your decisions about the future. I didn't say very much at the time, but now I feel I must write to you and not conceal what I was thinking then and still think. You have strong arms and the recklessness of infatuation is in your eyes. That was what I thought when you spoke of freedom. You said it was to be found up there in the mountains. Up with those people.

That may be correct. They do probably have freedom once they are out of our reach, out of reach of our schooling and our judgments about their lives. But I can sense other things as well. I saw the powerful Lapp clan heads when I was young. They are not your people, Kristin. Your mother's father was a poor man. The wealthy Lapp family heads had fingers jingling with silver. I recall their power and all the bowed heads and peering eyes that surrounded them. I sense that there may be a future Matke or Klemet in every boy who's been given a reindeer brand and deer of his own.

Will you bow down, Kristin? Will you be Risten and give up your seat at the hearth to your husband?

To you there is nothing better and nothing more important than freedom. That is how it is when you are young. The wind sings in the mountains, and the water roars. Your arms and legs are strong enough to endure freedom and to slave for it.

You might not believe me if I said that once upon a time I traveled up to these parts for the sake of freedom. I left behind hospital regulations, Aunt Eugénie's moralizing, and in the end, also a man to whom I was secretly betrothed, left behind his eternal anxiety that someone might discover there was something between us.

But there is more to life than freedom, Kristin. Health and security are also important. You have grown up here. You have slept in the room with the white furniture. Not even for a day have you ever been without wood or kerosene in our home. When you had a fever, I tucked you in and nursed you. I feel a great deal of anxiety about what could happen if you fell ill up there, far from all help. Do you remember when Ingeborg Gabrielsson got appendicitis and her temperature flared up? She didn't get to the doctor in time. She died of peritonitis, strong healthy woman that she was.

I think about your childbirths when they come. I think you would have understood my anxiety if I had told you all this when you were sitting here opposite me. And yet I didn't. I suppose because I know that every person has to make her own decisions. You have to choose your life.

You do so during the years when you are full of strength and recklessness.

Yes, recklessness, I say it outright. That is when you choose between freedom and security. Between infatuation and forethought. Between the mountains with their winds full of songs and the village with its drudgery and its envy and its everyday tedium. That's not a difficult decision, I know. You hardly notice you're choosing. You are so strong, Kristin.

Someday in the distant future you will be sitting as I am now at a kitchen table, perhaps up there in Langvasslia, looking out through the window and thinking about how things turned out. I hope to God that you will then have the strength, a different kind of strength, to bear your choices without bitterness.

Uncle Trond sends his heartfelt best. All is well here at home. Today we inaugurated the new road. It will be the link between us too, and for that reason I have chosen to write to you on this particular night. There was a brass band and an author who spoke. Afterward there was coffee at the community hall, and Myrtle had rehearsed with a few girls; they sang in parts. We were all there of course, except for old Haakon. He's going downhill. He trembles badly now. Myrtle says she'll be writing herself, but she sends a thousand kisses. And indeed, she's inconsolable because you are moving, as you know.

> *Much love to you, my*
> *dear girl, from your*
> *own Auntie Hillevi.*

Trond and Hillevi agreed they wanted to give Kristin a proper wedding.

No one will remember that she's lived with us for virtually all her life and had such a good education she can take a position as head housekeeper. That won't count, said Hillevi, but no one will forget that she's Meat Mickel's granddaughter. Believe you me.

Hillevi was distrustful of the Klemet clan. Except for her Uncle Anund, Risten didn't have any close relations of her own. Hillevi hoped the more distant ones would refrain from attending the wedding. If they turned up at the church they would, of course, have to be invited along to the dinner at the guesthouse. She sounded Anund Larsson out a little cautiously when he delivered the grouse.

Not likely. They wouldn't have the clothes, he said.

He, though, had hung a new black suit in the vestibule of the guesthouse.

Anund Larsson had snared the grouse up on Mount Giela. He arrived later than expected, and the lard she intended to slice thinly and tie over the breast pieces of the fowl had gone soft in the heat. She had to put it on the lump of ice in the box for a while. Still the fowl seemed tender and had been nicely plucked and cleaned, thank goodness.

Verna's daughter Hildur and her husband Erik Gabrielsson ran the guesthouse now. Both her younger sister Elsa and their mother were helping out for the wedding, and Hillevi had brought her kitchen girl from home too. She didn't want Myrtle, who wasn't much of a cook, in the guesthouse kitchen. There was no need for her hair to reek of cooking fat. She did help set the tables and had been out with some of the other girls picking whatever wildflowers were left so late in the summer. There were valerian and meadowqueen in the bouquets. Hillevi found the scent overpoweringly heavy, almost indecent, but she didn't say anything. Myrtle meant so well.

She had sent her home now to help Kristin with her hair. They had been in town and purchased, for an outrageous sum, an electric wave comb, the kind only hairdressers used. She had planned for Kristin to have lots of time to get dressed and have her hair done, but in the end she had to send for her.

It was all because of the corset.

They had been to Östersund, she and Myrtle, to be fitted for their dresses by Miss Lundgren, the seamstress on Church Street. Hillevi had also made up her mind to invest in a new corset. She wanted to look really nice, even underneath. When she tried it on at the corsetry shop, she thought it felt perfect. It was salmon pink satin with a pretty flowered pattern that was only visible when she twisted so the light fell just so.

Everything felt good at the final fitting. On the day of the wedding though, she made the mistake of putting it on first thing in the morning, thinking she'd be in such a rush before going to the church that it would be practical to have only the dress to pull on.

Now she was dripping with perspiration. It was hot as Hades in the guest-house kitchen with its AGA stove and a really hot day outside to boot. By ten o'clock she felt faint. Eventually she had no choice but to go up to a room in the guesthouse and lie down; she had heart palpitations. That was why she ended up having to send for Kristin in spite of her intentions. She didn't dare leave everything in the hands of outsiders, which Verna and her daughters were, regardless of how well she knew them.

So the bride-to-be ended up in the kitchen as if she had been hired to do the gravy and trimmings. In the old days someone was always brought in to put on the final touches. Now most people tried to do everything themselves. Pathetic, thought Hillevi, remembering her own wedding up at Lakahögen, where she had never touched a thing. She hadn't even curled her own hair.

When it was time to leave for church, Hillevi realized she needed to go home and have a wash. The young people from Blackwater had already left. There were ribbons in the horses' manes and birch leaves decorating the wagons. Risten was just heading off with Myrtle and Tore. He was harness-ing Silver Pearl now; she had bows by her ears and a brand new bridle. They had to laugh when the mare shook her head at the finery.

She's a smart old thing, said Hillevi.

Then they were alone, and Trond had to help her back into the new corset.

Why not just wear your old one? he asked.

If only she had listened.

Before they were even at the border stream, she could feel how unbearably tight the new one was. She must be bloated from the heat.

We're going to have to stop so you can help me loosen it from behind, she said.

It was hard to find a place to pull over where she wouldn't risk being seen by possible late arrivals. Trond backed up to a timber pile and got out to help her. That was when it became clear what a state she was in. Her midriff was bulging out over the top edge.

This thing's just too small, plain and simple, he said.

Oh come on, just loosen the lacing at the back a bit.

He picked and poked until she thought she would go insane. Then they started to quarrel. He walked away.

Please help me, she pleaded, her eyes brimming.

It was like a bad dream. He removed his watch from his vest pocket and looked at it. There was no need. She knew how late they were.

Just take the damn straitjacket off, he grunted and went and sat in the car.

There was the sound of a car engine. She rushed in behind the pile of birch trunks. The car stopped; a man's voice said hello. It was Isak Pålsson. Now she heard Verna's too and several others coming from the car. She removed her silk jacket and the dress with the lace inset in the bodice and, furious, started undoing the hooks and eyes at the front of the corset. Her fingers were swollen, and it was very slow work.

When she finally got it off and had her dress back on, the voices were still out there. They were obviously waiting for her. She had nothing to put the corset into; her handbag was in the car, and it would never have fit in anyway.

So there she stood with the flesh-colored garment folded under her arm, waiting behind the pile of wood while the men wrangled about which car was best: Trond's Chevrolet bought at Sandström & Ljungqvist in Östersund or

Isak's Ford v8 about which it was boasted *this pleasant vehicle will transport you silently and comfortably through the glorious landscape of Jämtland.*

Hillevi wanted nothing more at that moment than for Isak to transport himself out of sight, silently or not, so she could come out. But more time passed. Men were such fools, she thought.

We'd best be hurrying on, she heard Verna say. But they paid her no heed. They were bragging about their brakes now.

Hydraulic, said Trond. Instant stopping and double acting.

In the end it became clear to her that the Pålsa family wasn't going any-where until she came out from doing her business behind the timber pile, which they thought must be trivial and easily accomplished. So she had to stuff the corset into the pile as well as she could and come out. Then they could finally get going. It felt so good to be out of the corset she soon forgot all about the whole business.

The minister was standing outside the church, black as a raven in the sun and livid because they were late. Not to mention that he'd had to travel from Byvången all the way to Röbäck in the heat just because the local clergyman was on vacation bicycling around Lake Vättern—such new-fangled nonsense! Holding the ceremony in the chapel at Lake Boteln was nothing but an ad-ditional source of annoyance to him.

They say it was a Lapp chapel once upon a time, he commented, and after that a tannery. I think it might just as well have remained one.

Halvarsson's grandfather was the one who had it restored to its former glory, Hillevi said, sounding slightly more caustic than she had intended.

They weren't going to the chapel the long way by driving around the lakes. No, the entire wedding party was going across by boat. They'd all been wait-ing for her and Trond and the Pålsas outside the church, and now they stated walking down to the lake. Two fiddlers led the way and continued to play as they were rowed in the first boat, which in addition to them, contained only the bride and groom. The minister was in the Halvarssons' boat, sitting beside Hillevi on the aft thwart. Myrtle was sitting on the thwart at the bow; Trond was rowing. Old Haakon tried to insist on doing the rowing in spite of the trembling that shook his whole body, but he ended up on a thwart too, while Tore was seated on an upside-down bucket at Myrtle's feet to keep the center of gravity in the boat low. He was tall and heavy, and the boat was generally overloaded. Hillevi had an unpleasant flash of a story about a whole wedding party that had drowned in Lake Blackwater in a storm. Today, though, the water in Lake Rössjön was smooth as oil in the heat. Although the shores were rocky and all you could see above them was spruce forest, there was a scent of flowers in the air.

She could see Kristin in the boat with the musicians, her train rising and fluttering. Though there wasn't really any wind; it was the motion of the boat that stirred up the air around them. Myrtle's yellow voile dress was fluttering too. She hoped Trond wouldn't row too hard. Why in God's name did everyone have to behave as if it were a race! The fiddlers played as if they were trying to lure the devil out of hiding. Their music had begun to sound like the Wild Hunt as the boats flew across the water.

She asked Trond to call out to everyone to slow down or there would be an accident. He just smiled. She recognized that particular smile of his and was embarrassed to be sitting next to a clergyman when he flashed it at her—and in broad daylight to boot. It reminded her of the time he and she had their own private marriage ceremony under a spruce tree, though no one else ever knew it. That morning had been damp and naked as a newborn. Her neck went red when she remembered his moist mouth and the rain. Oh God, he had that impish look in his eye as if he could read her mind, and he went on rowing, harder than ever.

But the minister didn't notice a thing. He was sitting in his own elevated tranquility lamenting Kristin Larsson's chosen way of life. He said the Lapps were restless souls, always in transit between two worlds.

What did he know about Risten? He had met her for the first time outside the church just a few minutes earlier. Both she and Myrtle had been confirmed by the local minister.

She's twenty-two years old, said Hillevi. So I think she knows what she wants.

She wasn't really paying much attention to his talk. It was such an exquisite pleasure to sit down and rest after all those hours in the hot kitchen. They had to walk from the far end of Lake Rössjön along the stream to Lake Boteln. But walking without a corset felt wonderful too. They got back in when the men had portaged the boats down to Lake Boteln. The chapel was in sight.

By that time the minister had moved on to immorality, though she had no idea how he'd got there.

Fornication will be punished, he was saying.

Hillevi couldn't resist, in spite of how happy she felt in the sunshine.

Oh yes? How? she asked.

That gave him just the opening he needed. On his high horse he went on: Sinners bear mentally retarded and deformed offspring.

She didn't know if he was referring specifically to the Lapps or to people in general. Perhaps he assumed Risten was in the family way?

Well, what can you expect? Man did arise out of earth and murky waters, said Hillevi.

His indignation knew no bounds, perhaps because she was trespassing on his professional territory. Hillevi had been quoting the words of her old friend Sorpa-Lisa; she thought they were every bit as good as his sermonizing. They had rounded the point at Anteudden, and the people in the first boat were beginning to disembark, putting one finely shod foot carefully down in front of the next on the hard stony bank. The chapel was gleaming; Trond had financed a new coat of red paint. It was always difficult to get the church council to invest in this distant chapel, rescued from stench and degradation by the Laka King. He had even had a little bell tower added.

They went into the cool wooden sanctuary with its white and blue streaked walls. The young people had decorated it and the air was full of the scent of birch leaves and flowers. Hillevi had another flash of anxiety, this time for Myrtle. The night before, when they'd been there decorating, the fiddlers had been there too, and there had surely been drinking. It was a beautiful summer night. She didn't think the place seemed like a church at all. Although an odor of decomposition and death clung to the minister's black woolen garb, the bright room smelled of summer and soil and gentle lake water.

I could've licked my plate clean, old Wolf Spider said, having finished his roast grouse breast with gravy and potato croquettes. Lucky I know my manners.

Well, don't you hold back; there's no need, said Trond Halvarsson. There was food aplenty. It was certainly delicious, both the grouse and the venison roast. The char came in just as lightly poached as Hillevi had hoped. Nobody liked overdone fish.

The fiddlers, who were from Träske, played a bridal march as people took their seats and a different tune as each course was brought in. But when it was time for the gifts, there was no music.

Jonte, time for the presents!

Jonte Framlund was already very drunk though, and had fallen asleep. Erik Eriksson could only play the accompaniments, which were no good without a first fiddle. So the gifts were presented in silence.

At first Trond and Hillevi had thought of giving Kristin a set of silver-plated cutlery. They had even picked out a pattern in town, but then they started to wonder how much use she'd have for it up there.

And what's more, said Hillevi, I don't doubt that those Klemets people would let her know it wasn't sterling silver.

So they decided on a gold necklace instead and gave Myrtle an identical one when she turned eighteen.

Sorpa-Lisa was one of the first to come forward bearing a gift. She was a good-hearted woman but ugly as sin. Though she was the same age as Hillevi, forty-nine, she no longer had any of her teeth.

Magic forest roots and herbs to ward off evil and all that disturbs, she said, extending a leather pouch to Risten.

An old woman called Elle came forward with two bed sheets woven of hemp, old and soft as silk. Goodness—it's like going back in time, thought Hillevi. Others from the Norwegian Lapp clans came forward with soft tanned reindeer hides. Women gave them grouse-down pillows.

Well, said Verna Pålsa, shaking her head. I do hope you know what you're getting yourself into.

Getting myself into!

Wedding day or not, Kristin was provoked.

If anyone knows you're not used to stomping around in the deep snow and chopping birch branches for the floor of your shelter, it's me.

Dragging home dead spruces for firewood! Hildur Jonssa from Skinnarviken added.

Nila's got us a house to live in. He's rented a place in Langvasslia, said Kristin. We'll only be moving around in the springtime.

There's snow up there even in April! Will you manage, melting snow for your water? You're used to just turning on the tap. When you worked for that toothdoctor, you had a zinc kitchen counter with a built-in sink and an AGA stove.

Will you be able to keep up with the does when they run to the calving pasture? Uj, uj, uj. Your head's full of romantic nonsense, Märta Karlsa said.

And she's not even a full-blooded Lapp, said Hildur Jonsa to Hillevi.

Kristin looked ready to burst into tears and turned to Hillevi for support.

What about when you got married to Uncle Halvarsson? What did your people in Uppsala say? They must've had a sink and an icebox and all kinds of modern things even back then?

That's right, said Hillevi, who couldn't resist giving Verna a nasty look. And Halvarsson got them for us too. The first thing he did was order a horsehair mattress.

That just made people laugh.

Not everyone stepped forward with gifts for the bride and groom. Hillevi thought the ones who were not so well off had no presents until Risten explained they were embarrassed that their gifts were so modest and would probably give them to Nila and her later on.

Tore set up the phonograph and the records. Nils and Kristin danced the bridal waltz to a recorded accordion version of *The Mountain Bride*. Hillevi was impressed with Tore for having found that song. He didn't dance himself; he was ungainly as a bear around women.

Kristin and her fiancé had both stubbornly insisted on her being married in full Lapp attire, although she didn't own any. Her uncle had dug out an old cardboard case with Ingir Kari Larsson's dress, the one Verna had had made up for her when she started waiting tables at the guesthouse, but it turned out to be moth eaten. So an outfit was made for Kristin, new from top to toe. No leather leggings, though, since she was planning to wear stockings and dressy shoes. They had already been purchased when Nila came home one day with a pair of Lapp boots of finely tanned leather, so pale they looked almost white. She decided to wear them of course. The first time she touched them they brought tears to her eyes.

But Hillevi and Myrtle had been horrified when she tried on the cap.

They thought it looked like a tea cozy and persuaded her to add a veil with a long train to her Lapp attire. It looked lovely. Myrtle had given the veil a tuck behind each ear. She had done an excellent job of dressing the bride, though she had been crying almost the whole time.

The dancing started, and Nils Klementsson was handsome in his jacket with the fancy edging and his longshirt with its colorful front. He had silver embroidery on his collar, a broad belt with a silver buckle, and a knife with a white horn sheath. He had on ordinary trousers, thank God, said Hillevi, and wore black shoes, so new they gleamed. Risten's silver collar was heavy and solid and came, of course, from the Klemet family. She set down the huge bouquet of flowers that had been ordered from town; they had the entire dance floor to themselves. Whatever Hillevi thought of her choice, Risten was now *The Mountain Bride*.

After *The Mountain Bride* Tore put on a Viennese Waltz, and other couples joined them on the dance floor. Tobias Hegger went straight up to Aagot Fagerli and asked her to dance.

Hillevi had written to invite him, and Margit too of course, thinking it was time to let bygones be bygones. He had come alone. Now she was afraid of what she might have triggered because when Tobias put his arms around Aagot with her hand in his, it was clear that nothing was bygone at all.

What was worse: it was perfectly evident to one and all. Other couples were dancing too, but one had to step aside when Tobias took a wide turn, after which others too withdrew to the tables or to stand by the wall. Eventually even the bride and groom left the dance floor. Aagot and Tobias had the wide-planked floor to themselves.

Well, her cousin certainly could lead in a waltz; Hillevi couldn't deny that. She hoped it was the dancing the others were staring at. Tobias swung round, taking advantage of the whole large space, sweeping across the floor with Aagot, who was stately and light on her feet and, in spite of her thirty-seven years, still had the deportment of the easily offended strong-willed shop assistant she had been long before Boston and American coats and dresses with laced bodices. She was wearing thin silk stockings and showing off her legs—ten or fifteen years after everyone else of course. Aagot always had to be different somehow. She had refused to cut her hair short when everyone else was bobbed; she still wore it pinned up. That evening she didn't have a bun but a shiny black twist at the nape of her neck. There were wisps of gray at the temples.

They danced for a long time, looking straight into each other's eyes throughout. Then Tobias let go of her hand and put both of his around her waist, which was still narrow, although her bottom and breasts had become so imposing. She put her hands on his shoulders; they seemed to move even closer and had eyes for no one but each other.

Trond said softly to Hillevi:

Look. No one can take their eyes off a woman like her.

In fact he was looking too and so was Hillevi. She was thinking about how powerful attraction could be and how little others could influence it. Trond knew about what was between Aagot and Tobias; she had told him. The same night, lying in the darkness, she had confessed to him that she sometimes longed for him in that way. She realized there was no getting back what once had been. But he whispered to her that he longed for it too sometimes. He knew just what she meant when she said *that way*, and for a little while things had been almost like before.

She wondered if there were others who saw Tobias and Aagot as she did or if they were all just envious and full of ill will and their own self-righteousness. Love really must be given its due, she thought. Whatever shape it takes.

Trond put his arm around her waist, and they moved out onto the dance floor; other couples were quick to follow. She saw Risten and Nila looking each other straight in the eye the whole time too, his hand reaching for her waist. It occurred to Hillevi that Risten might in fact be with child. Things were hot between them of course. And they had become acquainted at Aagot's after all.

She was glad now she hadn't tried to talk her out of getting married. They had been intimate, and that was that, but she did hope Risten had taken precautions.

Hillevi knew all too well of course that there was only one way to prevent consequences. As Trond used to say: do your threshing between the walls but shake the bag outside the barn. He hadn't been all that good at it himself though.

It was smoky and noisy, but people were enjoying themselves. When a couple of men started to fight, Trond and Erik Gabrielsa managed to get them outside before things got too far out of hand.

The minister, thank God, had left early. Some of the gentry were still there: a few timber dealers, the doctor from Byvången, Tobias of course, and the dentist from Östersund who had been Kristin's employer for a whole year. The young people were dancing to jazz records Tore was playing.

This place sounds like hot times in niggertown, said Doctor Nordlund, going over to sit down among the men at the Bismarck table. Others were teaming up to play whist, but no one was playing anything with really high stakes, the kind of games lumberjacks and logrollers lost everything on, right down to the shirts on their backs. The conversations around the Bismarck table were mainly about timber prices, though some people were talking about war.

There was going to be another war. Everybody said so.

Gerry's like a wolf, said the aged head of the Matke clan. He won't be satisfied 'til he's slaughtered 'em all.

That got Doctor Nordlund hot under the collar: he said the peace had been an insult to Germany, so it was hardly a surprise that the Germans were rising up. The cards remained on the table for a few minutes, and the men drank their cognac mixed with Vichy water in silence, scowling and looking uncomfortable. Arguments associated with war and acts of war were deeply rooted, and people remembered from the last war how taken aback they had been when conversations quickly became so heated.

Well, it's worry that drives the works in watches as in the world, commented Haakon Iversen, which was enough to lighten things up.

Diamonds are out! said the glazier.

Well, I never. So you were sitting with a trump in your hand after all, dammit.

Myrtle's voice rang out from over by the phonograph:

I can't give you anything but love!

Baaaybeee! one of the Fransa boys shouted.

Myrtle was announcing the name of each record before Tore put it on. Although she had studied English when she did her upper secondary, she was bashful and didn't really want to, but people kept asking:

What'll the next one be?

So Myrtle shouted *Riverboat Shuffle* and *Honeysuckle Rose* and *Muskrat Rumble,* and everybody roared at the silly English sounds. Being laughed at was getting to her, and in the end Tore called out:

Oh come on folks, there's nobody in this room who doesn't have family in America! People are human over there too.

The younger folks were more accustomed to it all: in fact *Darktown Strutter's Ball* and *King Porter Stomp* were old hat to them; they wanted to hear the latest tunes. At the tables along the walls people were arguing about the right steps for old-time Swedish dances, the hambo-jump versus the hambo-stamp.

That's enough struttin' and stompin' now! Erik Eriksson shouted. Elin from Skinnarviken, who had such a powerful voice her cow calls could drown out all the others, started singing a folk song so loud she overwhelmed the phonograph. People had a good laugh at that, and the conversation turned to all the festivities—all the invitationals and harvest balls and the dancing after auctions—there had been in the old days here at the guesthouse and elsewhere.

In those days everyone danced, men and women and all the young-uns; things were lively as can be, and the liquor flowed, both store bought and home distilled, said one old man.

Trond saw to it that more aquavit and Kron vodka were brought in, in spite of Hillevi's raised eyebrows. She always said mixing drinks was just mixing for trouble. She didn't think he ought to serve anything but cognac right now; the aquavit was to go with the late night meal. But Trond didn't want anyone saying afterward that at the shopkeeper's family wedding there wasn't enough liquor to go around.

Tore put on a waltz every now and then at Hillevi's insistence so the older folks would have a chance on the dance floor too. When the Fisherman's waltz came on, bearded Kalle Persa beckoned to her from all the way across the room. Many a sturgeon and char had passed between them, and he had never accepted any money or let them give him any special favors at the store. But now he wanted a dance, and he came striding across to claim it, with a wide grin above his white and green-streaked beard.

It'll start off all right, Elin warned her. He'll behave himself to begin with. But watch yourself when he starts to growl!

At first Kalle just had a strangely old-fashioned way of dancing. He seemed to make his way across the floor in a spiraling movement, dragging one leg behind him. But then it was just as Elin said. The old man got going and it felt more like circling backward than waltzing. Then he got all steamed up and started growling, interjecting complaints about the music: it's a little slow, doncha think? He twirled her around so hard the other dancers started leaving them space, but they never tripped and fell, and when the record ended and they stopped dancing, everyone applauded and shouted compliments.

No one else had dared to come near them while Kalle was waltzing Hillevi from one side of the room to the other, but now lots of people wanted their chance, and they shouted for more schottish and hambo tunes so they could shake a leg without having to do that new-fangled strutting. Elin from Skinnarviken lamented about how the best dance music had never been recorded and hardly anybody was capable of playing it any more. It was no use even wishing for a decent polska.

The real polska went down in history, she said, once the hambo-polska took over.

Over at Elin's table, at which Erik Eriksson and Anund Larsson were also sitting, the conversation turned to circle dances, polkettes, and mazurkas. And then somebody called out from the other side of the room:

Hasn't anybody got a fiddle?

So Erik Eriksson raised his violin, and up at the front of the room, where Tore was sitting, old man Fransa swept the arm of the phonograph off the record with a big screech. Erik looked around for Jonte, but he'd passed out and been moved to another room to sleep it off.

Anund, dear Uncle Anund, Risten pleaded. *Jyöne* Anund . . .

She had gone to get Jonte's fiddle, and she passed it to him, but he fended it off. Then a young lad from Lakahögen came out with a fiddle he had been hiding in the cloakroom. His cheeks were bright red with embarrassment, but he really wanted to play. At that, Anund could no longer resist, so he went and got his accordion. He had planned to stay out of things and had not yet sung a single note. He was Risten's only close kin, and he knew what people said about him: that fellow's got no proper job; he just goes around playing. He plays someplace almost every single weekend and gets a meal and his coffee wherever he goes. But when Risten herself shouted and clapped her hands, he let caution fly and started fingering the buttons. The first dance was a hambo-jump, and the chairman of the local council invited Kristin onto the dance floor:

May I have the pleasure of a dance with the bride? Isak Pålsa asked.

Risten couldn't refuse him, but she didn't know the jump-hambo steps. Isak's old mother, Anna-Stina Isaksa, raised her skirts to show how to dance the part that differed from the traditional hambo. They couldn't believe their eyes when she showed her legs.

But ma'am, I thought you were religious, Risten gaped.

Indeed I am, she said. But back then I wasn't.

The lad from Lakahögen, who told them Jonte Framlund was his uncle, turned out to be a fine fiddler, and Erik fiddled away too, taking swigs between the dances.

Äcke's as crazy about his liquor as goats are about their piss, said Anton Fransa.

But it could have been worse; every time he looked ready to pass out, they revived him with coffee.

Risten really enjoyed that dance. Verna nodded and said of her husband:

He was one helluva hambo-jumper in our younger days.

Things got wilder once the fiddles and accordion had taken over from the phonograph. Hillevi said to Verna it must be about time to bring out the meatballs and the herring casseroles. The two of them went out into the kitchen to heat up the food. It was after two in the morning. A little something to eat might settle people down.

There was a gunshot outside. It sounded like someone was shooting out across the lake from right by the window. After a moment of total silence more shots rang out from around the guesthouse. People started laughing, and Anund Larsson, who had sworn he wasn't going to sing that night, did anyway:

He was the head of the logging team
when he shot that fateful round
right into me, poor girl, it came
and with child I soon was found!

The softboots are here! someone shouted.

Hell and damnation. It's a whole pack of 'em.

It wasn't just Lapps, though; it was people from the whole area. Peering out through the kitchen window Hillevi saw Gudmund and Jon Eriksson. They were keeping a bit of a distance. She knew a whole lot of Lapp lads and Värmlanders and other types who were more or less at loose ends that weekend were lodging with them. Now they'd got them drunk too. Gudmund and Jon weren't among the first to storm up onto the front steps howling:

Bring out the bride! Bring out the bride!

Nils took Kristin by the hand and went out onto the steps. She had recognized relatives of hers in the mob, and Hillevi couldn't talk her out of it. Trond showed no backbone at all, saying family is family. But surely Kristin wasn't family to a crowd of drunken Värmlanders, or to the Eriksson brothers. Those two, thank God, never came in. They must have had some sense in their heads after all.

Hillevi realized the brothers had got people drunk and riled up just to spoil the wedding party. It must have been a disappointment to them that the horde hadn't got going earlier. But presumably no one had wanted to go anywhere until every last drop in the jugs of Norwegian moonshine had been consumed.

Still, she thought, this was mild mischief and probably a sign that Gudmund and Jon really had no idea what had been behind their father Vilhelm's bitter hatred of her. Not to mention his father, Old Man Lubben. They just wanted to make a bit of trouble because they knew there was bad blood between their people and the shopkeeper and his family. They can't have the slightest idea what happened on the ice that time so long ago, she thought. And who would want to pass that kind of story along to their children anyway?

Once the door was open, it didn't take long for the whole gang to be inside; there was nothing to be done about it. They ate like wolves of course, as might be expected. Elsa told her not to worry. There were six herring casseroles waiting to be heated up. The newcomers were drawn to the liquor like flies to milk and started calling out toasts.

Jovkh! Jovkh!

Hillevi asked Trond not to put out any more liquor, but his eyes were glazed over, and he thought he ought to make another speech, so he started in just like the first time:

If ya don't mind me saying a few words tonight . . .

That only brought on more shouting and laughter and ended with him raising his glass. Anund Larsson finally created some kind of order by starting to play. The second round of present giving took place during the dancing as Kristin had predicted, though Hillevi hadn't believed it. Each of the Lapp lads asked her to dance, and while they were twirling her around, they took the opportunity to give her a little something. Mostly it was money; Hillevi had no idea how much. Then the dentist in whose household Kristin had worked came over and broke into her dance with one of the boys. He too twirled her around and gave her some money—several hundred-crown notes people said afterward—despite the fact that he and his old mother had already given the couple a silver-plated creamer and sugar bowl. Hillevi had a flash of a different future that might have been Kristin's. It was perfectly clear there had been something between them. Kristin had removed the heavy silver collar when the dancing began, and Dr. Öbring thrust the money as deep into her cleavage as he possibly could. Hillevi was glad Nils happened to be standing with his back to her at the drinks table and didn't see the look in Risten's eyes.

They left shortly after. They had reserved a room at the inn in Jolet for their wedding night, and in the morning Trond was going to pick them up and drive them to Langvasslia. Trond was pretty far gone though; Hillevi wondered whether he'd really be fit to drive the next day.

Once everyone had shouted hurrah and good wishes to the departing couple and tossed rice and been so generally rowdy the horse was ready to bolt, Hillevi told Myrtle it was time for her to go home. She asked Tore to walk her, see to it that she got inside and locked the door. But Tore was beyond reach; his face was slack, and his eyes wouldn't focus. So Anund Larson walked Myrtle home. He had to be quite assertive; she really didn't want to leave.

Anund's departure brought the music to an end since Äcke had collapsed and Jonte Framlund's nephew was too timid to play solo. At that point one of the Lapps decided to sing. All the older folks and gentry had left by then, and Trond was sitting all by himself at the Bismarck table, so it didn't really matter if they sang in their own way. They meant well of course. The fellow who was singing was a nephew of Mickel Larsson, so he was quite close kin, with a somehow both soft and powerful voice. Sorpa-Lisa, who was sitting next to Hillevi, told her he was singing about what a wealthy young man Risten had hooked.

What else? Hillevi asked, as his long meandering song continued.

Boantas poajhke
dihte dan vååjmesem åådtjeme . . .

Sorpa-Lisa was trying to hum along.

The richest lad . . . voia voia
she's won his heart
his heart she's won
and we're drinking to them tonight
to their happiness
nanana nananaaa
drinking just a bit

Which of course provoked laughter.

Who'll be the meadow's star now?
nanananaaaaa
Who caught the richest boy?
Who wore the silver collar?
Risten, the brightest star
nanananaaaa
Risten the clear star
the mountain flower
chosen by the wealthy lad
Nanananaaa

When he was done, a much older man, unusually heavy for a Lapp, came forward. Hillevi thought his singing sounded like the howling of a dog, but she still wanted to know what it was about. Sorpa-Lisa clenched her thin lips and wouldn't say. But now Anund Larson was back, and Hillevi asked him to tell her what the man was singing.

Aw, just nonsense, not worth wasting your breath on, Larsson answered. But she insisted, seeing the old man's nasty glower.

It's just, you know, stupid . . . foolish stuff, said Larsson.

Kill the reindeer voia voia
rich man's reindeer
damn your soul, you surly bastard
shameful wolfthroat
worthless crook

Well, there was certainly nothing worth hearing in that. Couldn't Larsson shut him up?

I'd have to bind and gag him, he answered.

The old Lapp went on forever, and Hillevi got to work with Elsa and Verna clearing everything away, even taking off the tablecloths and folding them. Maybe that would show the hangers-on it was time to get moving. But the first man came back and started singing again. She saw that Anund Larsson had sat down and was listening to him. He looked sad and happy at once; there were even tears in his eyes. When the man had been singing for more than a quarter of an hour and everything had been cleared up and every ashtray emptied, Hillevi told Anund it might be time to ask him to wind it up. He just sat there rocking slowly back and forth and wouldn't look at her.

Let the Lapp *yoik* so he won't lose his soul, he said.

Then he told her, still without looking at her, that the man was singing about the mountains that were dark at night now and about the wet clouds and the wind, that the wind was in his song.

It was Erik Gabrielsa who finally got everyone to leave, the Lapps and the Värmlanders, by sending them off with a bottle of spirits and a ring of smoked sausage.

The next problem was Trond. He was sleeping soundly with his head on the Bismarck table. She managed to get him on his feet, but his legs were liquid.

We'll never get him down the hill and home, Hillevi said, on the verge of tears with exhaustion.

Shall I go down and harness the team? Anund Larsson asked.

That seemed the best solution. She had tablecloths and candelabras and vases and her silver-plated coffee set to take home too.

Silver Pearl looked as if she were expecting the worst, having been dragged out of the stable at that early hour. There was a little sugar left in the bowl, and her soft lips took it from Hillevi's hand. Anund Larsson went in to get Trond. His legs were still giving way under him; Larsson had to carry him out.

He's as light as a lad, he said. Funny, he's always had all the food he wanted.

When they got inside, Hillevi asked him to lay Halvarsson on the kitchen settle. But he just kept going, carrying him up the stairs and into the bedroom, and put him in bed. Hillevi set out bread and butter and a beer for Anund Larsson and a glass of milk for herself.

It all worked out very well, she said. Though things did get a bit rowdy toward the end.

She wondered too if he was worried about Risten, about how she would fare with the arrogant Klemets clan. But she didn't dare ask, and he didn't volunteer anything.

Have another slice, Larsson, she said.

He'd certainly been very decent and helpful. He was a better man than his old babbler of a father. She had never got over what she had seen that time up at the camp: the little girl's body dirty, half-naked and freezing, and those awful sores. But she thought about it somewhat differently now. Not that the old man had done much for the child; she was sure he hadn't. But the sores might not have come from either eagle claws or human hands. Nowadays she thought Kristin had probably been playing with her grandfather's dog, who had been rough with her. She had said as much to her. But in spite of the fact that Risten was grown up now and sensible in every other way, except perhaps when it came to love, she stuck to her story: she had been abducted by an eagle, and she remembered it herself, being lifted and carried over the edge of the steep cliff, feeling the sharp claws in the flesh of her back.

Hillevi had no desire to talk to Risten's uncle about it. It was too sensitive. He probably blamed himself for Risten's having suffered when he was away. But there was something else she wanted to know.

Hildur Jonsa from Skinnarviken, she said, had a thing or two to say about this marriage.

He said nothing.

She's a gossip of course. But since she's married to a Lapp I couldn't help wondering.

She expected him to ask what Hildur had said, but he wasn't giving her an inch.

She said Risten wasn't a real Lapp, said Hillevi. Kristin's grandfather once told me the same thing.

He sat silent. In the end he had to give her an answer of course. But he just said:

I know she's got real Lapp blood in her, that's for sure.

Hillevi couldn't bring herself to ask outright who the girl's father was. They had their secrets of course, those people too. But Kristin had been like a daughter to her for nearly twenty years. She thought she had a right to know.

That Aidan Kristin talks about, she said. Where is it?

Aidan? he asked, looking up.

Yes, where is it actually?

Oh, Aidan, he said. It's a fairytale kingdom.

She saw him looking around for his hat, which he had set on the chair by the door, and realized he was about to leave.

Larsson, have you got a room at the guesthouse? she asked.

No, Aagot said I could sleep in her baking shed, he replied.

That was when she decided to detain him a while longer. She hadn't noticed when Aagot left the party, or Tobias either, though at some point she discovered both of them were gone. She didn't want Anund Larsson going up there if Tobias and Aagot were together. She knew now that he could keep his counsel about things like that, but she still found it upsetting. So she offered him another beer.

When he had uncorked it, they sat talking about old times for a while. She asked if he remembered having met her up at Thor's Hole when he was just a boy. Of course he did.

All those fine ladies strolling by the river while the merchant was out shooting grouse. And that minister who read them poetry.

Although it was all those years back, it still hurt a little to hear him say that.

Yes, he was something of a poet too, Reverend Nolin, she said. I think he was a very gifted man.

Oh, no, he didn't write it himself, said Anund Larsson. He only wrote sermons, if that.

I saw a poem that he'd written in the guest book with my own eyes.

In the guest book. So did I. That poem was by W. Goethe, and V. Rydberg put it into Swedish, Anund Larsson said with absolute conviction.

What makes you so certain, Larsson? she asked, taken aback.

Because the very same poem is in a book called *Blinking Lights* the school-mistress gave me when I left school. The binding's broken, but it's been really good reading.

It has to be a different poem, said Hillevi.

Two souls, alas, a dwellin' in my breast, Anund Larsson recited loudly. Don't think I've forgotten a word. I wouldn't claim to know every single poem in that book. But most of 'em. Two souls, alas, a dwellin' in my breast. That's how it goes.

That was when Tobias came in. He just stood in the doorway, leaning on the frame and smiling at them. The dawn light fell on his face, and she saw how ruddy his cheeks were and that he was very tired. His lips were swollen. Oh, honestly. She had to look away.

Recite it, Larsson, she said.

And he did:

Two souls, alas, a dwellin' in my breast,
each from the other strives to pull away;
one clutchin' at the world in earthbound lust,
and clingin' fast in passionate embrace;
the other risin' fiercely from the dust,
our forebears' lofty realms its endless quest.

The Same Sea as Every Summer
By Esther Tusquets
Translated and with an afterword
by Margaret E. W. Jones

Never to Return
By Esther Tusquets
Translated and with an afterword
by Barbara F. Ichiishi

The Life of High Countess
Gritta von Ratsinourhouse
By Bettine von Arnim and
Gisela von Arnim Grimm
Translated and with an
introduction by Lisa Ohm

To order or obtain more information on these or other University of
Nebraska Press titles, visit www
.nebraskapress.unl.edu.